Cover design: *The Poinciana Tree*
by Ann Arora (watercolour on paper)

FROM READERS OF THE POINCIANA TREE

Antony Jeffrey's book The Poinciana Tree recreates his mother's life and that of her family. We see through Aimée that there is no ordinary life as each person's life is precious and unique. We learn how Aimée lived, loved and coped with major challenges while leading her boys through to adulthood. A noble story well worth a read.

Carol L. Barbeito, Ph.D., Author, Consultant & Educator (Denver USA)

It was fascinating to read Antony Jeffrey's book The Poinciana Tree, and to understand his strong appreciation of his mother, so beautifully named Aimee.

Joan Carden, A.O., O.B.E., a.k.a. The People's Diva

Two parallel stories, written with a wry sense of humour ... One told lovingly from her son's memories ... the other from personal introspection of [the writer's] own life with the momentum of development of character, interests and relationships from childhood to adulthood.

Anne Dunn Snape (Balmain, NSW)

Beautifully crafted and wisely structured, The Poinciana Tree presents a wise tale, in literary language. It is, by its very origins, old-fashioned. Yet it is timely, and segues to the present with its inevitable end and sad verities. There is a grace and wisdom in Antony Jeffrey's writing which pierces into apparently ordinary people and exposes them as extraordinary.

Belinda Grieve (Orange, NSW)

[The Poinciana Tree] is a winner. It owes much of its charm to the memories of extended family and friends, faultlessly created through the extensive use of dialogue. The reader is drawn into an authentic world which visits [many places] at a seemingly more innocent time in Australia's history.

Margot Mann (Chatswood NSW)

A lively and brave account of a family in post war Brisbane. The portrait of his mother emerges as a strong, caring but vulnerable young woman having to navigate life as a widow. The description of his emerging love of music is fascinating.

Clark and Sandra Ingram (Brisbane QLD)

The Poinciana Tree is a novel about a woman and her family whose lives spread across the vast continent of Australia. On one hand it is a story of hardship, emotional deprivation and coping with the desperation of the Depression and war, but on another level it is a classic example of bravery, resilience, the joys and sorrows of family and the unswerving commitment of love and support to others.

The story is based on the real experiences of the author's own family. His mother Aimée Francis was born in 1908 in the remote goldfields of Kalgoorlie in Western Australia, but after her own mother's early death she moved to Perth, Melbourne, Sydney and ultimately to Queensland.

Our history is full of the bravery and resourcefulness of people like Aimée and those she loved, but rarely are they noticed. This book is a tribute to her and the thousands like her.

www.antonyjeffrey.com

ANTONY JEFFREY

The
POINCIANA
TREE

Aimée Francis at age 26

ANTONY JEFFREY

The
POINCIANA
TREE

*The story of an Australian woman's life and struggle in the
times before, during and after World War II*

Connor Court Publishing
PO BOX 7257
Redland Bay QLD 4165

First published 2022

Designed and typeset by Guy Jeffrey
Typeset in Adobe Garamond and News Gothic
Printed in Australia

National Library of Australia Cataloguing-in-Publication entry

Author:	Jeffrey, Antony.
Title:	The Poinciana Tree:
	The story of an Australian woman's life and struggle in the times before, during and after World War II
ISBN:	9781922449962

In loving memory of my parents Alan and Aimée

Contents

Part One

Origins and Destinies

*A*imée Francis stood at the rail of *SS Manunda* at the Port Melbourne pier waving to Janet below. She kept trying to brush her hair out of her eyes but in the brisk spring wind it was impossible.

Janet shouted: 'Give him my love!'

Aimée lent over the rail: 'Can't hear – what?'

The ship was pulling out, now a few yards from the pier. Janet shouted again and pointed to her ears, shaking her head and started waving. Aimée kept waving back until the ship had turned, facing out into the bay and the figures on the pier were indistinguishable. People lining the rail moved away, chatting excitedly at the prospect of the voyage up the coast. She stayed there on the deck, glad to be on her own, with the glossy white superstructure of the ship behind her and the huge buff coloured funnel above her.

She felt excited too, despite it being a mercy mission. Big ships like this were so full of promise of some unknown destination, or in her case full of dread. Only once had she travelled on a steamer, when she was twelve and her father had taken her across to Melbourne from Perth to her new school. That was certainly full of dread. How could she forget it. There were gales across the bight and she was so sick she thought she was going to die. Even when the weather turned bright and calm the void in her tummy was still there as if she was about to fall into a black hole. Her brother Owen had seemed to be in a daze the whole way. She knew he dreaded the prospect of Trinity Grammar as much as she did Merton Hall. She still remembered how she looked up at him and grasped his hand when they disembarked. He took it in a tight grip that felt like he never wanted to let go.

Unpacking in the little cabin was reassuring. The other passenger in the twin berth cabin was a middle-aged woman, a bit overweight, red-faced and cheerful.

'Where are you off to, love?'

'Brisbane.'

'That's nice. I'm going back to Sydney – been here for the Cup. Holiday for you?'

'Not really. My brother's in hospital and I'm going up to be with him.'

'What a shame, is he going to be alright?'

'I hope so.'

Later, back on deck, she watched the fading coastline until the sun neared the horizon, it got cold and she felt hungry. She thought she'd better find the lounge and wondered if she would be out of place huddled in her coat. She followed the sign for the Lounge. To her amazement, it was packed with people, all sitting at tables, smoking and drinking. Her first instinct was to leave immediately, her typical response to a noisy place, but a steward was at her elbow ferrying her across the room.

'Here's a table of young women about your age, miss, and I'm sure we can find a chair for you.'

Deftly he gathered up a chair and slid it behind her with a smile and a flourish. The girls at the table had plenty to say to him as he executed his manoeuvre. 'I can see you're on the spot, steward,' said a tall girl with an appraising smile.

'But I thought he was after me,' laughed a blue-eyed girl with curly black hair, 'anyhow I'm Dell.' She stretched out her hand across the table to shake Aimée's.

The steward flicked back his lank blond hair. 'You can call me Jimmy ladies, and I'm happy to get any of you another drink.' Turning to Aimée, 'What about you, miss?'

'I think I'll have a gin and tonic thank you.'

They giggled as Jimmy swept away and introduced themselves to Aimée. Judith and Kay were returning from a holiday in Melbourne. Dell was travelling with two friends, Maxine and Doris, all bound for a holiday in Cairns. Dell and Doris were secretaries with the Health Department, and Maxine, sitting next to Aimée, was a nurse. 'I'm a nurse too,' said Aimée, 'where do you work?'

'Royal Melbourne, in emergency at present – what about you?'

'I'm at the Alfred, and I'm nearly qualified for midwifery.'

Aimée was suddenly glad the steward had parked her amongst these friendly young women. Even though she was twenty-four, she had only started nursing the previous year. She had been studying art since leaving school but by 1930 with the Depression at its height, she told herself she needed to get a proper job and started as a nurse at the Alfred.

The bonhomie at the table seemed to get louder as the gin took effect. The noise level subsided when they got up to go to dinner, leaving Aimée with the tall girl who had introduced herself as Betty Jeffrey. She was also going to Brisbane, returning after a short holiday in Melbourne where her parents and sisters lived. Aimée liked Betty: she had twinkling eyes, a wry smile and an irreverent way about her. She had worked out all the other girls and made Aimée laugh with her imitation of Judith's and Kay's denial of being in Melbourne for the races. When Aimée told her she was going to Brisbane to see her brother Owen who was in hospital with diabetes, she was immediately sympathetic.

'How long are you staying? You could stay with us you know. I'm living with my two brothers and we have a huge flat in Kangaroo Point.'

'That's very kind of you but I've arranged accommodation at a nurses' home through the Alfred. And I don't know how long I'm staying. I've been told he's in and out of a coma with diabetes. I don't understand it because they have this new drug called insulin which is a sort of miracle for diabetics. He should have been treated with it.'

'I think you're incredibly brave going up there to get stuck into the hospital. We can help I'm sure. My elder brother runs the Brisbane office of a national accounting firm and seems to know everyone. We'll get him on to it too.'

They went into dinner and found a table for two. Aimée felt deeply relieved she had made such a feisty new friend.

That first night out of Melbourne on the *Manunda* she couldn't get to sleep. It was always the same: when she got stirred up by something important, she couldn't stop examining it from every point of view, over and over. That Owen was desperately ill was true, but was anything to be gained by her rushing to his bedside? Gwenda Lloyd as always had been sensible and objective. She was dubious that Aimée could do much but knew she wouldn't rest until she was there beside him. Though she was only ten years older, newly married with a baby daughter, Gwenda was both a dear friend and trusted authority figure for her. She had taught her English and History at Merton Hall and been an inspiration to her.

Hatty and Janet Alexander as usual had totally opposite opinions. Aimée lived at the big Alexander home in East Melbourne with the sisters and their parents. Always the enthusiast, Janet said she *must* go, *must* be beside her beloved brother. Hatty, broad, pragmatic and now nearly forty, shook her head and told her to go if she must but were the doctors going to take any notice of a student nurse?

Aimée and Owen were always very close. He was hardly more than a year older than her and they had been inseparable during their childhood. She was the youngest of four children, leading an idyllic childhood in a large rambling double-storied house in Kalgoorlie, Western Australia. Their father Arthur Francis was a successful surveyor in the Kalgoorlie goldfields. The goldfields were on the edge of the desert yet it was an exotic place, full of miners and prospectors seeking their fortune from every part of the world, many of them destitute or disreputable. Though generally dusty and ramshackle, Kalgoorlie had sprouted many large and pretentious buildings, banks, hotels, council chambers and even a couple of theatres. In the summer it was hot and dry and prone to stifling red dust-storms, but there was usually rain in the winter. She had always loved the profusion of wild flowers in the spring, especially in the expansive garden of their house on the edge of the town.

She had always been in awe of her father. When they grew up, her eldest sister Edna used to say their father had the air of a colonial potentate. In his white suit and straw hat, he cultivated a grand manner in the town and on his frequent trips to Perth. Their mother was gentle and quietly spoken, and never argued with her father, nor did any of the children, except Edna, who was cheeky and made him smile. They led a protected life, schooled by their mother until the age of ten, venturing out to the town only with their parents or the nanny, and never on foot. Arthur Francis often referred to the 'riff-raff' in the town which they assumed to be the raggedy children that passed along their wide street. This meant their playground was their own large wild garden and their companions were each other. For holidays the family moved to their house on the Canning river in Perth where they swam and boated. This was their happiest time when their father let his hair down and swam and played with them.

At seven in the morning the promenade deck of the *Manunda* was deserted. The horizon was shrouded in mist and the soft grey blue of the sea seemed to have the dimpled quality of Chinese porcelain. Only the vibration of the ship indicated movement. Aimée wished she had her painting things with her. To find the right texture of the water and the sky at this moment, perhaps contrasted with the bow of the ship, would have been the perfect challenge. A pang of anxiety about Owen broke her early morning revery. She turned a corner of the deck next to the swimming pool and was riveted by the sight of a lone woman powering through the water swimming laps as if her life depended on it. Leaning on the railing from the deck above, she watched with fascination: the churning of the water, the urgency of the turns and the sleek powerful body movements. At the far end, the woman stopped, slumped against the bar at the end of the pool. Slowly she pulled herself out of the pool, wrenched off her cap and walked back. She was surprised to see it was her new friend Betty.

All the girls from the night before had gradually gathered together at the breakfast table and the atmosphere was just as noisy. As if no one could tell from looking out the window, Dell announced it was a perfect day, the first real day of the voyage, and who was coming up to swim and play deck games? Relaxing on deck chairs between games of deck quoits and quick chilly swims, Aimée told Betty she had watched her swimming and how impressed she was with her speed and strength.

'I've always loved swimming and all games really but I've decided it's high time I got serious about it. I was runner up last year in the Victorian freestyle 200 and I reckon this year is my best chance to win the Queensland 200. I'm twenty-four and reasonably fit so it's the right time.'

'Did you try out for the Olympics this year?'

'Nice of you to ask, but I didn't. If I'd thought about it seriously last year and really trained hard I might have made it. Some of my swimming friends said I could. But you know it's so hard if you really want to succeed as an athlete, especially for a woman. You know my eldest sister Jo's fiancé is a champion athlete and got a Bronze medal in the 400 metres hurdles at the 1928 Olympics. He trained hard for this year's Olympics but his employer, the Melbourne Sports Depot, told him it was the Olympics or his job. Can you believe it? Already an Olympic medal winner and he works for a leading sports company. Of course they told him there was nothing else they could do because of the Depression. Bloody hypocrites.'

She was intrigued by Betty and her family. 'With brothers in Brisbane and sisters in Melbourne, it sounds like you come from a large family.'

'You could say that. Large in numbers and the racket they make, but not in stature. Believe it or not I'm by far the tallest even including my two brothers.'

'How many are there?'

'Two boys aged thirty-four and thirty-two, then four girls and I'm the second last, all still on the shelf, except Jo. Anyone else in your family besides your brother?'

'I have two elder sisters, one in Perth and one in Sydney, but none of us is married yet.'

Betty screwed up her face and wondered: 'Funny we're all at the marrying age but nobody has tied the knot. Don't look at me – I'm having far too good a time to think of marriage, even if I knew someone eligible.'

'Most of my friends in Melbourne haven't married. Do you think it's the Depression that's stopping our generation from getting married? I never think of marriage, I just hope I can keep on being a nurse.'

'What rubbish! You have the pretty face and demure manner men go wild about!'

They laughed at each other and got up to dive in the pool. She felt a real bond developing with Betty, such a contrast to herself, so much taller, stronger – like a beautiful young Amazon.

When the *Manunda* docked at 7 am at the Eagle Street wharf in the Brisbane River, Alan, Betty's eldest brother, was there to meet her. He wore a three-piece light grey suit, holding his hat to reveal his wavy silver hair, complete with neat dark moustache and the family characteristic upturned smile and opposite down-turning eyes. Betty turned out in a boldly patterned dress and slanting hat with feather for their arrival. Aimée in a cream silk blouse tied at the neck and dark tailored skirt, had not seen Betty looking so splendid and wondered about Brisbane's dress code. After Betty's cheerful introductions on the wharf, Alan turned to ask Aimée about the voyage but Betty regaled him with the dreadful story of the storm on the second night out of Melbourne. All the food, wine and plates had slid off the tables. One large lady had fallen off her chair flat on her face on top of roast dinner. Betty's hilarity was ignored as Alan whispered to her to bring Aimée home for breakfast. He led her off the wharf to wait for the luggage in the arrival hall chatting with solicitous interest. Betty needed no prompting to invite her back for breakfast, but Aimée said no, she must settle in and go to the hospital as soon as she could. Betty said: 'Alan, she's going to stay at the nurses' quarters at Brisbane General Hospital in Herston and we must take her there. I invited her to stay at Kangaroo Point, but her brother's very ill at the Hospital. Did you come with Dora?'

'Yes of course, let's go now.'

Dora, Aimée thought. Who's Dora?

Betty was reading her mind. 'Dora is Alan's new car, Dora the Dodge.'

Alan was the partner in charge of the Brisbane office of accounting firm Flack & Flack. The spacious flat he shared with Betty and their brother Rex overlooked the river at Kangaroo Point. Betty had told her on the ship that they all led busy social and sporting lives: Alan was regarded as among the most eligible bachelors in Brisbane. Rex frequented a less reputable horsey set, but they all played tennis, golfed, and there were always parties.

Brisbane General Hospital was a huge rambling place, reputedly the largest hospital in Australia. Neither Alan nor Betty knew their way around it so it was mid-morning before they were able to deliver Aimée to her accommodation and identify where Owen was. Neither wanted to leave her in this vast, confusing place, so they insisted she come for dinner and they would collect her at six o' clock. She reluctantly accepted, but as soon as they left she made her way to the diabetic ward, her heart beating desperately in dreaded anticipation. She climbed stairs, followed long clanking corridors, into another building and finally found the diabetic ward, seemingly hidden away, quiet and still. She faced the nurse's station and asked to see Owen Francis.

'You can't see him without his doctor's permission.'

She took a deep breath and instantly decided she must assume

Betty's confident no-nonsense manner. 'I'm his sister and I've just arrived from Melbourne. I'm a nurse and I need to see him. I spoke to Dr Taylor from Melbourne on the telephone. Where can I find him?'

'Oh, I see. Dr Taylor's not here on his rounds until four o'clock but I could try ringing him in his rooms and tell him you want to see him when he comes in.'

'Thank you but I also need to see my brother now.'

'Come with me.'

Owen was asleep when they arrived at his bedside. She knew he would be pale and thin but even so she was shocked at his pallor and death-like appearance.

'He sleeps most of the time and is quite weak because he can't keep much food down.'

'Is he having insulin yet?'

'Yes he was started on it last week but his response was compromised so they've taken him off it until they've done some more tests.'

'Why? It's essential that they have someone in his condition on it. Goodness me!'

The nurse looked helpless at Aimée's anger and anxiety. 'I'll sit by his bedside and wait for the doctor. Please let him know.'

She sat there feeling utterly helpless and pushed back the tears. She leaned over and spoke to him quietly: 'Owen, are you awake, it's Aimée.'

He opened his eyes slowly, smiled faintly and almost inaudibly said 'Aimée, how nice …'

The smile stayed on his face but he seemed to fall asleep again, so she decided she should just sit there and let him rest. This inaction felt so strange and inadequate to her; as a nurse, she was so used to constant activity with both patients and visitors. She had almost fallen asleep when the same nurse tapped her on the shoulder and said Dr Taylor had arrived and would see her now.

He met her at the nurse's station and took her aside to a bench at a corner in the large room. She steeled herself to be demanding, but looking at him, knew there would be no purpose in that. She recalled his Scottish accent from the telephone and now was able to add crew cut greying hair and a heavy grey moustache. He listened politely as she told him she knew from senior staff in Melbourne insulin treatment should be administered urgently in such debilitated cases as Owen's. She felt he would give the same explanation to everyone who asks every day: '... we need to build up his strength beforehand ... otherwise it can be too dangerous ... it's a new drug you know and the compound is unstable ... depends where it is sourced ... we have to analyse every new shipment ... he's in the best of hands as we have the best facility in Brisbane...' She found herself shaking his hand and thanking him for his care, yet sick in her stomach as she sensed his complacency and she would have to get Owen moved. But where? She went back to Owen's bedside and found him awake, half sitting up, being fed by the same friendly nurse. A real conversation was impossible; he seemed unable to concentrate. She realised this was an aspect of his condition where he would relapse into a comatose state.

A shadow appeared over her shoulder as Owen lapsed into sleep again. It was Betty.

'How is he?' she whispered.

'Not too good – comatose most of the time.'

'Have you spoken to the doctor?'

Aimée looked up and nodded, making a face.

'Come on now, I've got the car, come back to our place and I'll feed you up.'

By the time Betty had coaxed her away from the diabetic ward and found Dora, it was almost dark. They snaked through the Valley, up Queen Street, across Victoria Bridge and along the river to Kangaroo Point, all the time Betty cheerfully talking up the architectural and scenic marvels of Brisbane in a vain attempt to distract Aimée. She noticed nothing except that it looked dusty and bedraggled.

Kangaroo Point was different, with houses and blocks of flats nestling on a 180 degree curving hillside overlooking the river towards the city area. The flat was up a flight of stairs into a huge lamp-lit living room with windows along its length, the view of the bend of the river below and the twinkling lights of the city on the other side. Alan was there and offered them a drink. She found the effect of the beautiful room, its view and the friendly reception almost overwhelming, so much so that she needed to sit down, accepting a drink from Alan with nothing more than a faint smile and a word of thanks.

'Rex, come and meet Aimée,' shouted Betty, craning towards the kitchen. 'How's dinner coming along?' Rex appeared with a broad smile clad in a blue and white striped butcher's apron. He went up to Aimée and bent over to shake her hand. He was a short man with shiny dark hair parted in the middle, giving him a racy look.

'I'm Rex, the ne'er do well brother, only good enough to slave over the hot stove,' with a quick grin at Alan. 'We're very sorry to hear about your brother. Have you seen him today?'

'Yes I've been with him all afternoon; he looks very frail and seems to sleep all the time. But please, I'd rather not talk about it at the moment. It's so good of you all having me here in this lovely place.'

After a short while, Betty ushered them to the table beside the window and Rex served up a delicious dinner of lamb chops, mashed potato and buttered asparagus. He said he was especially proud of the asparagus which he'd found in a Chinese green grocer in the Valley. Aimée hadn't realised how hungry she was and felt herself relaxing as the four of them chatted over dinner and cups of tea. Like meeting Betty on the *Manunda*, she felt a strong attraction to these siblings though they were so unlike her friends in Melbourne or even her own siblings. They all liked to talk, often interrupting and talking over each other. They laughed a lot and obviously knew each other closely and were very affectionate, though disguising the affection with teasing and ribaldry. Her father might disdainfully have called them 'noisy'. Rex had a job as an electrical salesman. It involved tramping the streets of the city, the Valley and

South Brisbane dragging a large trunk on two wheels he called his 'gear' full of his smaller samples and his leaflets. His real interest was racing, preferably horses, but dogs would do. He had what he called a 'system' which seemed to be quite effective from what she could tell from the effort and planning he put into it.

During all the verbal horseplay between Rex and Betty about the glories and desperadoes of the betting ring, Alan had sat on the sidelines with an amused smile saying little, offering occasional explanations to Aimée about the peculiarities of racing lore. When Rex got up from the table to fetch the bottle of whisky, Alan put his hands on the table and looked around at them all.

'Well I've got some news for you all.' Rex paused in mid-room with the bottle in his hand and Betty went suddenly silent, looking shocked. 'You're not getting married are you?'

'What me? Hardly! No, but it's just as amazing. Dad is being transferred to Brisbane and the whole family is coming here in January!'

Betty put her hand to her mouth – stunned, speechless.

'When did you hear this – how long have you been sitting on this?'

'Just today. Mum rang me at lunch time. She's speechless too. They both are but I suspect he's known a bit more for a while. In fact I think he might have engineered it.'

He turned to Aimée. 'Our father is a senior accountant in the GPO. He's spent most of his career in Melbourne but he's had a stint in Adelaide as chief accountant and has been a bit frustrated being back in Melbourne taking orders from someone else. So knowing how devious he is, I reckon he's been ferreting away it this for some time without telling anyone. And Rex I would take a bet he's used the fact that half his family are in Brisbane as a bargaining chip with the top brass at the GPO.'

Betty was still speechless, until the dam broke. 'I can't believe he didn't say anything when I was there. He certainly didn't say anything to her – in fact she was grizzling away how much she missed all of us and wished we could all be together. In a normal family you'd all be part of the plan,' she said to Aimée, 'but the cunning old cow has this evil delight in not telling anyone what he's up to until it's too late. But how *fantastic!* She jumped up and hugged both her brothers with whoops of joy.

All niceties of hospitality were forgotten. Betty got on the phone and rang her mother, but she told Betty it was all so new there wasn't much to tell. No, she had no idea where they would live. Yes, Mick and Mary would come but she wasn't sure about Jo. Will says we are to be in Brisbane by the end of January, but that's impossible unless he goes on his own …

In the morning Aimée found two messages on the desk at the entrance to the nurses' quarters, one from Janet Alexander and one from Betty. She knew Janet would want to know about Owen but there was little she could tell her so it could wait. She wanted to get to Owen but she'd better ring Betty. There was a telephone on the wall beside the door for the nurses, but already there was a girl on the phone and another waiting. She couldn't wait any longer and headed for the door, only to run into Betty coming in.

'Did you get my message?'

'I've been waiting to ring you.'

'Alan wants you to come and meet Ken Fraser who is a top doctor and a good friend. We've got an appointment at 10 o'clock and I can drive you there. Can you come now?'

It was Saturday morning and they arrived in minutes at the large building on Wickham Terrace where all the medical specialists had their rooms. The building seemed empty but eventually they found Dr Fraser leaning back behind his desk talking rapidly and gesticulating busily to Alan. Both men leapt up and Alan introduced Betty and Aimée.

'Ken it's very good of you to come in this morning to meet Aimée, but I think something has to be done urgently about her brother's illness. I know it's not your speciality, but I can't think of anyone else who knows more about what's happening in Brisbane's medical world than you, and gets things done.'

'You can cut the flattery Alan but I'm only too happy to help you Miss Francis. I know some of the people at the General and they tend to think they know it all.'

After her explanations about Owen's condition, he said he would speak to Dr Taylor whom he knew slightly, but not before he spoke to Dr Alexander Murphy, a personal friend.

'Pat Murphy is the most knowledgeable physician in Brisbane and he will know the best diabetes person we need to talk to. I think it's essential we get him out of the General next week and almost certainly into the Mater.'

She felt faint with relief and wanted to fling her arms around this voluble little man! He picked up the telephone on his desk, rang a number, joked with a woman on the other end and told her 'tell him to ring me as soon as he comes in from golf.'

'Don't worry Miss Francis, Pat Murphy will ring me this afternoon, and we'll get it moving. Can I call you Aimée? Any friend of Alan's is a friend of mine.'

Alan put his arm around Ken's shoulder as they got up. 'Ken, I can't thank you enough for doing this. It's a hot morning, let's all go down to the Club and have a drink. It's on me.'

And so they did. The four of them crowded into Dora and drove down Edward Street to the Gardens where the huge old colonial pile of the Queensland Club stood amongst Moreton Bay figs on the corner of George Street.

Ken Fraser's intervention sparked a rapid improvement in Owen's health. He was moved to a private hospital and quickly responded to more aggressive insulin treatment. But he was very weak and needed extended recovery time and medical supervision. Aimée decided she would move to Brisbane to be with him until he was strong enough to be on his own. She wrote to the Alfred in

Melbourne and they agreed to an indefinite transfer to the General in Brisbane where she could continue her midwifery. She found a little flat for Owen and herself on Gregory Terrace, high above the playing fields of Victoria Park.

It was a strange feeling: gathering Owen's things, not many – a few clothes and mostly books. Betty drove them over to the flat and they sat out the back with cups of tea overlooking the vast Victoria Park. The prospect of living and caring for Owen seemed life-changing. Though she could see she had a serious task in getting him ready to go back to work, in a way it seemed like going back to childhood when they had been so close, when their mother had died, and they had felt so abandoned.

Betty looked around the sloping back yard approvingly: 'You were very clever to find this place. It looks perfect for what you both need. I suppose you can walk to the hospital from here.'

'I can walk it in fifteen minutes,' she said proudly, 'but it's harder coming home up the hill.'

Owen said, 'I hope it's convenient for you Aimée, because I'm sure I can manage if you'd rather stay at the hospital.'

They both fell upon him in protestation. Betty said of course she's staying here and Aimée made it clear she couldn't wait to get out of the nurses' quarters. Owen was naturally reticent and never wanted to trouble others. She could see his illness had made him become even more withdrawn and introverted. Part of her task would be to bring him out into the world and away from his books.

She cooked Owen their first dinner together. His quiet presence made her feel more relaxed and even happier than she had been for months, maybe years. For the first time as adults they found they could talk about their past, their childhood and even the deep family sadness.

In their childhood in Kalgoorlie, she and Owen were inseparable and played together all day, and both adored their mother. When Aimée was eight, her mother suddenly fell ill. She had contracted meningitis, not uncommon in parched Kalgoorlie. She always carried the memory of the terrible weeks in the silent house as her beautiful mother lay desperately ill, and finally died. The children's lives were changed irreparably. Their father Arthur was an ambitious man who liked the trappings of success and found he could not cope with looking after four children, two of whom were on the verge of secondary school. All four were packed off to boarding school, the two elder girls, Edna and Olive, across the continent to Melbourne Girls Grammar, and Owen and Aimée to the nuns in Perth.

'Do you remember that terrible time when she was so sick Owen?'

'I don't really remember much about it. I do remember our father wanted me out of the house and kept arranging for me to be at school friends' places after school, and even taking me on excursions, or he seemed to be, I'm not sure. It was so unlike him to take an interest in me.'

'I hated that convent in Perth. I don't think I have ever felt so lonely and bereft of any loving face. I only seem to remember the horrible things, like having to practise the piano on cold winter mornings before breakfast and the nun watching me and if I played wrong notes she'd hit me on my fingers with a ruler.'

'I never knew that, how terrible for you. It probably wasn't so bad for me and that was when I discovered books. They didn't seem to mind that. I think they thought I was going to be clever.'

'Well you were!'

All those years ago, when their mother died, the terrible hollow on her heart was made worse by the virtual loss of her father. She remembered painfully how distracted and remote he became, and the way her siblings whispered in corners like a little group of lost souls. When her elder sisters were sent off to boarding school in Melbourne she missed them dreadfully, but learnt to push down her misery – she became a natural stoic. Arthur took up with a stylish woman called Anna, tall and elegantly dressed with her dark hair cut squarely along her jaw line. In 1920, when Aimée was twelve, they were married and sailed off to England on a lengthy honeymoon, regularly replicated in the coming years. In due course all the children took the endless journey across Australia to boarding school in Melbourne. They chaperoned and clung to each other for affection. The stepmother Anna was a distant figure whom they all distrusted. From their adolescence onward, family life was essentially over.

The emotional bond between them became deeper as the years passed into adulthood though eventually they would live in separate cities and see little of each other. Their common characteristics were their quiet introspective ways, their gentle humour (except Edna who was more boisterous), their acute sense of personal responsibility, distaste for religion and their avoidance of any display of emotion.

She wanted a cigarette after dinner with Owen, but resisted in deference to his health. She had noticed he was no longer smoking. She wondered if he had ever thought seriously of marriage. When he was restored to health he would be such a catch – at least *she* thought so. She hesitated, then plunged in: 'Owen, you'll probably be embarrassed by this, but ... have you ever thought of marriage?'

'Oh, goodness me, how could I ever think of that in my condition. I don't even know if I'll have a job to go back to.' He did look embarrassed. She felt foolish.

'I wasn't thinking of now or of anyone you might have met, simply the idea.'

'Since I was diagnosed with diabetes, almost ever since I've been working in Brisbane, I've had no social life at all and really haven't felt like it.'

'Well the insulin is transforming you and it won't be long before you'll be better than for years, and you should start planning to see people. Betty and her brothers would be a good start. They're very friendly and hospitable people.'

Aimée had been puzzled before when she heard Betty use the word 'surface' in a way that didn't seem to make sense. This time

Betty had rung and told her they were going to surface next week-end so you and Owen must come.

'Going where?'

'Surfer's Paradise. You know Alan's building a house there?'

'Oh. I see, now I understand. Yes I had heard he wanted to build a house at a beach.'

'It's a gorgeous place. It's only fifty miles down the coast, but it takes forever to get there. Three car ferries and a dirt road.'

It was quite an expedition, five of them crammed into Dora plus overnight sleeping gear. It was a full three hours before they arrived at a large inlet bound by sandhills they called the Broadwater. Another ferry took them across a river from a village called Southport until they reached a little settlement behind the sandhills that seemed hardly more than a few little cottages. There was an old house on stumps with a sign over the steps reading Laws General Store.

'This is Surfers,' announced Betty, 'population about thirty, Brisbane's great seaside resort!'

'It's not much, but it soon will be,' said Alan, pointing to a half complete art deco building with multi-coloured bricks and an embryonic six-sided tower. 'That's the Surfers Paradise Hotel, due to open next year.' They turned down a pine-tree lined street leading to the beach and along a sandy track behind the sandhills where there were a few holiday shacks.

'There, that's it!' said Rex proudly. It was a block of land almost totally covered by low coastal scrub, apart from a new stucco clad car garage with green double doors facing the street. Surely we don't all spend the night in there, Aimée thought. They all walked across the sandy track into the scrubby sandhills and looked down. The tide was a long way out, the sea a deep blue, the line of breakers endless to the north and many miles to the south to a single low headland. There was nothing else except the brilliant overwhelming white sand.

They picnicked on a grassy hollow in the middle of Alan's block of land, then went for a long walk on the beach. She found herself walking ahead of the others with Alan while he talked of his plans for the cottage. She already knew about his plans, so she knew it was a precursor to questions about herself. She didn't want to talk about herself, wanting to absorb the brilliance and isolation of this place. She had never seen anything like it before. You could live a whole life here and never be disturbed by anything.

'Was it the beach that attracted you to build a cottage here Alan?'

'Yes I'd heard about it from friends in Brisbane and knew I had to build a place here before I even saw it. Somehow, I knew inside me it was my place. It's amazing isn't it. In the morning you'll hear birds making such a racket you won't believe it.'

'Can you catch fish on this beach?' She knew men loved to fish.

'Oh yes, that's another passion of mine. Lots of bream and flat-head to catch here and whiting in the Nerang, half a mile behind us. Do you fish Aimée?'

She looked slightly shocked. 'No, only on the river bank with my father when I was a child.'

'I'd better teach you.'

Before it got dark, Betty and Rex drove to the general store, bought fruit and vegetables and some fresh fish to cook on a make-shift barbecue on the beach. They already had beer in the little ice chest in the car. They sat on a large checked rug Alan produced and laid out beside the fire and ate the delicious slightly charred fish. She looked up at the clear sky and shivered; the intensity of the stars in the night sky was astonishing. Was she shivering because it was now chilly on the beach? Or was it something else, more emotional or more primeval? Nobody was saying much. She looked at Alan who was sitting upright looking out to the sea. She thought he must be feeling the same thing she was. For a moment their eyes met and a shiver went down her spine. She shook herself like a dog and turned to Betty.

'How lovely it is out here under the stars – they seem almost on top of you. I suppose you'll be coming down all the time when the building starts?'

'There won't be much sitting under the stars when the real work starts, love,' said Rex tossing his head towards Alan, 'his nibs here will have us all at the grindstone. You'll be dragged into it too for sure. Seeing you're an artist of sorts, he'll line you up for painting the walls.' They all laughed and the moment of solemnity was broken.

'Betty rang for you earlier and wants you to go to her mother's for lunch tomorrow,' Owen told her as she arrived home from the late shift at the hospital.

'Why are you up so late?'

'I couldn't put down Aldous Huxley's latest book, *Point Counterpoint*. Apparently Betty's sister Jo is up here for a few days.'

Aimée had met the family at the house they had rented in Florence St Ascot including the other two sisters Mary and Mickey (everyone seemed to call her that though her real name was Frances). Maybe it was because she was so tiny – Mickey Mouse? She didn't dare ask.

She thought the family was fascinating, so different from any other family she'd ever met. Their father Will seemed a benevolent patriarch, gruff speaking, words always to the point and a constant tease to all the girls. He had one of those inscrutable faces that seemed to hover between disapproval and an almost-smile. The family was so noisy, always laughing and talking over each other. They all called their mother Mill, apparently a shortening of her full name Amelia Matilda, though when Betty really wanted something she called her mother Mum in a business-like way to make herself clear.

Betty collected Aimée in Dora to take her to the Jeffrey's. On the way she told her:

'You'll love Jo – she's the most genuine of all of us. Typical eldest sister, always fussing over everyone, keeping the peace and telling them to thank the milkman and smile at Miss So and So.

But she's had a really hard time over the last couple of years coping with the Depression. I told you about her fiancé Alf Watson who's an Olympic hurdler and his employer wouldn't keep his job open for the 1932 Olympics so he couldn't go. Poor old Jo has been scraping a living going from door to door offering to manicure womens' nails! Now they want to get married, gawd love 'em.'

The Jeffrey house was a typical Brisbane weather board painted white with a big front verandah overlooking a spacious front lawn full of budding rose bushes and neat gardens of colourful spring flowers. She knew Will was a keen gardener but he wasn't visible this time. As if reading her mind, Betty told her on the way up the front stairs that the boys had taken her father off down the bay so it's just girls for lunch.

Jo greeted them on the verandah with a big hug for Betty and a broad welcoming smile and arms outstretched for Aimée.

'It's so nice to meet you, I've heard so much about you. How's your brother going?'

'He's doing pretty well all things considered, and thanks for asking. In fact, he's planning to go back to Sydney to resume his job.'

Jo was small, compact, with huge blue eyes and a sunny smile. For a moment Aimée thought Jo could be a miniature Busby Berkeley showgirl, but in no time felt her shrewdness and maturity. The four sisters, their mother and Aimée gathered around a table on the verandah and of course everyone talked at once. Jo had already told her sisters where she was up to on wedding planning, but now that Betty and Aimée had arrived, it all had to be gone over again.

'I've made up my mind, it has to be in Melbourne and you'll all just have to come down.' Jo said this with an air of patient authority. 'Except for the family, all Alf's and my friends are in Melbourne, and a few in Hobart and Adelaide, and nobody's got any money to travel up to Brisbane.'

'I wish it could be here – it would be lovely in this garden.' said Mary wistfully.

Mickey shot back: 'That's only because your naval man's ship is here most of the time.'

'You can talk – with this doctor person you're always writing secretly to.'

'You little pest – what do you know?'

'You'd be surprised!'

'Girls, that's enough.' Mill was used to this bitchy banter. She turned to Aimée. 'I'm sorry, dear, I thought my girls had grown up by now. Personally, I would be thrilled if the wedding were in Melbourne. You all grew up there and we have the happiest memories. Have you a church in mind Jo?'

'No Mum, I hope you won't mind, but we're thinking of a garden wedding …'

'Not a church? Or do you just mean having a reception in the garden?'

'Well neither of us is religious, and our friends the Ramseys have offered to have it in the huge garden at Labassa in Caulfield, and they have a big flat in the house, if it rains …'

'Oh I see, Labassa! Are they having weddings there now? Well if this is what you want.' She looked very dubious. Mickey and Mary picked up on her disappointment in a flash. Mickey looked at her nails:

'We all go to St Augustine's here – it's such a lovely church.'

Mary laughed: 'Wasn't Dad terrible last Sunday in church! You were there Bet.'

Betty grinned. 'Yes he was!' She explained to Aimée: 'You see the Luya family sit on the other side of the aisle to us Jeffreys in the church and we see their daughter Mary all the time. Last Sunday when we were singing "Alleluia, alleluia" in the hymn, Dad was at his worst. He sang at the top of his voice "Mary Luya, Mary Luya". If that wasn't enough, when we lined up for communion, he took off at the rate of knots to be first in the queue, and we all trotted after him but he suddenly stops and puts his hand out with a stop sign and we all run into him. I reckon everyone in the church thought he was drunk!'

'Yes it was so embarrassing. I didn't know where to look. And when I scold him he just giggles.'

Mickey said: 'Mill I saw you – you were giggling too!'

Aimée saw Jo was looking very put out. 'I think it would be lovely to have the wedding in the garden at Labassa – it's magnificent. I used to know a girl who lived in one of the flats. Have you been there Mrs Jeffrey?'

'Mill, dear.'

'Mill …'

'No I don't think so.'

'Yes you have Mum,' said Jo, 'and you've met the Ramseys.'

'Are they those theatre people you used to know?'

'Yes but they're not "theatre people", they actually *go* to the theatre.'

Betty intervened and said it was time they got some lunch together and disappeared with Mary and Mickey to the kitchen. Mill looked at Jo and assured her a garden wedding in Melbourne would be lovely. Jo smiled briskly and said it would be very small and simple, then changed the subject and asked Aimée:

'But if your brother goes back to Sydney, does that mean you would go too?'

'I'm not sure. If he's strong enough, probably I should go back to the Alfred in Melbourne.'

'Oh that would be a terrible shame,' said Mill.

'Yes all the girls say you are so well settled here. Why wouldn't you stay?'

She looked at them both. It dawned on her there was an agenda going on.

'Well I love being here and your family has been so good to me – to us both, but I always promised the Alfred I would return when Owen was recovered.'

She was relieved nothing more was said on the subject. Of course she knew what they were thinking but it surprised her because nothing had happened between her and Alan, except a few curious glances and self-deprecating comments. Lunch proceeded with much banter when Betty and her sisters re-appeared with a delicious array of salads. Everybody became enthusiastic about a garden wedding at Labassa and it was agreed it would happen in early December and Mickey would go down a few weeks in advance to help. She even reluctantly admitted she might see a little of her mysterious doctor friend.

Aimée was at the maternity ward at the hospital on Monday morning when she was given a message that Jo Jeffrey wanted to come over to the hospital and have a cup of tea when she had a break. They met in the canteen and Aimée said with a big smile:

'What a lovely surprise for you to come to the hospital!'

'Oh I just wanted to see what you do and get to know you a bit better – I have to go back to Melbourne tomorrow. And I needed a breather from the family.'

'I just adore your family and all the carry on, but it's wonderful to put a face to you especially as you're the only one I hadn't met.'

They queued up for their cups of tea and went and sat in a quiet corner of the vast canteen. She had really warmed to Jo. She felt curiously honoured she'd come to the hospital to see her. She could tell there was something about Jo that seemed to make her the emotional centre of her siblings.

'Your family are so friendly. Betty tells me you've lived in several cities following your father's work. Was that hard for all of you?'

'Not really, there were always so many of us that you never got lonely. And you know Mill and Will are joined at the hip, probably because they were both from large Tasmanian families. Tassie families are always very close. When he left school Dad joined the post office in Hobart as an accounts clerk and worked his way up all round Australia till he's now one of the top people.'

'Do you remember Hobart?'

'Do I remember it? I spent my first twelve years there and we had a wonderful childhood there. You wouldn't believe how many cousins and uncles and aunts there were – on both sides of the family. We roamed the streets in New Town – like the whole area was our backyard! Then Dad was transferred to Melbourne and I spent my teens there and most of us had our schooling there, but after that he kept on being moved around. Now here they are in Brisbane! But what about you Aimée?'

She looked away and shook her head. 'Our childhood was happy for a while but my mother died when I was eight and it was pretty grim after that.' She told Jo the sad story of the lonely lives and schooling in Melbourne. Jo thought it was a terrible way to treat bereaved children and asked if it had damaged any of them for adult life.

'Actually we came through it remarkably well in the end, because like your family we were very close, but I think it has made us all self-sufficient and rather too private. I was miserable the first year at Merton Hall in Melbourne, but I learned to love it. There was a serious blue stocking atmosphere that seemed to suit me and I found I was quite good at art.'

'None of us was any good at that – we were all too busy mucking up. Did you take the art any further?'

'Yes when I left school I enrolled in the National Gallery of Victoria Art School, but then we had the Depression. I had to get a real job so I became a nurse at the Alfred and did midwifery.'

'What a shame to give it up. Do you still do art?'

'Not much, I don't ever seem to have the time.'

She didn't tell Jo the full story as she thought Jo and the Jeffreys wouldn't approve. What she had really loved about Merton Hall and her two years studying art was how she came under the spell of a young teacher at the school called Gwenda Kent-Hughes, whom she thought was the cleverest person she'd ever met. Despite being a teacher in a very established private school she threw herself into organising and haranguing for better education, women's rights and the political left. Looking back on it now, it said a lot for Merton Hall's advanced attitudes. At the time Gwenda's brother Wilfred was a young politician in Joe Lyons' United Australia Party. Gwenda was the complete opposite of Wilfred and regarded her brother with amused derision. She found Gwenda and her friends completely fascinating. She resisted her politics but loved her enthusiasm, intellect and protective friendship. When Gwenda had married Ian Lloyd, a music-loving lawyer, she became deeply attached to them both and looked to them for moral support and guidance. She loved the ferment in the Lloyd's large ramshackle house in Kew where musicians, artists, composers, European emigres and disreputable lefties thronged.

Aimée looked at the clock on the wall and realised she had to go back to the ward. 'Jo, I'm going to have to go but I'm so thrilled that you came over here. Can we keep in touch after you go back?'

'Yes of course we can, and we must. You know you've become part of the family.' She took a deep breath and went on, 'and of course you know, don't you, Mill thinks you are the right girl for Alan.'

'Oh, don't be ridiculous, I hardly know him and there's nothing going on between us.'

Jo looked at her with her big eyes and lazy smile. 'Alan is like a tortoise, but I'm warning you I have it on good authority he's head over heels!'

For the next few days, she was in a daze. She had never allowed herself to think about Alan, but then life and work had always been so serious, she had never really thought about a relationship with any man. You went to dances with men and met them on outings with your friends. Mostly they seemed awkward and rather boring and wanted to loom over you in dark corners. She had never been with Alan on his own but had got to know him quite well socially, usually with Betty. She could tell he was intrigued with her and sometimes it had given her a little shiver of pleasure. He was a lot older, had mature friends and she knew his sisters thought the world of him. The idea that he might want her was overwhelming. It turned the world upside down, because .... because when she opened her eyes to herself, ever since she first met him, she had liked him a great deal, as a really substantial and kind person with an attractive personality, and, she had to admit to herself, as an attractive man …

What should she do? Owen was returning to work in Sydney in the New Year. Her conscience told her she should go back with him; he would need looking after for some time yet. Janet Alexander was always writing and asking when she was coming back to Melbourne. She had lived with the Alexanders since she had left school, and Janet had been her constant companion despite being several years older. She would love to go back to Melbourne; her life there had been so varied and interesting and she had made many friends from all sorts of walks of life. So she did nothing. She didn't answer anyone's questions about what she would do when Owen left for Sydney.

Then out of the blue Alan rang up and asked her to be his partner at his firm's annual dinner for clients and senior staff at the Queensland Club. She was sure Mill had put him up to this and she accepted reluctantly. Everyone would look on her as a sort of de facto fiancée, yet in reality there was *no* relationship. She agonised about this and decided to ring him up and say it would be unsuitable and embarrassing for them both. Fate intervened. That very evening she had just arrived home at the Gregory Terrace flat and was having a drink with Owen when the doorbell rang and there was Alan.

'I've never been invited to your flat before so I thought I would just have to invite myself on my way home from work.'

Owen smiled at him: 'Perfect timing Alan, what would you like to drink?'

They sat on the little balcony overlooking the playing fields. The two men chatted and she couldn't take a smile off her face. 'Would you like to stay to dinner Alan? I'm just about to put something together for Owen.'

'That's very kind of you Aimée, but I want to give you a bit of background about the firm's dinner at the Club, so I wonder if Owen would mind if I carry you off down to the Valley for something to eat – there's quite a nice little place I've been to a few times.'

They went to his nice little place. It was softly lit and they talked for hours, about his job, about their mutual love of Melbourne and the things they each used to do there, and about her own sisters. He was excited about his plans for Surfers Paradise; the builder was starting in January. He didn't mention the dinner at the Club.

The time in Brisbane was a real Indian summer for Will Jeffrey and his family. Alan's open personality attracted friendship amongst his professional colleagues and their friends and families. Mickey, Betty, Rex and Mary were all gregarious so the family home in Florence Street Ascot was always full of young people going or coming to parties, tennis parties or 'going down the bay' on somebody's launch for a fishing weekend. Aimée was always invited and now that he was stronger, she encouraged Owen to come along too. Brisbane has always been fond of parties and young men and women with pretensions to being fashionable never shirked opportunities for dressing up – the more formal the better. Exhibition Week in August was always the apex of the social scene, even in the 1930s. The Bushwackers Ball, the Bachelors and the Girls were the big events of the year and mostly took place in the huge Cloudland Ballroom with its famous sprung floor high up at Bowen Hills overlooking the river. Now that she and Alan were going out together (though neither of them said anything to each other about a 'relationship'), she found the social whirl a little beyond her. They all seemed to lead frenetic social lives, and Alan squired her to parties and business functions. But he was so busy with his office responsibilities that there seemed no time for them to be on their own.

But the Jeffreys were dispersing. After less than two years in Brisbane, Will was promoted to Chief Accountant for the GPO and the family was transferred to Sydney for his final stint before retirement. Everyone went down to Melbourne for Jo's wedding, and Mickey announced her engagement to her mysterious doctor friend Charles 'Breezy' Gale, and went back to live in Melbourne. Aimée's dedication to nursing and the impressive way she intervened in Owen's diabetic illness, convinced Betty to enter the nursing profession. She had often thought of becoming a nurse, but at twenty six, she wondered if she would be accepted. Aimée encouraged her and put in a word at the Alfred. Betty was thrilled when the matron told her that to start nursing at a mature age was the best way to a successful career in the profession so she too made her way back to Melbourne.

Aimée's dilemma about her own future intensified with all these comings and goings. When Alan took her down to Surfers one weekend to see the start of the building of what he now called *Breffney*, it was too much for her, and she confessed her confusion to him. She didn't tell him she now realised she was in love with him, but she thought he probably knew.

'I feel I have to go to Sydney at least for a while to make sure Owen's on his feet. He's pretty helpless in the house you know with his head always in a book.'

'I understand, but what will I do without you? Who'll look after me with Betty gone? Rex?'

She gritted her teeth and hit him on the arm.

'I have an idea which I've been turning over in my mind.' He suddenly looked serious: 'Why don't we talk to Mill and have you live in Sydney with them? They're renting a big house in Mosman and there's only Mary at home now. If you like, you could both stay there. When Owen's on his feet you can come back here, and stay in Kangaroo Point in Betty's room?'

Mill and Will were thrilled with the idea. So was Aimée, though again she felt it had been a set up between Alan and his mother. She was a pawn in their game. It didn't matter: she loved Mill, she was like a replacement for her own lost mother. It was a privilege she thought, living with a woman who had six children, all of whom loved her dearly, and a husband she had lived with for nearly forty years who worshipped her. And Mill loved all her family back fiercely. Nothing could pull these people apart and they have welcomed me into their lives. What good fortune for me.

Nevertheless, Sydney was a pause in her life, a frustrating pause. Alan's life seemed to go on as before, incredibly busy, his letters distracted by work, leavened only with progress on *Breffney*. Owen had found rooms in a boarding house run by a caring landlady, and told her he was even going out from time to time.

The brightest spot was living and talking with Mill. Aimée's routine of travelling every day to Sydney Hospital where she was working as a midwifery sister, was always changing depending on her shift, but Mill insisted on cooking and eating her meals with her whatever the time of day. Aimée found their conversations took her into a new realm of understanding. The subject of midwifery was the starting point. Having given birth to six children, Mill seemed to know more about the subject than she had ever learnt. Aimée had always thought Gwenda Kent-Hughes was the wisest woman she had known, but Mill knew about people and what made them tick. She talked about all her children, even Alan, with such understanding. Though she loved them all, she also knew their faults, and she knew how to balance this knowledge without preaching to them. The intimacy Mill gave her was a gift, allowing her to unburden herself of the sadnesses and loneliness of much of her childhood.

One afternoon when she came home from the early shift, Mill said:

'You look rather pale and tired dear. Do you need a rest? Is everything all right?'

'Yes I'm fine thanks.' She looked anything but.

'Have you heard from Alan recently?'

'No, not for nearly three weeks.'

'Yes he's not a good letter-writer. Quite unlike Will who wrote almost every day when he was away from home. Why don't you ring him and shake him up?'

'I don't think it's my place to ring him, but I do worry that he works too hard and doesn't look after himself. When Betty was there it was different.'

'Alan has always had such a strong sense of responsibility. He was the one who had the best education and I think he felt he had more privilege than the others and he had to help them and show the way. He deeply respects his father and I often feel Will should tell him how much he admires him. It would take some of the weight off Alan's shoulders. Ring him dear and ask him why he hasn't written.'

She thought about this for a day or two, then steeled herself to pick up the phone when no one was around.

'Hullo.'

'Alan, it's Aimée. How are you?'

'Aimée, how nice to hear from you. Is everything alright, are my parents behaving themselves?'

'Of course, they're wonderful. But I'm ringing to see how you are. You always work so hard and never have time for anything else. Your mother worries about you and … we all miss you.' They talked on for a while but it seemed stilted. She knew they had to be face to face for him to be relaxed with her.

It took a major family event to introduce new dynamics into the situation. The advent of the debonair John Denny into Mary Jeffrey's life and his new and prestigious position as a senior officer on the navy flagship HMAS Australia, added a real touch of glamour for the family. Mary with her infectious giggle seemed to flirt with all the eligible young men, but John was different and persistent. In the autumn of 1935, the officers of HMAS Australia put on a big reception for the city's bigwigs when the ship visited Sydney. Mary was invited and insisted to John that Aimée should also be invited. Knowing Alan was slow off the mark, she also wangled an invitation for Alan who agreed to come down from Brisbane. Betty rang Aimée and told her that if he finally gets around to 'popping the question', in the immortal words of the then-current popular song: 'You must say 'yes' to Mr Brown'. No doubt Betty had given Alan a pep talk before he got to Sydney, as the day after the party on HMAS Australia, Betty received a telegram from Aimée that read: 'Have said yes to Mr Brown!'

In September 1935, Aimée and Alan were married in the Melbourne Grammar School Chapel, Alan's *alma mater*. A reception was held at the Alexanders in nearby East Melbourne. In addition to her nursing and art school friends, she invited several of her old school friends including Gwenda and Ian Lloyd who had been so caring for her in the lonely days after she left school. Owen came down from Sydney with their sister Olive who had married a Sydney doctor, Bruce Fry. Edna came across from Perth but their father Arthur Francis was overseas on one of his trips and only could manage a telegram of good wishes and the promise of a special gift from England on their return. All the Jeffrey clan were there and collectively turned the gathering into a real party. Aimée, in a flawless cream silk ballerina length dress, looked serenely happy. She felt she didn't need to say much, just stand beside her new husband and drink in everyone's enthusiasm. Alan with a big grin on his face, talked to everyone, explaining about life in Brisbane, how enjoyable it was, the cottage at the beach he was building and how he couldn't wait to take Aimée back there and start their life together, especially seeing she had already met most of his friends.

When Alan made his speech, she glowed with pride. He was humorous, but also confident and even commanding as he spoke of his devotion to his parents and his family, the pleasure he had from the many friends he had made in Brisbane, and his keen anticipation of the life they would share there in the years ahead. She was thrilled at the words of love and commitment to her that concluded his speech. She realised he was a man of fine character and how serendipitous it had been to meet Betty on that ship, then to meet Alan and to now know without a shadow of doubt he was the man for her. After all, she thought, he was a mature man of thirty-seven; already his hair was white and he knew a great deal of the world. She could feel the pride in the eyes of her father-in-law Will sitting at the end of the oval table, as well as the adoration for her son shining in Mill's eyes. It was an extraordinary moment.

On their honeymoon they drove along the coast to Adelaide and took the ferry over to Kangaroo Island, for them a remote and isolated place they had never visited. Neither of them could recall having two weeks to themselves at any time in their lives. It would have been challenging to either of them if alone; being together for the first time in this place was at first difficult. Alan was a gregarious man and eldest of a large and rowdy family. He had a job running a sizeable office. He had never been faced with such intimacy before. Despite being to some extent in awe of her new husband, it was easier for her. She was used to quiet places; close friends were more important than outward sociability.

He watched her looking calmly out to sea sitting at breakfast in their little guest house in Kingscote:

'What are you thinking?' he asked putting his hand over hers.

'Looking out at the peaceful bay reminds me of the wide reaches of the Swan where we used to play as children on holidays. Did your family swim in the Derwent?'

'Not much where we lived at New Town in Hobart, but we had these great expeditions to Kingston for Christmas holidays where we swam all the time. The Derwent looks like a lake from there.'

He was looking at his watch, an oblong silver object, linked by one of the cream canvas bands she noticed he washed each morning.

'Do we have to be somewhere soon?'

'Not yet, but if we're going to catch the bus to the end of the island to see the seals, we need to get ready.'

She noticed he always seemed to be planning the next step. He was not an impatient man, but so far seemed unable to relax.

Unlike the ferry ride from Adelaide, where he strode from one end to the other looking at everything and talking to the captain, the long trip on the rattling old bus to the seal colony, squeezed up against each other, seemed to relax him. He chatted about anything that came into his head, and she saw the crinkling up of his eyes she loved so much. They held hands as they walked around the edge of the rocky escarpment where hundreds of seals sunned themselves. When they looked and smiled at each other, no words seemed necessary. The great colony of seals on the rocks was yet another new experience and made her think words *were* necessary. They needed to learn about each other before they could genuinely lead a life together.

She said: 'All those seals remind me of a beach full of people sun-baking. They must love being here.'

'Yes I suppose they do – like we're going to love sun-baking at Surfers.'

'Are you going to want a family – like your own?' She had never raised this question before.

'I would like children though I had never thought of a big family like ours. But this is a question I should ask you.'

She paused for a moment. 'Yes I would like children, but you know I never really expected I would have any. Even now the thought feels extraordinary.'

'Why? All loving married couples expect nothing less.'

The sun had gone in and the wind was quite cold. They walked along the road to a little cafe, the only sign of life, except the seals. They ordered a cup of tea and sat down beside the window. She had not spoken for a while.

'I don't think we can expect children. We have to think if we are able to give any child what they need. I hate to think any child of ours would have to go through what my brother and sisters went through. I'm sure we could be loving parents, but is that enough today? I could hardly believe my eyes when I saw the dreadfully poor and deprived people brought into the hospital in Sydney, and it's even worse in Melbourne with crime added to poverty. And it worries me terribly what's happening overseas. You've said yourself there could be another war.'

He looked at her carefully as if he'd never seen her close up before.

'Yes you're right. I'd never thought about it that way before.' He shook his head gently, smiled and went on: 'I love the way you care so much about people and about our responsibilities. I completely agree with you. But we have to realise we are the sort of people, with our experience and education, that must do these things, have children, give them the great opportunities.'

'I do hope you're right Alan. I want you to be right.' She smiled but she wasn't convinced.

It became the way for them. He was always the optimist, comfortable with people, confident in his ability to work through and solve problems. She was not a pessimist, but she worried about people and their circumstances and felt the burden of her responsibility. She totally trusted him and felt his opinions and instincts were well founded. At first she was inclined to bend completely to his mature authority, but she came to understand that his confidence was not bombastic, that he needed her opinions and support. One day he told her he needed her wisdom and could not do without it. 'Soon after I got to know you, I realised I had missed out on feminine wisdom ever since I left home and I was in danger of becoming the wrong sort of man.'

Setting up in the Kangaroo Point flat overlooking the river was a tremendous thrill for her. Alan had insisted she give up her full-time nursing, saying she could do part-time private midwifery if she really wanted to, once she had fully settled in back in Brisbane. She quickly acquiesced, having no desire to return to the General. The flat was airy and spacious. Rex had gone back to Melbourne to live and it was the first time in her life she could call a place her own. She could almost see Alan's personal office across the river from the kitchen window.

With his assurances, her reservations about having children had receded, if not vanished. They took to the process of fulfilling that dream with enthusiasm. A routine developed where every second Friday, he came home at lunchtime and they drove down to Surfers for the weekend. *Breffney* was nearing completion and Rex's prediction came true that she would finish up painting the house. Before long to their mutual delight she became pregnant, but the weekends at the beach didn't slacken. Alan worked tirelessly to create a garden around the house enclosed on all sides by the bird-filled native bush. A narrow exit to the sandy track at the front led straight on to the sandhills, the roar of the surf and the deserted beach in both directions.

A boy was born the following spring. They named him Antony as she was fearful he would be referred to as An*th*ony, which she regarded as both ugly and incorrect pronunciation. For her, life with Alan and Antony was completely fulfilling. When she was feeding Antony in the morning looking out to the river, she found herself marvelling at its perfection. There were plenty of problems every day, some serious. It was her obligation to deal with them and even solve them. She knew that her happiness, the feeling she was experiencing *now*, gave her the ability to face everything that lay ahead. The reality was that her new married life was indeed crossed with shadows.

She had not understood until now how demanding and even exhausting Alan's job was. He was the partner in charge of a busy and rapidly expanding accounting practice. Not only was he supervising all the client work, but he was out day and night meeting new clients explaining how his firm could meet their needs. She was increasingly drawn into after-work entertainment of the clients. To her surprise and some alarm, she realised he sometimes depended on her being beside him. From time to time the senior partner in the Sydney office visited Brisbane to look over the management of the practice. Mr Chancellor was much older than Alan. It was obvious he was a very important person in the world of business and accountancy. Tall and straight with neatly combed grey hair, he had a quiet humour and she felt he understood the demands Alan was facing. He confided to her that Alan was the most talented of the younger generation of partners in the national firm and in due course would be needed in Sydney or Melbourne. She was relieved he was sympathetic to the situation of balancing work with a young family, but the message was clear: she had to be an integral part of Alan's career.

Up to a point Alan thrived on the demands of his work. When he came home late from work, often looking grey and exhausted, he quickly revived when she told him of her day's domestic doings and he in turn unloaded his office dramas and absurdities.

'I don't know what I'd do without Ernie Flook. He saved my life today.' Ernest Flook was one of Alan's brightest colleagues, who some years earlier had arrived fresh off the boat from the East End of London, replete with the broadest Cockney accent. His habitual response when his office phone rang was 'Flook of Flack and Flack 'ere', invariably raising a smile with clients and staff.

'I had this new client from a big English company. You know how pompous some Englishmen can be, and this man is the head office accountant of their Australian operations in Melbourne and he was obsessed by the clash of Australian tax laws with British tax law. He kept telling me nobody in the firm in Australia could solve these tax problems. None of us in the Brisbane office could, but in desperation I called in Ernie because I knew at least he could bamboozle him with technicalities. Well you should have seen his face when Ernie came in with his accent and his waistcoat covered in ash from the cigarette always hanging from his mouth. Luckily I had to go out to another meeting, but when I got back the room was full of smoke like a gambling den. The two of them had papers everywhere and had become firm friends. Ernie is off to Melbourne next week for a week to solve all their tax problems. I had no idea he was such an expert.'

The work was not the problem in itself; he enjoyed his job and the people around him. She could see he drove himself too hard and it was affecting him physically. Every few weeks he had severe pains in the stomach and his doctor prescribed medication to settle it down. With her nursing knowledge, she worried more than he did and kept at him to have specialist tests to diagnose if something was seriously wrong. He was told he had ulcerative colitis and must be careful what he ate and not drink alcohol at all or in moderation. She was meticulous about his diet in the food she prepared but much of the time it was trial and error.

The compensations for his busy life included the friends he had made in his time in Brisbane, and new friends they met together. Friendship through being the wife in a married couple was a different experience, especially with a baby. When she became pregnant a second time, they reluctantly agreed they needed to move from the Kangaroo Point flat to a house with a garden. A house with a large flat back yard in salubrious Palm Avenue Ascot was rented. The role of being a suburban housewife with a small child and another on the way was certainly different and sometimes she wondered if it was more of a challenge than a delight. Nevertheless she made many new women friends, most married to men Alan knew and most either pregnant or with young children.

Two families became close friends and became very important to her.

She took a great liking to Ken Fraser, the doctor whose intervention with Owen had probably saved his life. A small, bustling man with boundless energy and good humour, Ken was arguably Brisbane's leading paediatric surgeon. He had Scottish ancestry and played on his heritage at every opportunity. Kilts were worn whenever possible at a suitable occasion. Robert Burns, Scottish phrases and the histories of the clans were constant elements of life in the Fraser household. Ken's wife Patricia came from a large Brisbane family much involved in the medical profession and she became a close friend. She had three little children, the youngest the same age as Antony.

The other family was rather different. Thomas Brown and Co were leading retailers in Queensland. The current scion was also Thomas Brown, known unsurprisingly as Tom. The Browns were as near as possible to local aristocracy. They had played a prominent role in Queensland's development for a very long time, and on the family's maternal side were descended directly from one of Queensland's great pioneers and former chief justice Sir Samuel Griffith. Tom and his wife Betty Brown lived on the upper level of a huge old weatherboard mansion on Brisbane's premier residential street Windermere Road, Ascot. The house nestled at the head of a circular gravel drive. Surrounded by luxuriant trees and great banks of bougainvillea and flowering shrubs, it had the appearance of a wild suburban rain forest. The lower storey of the house was occupied by its owner, old Mrs Brown, Tom's mother, who lived alone in its gloomy cavernous rooms and was always dressed in ankle length black. Aimée loved the Browns; Tom was blue-eyed and ruggedly handsome, monosyllabic, but with a wry humour. He and Alan got on very well; Alan was one of the few men who with his observant wit made Tom laugh uproariously. His wife Betty had a keen sense of the frailties and pretensions of people around her. She needed to be engaged in activities that stretched her and she felt were worthwhile. She made Aimée laugh and fostered her dormant sense of mischief.

The friendships with Betty Brown, Pat Fraser and other young married women became a boon and refuge from the alarming news of impending war filling the radio and newspapers. Her sister Edna's husband Norton Dillimore from Perth had already enlisted in the army. Alan's sister Mary's husband John Denny was a senior naval officer and Aimée knew through Mary that the navy was on high alert for action in the region if it was needed. Her brother-in-law Rex took a different view to the political situation around the world. Thoroughly fed up with the drudgery of a salesman's life, he couldn't wait to see some action overseas.

Dora the Dodge had been pensioned off following an accident in Lancaster Road one afternoon when a car driven by an old man, blinded by the sun in his eyes, wandered across the road and crashed into Dora parked on the other side of the road. Antony was sitting in Aimée's arms and went hurtling into the windscreen, receiving a wide cut over his eye. Flossie, a green 1937 Ford V8, took Dora's place and every possible weekend they took the baby off to Surfers. Several of their friends from Brisbane were building holiday cottages, some in the same style as *Breffney*, as log cabins or simple fibro shacks. The pristine beauty was a magnet for Brisbane families looking for a hideaway. For more than a hundred miles north of Brisbane to the NSW border, there was virtually uninterrupted fine white sand beach, comprising from the north, Moreton Island, North Stradbroke and South Stradbroke Islands, then endless mainland beach to the border at jutting Point Danger and its lighthouse.

It was their true retreat, almost magical in its brilliance and remoteness, but leavened by the presence of a few like-minded friends. There were no distractions, no social life apart from an occasional barbecue or an early evening picnic in the sandhills. There was body surfing on the endless beach, playing cricket on the beach at low tide, fishing in the surf and the quietness of just being there. *Breffney* seemed to enclose them from the outside world – for brief interludes they could think only of themselves.

Her second boy arrived in June 1939 and they called him David. He had blue eyes and from his first months, fair curly hair. Antony was nearly three, already with almost black hair, but her newborn's angelic appearance gave her constant delight. Even so she knew it was a chimera and at night the sense of dread spread through her consciousness as she fed the baby. Rex joined up; her sister Olive's husband Bruce Fry, a radiologist, had responded to the urgent call by the army for radiologists. Soon after war broke out in September, Alan received notification from the Defence Ministry in Canberra that his job as head of Flack and Flack was a 'prescribed position.' Accordingly he was not eligible to join any of the armed services while Australia was at war. In one way this was welcome news for Aimée as she knew his health needed her day to day support, but in another sense it was worse. Many of his staff were joining up and his work-load was becoming impossible.

It was not in her nature to air her concerns to all and sundry. She had the discipline and sense of responsibility of a nurse and the life-long practice of internalising her worries. Knowing the commitment she had to make to Alan and his job, she engaged a nanny, Kathleen, to help with the boys. Kathleen loved the boys and Aimée became grateful for her help in giving them an idyllic early childhood.

She gave no thought to her burdens in relation to herself. Not for a moment did she feel resentful that her long-awaited happiness was being compromised by the danger to almost everyone in her family let alone to the country. Outwardly she was the calm and serene young wife and mother, helpful and solicitous to her friends and everyone she met. At times she felt like an impostor acting out the life of middle-class urban Australia in its most carefree mode. Alan had a naturally optimistic personality and made it his business not to talk about the dire world situation at home. He treasured his home life with his little family, was aware of the tenuous nature of their circumstances, and even put a gloss on the political situation to try to reduce her anxiety. It was not easy as he was usually home late, feeling exhausted. After dinner, he liked to listen to music on the wireless or talk to her light-heartedly about the day's doings in the office. He wanted to know every detail about what the boys had done during the day. Though their life was outwardly peaceful and companionable, there was an underlying tension both tried to hide from each other.

Early in 1940, Betty rang to tell them she had decided to join the Army Nursing Corps. This was a shock to them both and the trigger to the serious discussion they had been avoiding.

'Betty told me the nurses are likely to be sent overseas. Does that mean she would be sent to a war zone?'

'Not now, but later on it could be. One of our biggest logistic problems if Australia gets caught up in real battle is evacuating wounded servicemen. They are converting passenger ships to hospital ships, even the *Manunda* where we first met.'

'But surely they wouldn't send nurses to Europe?'

'Probably not, but quite possibly to places in Asia where there is likely to be fighting. India, Malaya, Singapore, New Guinea are all possible.'

'Alan that's terrible. I had no idea it was likely to be so close. Do you think we'll be safe in Brisbane?'

'Brisbane's a very long way from any of the conflict zones so we should not worry for ourselves.'

'I don't think we can look at it like that. It only seemed a few weeks ago that this was happening only in Europe, and most of it was just angry talk between world leaders. If war can happen in such a short time on our doorstep, how can we protect our family?'

Alan rubbed his eyes and shook his head. 'I can't answer that. All I can say is that I don't think it will happen – it's too far away.'

It gave her a cold feeling in the pit of her stomach. For the first time, she understood he knew no more than she did.

Her realisation of their vulnerability had changed the atmosphere of their marriage. She had always felt he was so mature and knowledgeable, could be relied upon to know each step along the way. It was not that she respected him the less. If anything she loved him more, feeling he needed her protection as much as she needed his. The worst thing was that their happiness had plummeted. Their chats over dinner after putting the little boys to bed had a false humour. Sometimes she thought they were like actors, playing the parts of the contented parents. She disliked herself for her feelings of negativity, fear and helplessness; it reminded her of her early time at school in Melbourne.

Every morning she scanned the papers, trying desperately to find good news amongst the bad. It seemed all her family were involved in the war in some way. She vaguely thought if she knew what was happening in the war she could somehow help them. Betty had been sent to Singapore to be a nurse for Australian soldier casualties if fighting broke out on the Malayan peninsula. As always her letters were full of the fun they were having mixed with an underlying alarm she was not allowed to express in words. Then in December 1941 came the terrifying news of the Pearl Harbour raids. Even worse for Alan and Aimée was the Japanese declaration of war against the British and the rapid advance of their army down the Malayan peninsula. Christmas at *Breffney* was a sombre affair. Their friends in the nearby beach cottages all shared the same gloom and apprehension for serving family members. Most of the men were not there but on active service. Stephen King was in the airforce in England. Harry Mort, Byrne Hart and Alan's own colleague George Capper were all away in the army.

Early in 1942, several terrible events shook their lives to their foundations. The British battleships *Repulse* and *Prince of Wales* were sunk by Japanese air attacks in the Malacca straits. Worst of all, Singapore fell to the Japanese. They heard after a few days that Betty and her army nursing unit had been ordered to a small hospital ship, the *Vyner Brooke*, which escaped Singapore harbour with a large contingent of injured service people. Two days later, barely 200 miles from Singapore, the *Vyner Brooke* was bombed and sunk and most of its complement perished in the Malacca Strait. At home there was no news of the dead and whether there were any survivors.

All the Jeffreys were devastated – the brave and irrepressible Betty was the life of the family. The Japanese advance continued apace: Darwin was bombed, Papua New Guinea was invaded and their navy entered the Coral Sea to Australia's north-east. Queensland coastal towns and cities as far south as Brisbane became very alarmed; for the first time in its history, Australia seemed on the verge of invasion.

Aimée went about the daily routine with the children in a kind of nightmarish dream. She would sit with Kathleen in the nursery playing over all sorts of fanciful scenarios for keeping the boys safe. Alan seemed unreachable. In the office all day and most of the evening, whenever she saw him, he was remote and grey with exhaustion. On a Friday two weeks after the news of the *Vyner Brooke's* sinking, he came home early and told her they must discuss what they should do. When she had put the children to bed, she sat down at the kitchen table facing him, her eyes huge and anxious.

'You and the boys will have to go away to the country ...'

'No, not without you. I've already made up my mind. We must stay together.'

'Most families with children are getting ready to go …'

She interrupted him again, 'Alan I'm not going anywhere without you.'

'It's impossible for me to leave Brisbane, certainly when there's no immediate danger. The real point is that we must make arrangements for you and the boys while it's still safe. I've already had a talk with Joan.'

'Joan? You mean Joan White?'

He nodded.

'Why? What for?' One of her first friends when she came to Brisbane was Joan Perry (anointed as Antony's godmother when he was born). Joan later had married Henry White from a pioneering NSW grazing family and had gone to live on Henry's property *Talbragar* near Coolah in central west NSW.

'I think you should take the children to the Whites for a while – until this danger is over. I talked to Joan on the phone and she would be delighted for you all to go.'

'You talked to her, without consulting me? No Alan it's out of the question, unless you come too.'

She agonised for the whole weekend. She could see the sense but she could not get her head around being separated from him. It was not just the idea of being apart if there were an invasion, it was her constant concern about his health and the diet she oversaw daily. On Sunday she rang Joan. Joan was a noisy, larger than life personality who blithely insisted she should come, telling her that her presence would liven up her boredom with country life. Their son Michael was the same age as Antony and it would be good for both boys. Alan tried not to say too much while she wrestled with the issues. That evening he said to her:

'Why don't I come with you to the White's, and stay a couple of days until you're settled in.'

'It's not that Alan, I can manage the boys on the train, but it's you I am worried about. You'll work too hard, come home late, not eat proper food and get sick again.'

'No I won't – I now know what I have to eat for the right diet, and you must realise our friends will always be asking me over for meals.'

'That's just the problem. All the men are disappearing into the services and you won't get invited and you'll just work harder. I don't think we should go.'

'You must. It won't be for too long. When the Americans bring more forces, the tide will turn. The danger to families like ours is now, and if it lasts longer I promise I will join you at *Talbragar*.'

Six weeks later, Aimée and the children set out for *Talbragar*. All her instincts were against it but she was good at gritting her teeth and pushing down her deep emotional misgivings. Kathleen had left to go back to her family in Sydney. They took the train to Tamworth where Joan met them in her big Buick with the cumbersome gas producer attached to the rear. Despite the long drive through almost deserted drought-stricken country, Joan's loud effervescence was infectious and the arrival at the big spacious homestead with its wide verandahs and colourful garden was like arriving at an oasis. Henry, tall and lanky, was a welcoming host, the epitome of the laconic, hard-working grazier.

She rang Alan immediately and told him the Whites were wonderful and she was glad she had come, much to his relief.

She quickly fell into a routine, starting Antony in correspondence lessons at which he thrived. In addition to Michael who was Antony's age, the White's had two little daughters, aged three and twelve months, so Aimée threw herself into the nursery and helped in the huge kitchen where the food was produced for all the employees. It was like a small town with a store, several cottages for the men and their families, large shearing shed, blacksmith shed, yards for the stock and even a little building for the school of which there were half a dozen pupils.

As the weeks wore on, while her concern for Alan's health did not diminish, she found the rhythm of life at *Talbragar* almost soothing and found she could give herself time to gather her thoughts and even plan (or dream) the life she wanted with Alan and the boys after her return. Alan seemed to be in good heart and felt the war situation was turning and, fingers crossed, they could be home by Christmas. She noticed that her nursing training and strength of mind had good effects within the White family. Joan was not an easy person to be married to – she was often impatient with Henry whom she seemed to think was too staid. She was used to bright lights and having fun and none of this was available at this time and place. Joan unburdened herself with Aimée and would say she didn't know how she could manage Henry and the children without her.

Antony loved that time at *Talbragar*. His mother took him there when he was five, with David his little brother. It was a big sheep station near Coolah in NSW. She told him they had to go there because the war was getting closer to Australia and his father said it was dangerous for children to stay in Brisbane. It was a long way to *Talbragar* and they went by train and then in a big car with a gas producer on the back driving through very dry, grey land with lots of dirty sheep. He saw a dead horse and some kangaroos.

The homestead had big verandahs and he used to sit there doing his correspondence school work. Sometimes a bundle of Correspondence School papers came in the post and had coloured pictures of letters and numbers so it was easy to learn how to write. He liked trying to make letters and numbers look as good as the Correspondence papers that came in the mail. One day when he was doing his correspondence school work, he saw a huge cloud of dust in the distance. Auntie Joan who was rather fat and had a loud voice came out and leant on the verandah rail looking out and said the cattle are coming. This made him feel strange in the tummy and he asked why they were coming. She said they have to be mustered and would soon be up near the yard. The yard was a really exciting place where the horses were saddled and stockmen cracked their whips. At one end was the blacksmith's shop where the horses were shod. But he got really scared because he thought all the cattle charging about with their horns in the yard would be very dangerous. He ran into the house to tell his mother to come and look as the cattle were coming but really he wanted to be beside her. He found her and they both came out on the verandah to look. The cattle were much closer and he could see all the animals and hear the noise and felt even more scared. He was glad when they weren't put in the yard but kept in the home paddock which wasn't too close to the homestead.

The things he remembered best about *Talbragar* were the smells: the Pears soap from the big bathroom and the porridge you had for breakfast even though he didn't like it much. The smells in the kitchen were best. There was a huge wood-burning stove which warmed the whole big space and the mixture of the woodsmoke and roasting beef or mutton always made him hungry. In the garden, not far from the kitchen, was the store. This was his favourite place and it was where all the food was kept because it was sometimes a very long time for supplies to arrive from Sydney and you could never rely on getting what you wanted. The store was full of tins and bottles and packets of everything a sheep station might need, sacks of potatoes, stacks of corn flakes, honey, soap, bottles of jam, cordial, fruit, beer and the delicious tins of pineapple juice which were scarce and you were only allowed little drinks. It was like a shop, only better as there were no customers buying things and taking them away.

Bill, the blacksmith often took him and Michael into the blacksmith's shop to watch him bashing the horse shoes. There was always a glowing fire and the ends of the implements red hot. Michael's parents were Auntie Joan and Uncle Henry though he knew they weren't his real uncle and aunt. Michael was his best friend at *Talbragar*. He had yellow hair but his own was black. It was the next year before they went back home to Brisbane but it wasn't nearly as much fun as *Talbragar*.

In early 1943, Alan rang her at *Talbragar* and said he felt the Japanese danger had receded sufficiently for them to come home to Brisbane. Her heart leapt with a lightness she hadn't felt for months. As the tenancy on Palm Avenue had lapsed, he had found another house at Creswick Street Clayfield. It wasn't as nice but it was comfortable and he set about making it spruce and planting the garden. He found close by a big seed pod of a poinciana, broke it open and planted it. He knew poinciana trees grew quickly in Queensland and it could be a living symbol of their life in Brisbane, which he felt would flourish when the war was over.

When Aimée and the boys arrived home he noticed right away a new maturity and strength of purpose in her. She seemed to have shed the lost and fearful look he remembered before her departure. She took over his domestic life, insisted he be home for dinner each night, take Mondays off so they could stay longer at the beach on weekends, and watched his diet like a hawk. She had learnt a lot about where and how to obtain decent food and supplies from her experience maintaining the store at *Talbragar.* She engaged a lanky young girl straight out of school called Gladys as a live-in house-keeper, giving herself more time to look after Alan's needs.

Their time at the beach with the boys, snatched between the rigours of war-time Brisbane, was so fleeting, but it was their true life, where they could hold each other for themselves, where for a moment nothing else intruded. She loved the way Alan took time every morning for the little routines of chopping wood out the back of the house for the fire, chatting to the neighbours and taking the boys hand in hand to the beach. More than anything, she loved the way he would stop anything he was doing, and chat to her about little events in their lives, funny stories of the office, the absurdities of coping with the lack of essential supplies, Miss Laws' canny observations at the general store. When they were at the beach, he never referred to the war. She hung on his every word, wanted to touch his silver wavy hair, gazed at his smiling eyes, letting herself surrender to these moments like a child, suspending her awareness that the real fearful world awaited her on their return on Monday night to Brisbane.

The news finally came through that Betty had survived the sinking of the *Vyner Brooke* and was in a Japanese prison camp on the occupied island of Sumatra. It was hardly encouraging as it was well known that most of the prison camps were hell holes, but at least it gave some hope. 1944 brought more hopeful news about the progress of the war in the Pacific and they had confirmation that Betty was still alive. They heard from a soldier who had escaped Sumatra and returned to Australia some news about the prison camp where Betty was imprisoned. It was second hand information and told a grim picture of conditions in the camps. While Betty's continued survival was a ray of light in the gloom of war, her well-being and even her whereabouts were uncertain, so in no way did it relieve their anxiety.

Nevertheless a glorious summer weekend at Surfers Paradise shortly after getting the good news of Betty seemed a portent of the future. So it was an unexpected shock when Alan fell ill. His stomach pains were worse than in any previous episodes he had suffered. She insisted he stay home from work and she installed him in the little bedroom off the verandah where it was cooler and he would be less disturbed. All her old stoic agonies returned and she found herself ministering to him like a nurse, smiling and caring, but speechless, willing him to rest and sleep, but silently wringing her hands in another room.

Ken Fraser called regularly and prescribed a new drug which would relieve the discomfort. But Alan was not improving; Ken and other doctors he called in were puzzled about an accurate diagnosis. Cancer of the stomach had been ruled out but in any case he had suffered this colitis for years. She sat beside his bedside every day while Gladys looked after the children. He slept most of the time, though even when he woke he was drowsy from the drugs he was taking. Conversations always started with the mundane:

'How are you feeling?'

'A lot better. I think I'll get up and go and sit on the verandah.'

'That's a good idea.' She helped him get up and took him out, settled him in a chair and went to get him a cup of tea, horrified at how weak he was. She brought him his tea and sat beside him and they talked of the boys, always bringing a smile to his face. Soon enough he was leaning back in the chair with a look of pain.

By early April, after he had been ill for several weeks, Aimée told Ken he should go to hospital as he was having such dreadful nights, so it was decided he should be admitted to Turrawin Hospital and an operation undertaken. The Browns took the boys so Aimée could stay near to Alan. She stayed beside him night and day, numb with silent horror at his condition. The operation was not a success. He hung on for a few days either comatose or sleeping with Aimée sitting beside him. Each day Pat Fraser brought her home and gave her something to eat. Three days after the operation she watched as he died peacefully.

When Alan died she could hardly take it in. Though he had been ill for weeks and had been in poor health for a long time, she had always firmly believed her nursing skills would gradually restore him to health as she had done for her brother Owen. The shock and disbelief soon gave way to bitter grief and fear for the future of her children. She was thirty-five and as had been her habit for so long, she pushed down her emotions and determined she would not be overwhelmed. She sat alone in her bedroom looking out to the garden for hours in between visits from her friends which became less frequent as the weeks went by. The young house-keeper Gladys could not cope with Aimée's grief and told her there was no need for her in the house any longer and did she mind if she left.

Brisbane in the mid-forties as the war drew to a close and service men and women returned home, usually exhausted, emaciated and worse, was a listless and sleepy town. Food rationing still persisted though healthy food staples were plentiful. Social behaviour was cautious and conservative: men still went to work in three-piece woollen suits and grey felt hats despite the sticky sub-tropical climate. Aimée felt a despairing langour, a feeling that she was trapped in this dull listless place. The end of the war was clearly in sight but Brisbane seemed locked in the motions of the past. Families were slow to accept anything new. It was enough to try to resume normal pre-war life and deal with the sadness of lost loved ones or sick and traumatised relatives returning from the war. The long years of the Depression followed by the war had added to the impression (and reality) of Brisbane as a shabby, dusty place full of skimpy wooden houses on stilts with peeling weatherboards and rusty tin roofs.

Why had she finished up here? Even when she looked at her boys and their happy faces, she found herself resentful of their presence. Pat Fraser worried about her and came around and sat with her most days. Aimée refused to talk about Alan and was reluctant to even talk about the boys. So Pat talked about anything that came into her head. She found it was best to talk of her children, their arguments, bad behaviour and their funny interactions. She now had four, two boys and two girls aged from thirteen to four. It was a rumbustious household with lots of argument and noise. Ken was an extrovert man, never still for a moment, issuing streams of instructions over his shoulder as he rushed from one activity to the next. Antony and David were included in activities and outings with the Fraser children. David Fraser and Antony became best friends, being ten days apart in age. It was good therapy for her. She found herself laughing at the Fraser antics despite herself.

Trying to help but revealing the prejudices of the times, Ken told her the boys might be adversely affected by the loss of their father and she should avoid undue maternal physical contact as they might become susceptible to homosexuality. She thought this strange, but accepted his authority. Throughout their later childhood and adolescence, she resisted her own desire to kiss or hug them and after Alan's death, never again spoke of their father. This was not because of hard-heartedness, simply that she knew she could not cope emotionally to talk about him to the boys, without revealing her helpless vulnerability.

The best thing Antony remembered was going on holidays to the beach at Surfers Paradise. His father drove them in Flossie the Ford, but because it was the war and petrol was scarce, they sometimes went by train from South Brisbane Station which took forever. Flossie was green and had tail-lights that stuck out on stalks and the engine made a throbbing sound like Antony was able to make in the back of his throat.

His parents had a house called *Breffney* in the bushes over the sandy track behind the beach. It had a big hollow in the middle of the front garden which the kids rolled into and played games and sat in the tree beside the road and listened to the sound of the surf. The garden was much wilder than Brisbane and the birds cackled and there was always a wind off the sea. *Breffney* had green shutters on the windows and the Morts next door had blue shutters on *Hamerton* and the Cappers further up had red shutters on their house *Piri-Noa*, but the Harts had no shutters on *The Log*.

When he was a bit older, he was allowed to go on the beach with the Capper boys and sometimes they played all day in the sandhills. In the afternoon when the tide was out, the beach was hard and flat and the waves a long way out. From the sandhills he could see the beach going on forever in both directions. He liked to sit in the highest spot watching the change in the colour of the sea and the sky. The blue got softer and softer and then became mauve before it went grey and then he always had to go inside.

John Capper was often sent by his mother around to the Pacific Highway to buy fish and chips at the fish shop or to Miss Laws' general store and Antony went with him and sometimes his mother asked him to get something from the shop too. John had eagle eyes because he was always finding two bob pieces in the sand beside the road. Antony only once found one when he was with him but when he came past *Breffney* on the way home, he would sing out, hey guess what, I just found another two bob piece and showed it to him. Antony always looked very hard but never found any. John bought lollies with the two bob pieces he found and sometimes gave him one. In the end he didn't believe John found all those two bob pieces in the sand beside the road and wondered where he got them. When John showed him the two bob pieces, he looked like the cat who'd caught the canary and this made Antony suspicious.

At *Breffney* it was better because his father was there most of the time and friends of his parents came to stay. When he sat at the table having his breakfast, his father drank his tea from a wide cup which had six sides and red flowers and strange patterns on it. After breakfast he went with him to the woodpile where he chopped wood for the fireplace. He was told to go into the bush at the back to look for sticks to start the fire at night. His father often went to Mr Fogarty's next door to have a talk, or to wash Flossie, or sit on the step outside the kitchen and talk to Gladys, who had a tiny room next to the kitchen. Gladys was the maid and he liked her a lot but she has gone now. She was very tall and liked talking to his father who made her laugh.

But all the talking and washing and getting sticks was boring as he wanted to go to the beach with his father. He would say be patient Ant, we have to wait till the iceman brings the ice, then we can all go to the beach. The ice chest was next to the kitchen, and the iceman could hold two huge ice bricks in his big black tongs and dump them into the top of the ice chest. Next morning they would be completely melted, but the milk and other things inside would still be cold.

On the beach they swam in the surf and his father held his hand if it was too rough and usually his mother looked after David who was always running to her to be protected. His father built wonderful sandcastles with deep moats around them and shells on top, and tunnels through them to push pretend cars. In the afternoons when the tide was out, he played cricket with the grown-ups, but any kids about were given a bat and chased the balls when they were hit into the sea or far along the beach.

At *Breffney* the whole family sat beside the fire at night and

Gladys played her mouth organ in the dark with only the light from the little crinkled paper lamp. He sat on the floor leaning against her legs and David sat in his mother's lap sucking his thumb – he always sucked his thumb. The sound of the mouth organ made him think of other things and places he had never been to but really wanted to go to some day. Gladys held the mouth organ between both her hands, one on top and one below and made the sound vibrate. When she did this, it made him feel sad and excited all at once. The grown-ups stared into the fire and smiled and thanked Gladys when she finished a song. They were worried about Auntie Betty who was a prisoner of war.

At home his father got very sick and was in bed in the little room off the verandah most of the time. Dr Fraser came around to see him a lot and sometimes another doctor too. Dr Fraser lived in the next street and had four children. David Fraser was bossy and when they played after school, told him all the time what games they had to play. When he got sick of David Fraser's games, Antony went down to the end of the street and sat on the corner and watched the trams. The 400s were silver and were the newest and had pointed ends that sloped out. The 200s and 300s also were silver or grey really, but much older and more fun because you could sit on the outside. Late in the afternoon the red trams came along and he liked them best. They were smaller and rocked as they had only one set of wheels and the driver stood at the front with no window and kept twirling the handles. He badly wanted to ride on a red tram.

He was asleep the night his mother turned on the light and came into the nursery and untucked the mosquito net and sat down on the edge of his bed and said very quietly that his father had just died. Nothing like that had ever happened to him before and it was strange because at first he wanted to laugh but he knew it was very serious and that would be terrible so he made sure he didn't even smile. He asked her why he had died and she said it was the awful tummy trouble that kept making him so sick. She talked to him for a while about what a good man he was and he had be very brave and look after Davy, and then she tucked him in again with a kiss and went out and turned off the light.

She never talked about his father any more.

Getting on with her life was grim and hard going for Aimée. For years they lived in the black-oiled rented house in Creswick Street which gradually crumbled through neglect. Innately neat, dignified and elegant, she was reduced to painting the threadbare carpet in the living room and dining room in an acceptable forest green to cover the holes. While the boys were aware of the household poverty, she strove valiantly to make their lives seem normal, and apart from loss of a father figure, which deeply affected their later lives, in most respects their lives went on as before.

Even holding on to the house was perilous. When Alan had died, she had never known how much the rent was for the house. She had found the folder with the lease documents in the top drawer of his desk and saw there was still over a year to go on a three year lease at £10 a week. She recalled nearly fainting with horror. She knew there was no way she could pay anything like that. She had no money and virtually their only asset was the cottage *Breffney* at the beach. Even though Alan was the resident partner in his accounting firm, there was minimal residual value of his partnership.

The very day after her discovery of the rent situation, she rang Jim Irwin at the Flack and Flack office. Even though Jim was not a partner, Alan had told her he was the one to ask about any financial matters. Jim told her he would work something out and that she should not worry. Alan's partnership monthly advance would continue for at least the end of the next financial year, and he would find a way to cover the rent for the next few years. The stark reality that survival was in the hands of Alan's bright young colleague's financial ingenuity exposed her awful vulnerability.

But at least the talk with Jim Irwin hardened her realisation she must put aside emotion and find an income. Jim had come back two weeks later with a formal offer from the firm. She could tell from his embarrassed look that he had gone to some lengths to cobble a proposition from the firm that was beyond what Alan was formally entitled to, especially in wartime. They would pay her rent until the boys had left school and for their schooling, (unless she married again when it would stop).

She decided the one bankable skill she had that allowed her to work from home was to sew. She had always enjoyed sewing and at *Talbragar* had taught herself to be something of an expert. Smocked clothes for babies and small children were fashionable: it involved gathering the material of the dress or shirt into tiny ribs, less than a quarter of an inch deep, sewing them together and decorating the smocked section with little sewn motifs. She became outstanding in this intricate and painstaking work. Her friends rallied round and ordered their children's clothes from her.

It was dreadfully hard and time-consuming work. During the day, she sat at her sewing machine. After early dinner for the boys, she sat up late at night in her chair under the lamplight doing the decorative stitching with needle and thread. Later, and for many exhausting years she made beautiful baby clothes for an expensive shop called Snow White owned and run by a hard-nosed and sanctimonious woman she always referred to with disdain by the same name.

Even the one bright spot in her life, her love for her two boys, was tainted by the guilt and frustration of having such little time with them. When they were at school she sewed at the machine, and after school, she would send Antony off to the shop at the bottom of Creswick Street to get basic household supplies. Then she had to rush to cook their dinner and get them off to bed as soon as possible so she could do the detailed stitching until late at night. Her neglect didn't seem to affect Antony who was self-sufficient and read comics and books or played endless self-invented games with his model cars. However Davy was different, and at the kitchen table at night eating their dinner, she watched him anxiously as he toyed with his food, and hung on the words of his more assertive elder brother. She didn't like the way Antony ignored him unless it was to criticise or tease him. Despite Ken Fraser's advice, it was a consolation when she continued cuddling Davy in quiet moments, as she had always done. She adored his light brown curly hair, his big blue eyes and even at the age of seven or eight, his evident satisfaction at her loving attention.

Antony thought the nursery was a stupid name for the bedroom he shared with his brother David – as if they were both babies. It had a verandah off it with wooden blinds that looked out into the back garden with lots of trees including a persimmon tree full of messy yellow fruit which fell on the ground and were horrible to eat. He used to be scared of cats, especially black ones, and had nightmares about them. When they yowled on hot nights in the trees near the verandah, he thought they were going to pounce into his room.

His mother used to read books to him sitting on the bed before he went to sleep. David sat beside her too but he was too little to understand properly. Now most of the books he could read by himself. The *Just-So Stories* was his favourite. The cover was all messed up because he read it so much. He loved the way she said 'the great grey green Limpopo' in a low spooky voice. And he never got sick of looking at the drawing of the four djinns lifting up the whole city when the butterfly stamped its foot, and the drawing of Small Porgies, the smallest of all his brothers, sitting in the harbour and the ships around him looking like tiny toys! His next favourite was *The Meeting Pool* which was all about animals in the jungle. The *Way of the Whirlwind* had coloured pictures of magical creatures and black children. His mother loved this one best because it all happened in Western Australia where she grew up and she thought the person who painted the pictures was very clever.

When she sat at the sewing machine, listening to it drone away endlessly as she pedalled furiously, the boys' futures constantly in the back of her mind, she felt a kind of peace and calm from the very routine of the days. In the early morning, she was usually woken by the noisy drone of the newsagent Mr Myers' old cut-down Vauxhall as it turned around at the lane just down from the house, then roared slowly up the hill, with Mr Myers flinging the rolled up *Courier Mails* into each of the front gardens. The milkman was always prompt at eight, filling her enamel jug at the bottom of the stairs from his big steel jug, and replacing the saucer she left on the top of the jug. The baker came later, around ten o'clock. He came up the stairs to the kitchen door with his big wicker basket, full of sweet smelling loaves. Usually there were other callers of a more casual nature trying to sell their wares, and she didn't mind breaking her grind to answer the door.

The Model One Teacher School at Ascot State School was one of the few positive aspects of their lives. Antony had started there in 1944 at the age of seven and his news of the day's doings always entertained her. It was a school within a school specifically designed to demonstrate to trainee teachers how small country one-teacher schools operate. It had six classes ranging from ages six to twelve in a large airy classroom and its own small playground out of bounds to the main school. The teacher, Bill Gordon was himself a country teacher and had become an institution in the district.

She had found out about the school from several of her friends before Alan had died. Betty Brown had been worried about her son Thomas who was Antony's age but painfully introverted and shy. She was dubious about any of the state schools she had seen in the district, and was determined he should not board at a private school. She told Aimée:

'I've heard about this little school inside Ascot State School. Meryl Cullen says the teacher is superb and teaches six little classes together. What's really amazing is that he insists on recommendations from parents of existing or previous students before he accepts anyone. I can't imagine how he gets away with it.'

'Have you met him yet?'

'I took Thomas down to meet him the other day. He's a funny looking man who seems to be from a past age but he has a sweet manner. The classroom is huge with lovely full-colour illustrations on the walls that look almost like frescoes. He actually asked me who recommended us to the school, but he wasn't impressed until I mentioned the Harrises who have two boys there.' She laughed, 'It seems like an exclusive prep school except there are no fees.'

Betty's discovery of the school led to an influx from amongst their friends. She sent Thomas there and her daughter Erica; the Frasers sent David and the Cullens their eldest daughter Lindsey. Alan's colleague Russell Cuppaidge sent his son George.

Antony wasn't sure what to make of Mr Gordon. He told his mother:

'He has round green glasses but one of his eyes is white and doesn't see, but it's amazing because when he writes on the board he looks across with his good eye on to the other green glass and sees the reflection of what everyone's doing in the class, and if anyone mucks up, he's on to them in a flash.'

Like most of his mates at the school, Antony liked the independence from the 'big school' Mr Gordon fostered. At the bottom of its own little playground there was a hen house where they kept Australorps, White Leghorns and a few Rhode Island Reds. Every morning two kids collected the eggs and sometimes he got to take eggs home to his mother. He reported to her that Gordo would roar at any big school kid stupid enough to come in to their little playground or dare to enter the hen house. Apparently even Mr Gordon was reluctant to have his children involved in any big school activities, except for the sports days when the tiny One Teacher School team held its own with the big school's four sports 'houses'.

Mr Gordon's gruff manner masked a deep understanding of how to teach children. In his view the school was an ideal way of teaching children and its demonstration function an irritating distraction. Aimée was amused at Antony's sympathy with the student teachers when he said the kids felt sorry for them because most of the time Mr Gordon said nothing to them or if he did it was to tell them to keep quiet.

After the war ended the city slowly recovered its pre-war bustle. The Browns invited them from time to time for weekends to their farm at Mt Glorious. Davy's friend Jim Harris's father was a car dealer whose family lived up the street. From time to time they took Aimée and the boys on long drives into the country in the latest car. Other dutiful invitations were received from Alan's friends or colleagues for Sunday outings. She accepted them with gratitude but realised the boys were usually bored stiff. Sometimes there was a children's birthday party on a Saturday afternoon that she enjoyed more than the boys as it was a chance to get out of the house and meet people.

The Fraser's had regular booked seats on Saturday nights for the pictures at the huge old Savoy Theatre at the terminus of the Clayfield tram. Usually they would invite Aimée to join them, and sometimes the boys too if it was a suitable picture. She enjoyed this, but though a light smoker herself, found the fug of cigarette smoke hard on the eyes and it was sometimes so thick it obscured the distant screen.

Often the boys and others from the neighbourhood went to the Savoy on Saturday afternoons. It was always a treat, watching Batman or other terrifying serials, but most fun of all was rolling empty Coca Cola bottles down the endlessly long sloping aisles of the theatre, gathering speed and noise until they crashed into the stage, infuriating the attendants. If you were caught, you were bundled out unceremoniously, but if you weren't you nearly wet yourself laughing.

In those hard years during and after the war, survival and seeing the boys through their schooling was her main preoccupation. Seated in the armchair under the lamplight sewing away night after night, often Pat Fraser, Betty Brown or another friend would come around after dinner and sit with her and they would chat in low, companionable voices. All her life she had bottled up her emotions: now more than ever.

The one time she let her guard down was in 1946 when one morning, she sat with Antony on the dining room window seat, and on the 7.45 ABC news on 4QG, the names of surviving Australian Army nurses rescued from Sumatra were read out by the newsreader. She sat on the edge of the seat leaning forward like a frozen statue. When the announcer read out the name 'Agnes Betty Jeffrey', she couldn't control her sobs and an amazed nine year old tentatively put his arms around her.

The Kindness of Others

'... nd now I'll say goodnight till ... next time.' The quavery old voice of Dr AE Floyd farewells listeners to his classical music program every Sunday night at 8 o'clock. Aimée looks up from her sewing to see Antony standing like a stork in the middle of the room.

'Why does he always say exactly the same thing every time?' he asks.

'Do you know he used to teach me music at school in Melbourne, and he always sounded just like that, all those years ago.'

'He knows an awful lot about music – was he the one who used to hit you over the knuckles with a ruler when you were practising on cold mornings?'

'No, that was one of the nuns in Perth – Dr Floyd was a sweetie. It's time you cleaned your teeth and went to bed, and be quiet and don't wake up Davy.'

Later when she goes to bed, she sits for a while on the end of Alan's bed next to the window and looks out at the garden and the lights in the houses further away, and lets her mind wander. I'm usually too tired to sit here dreaming, she thinks, but it was interesting in the front garden today when that army girl stopped to chat, looking for someone but she was in the wrong street. Winifred, the daughter of the Dean of Ballarat – and she went to school in Melbourne too. You can tell because she spoke so nicely, though she'd be a few years younger. She wonders what made her ask Winifred to come to dinner next weekend; she was nice to the boys when she talked over the fence and has a lovely smile.

On Tuesday Pat Fraser rings up and asks can she come around after dinner. She is making a dress for her youngest Leith, and needs help, or so she says. Of course she's only too pleased and suspects Pat really just wants a chat. She gives Pat a few bits of advice about the dress which is cut out quite poorly but she tells her how to make it work. Pat says she's worried about Leafy because she's always getting colds and sniffles and seems to be losing weight. Ken's so busy running around to all his meetings and visiting his hospitals he hardly has any time for his patients at his rooms, and none for his children. Aimée thinks Leafy is spoilt and needs a smack on the bottom, but just nods sympathetically.

'I met an Army person called Winifred Best on Sunday and invited her to dinner,' she says, 'she says she's being demobbed and is looking for a place to live. I wondered if I might offer her the little room off the verandah.'

'Could she help you with the boys?'

'I hope so.'

'Are you managing?'

She says it's fine, but Pat probes, and after a silence while Aimée starts a new thread, she admits she gets worried sick about the boys. Antony has already had three operations including that botched appendix by silly old Dr Maddocks and now he has to have another hernia operation. And Davy struggles at his lessons and hates Mr Gordon's school. She sighs.

'I know your David thrives there and Ant seems to like it and so do Thomas and Erica Brown and the Cullen girls, but Davy really flounders, and I don't know what I can do about it. I don't have time because I get so behind in Snow White's orders.'

'Aimée why don't I get Ken to talk to Mr Gordon – he can drop the boys at the school in the morning?'

'No you both do so much for me and I can't tell you how relieved I am that he will operate on Antony. No, I'll sort it out.'

It's a moment like this when she finds she can't speak for wondering what Alan would do. All those resolutions about taking charge of her life and here she is with no idea of what she can do except sew, sew, sew for that awful woman, and if she says another word to Pat she'll cry.

A few weeks later, Winifred comes to live at Creswick Street. She accepts with apparent delight the little room off the verandah.

Aimée feels relieved rather than pleased. She doesn't tell her Alan slept there almost until he died, but now she has got to know her a little, probably it would be of no concern to Winifred. For someone who must be well over thirty and has spent years in the army, she seems strangely naive, as if she hasn't seen much of life. She's like a big sister to the boys and she and Antony get on so well.

Winifred has taken a job as receptionist in Dr Scholes' rooms, a leading eye surgeon. He is a rather pompous grey-haired man of about sixty but every night he drives Winifred home and parks outside the house where they chat, sometimes for as much as an hour, before she comes in for dinner. She thinks Winifred is being very unwise. Being soft-hearted and lonely, she's liable to become entangled with a married man. She can't be too worried about her – it's her life and at her age she doesn't need advice from a landlady with enough worries of her own.

Antony complains bitterly about Winifred making him eat all the left-overs from the previous night's dinner. Worst of all, she makes him eat the porridge left over from yesterday's breakfast.

'If you don't like it,' Aimée tells him, 'eat it when it's fresh and stop being so fussy – Davy eats all his.'

'But it's horrible and she actually scrapes if off my plate and puts it in the fridge and it might have been there for days. It makes me sick.'

With Christmas approaching, she invites Winifred to join them to spend the school holidays at the beach. She knows she must sell *Breffney* as it's her only asset and it's wasted for her as a holiday house, but she loves it so much – the children do too. It seems like the only place and time she has been really happy. She has sold Flossie the Ford as it ate up too much petrol and has bought a little black Ford Prefect, very upright and bumpy and inclined to kangaroo hop if you let the clutch out too quickly.

They haven't been at the beach more than a day when she is overwhelmed with the conflicting emotions of bitter sadness and the joyful memories and sensations of this place, the boys' delight at being in their bedroom, rolling in the hole in the front lawn and rushing down to the beach. Joyce Hodgkinson calls and asks them all to a barbecue in the sandhills and to a Christmas Eve party for all the children around and about. Nell and Harry Mort next door seem really pleased to see them, and the Cappers are arriving next week. She decides instantly she can't sell the place. There are too many friends around, welcoming them. Oh Alan, if only you were here, we would be so happy.

They spend Christmas Day with the Cappers. On Boxing Day Alan's old friend Warwick Ramsden arrives and after lunch they stretch out and listen to the ABC description of the test match against England from the MCG. Antony is riveted and can't be torn away from Alan McGilvray's broadcast. A few weeks earlier Ken Fraser had taken him and his own son David to the test match in Brisbane and they had seen Bradman bat but Antony was more interested in local hero Colin McCool. Antony is always Colin McCool when he plays cricket with his friends in the lane after school.

Warwick is tall and slender; Aimée thinks he's a 'dish' and expects Winifred does too. He talks to them about mutual friends in Melbourne as the afternoon idles away and asks Aimée if she plans to move back there.

'I don't know,' she says, 'I've made such good friends here in Brisbane who are unbelievably supportive and I can't imagine leaving, but I do miss my Melbourne friends. My brother Owen is now married and is living there but his health is not good so I'd love to be near him. I think most of all I miss old Mill Jeffrey, my mother-in-law. She is such a wonderful woman and was a real mother to me as well as to her own daughters. I think they are the happiest family I've ever met.'

For a while she thinks Warwick might cast his eye on Winifred. He must be over forty now and is such a catch. But just before he leaves, he takes her aside and says he is about to announce his engagement to a Melbourne girl called Phyllis – Phyl for short. Oh Warwick that's wonderful, she says, tell me about her and do you have any snaps? For a moment she forgets propriety and hugs him.

When they get back to Brisbane after the holidays, she feels deeply depressed, and again lassitude and indecision envelop her. Do I sell *Breffney*? Do we go back to Melbourne? I must try to get a job as I'll go mad sewing for Snow White. At least she worries less about the boys. Davy spends every spare moment up the street with his friend Jim Harris. Jim's father Jack is a car dealer and always has a nice new car. Antony is different in every way and has odd tastes and obsessions like his fleet of plasticene warships he spent weeks making and if he's not making something, he's sitting on the verandah happily dreaming.

She encourages the friendship between Antony and David Fraser. The Frasers live in the next street and Pat has become her closest friend and of course she relies on Ken so much for guidance about the boys' future. David is exactly Ant's age but is so much more confident and she hopes his influence will help to overcome Antony's introspection and shyness. The problem is not his personality, she argues with herself, but his lack of a father in these crucial years. Ken is so opinionated, such an organiser and doer. With two sisters and an elder brother, it's no wonder his son David is so extrovert and confident.

But it is not all plain sailing. Late one afternoon, she asks Antony how was his day at the Fraser's.

'Not much. Mrs Fraser said we had to play in the garden most of the morning, and do you know what?'

'Well?'

'When we came into the kitchen for lunch, she gave us some sandwiches and a bottle of lemonade, and do you know what? David took two glasses, filled up the first one and put the rest in the other glass but it was only half full, and he took the full glass and drank it straight off and gave me the other half full glass.'

'That was a bit mean, what did you do?'

'I said, hey! But he just smiled and walked off. So I said, well I'm going off to watch the trams, and he said you're mad going to watch those stupid trams again, and I said I'm not and so I said hooray and went off down to the corner of Sandgate Road and sat on the kerb and watched the trams. And do you know what, I saw an old red tram number 27 and it's the oldest I've ever seen and it only has one bogie and it rocks all over the place and you can see the driver spinning these two brass handles to keep the old tram going.'

'Before you left did you thank Mrs Fraser for lunch?'

No answer.

'Did you?'

'No.'

'Well you go straight back now and thank her.'

'Now?'

'Yes, now.'

'I couldn't do that!'

'Yes you can – off you go.'

He is appalled at the prospect of such humiliation and argues, but she is adamant, so he trudges off. He goes slowly up the back stairs of the Fraser's house and peeps in. Mrs Fraser is preparing something at the kitchen table and looks up surprised and says:

'Hullo Antony, I thought you'd gone home ages ago – did you leave something behind?'

'No.'

'David's in his room I think. Did you want to see him?'

'No, not really.'

'Oh. Then would you like one of these biscuits?'

'Um, well, yes… thanks for having me today Mrs Fraser.'

'Oh it's always a pleasure, you can come any time. Did you come all the way back to say thanks?'

'Um … sort of.'

She smiles at him: 'Well you're a very well-mannered boy. David could take a leaf out of your book.'

Winifred is making a huge difference in his life. Discovering his passion for trams, she offers to accompany him on a day's tram travelling. On Saturday morning, Aimée is pleased to have a day to herself. David has gone to spend the day at his friend Jim Harris's place. Antony and Winifred have cut their lunches and marched up the hill to the Clayfield tram stop. They catch the tram to the city and he says they are going to catch the Adelaide Street trams as he has only ever caught Queen Street trams before and usually only those going to Ascot and Clayfield. He looks at Winifred solemnly and asks whether she'd rather catch the Rainworth-Kalinga tram, or the Bardon-Stafford tram, or maybe even the Ashgrove-Grange, but the Grange doesn't go very far, so probably not that one. As they arrive in Adelaide Street, she suggests, 'Why don't we catch the first one that comes along?'

'OK.'

'This one's going to Bardon, will we catch it?'

'I really wanted to go to Rainworth – I don't know anything about that suburb.'

'Government House is near the Bardon terminus – we could go and have a look.'

'Oh yes that's good – quick.'

So at the last second they scramble on the Bardon tram. When they reach hilly, wooded Bardon there's almost no one on the tram. He is absorbed in the streetscape. They alight and walk to Government House, peer through the gates, catch the next tram back to the city and out the other direction to Stafford. That day they travel to all the Adelaide Street tram destinations, and even manage to get to West End and New Farm Park as well.

He regales Aimée with details of all their travels when they get home, but he can tell she's not really interested. She asks questions like where did they have their lunch and whether Winifred managed to get time to find that scarf she was looking for, but all she says to his descriptions of the different tram routes are, 'Oh yes', or 'Really?'

After dinner when she sits under the lamp sewing, she thanks Winifred for spending the day with him and tells her how grateful she is for the interest she shows in them, but she mustn't feel obliged to spend her free time with them.

'Oh no,' Winifred responds instantly, 'it's not a chore, it's wonderful living in a house with such interesting boys. They tell me all sorts of things I would never have known.'

'But it must have been so boring sitting on a tram all day.'

'No we never stopped talking all day. He asks endless questions about where we are going and what do I think – he's a very unusual boy.'

'Yes he's a bit strange, I worry quite a lot about him.'

'You know he's very musical – he really should learn the piano.'

'I have thought about that but I can't afford a piano let alone paying someone to teach him, and he seems to be happy with his records. He doesn't ask to learn an instrument.'

'I should take him to concerts – would you mind if I did?'

'Of course not, but Winifred, you should go with your own friends, and enjoy yourself.'

Winifred looks rather crestfallen: 'The trouble is I don't really know anyone to ask to go to concerts with apart from Philip. He's a dear but it's rather hard going. The police thought he was drunk when we were walking down Queen Street the other evening.'

Philip Hart is Pat Fraser's younger brother. He is tall and good-looking but is badly disabled with cerebral palsy, has difficulty walking and his speech is hard to understand. Poor Philip is intelligent, amusing and loves fine music but is desperately bored. Winifred being a trained organist and music lover, Pat and Aimée thought she and Philip might hit it off. At least Pat did, Aimée was not so sure. Philip lives with his mother in a vast old house in Ascot surrounded by Moreton Bay figs and as dark and sepulchral as a cavern inside. As well as Philip and old Mrs Hart, his other sister Beatrice lives there with her husband but you would hardly know because the place is as silent as a tomb except for the cries of the flying foxes nesting in the trees on hot summer nights.

The first time Winifred takes Antony to a concert, they walk nearly a mile to the Hart's house to join Philip. Old Mrs Hart invites them in and gives Antony a lemonade before the three of them set off to catch the Ascot tram into town. Antony is speech-less with embarrassment as he can't understand a word of Philip's noisy chat. He thinks Philip is telling jokes about him as he and Winifred both keep laughing. And Philip staggers as they walk and nearly falls over all the time, and people keep looking. On the tram it's worse, because Philip talks so loudly and *everyone* on the tram is looking.

At the City Hall, a large round auditorium with hard wooden seats and huge pot plants on the stage, the Queensland Symphony Orchestra is ranged up on tiered rows. The conductor is an expansive man called John Farnsworth Hall with tinted glasses and a magisterial way of waving his baton. Antony wonders how all the players seem to know how to follow him. After a short piece for the orchestra, a balding grey-haired pianist called Walter Gieseking walks on to enthusiastic applause. He is to play Beethoven's Emperor Concerto and from the moment of the great opening chords and the pianist's scales up the keyboard, Antony enters another world, previously unknown. Indeed Winifred, Philip and the whole audience is entranced. The seventh symphony of Beethoven follows after the interval and as they walk back to the tram, Antony is lost for words. Philip goes home alone on the Ascot tram and Winifred and Antony catch another tram to Clayfield. He questions her about the different instruments, where did the pianist come from, how do the players follow the conductor, when can they go again?

Aimée is pleased with the success of the concert outing and Antony's constant chatter about it. She buys him a record of her favourite singer Joan Hammond singing *One Fine Day* and *They call me Mimi* which he plays endlessly on the gramophone. He gets these crazes. Once he told her of the strange thrilling feeling he got whenever he played *Nymphs and Shepherds* sung by the Manchester Children's Choir on that worn out old record – 'Mum, the label says there are 250 kids in that choir.' Winifred buys him a two-record set of Franck's *Symphonic Variations* played by the same pianist they heard at the concert. He handles this with reverence. It's the first *real* record set he's ever had.

Mr Gordon's One Teacher school is more than a mile from where they live. The boys walk there and back every day, though sometimes they catch a bus if it's wet. Aimée's kitchen is at the front of the Creswick Street house. From the sink at the window, she can see down the street, along the lane where they play cricket and where they emerge from the long walk home from school. Usually she stops sewing at the machine in mid-afternoon and has a cup of tea at the kitchen window to be sure the boys arrive home safely.

He likes to walk home slowly. There are always kids to walk with and so many places to play games. There is the overgrown field under the cliff next to the convent. It's one of the best places in the whole district to hide when they play the chasing game, especially when they are getting away from the Walsh Gang. Then they always stop at the chalk cliff in the cutting where they write messages with chalky stones. The best thing is playing cricket in the lane when they get home. There's usually Peter Biggs and Neil Roberts and Jimmy the black boy. Sometimes David Fraser comes around but the kids like it best without him. It can go on forever until his mother leans out of the kitchen window and claps her hands, the signal to come in and have a bath.

He never forgets the day they were all playing cricket in the lane after school. His little brother David was sitting in the Biggs' backyard reading a comic. Jimmy was bowling to David Fraser (who was a better bat than any of them) and Fraser hooked the ball through a gap in the fence and it hit his brother David square on the nose. He fell back and his face was a mess of blood. He was horrified at the sight of his brother – he thought he might have been killed. He turned around and ran home shouting to his mother that David had been hit by a cricket ball. It was all a blur: his mother running down the street; Mrs Biggs cradling David; the kids standing around silent...

The cricket ball incident shocked Aimée terribly. Davy's nose was crushed and probably permanently altered, though after a few weeks he seemed fully recovered. Although he was only eight at the time, she recalls how it brought her face to face with the boys' vulnerability as they grew up, and how little her care and concern really counts in the reality of the world outside their little cocoon.

Later that year her elder sister Olive invites her to bring the children to Sydney for the Christmas holidays. 'Bruce will pay for you all to come by aeroplane and we'll drive down to Shellharbour for a couple of weeks. We can go and see Owen and Honor too. Please don't argue about it – Bruce is insistent and you know what he's like when he's made up his mind.'

The flight on a DC3 to Sydney is a great event and Antony gets to sit in a single seat next to the window. At first, the seat slopes upwards but as the plane gets up speed it levels out and he can look at the city and the water and when it tilts over it's really scary. It's also cold and noisy and sometimes it gets in air pockets and you think you're going to crash.

Olive and Bruce Fry have four children, two boys a few years older than Antony and two girls his age and younger. Bruce is a radiologist and in charge of Randwick Base Hospital. Aimée thinks he is very kind and generous but a little of him goes a long way. She is glad she's not Olive, being instructed by Bruce about every arrangement and household matter, but then Olive has always been very calm and soft spoken and never seems to mind.

The Frys live in a small semi-detached house near the hospital and despite the squeeze, happily find room for Aimée and the boys. Seeing Olive after such a long time brings up a huge well of emotion for Aimée. Olive always has been introverted but they understand each other so well without needing to say much. Seeing her with her lovely children is really heartwarming. She watches as the girls brush their long waist-length hair; Olive patiently makes two long plaits for each girl as they get ready for school. The girls are full of laughter and hug their mother and Aimée as they rush off.

She feels a tug of envy – boys are not like this.

Antony sleeps in the sleep-out at the back of the house with his cousins David and Michael and Uncle Bruce as well. In the middle of the night, he wakes up to find Uncle Bruce lying awake smoking a cigarette who after a while asks him how he's enjoying school. They then talk about all sorts of things, including cricket, fishing and rabbiting which Uncle Bruce promises when they get to Shellharbour. He decides he likes Uncle Bruce but he's not sure about his cousins Susan and Jane who are both tall, talkative and very pretty. He doesn't know what to say to them and has a really strange feeling about them. It feels like they are like, well, it seems stupid, but like they are princesses, like the real Princesses Elizabeth and Margaret Rose. Being with them and looking at them makes him feel a bit faint and his tummy seems to churn and he can't find anything to say. It's funny, they talk all the time to Davy and he chatters back non-stop.

Aimée's heart has the jitters on the day Olive drives her together with Antony, Davy and the girls up to Kurrajong to see her brother Owen and his wife Honor. She hasn't seen either since Alan's funeral four years earlier. She loves them both but she dreads seeing Owen's physical condition. After he got his diabetes under control, he was diagnosed with TB during the war and ordered to give up his senior government job and live in the clear air of the mountains. Olive has warned her they live in an unlined shack on a tiny passionfruit farm in the hills near Kurrajong, that Owen works from dawn to dusk and they are penniless.

Driving slowly down the little rutted lane to the neat white-painted shack, her worries are immediately put to rest. Owen and Honor are standing on their little verandah looking strangely like two toy soldiers, both dressed in pressed khaki shirts and trousers, small and trim with beaming smiles. They are both deeply tanned and seem to represent the epitome of the healthy outdoor lifestyle. Owen is overwhelmed to tears seeing Aimée and for a moment is hardly able to speak. Honor has taken Davy by the hand and leads him to a holly bush where (she tells him) someone has left something sticking out of the ground. It turns out to be a little parcel addressed in large handwriting to 'Master David Jeffrey.'

She is further relieved to find the three-roomed shack is charming and the main sitting room kitchen with its unpainted wood walls is warm and inviting and full of their treasures. The bedroom is spartan but there is a bookcase packed with Owen's books, and as expected, pride of place given to his library of Proust: *A la Recherche du Temps perdu,* in the original French and in Scott Moncrieff's translation and with many volumes of analysis and criticism.

Honor is a small bird-like person with big eyes and piled up hair, a soft voice and great empathy with children. Aimée has known her and her family since her Melbourne days and nothing has ever pleased her more than that these two gentle studious people found each other, and that Honor has been Owen's rock through his illnesses. The only problem, it seems to Aimée, is the presence of Honor's older sister, Elizabeth, who has come to live with them. Elizabeth has the third room, the largest, has had it lined and gaudily decorated, and dominates the conversation with her loud pretentious drawl. Elizabeth says she has come to live with them, to help. Poor darlings, they had no idea what to do when they came here, but I was able to help them pull it together.

Owen takes Aimée for a walk around the farm and admits it's back-breaking work, but Honor works on the farm too and it has been wonderful for his health and he has not been so well and fit since he was a youth. He reads every night, listens to music on the wireless and feels very fortunate and content.

'How do you both manage with Elizabeth here?'

'Well it is hard for Honor and that's one of the reasons she works all day on the farm. I'm afraid I bury myself in a book at night, and there are programmes on the wireless I insist we listen to.'

'Do you earn enough on the farm?'

'Not really but Elizabeth does pay us board.'

'Have you made any friends in the district?'

'Honor has – she goes into Kurrajong at least once a week and is looking for a job.'

'What a good idea, I'm sure she'll get one, she has such a way with people. But you mustn't work too hard on the farm Owen. You've always worked too hard and I hope you spend enough time with Honor.'

'Well, you know what she's like, she never stops, is up at the crack of dawn and often falls asleep if she doesn't go to bed early. We manage pretty well.'

Back in Sydney a day or two later, after school has broken up for the Fry children, all nine people pile into Bruce's Oldsmobile, the three adults in the front and six kids in the back plus two wooden boxes of fruit squeezed on the floor behind the front seat. Skinny Michael decides to lie along the ledge behind the back seat. All the luggage is piled into the trailer. The journey to Shellharbour seems to take forever as Uncle Bruce drives very slowly. Antony thinks nobody understands how uncomfortable it is in the back seat with no room to put your feet anywhere.

The house at Shellharbour is primitive but perfect. Set on a headland overlooking the beach, it has wonderful views of the sea and the hills behind the village. After seeing Owen and sharing the double bed with Olive for several nights in Sydney Aimee feels like a new person. She has at last been able to unburden her grief and worries and hopes. The sea breeze at Shellharbour is brushing away all the cobwebs. She is so grateful to Olive, just for listening sympathetically. In a way she's surprised as she has never talked like that to Olive before. In fact, she has never talked to anyone like that before.

Antony and Davy have connected with Susan and Jane and the four of them spend whole days playing games on the beach and especially in the large protected rock pool. Michael and his elder half-brother David are older and more worldly and roam further away. Aimee loves the sense of independence in their family, how the children feel free to go off anywhere, and perhaps are not seen all day until they come back for dinner with laconic explanations of what they have been doing. Bruce is a solid and authoritative presence: short and stout with crew cut greying hair, he sometimes seems intimidating, but laughs easily and teases the girls. He is insistent on everyone's household duties before they can go out, supervises what they eat, and enforces the rule that all children, without exception, must do their business after breakfast in the dunny up in the back corner of the yard. Antony is appalled by this. It is full up to the brim as the night cart hasn't come for two weeks. He whispers to his mother that it's disgusting and you can't even sit down. Next morning Bruce relents and orders David and Michael to dig a pit behind the dunny and empty the can's contents into it. Antony makes sure he's nowhere near this piece of action and is safely occupied in the rock pool.

Some afternoons Bruce takes the boys rabbiting in the Oldsmobile, an activity Michael and Antony find totally absorbing though David Fry usually avoids it, having chased rabbits many times before. They drive out into the hills behind Shellharbour. Both boys become very adept at identifying 'rabbit country' and more particularly spotting rabbits. Each boy is glued to opposite windows, Davy sitting in the middle making one of his sticks and rubber bands contraptions. When a rabbit is spotted, Bruce stops the car, picks up his rifle, a .22, and without moving from the driver's seat, swivels round until he has the rabbit in his sights, and with unerring aim, picks it off. The boys leap out of the car, run up the hill side to gather the dead animal or wring its neck if it's still moving. Michael, who considers himself an expert, does the dirty work. Michael and Bruce agree five rabbits in an afternoon is a decent haul. Then the expedition heads home where the women are expected to produce delicious rabbit stew or roast rabbit for dinner. The sack of bloody dead rabbits is produced in the kitchen while Michael and Bruce set to skin and gut them. Olive patiently rolls her eyes, but Aimée has to leave the house and go for a walk, wondering how she tolerates it.

Sitting on the cliff overlooking the beach, watching the children play and swim one morning, Olive and Aimée reflect on their families' experiences. Olive talks of her own terrible loneliness at school and afterwards as she studied to become a pharmacist. She says: 'I often think I wouldn't have survived those bleak years in Melbourne at school and then studying, without the memory of our childhood and those holidays we had on the river in Perth. You were so young, do you remember them?'

'Oh yes, so well.'

'You were such a plump, giggly little girl – how did you grow up to be so slender and calm?'

'Oh Olive, I'm not calm, one thing Merton Hall taught me was to be strong and not to cry when I remembered our mother and our home in Kalgoorlie and those holidays.'

'Our father seemed so totally involved with us in those holidays. I could never understand how he could just go off with that woman and leave us year after year.'

'Probably she was completely demoralised by us. She was so cold and distant after Mother's sweet nature and I suppose we all hated her, or at least she must have thought we did.'

'You know she talks quite often to Edna in Perth. They run into each other at the Karakatta Club. Father turns eighty next year and Edna says he is quite frail now.'

She asks Aimée: 'Does he ring you at all? You know you should inherit a decent amount when he dies.'

'He writes a letter for my birthday and sometimes sends me a little present but I haven't had a proper conversation with him for years.'

She watches the children tearing off down the beach and changes the subject: 'Susan and Jane are wonderful with the boys – they are thick as thieves now. I wish we could see you all more often. Why don't you all come up to Surfers next holidays, before I have to sell the house?'

'That would be lovely, but I think it would be hard to move Bruce. He likes his familiar routines and hates travelling far. Why don't you pick your moment and ask him. He's very fond of you.'

That night at dinner, which is always interminable because Bruce eats so slowly, all six children, including David, who is sixteen, have left the table, their meal finished. Jane has told Antony and Davy her father chews every mouthful forty-two times and they all die of boredom waiting for him to finish. Uncle Bruce is now an object of total fascination to the Jeffrey boys, who gaze at him counting the chews for each mouthful. Do you have to chew everything forty-two times too, Antony asks Jane. Oh yes we're told to but we never do that many unless he is watching and counting, but I do try to get to twenty which seems to be enough. Antony says he chews each mouthful only about four or five times, and it would get terribly mushy if you chewed forty-two times.

Aimée and Olive sit with Bruce while he finishes his meal. Olive's patience is proverbial but she lights up a cigarette while waiting for him and offers one to Aimée who declines and waits for later.

'Have you thought where you will send the boys to school after primary school?' Bruce asks Aimée.

'Alan's firm Flack and Flack have promised to pay their secondary school fees, so if they do, it will probably be Churchie as our friends the Frasers send their boys there.'

Bruce fiddles with his pipe, strikes another match, and with the pipe poised in mid air, says: 'The right school is extremely important you know because of the influence, good or bad, on the boys' development, and helping them to find their vocations.'

'I haven't quite decided whether we should go back to Melbourne as Alan put Antony's name down at his own school Melbourne Grammar as soon as he was born.'

Bruce shakes his head, 'Don't go back to Melbourne. In your circumstances it's much better to stay in Brisbane.'

'Bruce, don't lecture Aimée', says Olive, 'it's up to her where her boys go to school. And in any case, there's Aimée's house at the beach to consider. She has asked us to spend the next school holidays there and I think that would be lovely for the children.'

Home in Brisbane, back to her endless smocking and sewing,

sitting in her chair under the lamp, she reflects intermittently between her concentration on the intricate task. Not unhappily, perhaps a little resentfully, recognising the prospect of the endless grind, but also strangely content that their lives seem to be falling into place. She remembers with a smile her exhaustion from the packing up and preparing for the expedition back to Sydney from Shellharbour, not to speak of the privations of the journey itself. Nine irritable people squeezed in Bruce's smelly old car. Only Bruce seemed oblivious to it all, in the best of humour, driving as slowly as he ate, explaining the significance of every scenic outcrop, frequently stopping to go into lengthy explanations. It was really the loveliest holiday. She can't imagine living the chaotic, crowded life Olive and her family live, but what a blessed family they are. She can't remember when the boys enjoyed themselves so much. It puts a new slant on their lives. We can all be happy if we have people like this around us. Why need I worry so much? We have such good friends in Brisbane too. Bruce is probably right, what is there to gain in going back to Melbourne?

And the boys are settling well. Of course there are always problems, and not only the money ones. Antony is odd with his strange crazes and obsessions, and Davy struggles with school. Friends tell her boys are like this – it's normal. But they are making friends and seem mostly to be happy.

Antony loves dogs, especially since a mangy little fox terrier he named Tuppy strayed into their lives a couple of years ago. Tuppy was white (for a while after he was washed) with a mostly brown head and a big brown spot on his back. He was a quiet little dog who looked a bit sad and you felt he must have had a pretty lonely or badly treated life until he was taken in by the Jeffrey family. He followed him everywhere in the district where he played with his friends, after school and in the weekends. Tuppy was always there, hanging around, following Neil, Peter, Jimmy and himself when they played cricket in the lane, or when they played the chasing game against the Walsh gang. Tuppy liked to chase the arrows in the paddock at the bottom of the hill when they played with the bows and arrows given to them by old Mr Grundstein, who got them when he lived in New Guinea.

Until the day that becomes the worst day of his life. After school, his mother tells him to go down to the shop on Sandgate Road to buy some butter, carrots and beans and a packet of Craven A. Sandgate Road is a wide busy road with lots of traffic and trams going both ways. He and Tuppy are walking down Creswick street to the shop when Tuppy suddenly runs ahead and straight on to Sandgate Road, and before he can even shout to him, a car comes along and runs over him. There's a yelp and there's Tuppy wriggling and struggling to get up and he can't. His first feeling is unbelieving horror, like the world has suddenly blown up. He shouts Tuppy's name and runs out on the road and bends down over him but he doesn't know what to do because he knows he would hurt Tuppy if he picks him up. A man comes across from the other side of the road and says: 'I'm afraid your dog is a goner.' He picks him up and takes him to the footpath and puts him gently down. Antony sits down beside him, in tears and speechless, but Tuppy is making no sound, just quivering and panting, until after a while he stops. Not only that terrible day, but the whole next week he feels awful and doesn't want to talk to anyone.

Winifred tells Aimée she will get him another dog. He is inconsolable and for a boy of his age it's the biggest shock of his life. Aimée nods and says she supposes so, but if you get the dog, I'll pay you for it. No, says Winifred, I'd like to do it. So Nicky, another fox terrier, but all white with black and white head markings, joins the family. He is a cast off from another family moving away, but is a livelier and more temperamental animal, sometimes giving her cause for regret about his joining the family.

Her cautious approach to Alan's successor Mr Flook (what a name she thinks!) at Flack and Flack confirms the arrangement to pay the children's school fees, so she is relieved to be able to make a firm decision to stay in Brisbane and send Antony to Churchie. Ken Fraser had already decided to send his son David to Churchie when he turns twelve and in the process skipping the final year of primary school. He tells her both David and Antony are very bright, are close friends, the same age and should go to Churchie together a year early. She is very dubious about this but Ken has been so influential in her life since Alan died that she accepts his advice without demur.

But these are not the reasons for her decision not to return to Melbourne. This comes about during a weekend staying with the Browns at their farm at Mt Glorious in the hills behind Brisbane. The Browns have been inviting Aimée and the boys for weekends at Mt Glorious for some time now. The farm at Mt Glorious is a haven for the Browns; it is a lush hilltop of red soil bounded by thick rain forest with picturesque views of rolling hills in all directions. It is always fresh and cool after Brisbane's humidity and she counts herself lucky they are invited there from time to time. The Browns employ a farmer who grows fruit and vegetables for the Brisbane market, mostly rhubarb, potatoes and onions, and runs a small herd of dairy cows.

Twice Antony has spent school holidays at the farm with Thomas and Erica, and has come to feel it is his own special place. He is always asking his mother when can they go again. He loves the earthy smell of the house. It's like a big shed because the front door is really a double gate locked with a padlock, and when you go inside it's dark and gloomy and it's a huge room full of farm gear and galoshes, and boxes of fruit and vegetables and there are lumps of red soil on the floor. The bedrooms off the front room have walls that don't go up to the roof so you feel like you are sleeping in the shed. But when you go through the door into the back part of the house, it's like a normal house, with tables and chairs and windows all around looking out at the view of the hills.

He especially likes to walk down to the cottage where Mr Hall, the farmer and his wife live with their little girl Laurie. If he gets there early he can watch the cows being milked. Mr Hall lets him try but not much milk comes out. Later he watches the milk and cream being separated and the butter churned. Most days he goes off through the bush with Thomas down to Cedar Creek where they climb down the waterfall and play war games in the bush where nobody ever comes to interrupt. But he also likes to stay in the back yard of the farmhouse and play school with Erica where she is the teacher and he is the star pupil. This game can go on for days and Thomas gets very cross and sometimes gives Antony a corked arm, because he thinks it's a pathetic game and he doesn't want to be part of it even though Erica asks him. Best of everything at Mt Glorious are the old colour picture books in the window seats that must have belonged to Mr and Mrs Brown when they were kids. They are full of fantastic comics of Tiger Tim and other animals and stories for boys that are old-fashioned but much better than modern comics. Mrs Brown lets him pull them all out and he spends hours reading them.

Aimée enjoys time at Mt Glorious too. Stepping out into the peaceful cool air after Brisbane's bustle is a physical pleasure. This Friday afternoon Betty Brown has driven her up with the children as Tom can't come till tomorrow afternoon. It gets cold quite quickly so fires are lit in the big fireplace and in the wood-fired oven in the kitchen. There will be no baths tonight as the water will take a long time to heat up but Erica organises games of Chinese Checkers and Ludo and asks which one the others want to play. Davy wants Snakes and Ladders and Erica, who is very considerate, goes off to rummage for it even though she's pretty sure they don't have it.

In the kitchen, before starting to get the meal ready, Betty pours Aimée and herself a gin and tonic and lights up a cigarette. There is a slightly hectic flush in her cheeks and Aimée can see she is bothered by something – in fact she has been aware of this coming up in the car but it's not in her nature to ask directly. Davy wanders into the kitchen, bored because he's been left out of the game, but still apprehensive, and asks:

'Is the bull still in the paddock?'

Betty laughs and replies in her hobgoblin voice: 'Don't worry Davy, there's no bull about this time.'

Last time he was at the farm, Davy came rushing up to the farmhouse shouting at the top of his lungs: 'There's a bull about! There's a bull about!' Betty thought it was hilarious and has been repeating it to her friends.

'Will I put on the potatoes and grill some of these chops?'

'No let's just boil some eggs and get them off to bed.'

Betty goes into the big room where the children are playing Chinese Checkers and tells them to clear it away because dinner's almost ready. Loud protests from Thomas, and even Erica is miffed.

By the time the so-called dinner is eaten, the children are packed off to bed with the older ones allowed to read. Betty has now demolished two gins and tonic. For a moment they sit quietly before the fire, feeling its comfort and warmth and Aimée wants to close her eyes and think of nothing.

'Aimée, I have to tell you – I'm pregnant. I should be excited but I'm devastated. What am I going to do?'

'But Betty, that's marvellous. What's wrong – is there a problem?'

'No it's not that – I'm fine, but it seems like Thomas and Erica are almost grown up and Sam's still little and what am I doing at my age with another baby? It makes me wonder what sort of person I am. I sit in that big house and wonder why I'm there – it's not even our house. I don't do anything that's really worthwhile. The older children hardly seem to need me. Thomas is off to Geelong Grammar next year and Erica is so capable – she even tells me what to do. I don't want Thomas going to Geelong. He's so shy and will probably hate it but Tom went to Geelong and his father before him and he won't hear of him not following in the family tradition. I feel I'm completely at odds with everyone.'

'But you're so clever and so helpful to everyone. You're wonderful to me – to us. You make me laugh and I always love being with you, and you always lift the clouds and I can see the bright side.'

'That's nice of you. It's silly, I shouldn't complain, but sometimes I feel depressed and so – bored. Sometimes I get impatient with people, even my friends and I wonder what's wrong with me. I have three beautiful children and everything I want. I try to help at St Augustine's but then I sometimes get sharp with some of the do-gooders, and then they think I'm insulting them. I probably am. Then I look at you and you're always calm and serene and don't seem to have a trouble in the world despite all that's happened. And all I want to do is go home and have a drink.'

'You're probably feeling like this because you are pregnant. Pregnancy brings out all your old worries and fears, often so irrational. Have you told Tom, what does he think?'

'I don't think he believes me – he just looks at me with a silly grin as if I'm mad.'

They laugh and Betty gets up to pour another drink. Betty tells the story of her contretemps with some of the 'ladies' at the church and how old Mrs Brown heard about it, and how Tom seems to get more puzzled by his wife's behaviour the longer they're married.

'What happened at the church?' Aimée asks.

'Oh you know how cherubic Canon Birch looks – well I said to him a few weeks ago apropos of nothing, how friar-like he looked that morning and one of the women must have heard it and was appalled and it got around like wildfire. People started looking at me and avoiding me. And then last week I took down some of my geraniums and put them around in some vases. I thought they looked quite nice – rather Italian window box effect. But again they made it clear they weren't wanted and someone whisked them away. It created quite a fuss. They think I'm an emissary from the Pope.'

She rarely drinks more than a glass, but sensing Betty's mood is more than about becoming pregnant, she accepts one or two more. As the evening winds on, they both become tipsy, and tell each other increasingly intimate and outrageous stories, Betty about her pre-marriage dalliances, some of whom are family friends, and

Aimée about the absurdities of her life in Melbourne as a nurse.

As she lies in bed with her head slightly spinning, she giggles at one of Betty's stories, and suddenly feels a strong sense of belonging, a feeling she hasn't been aware of during all her years in Brisbane. This is where her place is; above all it's where the children belong, where they have been looked after – by people who may have become more important to her than anyone else.

Antony starts at Churchie in 1949 and she needn't have worried. Along with David Fraser, they jump a year and enrol in the last year of primary school in the Remove class. Despite Ken Fraser's assurances, she is very dubious about him leaving Mr Gordon's school a year early, but he seems happy about it, especially the long journey by tram (two trams) each way. The trams seem more important to him than the school.

She doesn't want to pry too much into what he thinks about his new school, but he is quite happy to talk about it, usually when he thinks something or someone was strange or funny. While she thinks some aspects of the school are definitely strange she usually finds what he thinks is funny is incomprehensible. She feels she has a lot to learn about adolescent boys. One afternoon he came from school and wide-eyed told her that the history master Mr Chaytor got so mad with the class for constantly mucking up and giving cat-calls across the room that he lined up the whole class in single file and had each boy bend over in turn to be whacked on the bottom with his waddy. The result was apparently quite the opposite to what was intended, as many of the boys lined up for a second or even a third whack, and general hilarity ensued while Mr Chaytor finished up red-faced, exhausted and even more furious. When he finished telling her this he said it was one of the funniest things that he had ever seen at school, and 'the whack didn't even really hurt much.'

'But Ant, that's a terrible way to behave for all the boys to be so rowdy and take no notice of the master.'

'We weren't all being rowdy – I wasn't. Just a few of the kids at the back were.'

'Then why did he cane you all? Do all the masters cane the boys?'

'Sometimes – not much.'

She thinks this is very odd behaviour at such a reputable school. She was appalled when he told her the boys in Chapel sing 'Poley, poley, poley…' instead of Holy, Holy, Holy when the Prep School headmaster Mr Adams is present, because his nick-name is Poley. The poor man is terminally ill with cancer, not that the boys know. It is so disrespectful and undignified, she can scarcely believe it. She is also dubious about the Prep School building. It is an old weatherboard house grandly called *Palmyra* standing forlornly in the middle of the school grounds while brand new red brick double-storey classrooms for the senior school are being built around it. Classes are held in the musty old bedrooms and on the creaky-floored open verandah that encircles the house.

During Antony's first year there, Mr Adams died and was succeeded by his deputy, a craggy, unkempt-looking young man called Roy Hoskins with a head of unruly brown hair making him look like an overgrown child. She instinctively likes Roy Hoskins' no-nonsense manner and the way he seems to like and care about the boys. Despite the inadequacy of *Palmyra*, she thinks the boys are well looked after and Antony is losing his timidity and making friends.

He quite likes being at Churchie on the whole, but there are some things about it he doesn't like at all. He hated playing front row in the house under-14 rugby team, until the coach despaired of his constant failure to put his head and shoulders into the scrum and stuck him out on the wing. Being a winger is better as he's quite a fast runner but tackling is no fun as you're likely to get hurt. Eventually he discovers you can make a dive for the opponent's flying ankles, and with careful timing you can make a spectacular miss. His speed is his sporting saviour; he came third in the under-

14 100 yards and the 880, both times beating David Fraser. This gives him huge satisfaction, as David Fraser is both clever and good at all sports, and always ignores him at school and spends his time with smart or tough kids.

Worst of all is the pocket swim, an annual nightmare where every boy in the school has to swim the mile-long, mangrove riddled, stinking pocket in Norman Creek that winds its sluggish way through the school grounds. The moment he saw the creek and heard about the annual compulsory swim, he made a firm and uncharacteristic resolution that he would never put a foot in the putrid creek. Years later he felt it was one of his great achievements in five years at Churchie to manage to avoid all five pocket swims with varied and always suspect excuses.

Now that he is nearly fourteen and in his second year at Churchie, he has the constant challenge of homework, a task he hates in every possible way. He made it clear to his mother, ages ago, that he couldn't possibly do homework in the nursery bedroom he has always shared with David. She finally relented and reorganised her sewing room to become Davy's bedroom. He now has no excuse not to do his homework at the large old table in his bedroom, but mostly he contrives not to. He prefers to lie on his side on his bed and study his text books, head propped on his hand. He has a note book where he can scribble anything he absolutely has to, which isn't much. Nicky, his fox terrier, nestles in the crook of his legs at the bottom of his bed. Sometimes Nicky lifts his head and looks out the double doors to the verandah, listening. Antony whispers: 'Is there a pussy cat Nick?' Nicky swivels round and stares at him. 'Is there a cat?' – even more softly. Nicky whimpers and leaps for the bedroom door, races through the house, down the back stairs and hurtles into the back garden. The sudden uproar in the dark, humid garden is deafening. There is rustling in the trees: small animals, a cat, a possum, maybe a nestling bird move away for safety. Nicky hears every movement and redoubles his barking and yelping.

'For goodness sake, Antony, stop Nicky's barking,' shouts

Aimée from the sitting room where she is sewing.

'Why does Antony keep sooling Nicky on to the cats?' asks Davy emerging from his room, and for his trouble gets a corked arm on Antony's way downstairs where he loudly orders Nicky to stop barking, a lengthy process extended by a whispered 'Good boy' and pats on the dog's head. Antony enjoys these interruptions to his homework. Even more, he enjoys sitting on the verandah, staring out to the lights beyond the garden, and hearing the rumbling of aircraft engines down at Eagle Farm aerodrome. He often puts on one of his records like Mozart's *Eine Kleine Nachtmusik* or Franck's *Symphonic Variations* that Winifred gave him and listens from the verandah while he stares out over the garden, imagining flying on one of those planes to a long way away. He dimly remembers travelling with his parents at night time lying in the back seat of the car when they were driving to Melbourne. He must have been only about three. He'd like to go to Melbourne again, or England. He would love to go to England. Actually he would prefer to go on a ship.

The Poinciana Tree

An Epic Journey

*A*imée writes her letters at the little cedar desk in the corner of her sitting room. She does it early in the afternoon when the children are at school because in the morning she is at the sewing machine. Davy marvels at her smooth flowing writing. He asks her why her letters are really neat while everyone else's are so bumpy and stick out like barbed wire so much you can't read them.

She feels a deep need to take the boys to Melbourne for Christmas with the family. There has always been an open invitation from her mother-in-law Mill Jeffrey; her much loved sister-in-law Jo Watson is constantly writing and saying why don't you bring the boys down for Christmas. Until now she's never seriously considered it; there's always so much to do and worry about just to make ends meet. She thinks, why don't we drive down – in the little upright Ford Prefect – that would be an adventure!

'Winifred, what would you think if I drove the boys to Melbourne for Christmas?'

'In your little car?'

'Mm.' She put some pins between her lips as she negotiates an awkward stage in the little smock.

'It's a very long way in that car – it falls out of second gear all the time; it's not made for long trips.'

'I've got used to second gear. We drive to the beach at Surfers and I manage.'

'But that's only fifty miles. It would take quite a few days, probably a week.'

'I had a letter from my sister in law Jo yesterday and she painted such a lovely picture of what they do for Christmas. I do feel I must go soon and possibly this is the last opportunity to see old Mill who I love very dearly. She's apparently getting very arthritic and old Will has lost his memory and has become very difficult to manage.'

'Yes you should go, but maybe you should go by train,' Winifred adds.

'No, I think I'll drive; it'll be a real adventure, and I need to do something adventurous before I get completely stuck in middle age.'

'Antony could be your navigator,' says Winifred, 'he loves maps.'

So it is decided. They will leave as soon as school breaks up, at the end of the first week in December.

She and the boys get on a tram to the RACQ in the city to buy maps for the journey. Antony watches closely as the man behind the counter pulls out thin strip maps for the whole journey to Melbourne, about fifteen maps in all, one for a hundred miles. He then staples them into a booklet. His mother asks how far they should drive each day and if the RACQ can recommend suitable places to stay. Not only can he do this, but he can telephone the hotels and make bookings for us.

'You're taking on quite an expedition missis! Look, what we can do is make the bookings for you and post you the vouchers for each hotel. I won't book the smart hotels where all the graziers stop; they're too dear. We'll go for for good clean places where the commercial travellers go. In a car like a Prefect, you shouldn't try to drive too far each day – 250 miles maximum. It's over 600 miles on the New England Highway to Sydney and 550 on the Hume Highway to Melbourne. I'll book you two nights to Sydney – maybe it should be three? Then as you're staying with friends for a couple of days in Sydney, two more nights to get to Melbourne. That will be six or seven driving days in all – how does that sound?'

They all nod, even Davy.

They leave the RACQ stunned, with a bag full of brochures, an atlas of Australia and the stapled strip maps. They really are driving to Melbourne.

'Can I sit in the front some of the time?' Davy asks.

'No,' Antony interrupts, 'I'll have the maps so I'll need to be in the front.'

She says firmly: 'Of course you can sit in the front sometimes Davy.'

Packing the car is an event in itself. The boot can only hold the big suitcase and some odds and ends. The boys' bags are smaller and can squeeze into one side of the back seat. But where is the space for all the Christmas presents she's been making? Oh, she forgot about the box of fruit and supplies and suncreams and powders. And the boys' books and comics, and the paraphernalia Davy insists he can't do without? She can see this is a really serious journey for him.

'Davy, you can't take all this stuff. You can take one toy and one animal.'

'But I can't just leave everything behind. They'll probably get stolen.'

'No they won't,' says Antony impatiently, 'the house will be locked up, and who would want to steal your junk anyhow.'

'It's not junk!' He hits Antony who shoves him back against the car, and a scuffle ensues.

'Stop it boys! Here you are fighting before we even leave. I won't stand for it. If you're going to behave like this we won't go. I'll ring up Grannie and tell her we can't come.'

But they do manage to get all the essentials into the car, and they do actually depart, early on a fine Saturday morning as the sun comes up, just before six. Nicky is being looked after by the Newmans up the street. Antony feels the most exciting thing so far is leaving so early. There's a cool breeze and lots of dew on the grass and nobody's about. Even Mr Myers the paper man hasn't arrived in his noisy old Vauxhall. The car was all packed the night before so all they have to do is have a quick breakfast and hop in and leave. He sits in the front with the first strip map open on his lap.

That morning is passed mostly in silence. Aimée, head up, leaning forward, both hands on the wheel, her lower back propped by a brown cushion, concentrating, something she does so well, second nature to her. Antony, looking around, absorbing the vast landscape of the Darling Downs, map on knee, working out where he is, always asking questions, then answering them himself because no one else does.

'How long before we reach Warwick?'

Silence.

'I think it must be in about seven miles.'

Pause. No talk.

'No that can't be right – it says W 9 on that sign post. Does W mean Warwick?'

Another minute or two.

'I want to do a wee.' From the back seat.

'We'll stop in the next town sweetheart. When's the next town Ant?'

'I just told you, it's Warwick – in a few miles.'

'Can you wait, darling?'

'I s'pose.'

They arrive for the first night in a town called Glen Innes, looking dusty and forlorn in the afternoon sunshine. The Criterion Hotel is on a corner of the main street, with a big verandah all around on both sides above the bar which stretches the whole length of the hotel and around the corner. She parks outside and looks at it uncertainly. Open doors for the bars and the bottle department welcome the public all the way along the hotel front. She can hear muted but jovial conversation inside, but it doesn't seem to be where she should go. Then she notices at one end heavy double doors with glass insets firmly closed. She tells the boys to stay in the car while she investigates. Carefully the pushes open the doors and finds herself in a dark empty lobby with a maroon speckled carpet. Peering in the gloom, she notices a little counter in the corner with a hatch behind it. On the counter a sign beside a bell says: 'Please ring for service'. She rings it and after a long pause, a door opens and a small plump lady with elaborate curlicued glasses and a harassed look emerges.

'Yes, can I help you?'

'Good afternoon, do you have a booking for tonight in the

name of Jeffrey?'

'Let me see.' The large, scuffed leather bound accommodation book on the counter is consulted and pages turned with a deep breath and a weary concern. 'There doesn't seem to be a booking in that name. How do you spell it? G..e..?'

'No, J E double F R E Y. I have a voucher here from the RACQ.'

'The trouble is the front desk left last week – we're on our own.'

'But do you have a room?'

'Oh, yes we have a room – is it just for yourself?'

'For my two boys and myself.'

'So you want two rooms?'

'No, we booked one family room.'

'We don't have family rooms at present.'

'But we – the RACQ – booked a family room. It shows it on this voucher…'

'Well we have twins or doubles or singles.'

'Can you put an extra bed in one of the twin rooms? It need only be a small bed – he's only eleven.'

'Well maybe Jack can … (sigh)… sort something. That girl…' She shakes her head.

In the end, Antony gets a single room of his own, and he's delighted. It has a narrow bed that creaks – he rather likes that. It has its own wash basin, a small chest of drawers on spindly legs, an empty wardrobe, and a wicker chair. Best of all, it opens on to the huge front verandah and there are a few canvas slung grandfather chairs with long leg rests. He digs *Biggles Air Detective* out of his bag and settles in one of the grandfather chairs to read. But there's too much to do, so after five minutes he's up and investigating the Gentlemen's bathroom at the end of the long corridor. It has these slatted wooden frames in the bottom of each shower cubicle. Maybe that's so that you won't get the germs from all the feet on the floor of the shower. And the seats on the lavs have a gap at the front. What's that for?

He goes down the corridor to find his mother's room. It's much bigger than his and has a bed on either side of the room and opens on to a smaller verandah looking out on to the yard and the hills in the distance.

'My verandah is much bigger than this,' he says peering out the double doors.

'But yours is noisy and you probably won't sleep. Mum changed our room to the back because it's quiet,' says Davy with satisfaction.

'They have a dining room downstairs, I went and had a look. It looks quite nice but it smells rather cabbagey. Do we have dinner in the dining room, Mum?'

'I'm not sure. The whole place isn't very clean.'

'It certainly isn't. My verandah and the old chairs out there are covered in dust.'

'When I've got our things organised, we'll walk down the street to where the shops are and see if we can find a good cafe. I'd love a cup of tea.'

After a while Davy returns slowly clutching a sloppy cup and saucer of tea and a couple of Arrowroot biscuits, watches her drink her tea and in return is offered one of the biscuits, Antony having disappeared to explore the hotel.

'Ah, that's better,' she says, 'now see if you can find your brother.'

The woman with the glasses who seems to run the hotel has introduced herself as Beryl, told her to park the car in the hotel yard, then says she has to go and help Jack in the bar otherwise they won't be ready for the six o'clock swill.

'We're shorthanded at the moment and he just mags away at the customers so I have to keep washing up the glasses. I'm sorry but I'm telling guests they'd be better off having their tea at the Athens, except Stan Carruthers and old Miss Benson who both live here and of course I always cook up something for them. Or if you want a slap-up tea, the Royal on the corner can do a good job. It can be a bit hit and miss but if you decide on the Royal, tell them Beryl sent you.'

'Thanks very much – we'll go and try the Athens.'

The Athens is altogether more satisfying and the boys love it. She likes it too. It has dark stained wooden booths all down one side and at the back, with a huge juke box in the middle. The counter on the other side has several milk shakers, six or seven large round bottles full of many-coloured sweets, ice cream tubs and many other goodies for the boys to feast their eyes on.

'This is one of the best cafes I've ever been in,' whispers Antony after they take their seats in one of the booths. 'Can I have a go in the juke box?'

'Can I have a milkshake?' asks Davy, eyeing the rich bubbly milkshake delivered to the next booth.

'If you have a milkshake now, you'll spoil your dinner. It's only five o'clock.'

Antony is circling the juke box gazing at the list of records.

'Can't we have dinner now?' pleads Davy.

Antony is back beside the booth: 'They have *The Runaway Train* – do you remember that Mum? Can I have a bob to play it?'

'How could I ever forget,' she smiles.

'The runaway train came down the track and it blew, and it blew.' sings Antony in an undertone, 'the runaway train came down the track and it *blew* and it *blew…*'

'Alright here's a shilling.'

'I really want a milkshake – they're so *full…* '

'Well it looks like we have to have an early dinner and it's probably a good idea so we can get an early start tomorrow.'

The boys order steak and chips from the large lady with her black hair pulled back in a bun and a big smile. Aimée tells them they both can have a milkshake. Antony promptly orders chocolate, but Davy can't make up his mind.

'Hurry up,' whispers Antony.

'It's OK, I can wait,' the lady says in a heavy Mediterranean accent, smiling at Davy, pencil poised on notebook.

'What about vanilla, you like vanilla? I'll have a corned beef salad please.'

'Alright I'll have vanilla. No I'll have caramel.'

'Please,' says his mother.

'Please.'

The steaks are huge and come with a pile of grilled onion rings on top at which Davy crinkles up his nose. But the milkshakes are fantastic and nothing is said until Davy groans and admits he can't eat any more.

Lying in bed awake with the doors onto the verandah wide open, Antony listens avidly to the night noises. He works out that he can hear a train approaching the town and then receding into the distance for a quarter of an hour! Then all he can hear is the sound of people in the street, over the other side of the road with their heels clicking down the footpath. The door from the bar opens below and two noisy men come out laughing and swearing. He tries to hear what they are saying, gets up, goes out on to the verandah, leans over to listen, but now they are just mumbling. As he stands there, he can hear the roar of a big truck as it thunders nearer and is deafening as it passes underneath. Five minutes later, another huge truck with a trailer comes from the other direction that's even louder as it's on the other side of the road and he can see the driver with a cigarette in his mouth. He goes back into bed and this time, shuts the doors so he can go to sleep.

He is woken by a bang on the door. It's pitch dark and Davy lurches in telling him to get up as Mum wants to leave before it's light. He gets up, throws his things into his bag, and joins the others in the yard packing luggage into the car.

'It's so cold,' he complains, shivering in striped tee shirt and shorts. 'Why aren't we staying for breakfast?'

'We'll stop at the next town. I want to get on as far on as possible before the big trucks start.'

The sun slowly comes up through the mist as they chug along, revealing an undulating pale yellow landscape until they come to a flat sleepy little village where there's a petrol station. A man comes out to pump the petrol and fill the car up .

'Which do you want?' he asks.

'Can we have Vacuum?' asks Davy, he likes the flying red horse on the top of the pump.

'We usually have Shell,' says Antony.

'Vacuum please. Is there a cafe nearby where we can have breakfast?' Aimée asks.

'Tony's is around the corner – he's always open early for the truckies.'

There's no truckies breakfasting at Tony's, in fact there's nobody at all having breakfast and they sit down in the gloom.

'It's freezing.' Antony frowns, hugging his shoulders.

'Go and get your jumper from the car.'

A sad looking woman comes up with a menu.

'It's very cold here for a December morning,' says Aimée.

'It's always cold in Guyra, 'the woman intones in a sepulchral voice. 'It's the coldest town on the Tableland.'

It's good they got an early start as it becomes a very long day. Soon after leaving Guyra, the highway becomes a dirt track with signs saying 'Roadworks in progress' except that there's no evidence of any progress. Dust is everywhere and windows are wound up. The car hates the corrugations in the dirt road and even more the potholes. It has not been designed for this sort of terrain and it bumps and slips and rattles as if it is next to death.

'I hope we don't get a puncture,' says Davy anxiously.

Aimée is grim-lipped as she stops at a huge trench in the road. She is hating this, the dust everywhere, and wonders fatefully if they can really continue like this.

'Ant, can you hold the gear in second when I ask you because I need to have both hands on the steering wheel?'

Then there's lights behind them in the dust and a big transport blows its horn and thunders past in a storm of dust. That's enough for her. She pulls over where there's just enough space for the car off the road. She walks off into the scrub for a wee and wonders why she got herself involved in this foolish exercise. She has been irresponsible; the boys are too young to be put at risk like this. They are not tough kids from the bush who have grown up with all sorts of practical skills. We could catch a train in Armidale but what would I do with the car? And she hates to think what would happen if they actually do have a puncture. She could ring the NRMA now they are in NSW, but if it happens in a place like this where on earth would she find a telephone?

She gets back to the car to find the boys playing hopscotch in the dust.

'That's very dangerous playing on the edge of the road boys, you could be run over.'

'Run over?' replies Antony sarcastically, 'there's no cars anywhere.'

'There's been no cars since you went into the bush for a wee.'

'Come and get in the car. We had better get going or we'll never get near the hotel tonight.'

The road improves once they are past Armidale, the biggest and most attractive town she has seen so far with well-built brick houses and real streets that could almost be like a suburb of Melbourne. Their morale lifts on their way to Tamworth after Armidale. The road is bitumen, the day is warm and sunny and all that is left of the horrible morning is a thick coat of dust over all their belongings. Antony feels personally triumphant as if it was his own navigational skills that got them through and put them on this smooth road towards Sydney and Melbourne. Then disaster strikes again. Another dirt road, dustier, more potholed and corrugated than ever. They plough on, endlessly. There are no trees, it is hot and there are flies as well as dust. He is hot and sweaty, trapped in the back seat as it's Davy's turn in the front. Then, finally they come to a little town – Werris Creek. This can't be right, he thinks with a sinking feeling. He grabs the strip map. There's no Werris Creek, they should be near Murrurundi. He looks harder at the map and sees a little road branching off to the right and off the map with the fateful words 'To Werris Creek 32 miles'.

'Mum, we're on the wrong road!' he shrieks in despair.

They creep into Muswellbrook shortly before seven, filthy, despondent and exhausted. They have been driving for nearly twelve hours and all they've had since breakfast in Guyra is warm lemonade, some damp sandwiches and for Aimée a thermos of tea. They find their hotel on the main street with a dark green awning shading a gloomy entrance. Their room is large, painted pale green, with four single beds in a row. She finds a bathroom and she soaks in an old-fashioned bath with rusty water stains. The water is already brown from the grime she has shed. Despite her exhaustion, she feels almost elated that they have got through so far without major mishap. She is amazed the little Ford Prefect has stood up to the test. Getting to Sydney tomorrow will not be so far she thinks. Surely as they get closer to Sydney, the road will be better.

How nice it will be to see the Frys again. Olive is her truest link with her own family. Her patience and good sense is like a balm. She enjoys taking in Olive's practical views and ideas, almost as if she were temporarily exonerated from having to even think about any decisions of her own. She wants to talk to her about finding a different way to earn her living than the constant sewing and smocking that will ruin her eyes and makes her so depressed. Most of all she wants the news about Owen and Honor because she knows Olive has seen them recently.

The road into Sydney is spectacular. After Newcastle it is all curves and glimpses of lakes and the sea. Davy complains of being car-sick so she stops and has a rest from time to time. She has discovered it is the only way she can avoid exhaustion. She can have a cup of tea from the thermos and the boys can stretch their legs, squabble a bit and relieve their boredom. They come down a long hill and a huge river confronts them. Wide-eyed, Antony tells them it must be the Hawkesbury.

'Tweed Richmond Clarence McLeay was a **hasty man**. He went hunting for **hawks** on the Shoalhaven. Gordo taught us this to remember the Northern Rivers of NSW. You see **hasty** means the Hastings river and **man** means the Manning river. **Hawks** means the Hawkesbury,' he explains.

This arcane wisdom is gobbledegook to Aimée and Davy, but no comment is made.

By mid-afternoon, they are driving cautiously along the Pacific Highway through Sydney suburbs of Gordon, Killara and Lindfield, the boys staring out at the big prosperous houses. Eventually, the road widens and they come over a hill and the vast prospect of Sydney Harbour is laid out before them with the Sydney Harbour Bridge in the middle rearing up in all its splendour.

'Wow!'

'What's that bridge?' asks Davy.

'It's the Sydney Harbour Bridge, and the main city buildings on the other side,' says Antony with the tenuous authority of a boy who has never seen it before but is *sure* he is right.

She stops to pay the toll and they drive under the girders and across the bridge, marvelling at all the tall brick and sandstone buildings spread out before them. As they drive off the bridge, they look frantically around for signs pointing to Randwick or Coogee where they are headed.

'Do you think Eastern Suburbs would be Randwick?' she asks anxiously.

'I don't think so,' he replies, 'that sign says Bondi – that's the beach next to Coogee isn't it?'

'Yes I think it is, let's go that way.'

They finally find their way to Avoca Street, Randwick, where the Fry's now live in a brand new house they were given when Bruce was appointed head of radiology. Olive greets them with hugs, apologising for the absence of everyone, with the children due home from school shortly and Bruce at the hospital.

'How on earth did you find your way in that little car?' she laughs in astonishment.

'Yes I can hardly believe we got here, but the boys have been a great help.'

'I was really worried about you – that road can be terrible in places. Did you get lost?'

'Well, not really, but it was very gruelling some of the time, and the dust...'

'Oh you must come in and have showers and clean up. Would

you like a soft drink boys? Do you need a whisky Aimée?'

'A good cup of tea will be perfect.'

The two days at the Fry's give her the space she needs and she quickly relaxes talking to Olive and also to Susan, tall, sweet-natured and mature in outlook. It's strange how a year or two changes everything with these young people. Susan has become a full teenager and Michael, a year older, is charming and has a nice sense of humour and perfect manners. She wishes Antony could learn a thing or two from him.

She rather dreads getting on the road again, but the way to Melbourne turns out to be easier; no dirt roads and not so many miles each day. The weather is hotter and the flies terrible. On the second day they finish up in Albury on the Victorian border, at a large, quite modern establishment with art deco curved red brick walls and a multi-coloured tiled roof. She thinks it has the largest bar she has ever seen, perhaps, she ruefully thinks, the largest bar in the world, an unending effusion of cream tiles with forest green trim, fit for the Guinness Book of Records. Swatting away the flies, they check in and are shown to a large room with three beds and a window through which the unrelenting sun pours. There's no option but to change into clean clothes and go down and sit in the lounge which at least will be cooler.

The lounge is very stylish with big curved wooden chairs, round chrome standing ash trays and side tables. She shudders inwardly at the maroon carpet and huge circular yellow floral design that looks like great lumps of scrambled egg. At least it's a vast improvement on the horrible hotel they stayed in the previous night in Goulburn. It was so dirty and the room smelt of stale tobacco mixed with a sinister mouldy odour.

Now feeling relatively comfortable and relaxed, she feels the need for something stronger.

'Ant, will you go into the bar and ask the barman to take an order for our drinks.'

'Can we have a Coca Cola?'

'Yes but ask the barman to come in here. You are not old enough to order drinks in the bar and I would not be welcome.'

The barman arrives and she orders a gin and tonic and Coca Colas for the boys. While waiting they are intrigued at a family that arrives in the lounge: parents and a girl about Davy's age and two older boys. Antony and Davy stare so hard she is reduced to tapping them on their knees and hissing at them: 'Don't stare!'

'Why do they talk so loudly?' asks Davy.

'Don't be rude Davy.'

'That boy's only got one hand.'

'Stop it Davy.'

The lounge that was empty when Aimée and the boys arrived, now seems to be full, such is the impact of the other family. They are all big, rangy people with loud voices and the father and the elder boy keep on going in and out of the lounge, bringing in more gear. The mother has ordered drinks for them all as well as cakes and biscuits, but the elder boy has complained that he is hungry and wants chips too. When the chips and salad arrive in large quantities, the mother realises another table is needed. At the same time, the father arrives with a big canvas bag and three fishing rods. Despite her instructions, Antony and Davy are goggle-eyed at all the activity, and even more so when the chips arrive. The mother leans across towards Aimée and with a broad smile says:

'Sorry for all the kerfuffle, but Cec and the boys are planning to go fishing early tomorrow on the Hume Reservoir. I tell them they're mad but you can't stop 'em. By the way, I'm Jean and the boys are Stan and Eric, and this is my treasure Connie. Shake hands boys.'

Introductions are made all round and hands shaken.

'Hey I'm sorry, would you and the boys like some of the chips. There's plenty here and these greedy kids will keep eating till the cows come home.'

'Thanks very much.'

'Yes, thanks.'

They both need no further invitation and hoe in. Cec charges into the lounge again with a box of reels this time, and turns to

Jean:

'Did you pack my waders?'

'Would I forget your waders – they are in the trailer, underneath the tent.'

'So where are you off to?' says Cec with a big smile.

'Melbourne,' chorus Antony and Davy.

'Well how about that, so are we.'

'Where have you driven from?' Aimée asks, feeling quite the seasoned traveller.

'Cec works at the Broken Hill mine and we come from there yesterday.'

'Goodness that must be a long way.'

'About 600 mile from here; nearly 400 from Mildura,' says Cec. 'We got an early start at six today from Mildura, don't muck around. I've got a Ford V8 truck with a double cabin.'

'That's very quick, is it a sealed road?'

'Sealed road! It's dirt all the way but the old Ford makes mincemeat of the road, whatever shape it's in. We can average fifty the whole way. What do you drive?'

She admits apologetically: 'A Ford Prefect.'

'Ford Prefect! Where've you come from?'

'Brisbane.'

'Brisbane! I don't believe it.' Cec has stopped fixing the reels to the fishing rods and seems stumped for words as he stares at her.

'How long has it taken you to drive from Brisbane?' asks Jean.

'Well, three days to Sydney and then we stayed with my sister in Sydney and two more days to here.'

'That's really something,' says Cec, 'and in a Prefect …'

'Yes it's been quite a marathon, but I drive pretty slowly and the car has behaved quite well.'

'By the way, would your boys like to come fishing with us tomorrow morning on the Hume?'

'Oh that's very kind of you but we have to get away to Melbourne.'

'So do we, but it's only a few miles out of here to the Hume and we'll get up before dawn so we can be there before six. Best fishing in the morning. And I'll have them back here by eight, nine at the latest, in time for breakfast. What do you say?'

'Yes!' says Antony, 'can I go Mum?'

'There's only one spare rod, but I'm sure I can rig up a line for the youngster.'

She is unsure about this, but in this big room full of noisy, friendly people, she feels she can't refuse.

'How long will it take to drive to Melbourne?'

'Even if you leave at ten,' says Cec, 'you'll be in Melbourne by three, four at the latest, even in the Prefect. It's a good road all the way.'

'Don't worry love,' says Jean, 'he's a good driver, even though I can't stand him sometimes!'

Cec and Jean insist they all have dinner together in the hotel dining room. The boys are a bit monosyllabic with each other at first, but Stan and Eric are naturally out-going and before long the talk is all about boats and fishing. Antony has been down the bay a few times on friends' boats, so is able to keep his end up. Typically Cec and the three older boys sit at one end of the table and completely ignore everyone else. Poor Davy and Connie, about the same age, are left to stare at each other across the table.

Going to bed that night is quite an ordeal for her. The boys are excited and even in bed, keep chatting and asking her questions. She knows nothing about this family, not even their surname. She can see they are friendly and close-knit, but they couldn't be more different from her and her boys. She and Jean have briefly confided their stories to each other. Cec is a supervisor at the mine and they live on a twenty acre spread a few miles out of Broken Hill. While Antony chatters and Davy finally falls asleep, she sets the alarm for five and wonders if she should follow them to the reservoir in the car, or perhaps have an early breakfast, pack the car and go out there and wait for them so they don't delay any more setting off for Melbourne.

All these tentative decisions vanish in the half light of the morning. The truck is packed with all the gear and waiting outside with the motor running, his boys in the cabin and Cec pacing the footpath rubbing his hands to keep warm. Her boys hop in and she is left feeling rather foolish, reduced to telling them to be very careful and to do exactly what … Cec... tells them.

She feels completely lost, almost distraught, as she walks back into the lobby alone. There's nothing she can do, she feels utterly helpless and angry with herself that she allowed this to happen. She could so easily have said yesterday afternoon that they needed to leave for Melbourne early. It wasn't even a lie. Mill will have been expecting them after lunch and now they will get caught up in late afternoon traffic and the last thing she should be doing is having a frail old woman worry about their arrival. But even that's not important with the boys out on a lake with strangers!

She sits down on a chair in the lobby, her face a mask of concern as she wonders what to do. Suddenly Connie appears running down the stairs, sees Aimée, and asks:

'Have they gone?'

'Yes dear, did they forget something?'

'No but Mum said your little boy might be a bit lonely because he won't have a rod and I could show him how to use a line.'

Jean appears down the stairs in a dressing gown.

'They've gone have they?'

'Yes they've gone. Connie's been telling me how she was going to help Davy do some fishing.'

'Yes she's quite good with a line, aren't you girl.'

'It's very kind of you both to invite the boys this morning,' Aimée says, suddenly feeling much better.

'Why don't the three of us go and get some breakfast, seeing the men never seem to worry about us.'

She goes back to her room, packs everything up and takes everything down to the car and is back in the dining room to find Jean and Connie already finishing their eggs.

Jean says:

'Run upstairs love, and get all your stuff packed up so we can leave after the boys get back. I want to have a chat for a while and I'll see you up there soon,' When Connie has disappeared, Aimée says:

'She's so thoughtful, you must be very proud of her.'

'She's like her gran, my mum. She's always known how to handle herself – right from the beginning.'

'I wish my boys were like that. Life is so hard for so many people these days and I don't feel my boys are at all prepared for it.'

'They'll be alright – they're smart and what you've done for them is amazing. I couldn't have managed anything like that. Coming from them goldfields in the west to Queensland and all that sadness, and now driving to Melbourne in that tin Lizzie!'

'Were you brought up in Broken Hill Jean?'

'No, Moree in the north of the state. My dad started out being a stockman. He was a great rider. We had a farm out there but nothing much ever grew as it was always in drought. You had to have the money to have a decent sized property and raise cattle or sheep, and Dad was a hard worker and great with his hands – a fantastic carpenter. But all he really wanted to do was ride and when we were kids we went with him to all the country race meetings and the rodeos.'

'That must have been a wonderful experience as a child.'

'Yes we loved it. Dad learnt all the tricks of the trade from the aboriginal stockmen. There's big abo camps up there in Moree you see. Dad used to compete against them at all the rodeos and race meetings, but he always said they were far better than he was but at least he was the best white man. Me and my brother spent all our time with the aboriginal kids at school and when we went out to the rodeos with Mum and Dad.'

'There were lots of aboriginal families in Kalgoorlie too but my father wouldn't allow us any contact with them. How lucky you were to have that sort of childhood.'

'It was pretty tough, we lived rough most of the time. At the local school, most of the other parents thought my brother and me were abo kids.'

Jean stretches out her hands on the table, smiles and slowly shakes her head at the memory. Aimée is intrigued and feels almost envious of such a childhood, such a contrast to her own. There are now several people having breakfast, but it seems quiet and private in their corner and she wants to know more about this woman's life.

'In many ways that must have been a wonderful privilege. Did you go on to high school and matriculate?'

Jean gives a short laugh and presses her lips together.

'No! I was a real naughty girl. I told my Mum there was no way I was staying at school after Intermediate and went and got a job at the local milk bar. I was fifteen but it was only part of my plan to get away. I waited till I was seventeen then I went off to Sydney. Mum was mad at me but she came round and anyhow she was right, Sydney wasn't for me. I got lonely for the first time in my life and after a while I looked out for jobs back in the country and finished up at the BHP works in Newcastle.'

'Is that where you met your husband?'

'Not for a while, but yes, I met Cec there but not till I was a few years older. I liked Newcastle, it was a real friendly place and I still like it and we go back there quite often and the kids are good pals with some of the BHP families there.'

She feels real warmth towards this woman the like of whom she has never known before. She tells Jean about the Jeffrey family in Melbourne. She hears the terrible story of Eric's hand when at the age of seven it was torn off in a dreadful accident from the pump mechanism. Even now, six years on, Jean shakes in horror at the remembering and telling of it, and Aimée can scarcely bear imagining her devastation.

Suddenly there are loud voices in the lobby and she looks at her watch in alarm; it is nearly ten o'clock! The dining room door crashes open and four excited boys and Cec rush in full of overlapping stories.

'Mum I caught lots of fish,' says Davy.

'Cec had to throw some back – they were too small,' corrects Antony, adding, 'I caught a two pound Murray cod.'

'Cec and Stan had to help him.'

'That's wonderful boys, but we have to get ready to go – we are running very late to get to Melbourne this afternoon. Thank Mr Dobson and go and wash your hands and faces.'

Cec comes up and presents her with two large fish wrapped in newspaper.

'Here you are love, two good Murray cod, one caught by your boy.'

Feeling flustered, she turns and tries to say, 'Oh no you mustn't,' changes her mind, and gives him her nicest smile, 'Thank you very much Cec, that's so generous, the family in Melbourne will be thrilled.'

She rounds up the boys, says heartfelt farewells to the Dobsons, rushes out to pay the bill and bundles the boys and the fish into the car and sets off. It is only that night when she finally gets to bed in Melbourne, to her dismay she finds Cec has paid for their dinner at the hotel in Albury. She didn't even thank him.

It's just before dark when they arrive at the Jeffrey's house at East Malvern, a neat brick arts and crafts cottage dating from the 1920s. The welcome from Mill and Betty is overwhelming. Not that it's noisy and emotional, but it's overwhelming for her. The long hugs from the two women leave her completely unable to speak.

To break the atmosphere of emotional vulnerability, Betty shouts out:

'Where are you Dad, they've arrived. Come and see Aimée and the boys.'

'He probably won't recognise you, dear,' whispers Mill to Aimée.

After a little delay, while Betty and the boys unload the luggage from the car, Will appears looking neat in his grey suit and his hair brushed back tidily with the part, as she remembers, just left of the middle. Momentarily she thinks with a pang, he looks as he always did with the inscrutable humorous look on his face, hardly any more aged.

'Good evening my dear,' so softly and slowly that she realises he has really aged. 'It's Frances isn't it, you look like your mother.'

'No Dad, it's Aimée, Alan's wife and these are your two grand-sons, Antony and David,' says Betty impatiently, introducing the two boys who look on shyly.

They all move into the house and Mill fusses around the kitchen finding drinks for the boys and showing them the room where they will sleep, while Betty makes cups of tea.

'This is ridiculous,' she laughs, 'What are we thinking of? It's nearly seven and we should be having whiskies!'

'I'll have a whisky,' says Will from his armchair.

'And so you shall. Mill come on, leave those boys alone, it's time we had your famous roast dinner, it'll spoil if we leave it much longer.' She looks at Aimée, looking utterly drained but with a faint smile, 'Come on little one, you look like a stunned mullet, I'm running you a bath, the roast can wait.'

Around the big dining room table, feeling much refreshed and relaxed from the bath and ten minutes of quiet time, she senses for a moment the transforming feeling of being at home, returning home, being where deep down she belongs, even though she has never seen this house before. She smiles, as across the table Mill chats to the boys, quizzing them about the journey, school, what they want to do in Melbourne. She watches Antony describing all the adventures in detail, with a glow in his eyes revealing he is in his element, determined to revel in all the new experiences on offer. Davy is sleepy, struggling with his food and puzzled by the confusing conversation with his grandfather. Sitting next to Betty who does most of the talking, she is only half-listening, feeling sadness pervade the joy of homecoming. Her caring and affection-ate father-in-law, the teasing interspersed with wisdom, is lost to the world. Dear darling Mill looks so old and bent despite her undiminished enthusiasm. It is as if, after more than fifty years of marriage, six children, the depression, the moves from city to city, the war and the heavy pall it cast on the fates of her children, the gradual loss of her beloved husband is too much.

Aimée is also anxious to know how Betty is going. She is no longer the stick-like figure who returned, in the nick of time from the terrible privations of the prisoner-of-war camp in Sumatra, but the dysentery and TB have permanently damaged her health. During her recovery, she had written a book about her experiences in the camp based in part on secret notes she had made on miniscule scraps of paper. The book she called *White Coolies* was an extraordinary success and became a best-seller. Betty had found herself a celebrity and the experiences of the army nurses in Sumatra a talisman of the heroism of Australian women during the war. In 1948, she and one of her surviving colleagues Vivian Bullwinkel had set off for their long-planned journey (partly to raise money for a Nurses Memorial Centre) around Australia and to England where they met the Queen.

'You look so much better Betty, are you fully recovered from the TB?'

'Yes it's all much better now but I'm never going to win any races again! But I must tell you the big news, I'm to be appointed the Director of the Nurses Memorial Centre.'

'How wonderful, where is it to be?'

'In St Kilda Road, just near Melbourne Grammar, and it's almost finished. Viv will be on the Board. It's all happened because of *White Coolies*. You know I always wanted to call the book the 'little yellow bastards' but I didn't think that would go over very well with the family and just about everyone I suppose, but the one good thing that came out of it is the Nurses Centre.'

'But the book has shown the world what happened and how incredibly brave all you girls were.'

'Do you know Viv and I have been invited to Japan by the American nurses. At first it just disgusted me to even think of going to Tokyo, but the government would like us to go. I got a letter from Earle Page, the Minister for Health.'

'If you feel up to it, I think you should go.'

The next day Betty takes her to see the Nurses Centre and introduces her to some of the people she will be working with. It thrills her to see Betty so energised. They take the tram over Princes Bridge and sit in a cafe near the top of Collins Street and order coffee. She looks around the wide tree-lined street, the elegant grey buildings and the trams rumbling by. How special it feels to be in a Collins Street cafe after all these years! It is their first chance to talk properly.

'Are you going to stay living with Mill?'

'At the moment I have no choice. Mill can't look after Dad on her own and he's going downhill quite rapidly. He's quite difficult to handle. The more confused he gets, the more irritated he gets and he takes it out on her. Now that I'm going to be working full time, it's going to be worse for her, and she's pretty frail now.'

'Are the girls able to help?'

'Not really. Mick's in Geelong of course and Mary doesn't handle Dad very well. You know her, she gets flustered with his bad behaviour. As you can imagine, Jo's a tower of strength and is always coming over and taking him for a walk or taking them both out to the pictures, but she doesn't have a car and she's got problems of her own ...'

'Do you mean ... Alf?'

'Yes. Bloody men! He's so bloody charming. Everyone thinks he's the bees knees, and yes he is – he's a lovely man and he's wonderful with their kids Joanna and Anthony. But poor Jo as usual gets the rough end of the pineapple. She works herself to the bone and is always doing odd jobs to bring in a bit more cash while Alf is out there having a good time.'

'But as a liquor salesman, isn't that what he has to do?'

Betty has always been forthright and intolerant of male bad behaviour, but Aimée detects a harsher note in her voice and she hopes Jo's marriage is not under threat. But Betty is irrepressible and shoves aside family issues. She wants to hear all the news from the Brisbane she used to know: how Aimee is managing financially, who's been married and had kids? On a more sober note she asks after the boys that didn't come back from the war and it leads them to reminisce about the golden days at Surfers Paradise. The surf, the fun, the sun-baking, the irresponsibility ... . It was another age, like it happened on another planet. While he is totally present in both their minds, they don't talk about Alan. Betty would love to but she knows it is impossible for Aimée.

'You know, I used to think of the beach at Surfers when I was at the camp, not so much about all the people we knew, but the place, the happiness we felt, and the way we slept like logs and woke up in the morning, and there was the beach again, just across the street.'

'It probably helped you to survive, but I've decided I'm going to have to sell *Breffney*.'

'What a terrible shame, but I'm not surprised.'

'I can't afford to maintain it, and yes you're right, it's in the past and I have to look to the future. We are always being asked to go to the beach or down the bay with friends, so we don't need it.'

Betty has bought an Austin A40 of which she is very proud and offers to ferry them anywhere they want to go. Because of Will's condition and Aimée having to share Betty's room, it is agreed they will move the next day to her old friend Alice La Treille's place in Camberwell while Antony stays on at Ailsa Avenue seeing he loves being there so much. Betty promises to take them to Jo's in Caulfield and if there's time before Christmas, down to Geelong to see the Gales. Betty's elder sister Frances, Mick to everyone, insisted to her husband Charles (Breezy) that if he was determined to establish his medical practice in Geelong, the compensation must be a decent new house – at the top of the hill overlooking the bay.

Christmas Day for the whole family is to be at Mary's (the youngest Jeffrey sister) house in Burwood. Betty is rather cynical about that arrangement and mutters that we'll be lucky if we get anything to eat. She tells her that John will see to it everyone has plenty to drink and will finish up doing the cooking too, as Mary will be running around in the days before Christmas telling everyone she has no idea what she's going to cook.

He couldn't be more pleased that he is to stay on at Grannie's while his mother and David are to go to the La Treilles. He loves Grannie's house: the slightly dank smell of the laundry, the concrete floor and the soap, and the Christmas puddings! He has discovered she makes several Christmas puddings each December, wraps them in calico cloth, and hangs them in the laundry to mature for NEXT Christmas, not this one. The flavour is so much richer she says, if you soak them in brandy and hang them for a year. He likes the big sitting room too — it's so quiet and dark and sometimes you don't even notice Pa sitting there, so still and quiet until he says something like: 'Is the cricket on yet?' Grannie also cooks more interesting meals than Mum does, like roast pork or chicken fricassee. Best of all is the Dandenong Dairy across the road, where he is able to get fantastic milkshakes.

Betty (she has told him not to call her Aunt Betty) has asked if he would like to come with her to the Second Test on Boxing Day at the MCG. Would he ever! Cricket is by far his favourite sport but he's not much good at it himself though he'll never forget the brilliant catch he took when the Ascot One Teacher School played Norwell. When they're at *Breffney* for Christmas holidays, he loves nothing better than to listen to the tests being broadcast and to the commentaries by Alan McGilvray and Vic Richardson. Tests at the MCG always have the best atmosphere; you can actually hear the buzz at the ground on the wireless.

When Betty takes them over to see the Watsons, he can hardly remember meeting his cousin Anthony before: they must have only been about five. He is three months younger but it's like as if they've known each other for ever. Anthony likes the same things mostly and he loves cricket and Betty has now offered to take them both to the test on Boxing Day. Antony just loves Anthony's mother Auntie Jo; she is small but not skinny, has a red face, talks loudly and laughs a lot. She finds it's very amusing they are called Anth and Ant. He has a pretty little sister with dark hair called Joanna and she and David seem to like each other though he doesn't say much as he's so shy.

On first arriving at the Watsons, when his mother hugged Auntie Jo, they both were crying even though they were also laughing. The noise in the kitchen is deafening with both Auntie Jo and Betty talking and laughing over the top of each other. In fact he has never seen his mother chatting and laughing so much and looking so happy too. They are all laughing at the trouble Uncle Rex got into during the Melbourne Cup carnival in November.

'The problem was that apparently he told Beatie he was only going to the Cup on the Tuesday,' says Jo, 'she probably wouldn't have minded if he'd told her he was also going to Derby day.'

'No it's not like that. She rules him with an iron rod and he's allowed only two race meetings a month.'

'But Bet, the Spring Carnival is different. Alf would die if he couldn't be at all the meetings in Cup Week, even the Oaks.'

'It's not as if I'm barracking for Rex. Goodness knows he has it coming to him. But Beatie is as tough as nails and it's pretty rich coming from her. But I did laugh when I saw Rex's face at Menzies hotel. It was a complete coincidence; I was meeting Burtta Cheney and Helen Gadsden for a drink at six, and there was this terrific din coming from one of the reception rooms as I walked past on the way to the lav, and who should emerge from this party but Rex, pissed as a newt. He tried to dodge me as soon as he saw me and slink back into the party, but I yelled hullo Rex, where've you been? He looked so guilty and tried to brush it off as some boring function, except there was this big sign on the door saying VRC, Derby Day Winners. Then he hissed at me, for Christ's sake, don't tell Beatie I'm here, she'll murder me.'

Jo says: 'Well it's a wonder I didn't get murdered too though I don't think I can be blamed when she rang for Alf on Derby day afternoon to see if he knew where Rex was. Anyhow Aim, it's so wonderful you are actually here. I'd begun to think you'd never come. You must have been mad to drive all that way in that little car. You look lovely too, not like frowsty old me. How do you do it?'

'Oh Jo, I can hardly believe I'm here with you all. It's like a dream. And how gorgeous Joanna is and the boys seem to have hit it off right away.'

Antony and Anthony are in deep discussion about the respective English and Australian test cricket teams as they have both been following every match since the Englishmen arrived in Perth a month before. Antony tells Anthony,

'I think Hutton and Washbrook are the best openers for England since Hobbs and Sutcliffe.' Though even as he says that he realises how ridiculous he must sound because he wasn't even born when they were playing.

'Keith Miller's my favourite,' replies Anth, 'and with Lindwall and Johnston, they'll be too good for the English, even Hutton, I reckon.'

'Anyhow, Australia's been far too good for England for years now, at least since the 1946 tour, so I'm barracking for England this tour,' Antony announces.

'How could you do that? You just couldn't. You're an Australian, you can't barrack for England!'

'Well I am.'

So they decide they will pretend to play a test match in the Watson's back yard. There's a straight stretch of grass about fifteen yards long finishing at the back of the house, ideal for a pretend test match. Antony will be England and Anth Australia. Anth wins the toss and decides to bat, while Antony runs into bowl with that strange leaning run of Trevor Bailey's and the next over he jogs in like Alec Bedser. This becomes a huge though intermittent tussle and completely absorbs the boys for several days. Who wins? It doesn't seem to matter; playing test cricket is what it's all about.

On Christmas Day everyone is to meet at the Denny's house at Alonso Street in Burwood at 12 noon. In a way, Antony's disappointed as usually there is a pillow slip at the end of the bed (partially) filled with presents. As his mother and brother are staying at Mrs La Treille's, it doesn't happen this time. He also guesses he is now too old for it to happen anyway. Rats! He was hoping for that record of the *Coriolan* Overture.

Betty drives him with Grannie and Grandpa to the Denny's. It seems they are late because the house is very crowded. Anth is there with his parents and they ask Uncle John Denny if they can play cricket. He points to the back gate which opens on to a large space like a paddock, perfect for playing cricket. Anth has brought along a bat and balls and a set of wickets. Their cousin Tim Gale has arrived with his parents from Geelong; he is two or three years younger than Antony and Anth and the three of them set up a cricket match. Tim has sandy hair, is very good looking and is one of those kids who goes to a smart school and gets on well with the big sporty kids. He is a pretty good bowler despite being only eleven and seems to bat as well as Anth or himself.

Aimée wants to come early to the Denny's on Christmas morning, but Alice insists they stay to open all the Christmas presents, and there is a magnificent train set with signal box for Davy. She feels in the way at Christmas with the La Treilles, especially as Alice's husband Dick came back yesterday from his constant travels. Alice lives in a beautiful house and is as welcoming and hospitable as ever, but she feels out of place. The carpets are thick, everything is so quiet that you feel you have to speak in a whisper. Arriving   at the Dennys could not be more of a delightful shock after the La Treilles. As she walks in with Davy, all these big men sitting around drinking beers spring up in unison with a sort of roar of welcome and all hug her in turn. There is Rex, Alan's younger brother, looking more like Alan than ever, but so *unlike* him … irrepressible and elegant, cigarette in one hand and beer in the other, the unmistakeable aspect of the race track evident from the boldly checked sports coat and the VRC tie. Alf, Jo's husband, ever the charmer, takes her hands in his and with his head tilted to one side appraises her fondly, gives her a long and affectionate hug:

'Aim, my dear, how lovely to see you, how are you?'

'How nice to see you too Alf.'

Alf was a champion athlete, a great hurdler and represented Australia at the Olympics twice, appointed team captain the second time. Ever since the war ended when he was demobbed, his work as a salesman has meant a hand-to- mouth existence for his family, his handsome presence and charm apparently counting for little in the job stakes. Breezy Gale, a medico with a successful practice in Geelong, also gets up and gives her a hug of welcome, telling her he is looking forward to having them stay in Geelong in the New Year.

The door opens from the hallway and in bursts John Denny, host for the day, his tanned face shining with pleasure.

'Aimée, it's wonderful to see you and the boys here, it's been such a long time,' says John, always in a breathless hurry. 'Can I get you a drink? Another beer Alf? Time for a whisky Rex?'

She refuses a drink but is delighted to see John again. She is especially fond of him as he was a close friend of Alan's. John is a senior officer on the navy's flagship HMAS Australia.

'How are you all John, I'm dying to see Mary and the girls?'

'I'm not sure where Sara and Jane are – out the back playing with Joanna and Gretchen I expect, but the *real* girls are all in the kitchen waiting to see you.'

'You know this is all so exciting for us – we've been looking forward to Christmas Day and seeing you all together for I don't know how long. Are you still at sea?'

'Yes but not for much longer, I'm being posted for a senior shore job at the Flinders naval base at Westernport, and we'll be moving there next year.'

'Oh, will Mary like that?'

'I don't think she will …'

'Here she is girls!' shouts Betty coming out of the kitchen, and to the clamour of shrieks and loud laughter, Aimée is ushered into the kitchen. As well as Mill, Mickey, Jo and Betty, there is Mary full of giggles and rolling her eyes as she despairs of getting Christmas dinner together, and Beatie: foursquare, plain, red-faced, chain-smoking and with a voice like sifting gravel. While none of the

Jeffrey girls is a sophisticated lady of leisure, Beatie is altogether a different kettle of fish. The family has always wondered how debonair Rex got caught up with her, and caught up he is, as she has always ruled his roost.

John follows Aimée into the kitchen, surveys the party scene, and announces with scarcely concealed irritation: 'Alright everyone, I think it's time you took your drinks out into the backyard and looked after the children. Jo, can you help me? I think if we can have a real go of it we'll get Christmas dinner on the table in – less than an hour, or maybe a bit more, but soon!'

'Oh John, I can manage.' says Mary helplessly.

'No, off you go.'

Mill takes Aimée into the back garden and they sit down on a bench under a tree. It is now a hot midsummer day and Mill fans herself with a Chinese fan.

'Now dear, I really want to know how you are getting on up there in Brisbane. I can't see that you have any worries about the boys. We have loved having Ant, he's seems a very bright boy and asks me so many questions and many I don't know the answer to at all. But you are so skinny and you looked exhausted when you arrived. Are you still doing that lovely smocking?'

'Dear Mill, you don't need to worry about me. Actually I hope to start a new job when I get back. My friend Pat Fraser's youngest brother Dan Hart has joined their brother's eye surgery practice on Wickham Terrace and he has offered me the job of his nurse/receptionist. Dan is a sweet man so I'm sure I'll love it. It will take me out of the house and I'll be so relieved to stop sewing for Snow White. I should earn more money too.'

'But isn't it time you gave up working altogether? And isn't there some nice man up there suited to you? There were so many eligible men coming through the house when we lived there – all wanting to take Mick, Betty and Mary out. I suppose it's a long time ago now. Do you get a chance to go out and have a bit of fun? You're so pretty and have a lovely figure, even though you're too thin. You seem to have such good friends up there, so surely you will meet someone soon.'

She is not sure what she should say. She had intended to confess about her new friend Toby to Jo who would be the best one to understand and advise.

'I have met someone, but I haven't told anyone yet. He lives across the street from us and runs a shipping office. He has asked me out a few times, but I don't think he's serious. Nor am I.'

'Oh that's wonderful. I'm so pleased, he sounds just the ticket! What's his name? Has he been married before?'

'No, he's a bachelor and lives with his mother and his sister who is also a widow.'

She can tell Mill has become dubious. She's not surprised, she is dubious herself, which is why she wanted to talk to Jo first. The conversation is ended by an influx of little girls: her four nieces who have been (literally) playing with Davy. He is like the cat who ate the canary; he sports a broad grin and has shed his bashfulness. The girl cousins, aged between nine and five, have taken Davy over and dressed him up like a tumble-down fairy.

Jo comes out into the garden looking harassed and calls everyone to Christmas dinner, muttering to Mill and Aimée that we may as well get started as we'll never get finished. She whispers a loud aside to Aimée that John has drunk too much; he drinks this terrible naval concoction of gin and sherry.

John has organised two large folding trestle tables from the navy which have been set up under the wisteria-covered trellis outside the kitchen – one for the adults and one for the kids. They are covered in several table cloths and laden with traditional Christmas decorations. It is also John who found the turkey, quite how no one dares ask, as well as roasted it, and now he proudly carries it out and places it in the centre of the childrens' table.

'Where on earth is everyone; come on you slow coaches!' Betty is getting impatient. 'Now look you girls, stop mucking about with Davy and round everyone up – Christmas dinner's on the table!'

John is now bursting with activity, his florid face dripping with sweat, his lips pursed with concentration, as he carves the turkey.

Jo looks on anxiously, unsure if his commitment to total control is liable to collapse. What she dreads are smart remarks from Alf or Rex that will puncture John's desperate need to have everything go perfectly.

The turkey is carved, several large bowls of salad are on the tables, condiments of every kind, and Mill's superbly crispy baked potatoes are on large baking dishes on each table.

Aimée watches as Mill leads Will out from the sitting room and seats him at the head of the table. As Mill turns away to fill his plate with the turkey and vegetables, he mutters that he doesn't want to sit there and gets up and seats himself at the other table on a spare chair between his grandchildren Tim and Sara. Sara sweetly turns to him and asks, 'Where's your dinner, Pa, can I get it for you?'

'That'd be nice girlie.'

But Mill arrives with his laden plate and converges with Aimée who asks him:

'Will dear, would you like to sit next to me at the other table?'

'No.'

'Now Will, behave yourself and don't talk to Aimée like that.' says Mill, 'If you want to sit next to Sara that's fine, but be nice to her.'

Jo seats herself beside Aimée and in no time they are absorbed in conversation. Despite the excitement and noisy Christmas clatter around them, she is swept up in her old intimacy with Jo. For a moment she wonders how these friendships happen: it seems so fleeting, can go for years without contact but when it resumes, all the old affection, trust, and sense of being back home, safe, is there in a flash.

'How do you feel Mill is coping – I was rather shocked with how bent she is?'

'Oh she's not too bad – comes from pretty tough stock you know, she still tells Betty where to get off; I don't know how Bet stands it. Having six kids and carting them all over Australia for years was no pushover, and she still loves Dad and never complains about caring for him.'

'And you, Jo? Are you managing alright? Alf looks well – is his job bringing in enough? It's so hard these days for so many of the men who were in the war, coming home and trying to make a living.'

'Yes we're managing, but only just. I hate the work he does, going from door to door at the hotels and clubs, selling them Scotch whisky mostly, and other spirits and liqueurs. He doesn't complain but I think it's beneath him. He goes out looking so handsome and well-dressed, and traipses around all day and it's such hard going. And of course, all the time he's having to have a drink with his customers, so by the time he gets home, he's exhausted and had too much to drink. Sometimes he has to stay out late with a big customer as they all want a bit of him because he's so charming and was a great athlete. It's a dog's life. But let's not talk about that, how are you managing?'

'Jo, it must be really hard on you and the children.'

'Yes it's hard for us always having to move and finding decent places to live and changing schools. It was fine when we were living in the big house in Labassa Grove with the Ramseys and its huge garden. What I really want is for him to get a better job. I'd like to see him managing a good quality hotel where he's in one place and using his knowledge of the liquor business. The customers would love him and he would build up the business I'm sure. We've been looking around but nothing suitable has come up yet.'

'Are you looking near here or in the city?'

'Anywhere really. There's a hotel coming up in Ballarat. I'd be happy to go there. But Aim, I want to hear about you. Mum's just told me you're getting a job with a top doctor.'

'Yes I'm pleased about that. His name's Dan Hart and he's an eye specialist. He's a really nice man, quite young and his sister is one of my best friends.'

'Is he eligible?'

'Goodness no, he's ten years younger and anyhow he's married.'

'Are you seeing anyone?'

'Well, yes, but it's probably not going anywhere.'

'Why not? Tell me about it.'

By now the children are lining up for second helpings and Mill and Mary disappear to check the progress on Mill's famous Christmas plum pudding. Rex turns to Aimée and asks:

'How are you going love, I must say you're looking terrific.'

'Don't interrupt Rex, I'm having a heart-to-heart with her, you can talk to her later. Go on,' she says, 'what's the problem – is he married?'

'No, he's never been married.' Suddenly she doesn't want to talk about him, not today, perhaps not at all. After all, it's Alan's birthday and it seems shocking to be talking like this. She sighs and continues: 'He's a nice middle-aged bachelor, very popular with his friends, he laughs a lot, he's kind-hearted and I think, rather shy with women. You see he has a withered leg from polio, he's bald and has a squint. He's also a bit overweight and walks with a big limp!' She laughs ruefully.

'Goodness me!'

'Yes indeed.'

'Those things don't matter of course if you like him. He sounds rather a dear. He's probably a treasure.'

'Mmm... He lives across the road – that's how I met him. He has an old mother who owns the house – she's lovely and he has a widowed sister and her little boy who also live there. Toby is hardly ever there. He's always out with his friends or business colleagues, playing poker, sailing – he has quite a social life.'

'What do you both do? Does he take you out?'

'Yes he's very generous. He takes me to dinner to nice places. He sometimes takes me to concerts or the ballet. We have long talks after...'

Suddenly John stands up, looks around, bangs the table with a spoon a few times and clears his throat.

'Can I have a word everyone. I don't normally make speeches on Christmas Day and I can't remember when we last had a speech on a day like this.'

'I can,' interrupted Betty, 'Dad made a very funny speech on the Christmas Day after I graduated as a nurse. It must have been 1938.'

'Anyhow,' resumes John, 'it's a very auspicious day because all the Jeffrey clan are gathered here, and I know all of us who were not born Jeffreys are very proud to be numbered amongst them. But it is a very special Christmas gathering indeed because at long last Aimée and Antony and David are with us, something we have waited many years to have them back with us. Alan would have been fifty-three today and I feel sure he would be very proud to look down at his own little family and his whole extended family and see how we have all survived the terrible war and how well they are doing.'

There is complete silence at the tables apart from giggling between Davy and Joanna who are not listening. John continues at some length about the importance of families, the sanctity of the Christmas season and the untarnished future for our beautiful children.... Lumps in the throat are forming and a few eyes are starting to brim. The ever-practical Mill is standing holding the tray with the plum pudding, about to put it down on the table. Her quizzical stare speaks volumes: what is John on about? We don't get maudlin and emotional in our family. Jo grips Aimée's hand and whispers, 'Oh dear!'

'And finally,' says John, 'I want to propose a toast to Aimée and her boys on behalf of you all. Aimée you are a wonderful credit to the family and the memory of Alan. Your hard work and dedication to your boys' education and upbringing sets a great example to us all. Welcome back to the family today and I hope you will join us whenever possible on future family occasions. Here's to Aimée, Antony and David!'

'Here's to Aimée, Antony and David,' intones everyone.

'Thank you John.' Aimée manages with a wan smile.

Mill declares firmly: 'Now let's have the pudding. Mary, I've made the brandy butter but where's the ice cream for the children?'

Antony's mouth is open – he is astonished at all this. He has never before heard anyone speak about his father, or his mother, or himself, like this. He looks at his mother who looks very quiet. Is she embarrassed, or is she going to cry? He hopes not. He expects this is what happens at big ceremonies, probably in the navy, or at funerals.

'Where's Dad?' This is from Betty who looks around her, puzzled. 'Tim, he was sitting next to you, do you know where he is?'

'He hasn't been here for a while,' replies Tim.

'Then go and see where he's got to. Maybe he's locked himself in the lav. I hope he hasn't wandered off.'

Tim and Antony go looking, first into the sitting room where all the men had gathered before lunch. In the spirit of detectives looking for a crook, they hive off and look into all the bedrooms, in cupboards, under beds, out the windows; in the bathroom meeting Uncle Rex as he emerges, out into the garden, around the front, behind the shrubs and bushes, out the back gate into the field where they played cricket before lunch. No sign of him. They meet Betty and Grannie looking worried as they come back through the gate.

They chorus; 'There's no sign of him anywhere,'

'Dad's gone!' Betty shouts. 'Come on men, we need a search party.'

There is general consternation: half-eaten plum pudding and ice cream is left for the flies. The women do another search of the house and leap out into the street. Mary points to lanes running off the street and sends off Mickey and Gretchen. Jo commandeers Anth and Joanna and sets off in another direction. John grabs Mary and tells her to door-knock to the left and he'll door-knock to the right. Alf and Breezy each get into their cars. Rex, Beatie, Betty, Tim and Antony bundle in too. Aimée stays with Mill.

'Has he done this before?'

'He's gone off down the street a couple of times, but usually only as far as the shop, and I've told them to ring me if he appears.' She looks crumpled and distraught, suddenly very old.

Aimée takes her hand. 'He can't have gone far. Ant said he was eating his turkey only about ten minutes before Betty asked where he was.'

'The trouble is he gets disturbed and cross if his routine is upset and he's liable to rush off all confused. He doesn't just wander, he goes like a train.'

The door bell rings and Aimée gets up to see two large policemen just inside the open front door. 'Good afternoon, madam, we've had a call from a Commander Denny. Could we speak to him please?'

'Oh, I'm sorry, he's gone off down the street looking for his father-in-law, Mr Jeffrey. Would you like to speak to Mrs Jeffrey?'

Mill comes slowly to the door and explains: 'My husband is losing his memory and gets very disorientated. The whole family has gone off looking for him.'

'Well if you can give me his name and age and describe what he's wearing and what he looks like, we'll put it out on the police radio, and we'll find him in next to no time. Could you also give me your telephone number?'

Anxious and perspiring, John rushes in the front door and takes over dealing with the policemen. It seems none of the neighbours has seen Will. John and the police go into a huddle and Aimée takes Mill back to the sitting room.

Antony is in the back seat of Uncle Alf's car, sitting next to Uncle Rex with Aunt Beatie in the front. He is driving slowly and all of them are looking out on both sides. Being the middle of the afternoon on Christmas Day, there aren't many people about.

'You know,' says Alf, 'we've pretty well covered the ground on this side of the house. I don't think he's here.'

Beatie responds: 'I don't think the old bugger's going to be wandering around deserted streets for long. He's not completely gaga – he'll be looking for some sort of action, like a hotel or a cafe, even though he'll be hard pressed to find one open.'

'Good thinking Beat,' says Alf, 'let's go down Warrigal Road as far as Toorak Road.'

So he turns the car around and heads to the main road, but it still looks pretty deserted. A tram careers past with one person on board.

Eyes glued to the footpaths of the streets they are passing, Antony is worried about his grandfather. He's a really nice old man, and he's still pretty smart. He likes to escape from wherever he is, even from home at Ailsa Avenue. Antony doesn't blame him; it must be pretty boring just sitting around waiting for your meals with Grannie and Aunt Betty always calling out and telling you what to do. Pa really likes listening to the cricket; that settles him down, and sometimes he falls asleep. Antony can understand that as some of the Englishmen bat so slowly. He falls momentarily into a reverie ... tomorrow we are going to the Second Test at the MCG ... hey, is that ... along there ...?

'Hey Uncle Alf, is that him hurrying along the road ahead? See?'

Alf peers out ahead, shades his eyes: 'Where? Oh yes, I can see him, you've got eagle eyes my boy, that's him alright.'

Sure enough, there is Will, neat in his dark suit and tie, despite the summer heat, hurrying along, as if he's running late to catch a bus. Alf pulls the car into the side of the road and everyone bundles out of the car to greet him.

'Where have you been Dad – everybody's been out of their mind?' shouts Rex, anger pushing through his relief.

'Come on Will,' coaxes Alf, 'Mill has been very worried, get into the car and we'll go home'

Will rears back, looking horrified at the group surrounding him. 'Go away, leave me alone, go about your business!' He walks on.

The men are stunned. Beatie hurries after him. 'Your wife Mill is desperately worried about you; please stop and come with us in the car.' Alf and Rex have caught up and Rex takes him by the arm.

'Take your arm off me – go away!' shouts Will and shakes himself free. The two men and Beatie seem unsure of what they should do next. Will is off again and Rex hurries after him, catches him up, again takes his hand to bring him back to the car and a little tug of war ensues. Antony is watching this from outside the car, and then is appalled to see a man and a woman open the front door of their house and stare at the confrontation with his grandfather. They look angry and hurry out to their front gate and shout at Rex and Alf:

'Leave the poor old man alone. How dare you interfere with him. What do you think you are doing? If you don't leave him alone, I'll call the police …'

Beatie goes straight up to the gate in belligerent fashion, 'Now you two just pull your heads in and mind your own business. Go on, go back in and keep out of this, or I'll …!'

The woman at the gate turns and looks Beatie up and down with contempt: 'You horrible old cow, I can see you're drunk. I've a good mind to … all of you, get away from the old man.'

Alf walks after Will while Rex joins Beatie as she confronts the house-owners at the front gate. 'Come on old girl, this isn't doing any good …'

Beatie elbows back at Rex, 'Don't "old girl" me.' Then she turns back to the house-owners and raises her voice, 'Look you interfering nosey parkers, can't you see this old man is confused. We are his family and are taking him home. Now leave us alone.'

'Not bloody likely until we get the police.' They move out on to the footpath and approach Will. 'Come on old feller, you can come into our home.'

Alf and Rex form a moving guard around Will who is still trying to escape.

Beatie finally loses her temper and screams at them, 'BUGGER OFF, you pathetic creeps!'

At this point, a police car pulls up behind Alf's car – two burly officers are out of the car before it has stopped moving …

Early in the New Year after the eventful Christmas, Aimée and the boys move a few miles away to Kew to spend the rest of their

Melbourne holiday at the home of her former teacher at Merton Hall, Gwenda Lloyd. Gwenda is only ten years older and still teaches History and French at Merton Hall, where she has become an institution. Merton Hall is a leading Anglican school for girls; many of Melbourne's powerful elite educate their daughters there. Gwenda and her husband Ian are politically active left wingers but this is no barrier to the high regard and affection in which she is held by the school and its old girls. It says much for the tolerant culture of the school and its encouragement of intellectual enquiry amongst the girls.

Gwenda and Ian's home is a large ramshackle Victorian era brown brick house, nestling comfortably amongst vines, shrubs, flower beds and deciduous trees. It gives the impression that it has looked like this for generations with virtually no change. It is where the Lloyds have lived virtually all their married lives and brought up their children, Jenny, now studying at Melbourne University and Philip, a little older than Antony, who goes to Carey Grammar school, literally across the road. The Lloyds have no interest in elegance or upwards mobility. Their well-worn cloak of bourgeois respectability is no hiding place, it is simply an easy framework for living lives devoted to family, progressive ideas, music, art and facilitating the lives of immigrants.

As soon as he enters this house, Antony decides he likes it. It's unlike any house he has ever been in. It is not cavernous and gloomy like the Brown's old mansion in Brisbane, but it has big rooms, high ceilings, and is full of comfortable old furniture. It is cool and quiet inside and every door you open leads into an interesting room, different from the last one. He really likes the room his mother and David will sleep in. It has huge windows opening on to the front garden and is painted a yellow-peachy colour, and he notices a few days later that when the sun comes in during the morning, it actually looks pink. If he lived in Melbourne, and he wishes he did, he would like to live in this room.

Philip's room is totally different. It's tiny with a low ceiling at the back of the house and full of Philip's sporting gear and prizes. Philip is a real athlete: he is tall and strong and a champion Australian rules footballer at Carey Grammar. Antony can't understand why he doesn't have the big peach coloured room at the front of the house, but Philip just smiles and shakes his head and says this room is great and really private. Next to Philip's room is Uncle Ian's work room where he does his carpentry and has afternoon snoozes on the narrow bed beside one wall.

Over the next few weeks, at his mother's insistence, he helps Aunt Gwenda with the washing up by doing the drying up and putting away. She is always interesting to talk to, quite unlike any teacher he's ever met before. She has grey hair pulled straight back in a bun at the nape of her neck, and a rather red nose as if she has a cold. She usually wears a plain grey woollen skirt and a thin jumper with the sleeves pushed up to the elbows. She walks with a purposeful stride and he smiles to himself as he thinks she looks rather like a washerwoman, especially when she's carrying a wicker basket full of clean clothes. But behind her wire framed glasses, she has very observant and twinkling eyes.

'Have you been enjoying the holidays, Antony?'

'Oh yes I've been having a wonderful time.'

'What have you been enjoying most?'

'Oh well, staying with my grandmother and Aunt Betty and getting to know all my uncles and aunts and cousins. And getting to know Melbourne. Melbourne is definitely the most interesting city I have ever been to.'

'Yes Melbourne is a curious city. What do you like about it?'

'Well, it's hard to say. I like everything about it so far. It looks so different from Brisbane. The houses and city buildings look more solid. I really like your house. Our silver trams are better than yours but you have terrific electric trains and ours are still filthy old steam trains. But I think most of all I love all the trees and gardens in Melbourne, and especially the War Memorial in the Botanic Gardens and the view from the top.'

Gwenda stands back from the sink, mop in one hand, the other on her hip and looks at him.

'I'm afraid I don't like the War Memorial much. It celebrates heroism and valour, but also war. Do you think that's a good thing?'

He's unsure how to respond to this. 'Yes war's terrible, but at school we are always being told about bravery and the heroism of all the old boys that got killed in the war.'

'Yes that happens in most of our schools here too. Do they talk to the boys about ways to help the new migrants coming into Australia now?'

'No.'

'Do they teach music and art?'

'No, not really, but there is a brass band.'

He feels rather embarrassed for his school. It doesn't seem to be measuring up to Melbourne standards. He asks whether Philip's school teaches all these things.

Gwenda laughs briefly. 'Not with great enthusiasm; we prod them a bit and they are trying. Your mother says you love music – are you learning to play?'

'No, we don't have a piano, but I love music and I collect records.'

'Do you really? Have you looked at Ian's record collection?'

'I've seen it, but I haven't looked properly and I'd love to. Could I go in and play some of them?'

'I'm sure you could: ask him.'

She turns and wipes her hands on her apron and goes over to the stove and lights the gas for the kettle.

'And do you think your mother is enjoying the holiday too?'

'Oh yes, I've never seen her looking so happy.'

'I am pleased about that. She deserves a good holiday with her old friends and family as it's been hard for her for a long time now. We were encouraging her to come back and live here a year or two ago when you were about to start secondary school, but it seems she's decided to stay in Brisbane. I imagine you are a great help to her and help her with a lot of the chores.'

'Well ... yes.'

After all the drama of Christmas day, and the subsequent recriminations, coming to the Lloyd household is a boon for Aimée. Gwenda and Ian are not only dear good-hearted friends, but wise and reliable too. In the six or more years since she has seen her, Gwenda hasn't changed a bit. Still that friendly open manner, and the same self-deprecating laugh as if you can't worry too much about the foolishness of the world. When she tells them about Christmas Day, Ian throws his head back and roars with laughter, but Gwenda chides him, telling him it's not funny and could have been a disaster, but at least they now know Will will have to be put into care.

'The whole family's in a complete fluster,' she tells Gwenda, 'and it's not going to be as simple as that. I worry most about poor old Mill, who is devastated and can't even contemplate putting him into care.

'Well, there's nothing you can do about it Aimée, so don't get embroiled in it. Hide yourself away here and have a rest,' says Gwenda, 'families are contentious beasts, often best avoided. Anyhow have you caught up with your friends yet, the Alexanders for instance?'

'No, and I must. I've talked to them on the phone and Hatty is taking Antony to *South Pacific* next week. I haven't seen the Ways yet either and Doug is Antony's other godfather.'

The first night at the Lloyds she can't sleep, and despite Gwenda's good advice, she's sliding back into her old habit of worrying about everyone and what she should do. Driving to Geelong with Betty and the boys, Betty was holding forth about the impossibility of the whole situation, that nobody wanted to take responsibility. Of course she doesn't want her new job at the Nurses Centre to be compromised, but Aimee detected a new intolerance and impatience in her. She's not surprised: after all the privations she's suffered and the permanent damage to her health, what else can be expected?

At breakfast, Ian Lloyd announces that plans must be made for the next two or three weeks while the Jeffreys are here. Ian has a serious professorial look, high forehead, rimless glasses, completely bald. He is a strong athletic looking man, walks with a long, bounding stride, but then is likely to stop suddenly, swivel around and face another direction. When talking, he has a tendency to declaim as if there is an audience in front of him.

'Next Saturday, we are having a soirée. Felix Werder will be here. In case you don't know Aimée, Felix is a Jewish Viennese, a wonderful composer who escaped from Vienna just in time in 1939. Harold Blair the aboriginal tenor will come and sing and of course Liesel Jorg will play. Antony, as you like music, it will be really valuable experience for you.'

'Dad,' interrupts Philip, 'Antony and I want to go to Luna Park tomorrow. They don't have Luna Park in Brisbane. Can we go?'

'What do you think Aimée?'

'I suppose so Ian, but how do they get there from here?'

'Oh it's easy,' says Philip, 'we just catch the tram in Glenferrie Rd at the bottom of the street.'

'Remember Jenny is having a party here next week Ian, I think it's Friday,' says Gwenda.

'With all her Commie friends, I suppose!'

'They're hardly communists Ian, they're thoughtful young left wingers.'

'Anyhow, Aimée, I want to take us all out to dinner before you go – show you all what real continental food is these days. I thought the Italian Society, Gwenda?'

Aimée protests but Ian insists and it's put in the diary.

Even though it's school holiday time, Gwenda takes Aimée to Merton Hall one afternoon. She loved her years there but is amazed at the leaps and bounds in the school's buildings and facilities since she left twenty-five years before. Gwenda shows her the new library and the beautiful new classrooms for the senior girls.

'Having decent student facilities and a real reference library makes such a difference to getting the girls really involved in thinking.'

'I still found it fascinating when I was there. You seemed to be able to find out anything you wanted. My love of art came directly from the art books in the old library. And if it weren't for you I would probably have been completely ignorant.'

'Well I can tell you that now the place is not so fusty, it's much better to teach and the girls are more responsive.'

She slinks over to her old boarding house. With a pang of mixed feelings, she finds it completely unchanged. Seeing it deserted and shabby, it seems small, lonely and dank. With a shiver she remembers the icy mornings, the terrible showers and how impossible it was to get your fingers to work practising the piano. No wonder she gave it up so soon. But this was where she started to make those friendships which made such a difference to her loneliness. For a fleeting moment she recalls the flood of emotion she felt when she first met girls who confided in her, who felt almost as lonely and bereft as she did, if that were possible.

They leave the school and walk down to Toorak Road to find a café for a cup of tea. It's a blustery afternoon, chilly with the cold change that always happens in Melbourne after a series of hot January days. They hasten, shivering, into a teashop, closing the door against the wind, Aimée murmuring how she had forgotten how cold it can become in the middle of summer. When the tea comes, in typical style, Gwenda delivers a bombshell with no warning.

'I've been thinking about it, and there's really no question that you and the boys should come and live here.'

'What? Here in Melbourne?'

'Yes, you'd be much happier here. Here in Melbourne would suit you – and the boys, in so many ways. You have many old friends, you have the whole Jeffrey family whom you love, you have us, the schools are better, at least some are. Antony's school sounds completely unsuitable.'

'But Churchie is a good school, probably the best in Brisbane.'

'Well that sums it up. If Brisbane's best school spends its efforts promoting manly, heroic values and sport, teaches no art, no music, and nothing about contemporary Australia and the issues facing young people today, need I say more? Don't get me wrong, many of the schools here, particularly boys' schools, are just the same, but there are good ones, and also in the state system where you wouldn't have to pay. There is a very progressive culture developing in the education system here in Victoria. We could help you find the right school and Antony with his love of music, would thrive.'

Aimée is stunned, flabbergasted.

'Look dear, Brisbane's not right for you either, especially as the boys are growing up and in today's world, they need good education. I'm pleased you are giving up the sewing, but being a receptionist in a doctor's rooms is hardly any better. You should be getting back to your art – you are so talented. And you could easily get a job around here in South Yarra or Prahran in a book shop or an art shop, and you could teach art too. You would meet interesting people and before long you would … find someone suitable.'

'Oh Gwenda, it's impossible …'

'You mean you wouldn't want to?'

'No, of course it's not that. In many ways I would love to live here. But I've put down roots in Brisbane. I don't think I could change now, unless …?'

'I'm not going to push you against your will, but I do think you should think hard about it and take the chance to talk it through with Ian and me in the next couple of weeks. Being here on holiday catching up with friends is one thing, but it is also a good time to think about possibilities, when you are not bogged down with daily tasks.'

By far the best room in the Lloyd's house, Antony thinks, even better than the peachy pink front bedroom, is the big living room. It has a big bay window looking out through leafy shrubs to the side street. It is a huge room, with a grand piano, two big sofas piled high with old floral cushions, lots of faded tapestry covered chairs, little tables, standard lamps, brightly coloured modern paintings on the walls, and a massive cedar wall fixture. It is the cedar wall fixture that really fascinates him; it is full of records, all neatly stacked vertically, in big bound folders with heavy paper sleeves for a symphony that might take five records. Next to it is a bulky free-standing radiogram, where you can stack up to six records that fall one by one on to the turntable as the previous record finishes. His little plastic table-top radiogram in Brisbane is pathetic in comparison.

He has been into the room several times, usually in the morning when everyone was busy somewhere else. He sits on a sofa, taking out each record from its sleeve. He loves their feel and carefully reads the labels; some are very old. The Trout Quintet has five records and was recorded in 1929 by the Busch Quartet. On the inside of the cover there are notes on the music and players. He knows how famous the Trout is but has never heard it. He hasn't played any records yet as he hasn't permission yet from Uncle Ian, who has promised to play some after dinner tonight. He can't wait: he puts the first movement of the Trout on the turntable, turns the play knob, and immediately the catchy melody enthrals him. The violin sounds so sweet and gentle and he settles down to listen, but in five minutes the door opens and in comes David.

'What're you doing?'

'Listening to music.'

'Are you allowed?'

'Go away.'

David goes out, but Antony stops the music, feeling guilty. He continues looking at records, laying out those he wants Uncle Ian to play: Beethoven's *Pathetique* sonata, the Emperor Concerto, which he heard Gieseking play when Winifred took him to the concert last year. There's so much else he's never even heard of. He wanders around the room and starts looking through the book cases. History books, big art books, books on music, novels. If only we had a room like this … He finds a large book full of Norman

Lindsay's paintings and drawings and his eyes nearly pop out. Completely naked women posing and dancing, leering satyrs, he turns the pages slowly, utterly absorbed.

At lunchtime, Philip bounds in: 'Hey, I've been looking for you – want to come ice-skating? Mum says we can go.'

'I haven't ice-skated before, is it easy to learn?' He's not very keen, really preferring to hang around the fantastic living room.

'No problem, come on,' says Philip and rushes to get his satchel.

They race down the street to Glenferrie Road to catch the tram to St Kilda, and once on board, Philip explains how to skate, leaning forward into each step and pushing your legs half sideways and half backwards.

'We hire these big lace-up boots with skates on the bottom. You might have to try a few to get one that fits'

'Has the skating rink got ice on the ground? How do they keep it frozen in summer?'

'It's not on the ground you nong, it's a big enclosed space with a refrigerated floor, but it does melt quickly in summer so try not to fall over and get soaked in freezing cold water!'

The rink turns out to be a vast space with millions of kids and plenty of adults too, all skating around in one direction to horrible loud dance music. It's also very cold and he clumps out to the edge of the rink on skates that teeter with every step. Philip gives him a cursory grin and sweeps off into the streaming mass of skaters. Antony takes a cautious step on to the ice holding on to the rail at the side with both hands, and immediately nearly does the splits. This is terrible he mutters to himself, but he perseveres, edging grimly around the side of the rink.

Ahead of him in this trudging, rail gripping procession, is a girl about his age. He watches her struggling like him; she's pretty, at least what he can see of her from behind. Actually, she's even slower than he is. Maybe he's getting better at it, so he takes a risk and skates slowly past her, turning to smile at her as he edges past, and sees she really is very pretty and she smiles back. Then a total disaster. In an instant he slips and loses his footing, and frantically whirls around grabbing at anything as he falls. He catches her arm, desperately grasping for balance. With appalling grace, her legs slip forward and in a trice she's flat on her back, soaked from head to foot in an icy puddle. Worst of all, he manages to stay upright, ignominiously helps her up, and watches helplessly as tight-lipped and furious she stalks off to the dressing room.

Later, to his great relief, he and Philip emerge into the warm sunshine and buy ice creams. Antony admits he is not keen to return to the skating rink and prefers playing cricket. On the way back in the tram, they discover they were both at the MCG for the Boxing Day test. This talk on the tram and the prospect of coming back to Luna Park restores some face for him, and he quickly accepts Philip's suggestion that they play cricket the next day in the park down the street.

At dinner Jenny is there, just back from a camp down at Wilson's Promontory with some of her university friends. She's a tall girl with straight black hair and a look that seems to go straight through you. She's not especially friendly, and she talks to either her father or her mother directly as if what she has to say is very important and can't wait. Uncle Ian announces at the dinner table that because Antony is so interested in music, the two of them will shut themselves in the living room after dinner and listen to records. Anyone else is welcome to join them but they'll have to keep quiet. At this, Antony can feel a disapproving stare from Jenny.

When after dinner they sit down beside each other in the big living room in two armchairs, Ian asks what he would like to hear: Prokofiev, Sibelius or Stravinsky? He is totally at a loss. He doesn't know any Prokofiev or Sibelius and has only heard vaguely the name Stravinsky.

'Um, do you have Prokofiev's *Romeo and Juliet*? I don't really know it, but it's a famous ballet isn't it?'

'Good choice – I like your taste, and yes I have an excellent new recording of it recorded in Moscow played by the Bolshoi orchestra.'

At Ian's direction, he finds the set and puts on the first record.

After two sides Ian asks would he like to continue or try something else. Antony has sat bolt upright without moving. He has never heard anything like it; it's so savage, so rhythmic, so gorgeous...

'Oh yes, can we go on please.'

The Balcony Scene overwhelms him with its rapturous surging and sighing; the Death of Tybalt curdles his blood. The closing scene in the tomb seems to strangle his throat. He sits back feeling drained telling Uncle Ian it was wonderful.

'I thought you'd like it. Now, boy, I want you to try some tougher stuff. I have a great old recording of Sibelius' Second Symphony, the first recording ever made of it. It was recorded by the London Symphony Orchestra with the great Finnish conductor, Robert Kajanus, a close friend of Sibelius.'

It's a scratchy old recording and he can make nothing of its opening with its throbbing lower strings and chattering woodwinds that seem to have no shape or logic. But as it winds on, something begins to make sense and in the second movement a big tune starts to develop that makes his spine prickle. The last side of the recording is a huge blare of brass with long slow chords trying to pound through the constricted sound from the speaker. Even though he can't hear much detail, it sounds amazing.

'Well, what did you think of that, boy?'

'It's sort of strange and hard to understand but you can really *feel* it. Can I listen to it again tomorrow?'

'Yes, you should. That's music from a real genius who loved the landscape of where he lived in Finland. The recording is a bit muddy but the conductor knew what he wanted and had it directly from the composer.'

He can only sit on the edge of his seat and think about it. He knows he doesn't understand what the music is about, but he also knows it is extraordinary.

'Now it's getting late but I think we should hear some German *lieder*. Do you know what that word means?'

'It's German for 'song', isn't it?'

Ian gives him a blue label 10 inch record that reads *Auf dem*

Wasser zu singen, and adds that it means 'singing over the waters.' The rapid piano accompaniment has a lilting quality, in what seems like a slow waltz rhythm, and when the soprano voice joins with a carefree silvery tone, he sees it truly has a sense of dancing across water; in his mind's eye, a lake. He reads the name on the label and sees it is Irmgard Seefried. Ian watches him and tells him that she is coming to Australia next year to sing in concerts for the ABC. They play more Schubert songs before Ian declares that's enough for tonight. Antony feels absolutely entranced by the lieder, not just the beautiful melodies, but the sound of the singers' voices which give him a feeling of exaltation, especially Irmgard Seefried's.

Aimée is pleased the evening was such a success when Hatty Alexander took Antony to *South Pacific* at His Majesty's Theatre. He couldn't stop talking about it for days and kept on saying it was the best thing he's ever been to, and how Hatty is so knowledge-able, even if his subtext was that most women know practically nothing. Though she's never married, Hatty really understands boys, indeed all young people. Perhaps it's the wide generous phy-sique, the plain shapeless dresses, or the reading glasses that always hang around her neck that give her that owlish benevolent look. She always asks the right questions of the boys and then talks to them at their own level. Aimée wishes she had half the same skill of understanding boys. The first time she took them to Hatty's gift shop, she expected them to be bored in a minute, like bulls literally in a china shop. But Hatty had them in the palm of her hand in a moment. She showed them some of the more practical or mechani-cal items for sale, asked them how they worked, and took them out to the back of the shop to assemble them. Before long Antony was wrapping gifts and Davy ringing up sales in the till.

Aimée is going to see Hatty's sister Janet at her family's elegant old double-storied semi-detached house in East Melbourne, just over from the Fitzroy Gardens. She recalls perhaps the most con-

Above: William (Will) and Amelia (Mill) Jeffrey
near Flinders Street station in Melbourne

Below: From the Jeffrey clan (l to r): Aimée and Alan,
Mill and Will, Mary and John (Denny) with Aunt Eff at rear.

Above: Alan with Antony as a baby

Above: Antony at the Royal Exhibition in Brisbane

Below: Aimée with Antony as a little boy

Above: Aimée on her wedding day in 1935 with bridesmaid Betty Jeffrey

*Below: David Jeffrey, (left), Antony (2nd from right)
and friends in Brisbane*

Aimée in her retirement

tented time of her life, living there and studying art at the National Gallery School. Janet is thrilled to see her. Though she must be fifty, Aimée sees she is still vivacious and elegant but with that indefinable look of innocence that betrays a woman who has remained within her family. Thankfully her mother is not feeling well and has taken to her room upstairs.

'You must go upstairs and have a chat – she is dying to see you, and I'll come up in a while and rescue you for dinner.'

'How is she Janet?'

'Not bad considering she turned eighty last year, but she has become fussier than ever and runs me off my feet with all her demands.'

When she came to live with the Alexanders after leaving school, it was a quiet place with an established routine. Dr Alexander was a scientist, already retired, benevolent but settled in his ways, spending most of his time in his study redolent of leather bound books and the aroma of pipe tobacco. It was a retreat, a device to free himself from the concerns and minutiae of his wife's existence. Hatty had made it her business to make a separate life for herself as soon as she left school, travelling widely overseas. When Aimée first came to know her, she had returned from several years overseas and set up her successful book and gift shop in South Yarra.

Aimée adored, hero-worshipped Janet from the first. Having just left Merton Hall at eighteen, homeless, virtually an orphan, she clung to Janet, six or seven years older and full of life and ideas. Janet had graduated as an MA from Melbourne University and then had a job as a research assistant at the University library. For two years they spent their time together at galleries, the cinema, the theatre and concerts, as well as dances at university colleges. Janet was a favourite with many of the young men they met but never seemed to want to go out with anyone more than once or twice. Even then she could see Janet was becoming a captive of her selfish mother. Now she is saddened to see her unchanged, just older. She spends half an hour with old Mrs Alexander who chirrups away, delighted to have someone else to talk to about all the little events in her life. At dinner, Janet is eager to know everything that has happened in the last few years in her life.

'I think you have been an absolute heroine coping with all that and as for driving all that way, I don't know what to say. It seems to me you work far too hard. Your eye doctor sounds very nice, but will you have enough time for your painting if you start work with him?'

'I don't think so; I've hardly done anything for years. I just don't have time.'

'But Aimée that's terrible, you must put time into your art. It's what you do, and now the boys are older and better able to look after themselves, you must really try to find the time.'

'It's all very well Janet, but I have to earn a living. But you must be doing something exciting with that wonderful brain of yours?'

Janet smiles rather coyly: 'I've been ages researching the early days of the nursing profession in colonial Australia and am starting a book about it, and I'd love to talk to you about it. The trouble is my progress is so slow with all Mother's demands. I wondered whether you would like to join me in the whole project.'

She is astonished. 'That's a lovely idea Janet, but I can't see how I could do it from Brisbane.'

'That's the point – you should come and live here, in fact I thought that was your plan.'

'Have you been talking to Gwenda Lloyd?'

'No I haven't seen her for ages. Why?'

'Because Gwenda has been trying to persuade me to come and live here too.'

'With them?'

'No, in Melbourne. She's been so persuasive about it I've become quite confused. I even feel guilty I'm not doing the right thing by the boys by staying in Brisbane.'

'Well we can solve all that.' she says with a cautious smile.

'What do you mean?'

'Hatty and I have been having a long talk and we've finally decided to relocate Mother downstairs as she has so much trouble now getting upstairs. We are going to convert the big back room into a little flat with its own bathroom. This would then mean you could have her room and its own bathroom and there's still your old room for the boys. I know when Hatty comes home, you and she will argue about all the practicalities, but I want to say I would **love** you and the boys to come and live here. It wouldn't cost you anything, and if later on as the boys get older, you want more independence, we would completely understand. The next few years will be your biggest challenge, and living here will help you through.'

'Janet, I'm speechless, I don't know what to say. It's the kindest thing …'

'It would be like that time when you first came to stay – we had the happiest time.'

When Hatty arrives home about ten, she looks tired. 'I played bridge at the club and I nearly fell asleep from boredom. Don't send me off like that again without warning Jan. What have you two been up to?'

'Talking about everything. I love Janet's project about early Australian nursing.'

'Did mother dear deign to grace the table for dinner?'

'Don't talk like that Hatty. No she didn't but Aimée spent nearly an hour with her telling her everything. It will brighten her life for a week.'

Aimée tells them how Antony is over the moon about *South Pacific.* Hatty snaps out of her languor and says what fun it was to take him and she almost felt like a teenager herself joining in his delight at everything. 'It really is a wonderful production, as good as anything I saw in the West End.'

She can see from Janet's silence she is nervous about bringing up the momentous offer to have them come and live there. Maybe she hasn't even told Hatty? Hatty would have a very different view. Old Mrs A might have kittens about it? In a way it could solve so many problems. Ant could go to Melbourne Grammar where Alan had always intended to send him. Perhaps I could go back to my painting? But living in that house – the boys would drive them mad – Janet has no idea what it would be like.

'Hat, I told Aimée about the plans for Mother living downstairs, and … we also talked about … Aimée … coming here.'

'Aimée, this is Janet's absurd notion she's been carrying around ever since you announced you were coming down for the holidays. How she can imagine you would want to is beyond me. The two of us are mad enough, but with Mother it would be like a lunatic asylum.'

'Hatty, don't go on like that. For one thing, you're never here and Mother will love her little flat looking on to the garden. She won't budge from it. Aimée don't take any notice of her.'

'Jan, I'm sorry but be realistic. I would love to have Aimée and her gorgeous boys living here, but she and the boys would go mad living with three old witches plus their mother.'

Aimée laughs but Janet is becoming petulant, 'I knew you would be like this Hatty, you're just being idiotic.'

'You know it's rather funny watching you two argue. You're doing exactly what you both used to do when I lived here, with your father shaking his head and your mother threatening consequences if you didn't stop. But the whole idea is like a dream and most dreams turn out not to be real.'

Hatty looks rueful and smiles. 'Aimée dear, if you really would like to come and live here, both of us could think of nothing better. It would transform our dull old lives. If you really think the boys could cope with us, I for one would be thrilled. Boy oh boy we'd make them hop!'

'Now what are you going to do at the soirée tomorrow night Antony?' asks Ian Lloyd with a flourish at breakfast.

Antony is horrified. Do? It was bad enough at Jenny's party last night with all her strange friends looking like they came straight out of a gangster or spy film. When they started to sing those Russian revolutionary songs, he felt so uncomfortable that he hid behind one of the big armchairs and read the Norman Lindsay book. Does he expect me to sing or something?

Ian continues: 'Surely you know a song you could sing, or you could recite a big poem, like the *Rime of the Ancient Mariner*? Or perhaps you could sing one of the Schubert lieder you like so much?'

'I could recite some of the *Wild Colonial Boy*.' offers Davy.

'Bravo!' says Ian.

'Could I play one of your records, like *To Music* by Schubert?'

'You could but that's hardly the point of a soirée. Well think about it boy, and let me know beforehand and we'll squeeze your gem into the programme.'

Antony turns to Philip and asks him what he's going to do. He says he'll probably play his tin whistle.

The soirée is to take place on the last Saturday night before they leave to drive home to Brisbane. He's not sure what to think about it. He has been having such a great time doing all sorts of crazy things with Philip. Two days ago they had got up early and put tacks head down across Wrixon Street to see if they could puncture the tyres of the local yellow bus. They'd spent hours hiding behind the bushes on the side of the street watching to see what happened and racing out to turn over tacks that had fallen over, but so far nothing had happened.

Now on Saturday the women are preparing and cooking chicken casserole, corned beef and white sauce, salads, cakes and apple pies, and Uncle Ian has been setting up the living room for the concert, making a space for a tiny stage next to the piano. The big chairs have been pushed back to the window wall, the room set up with a few rows of upright chairs. He can tell it's serious when in the afternoon Liesel Jorg, the pianist and Harold Blair, the singer arrive and confer over their scores. Harold looks worried. He sings snatches of the song while she repeats a few phrases on the piano. Uncle Ian has explained that Harold is the first aboriginal man who has become a classical singer, and that he will go on to have a great stage career. Liesel is what he calls an 'emigre' who arrived in Melbourne from Vienna just before the war. She is a dignified lady with black hair going grey, an aquiline profile and long elegant fingers. When Antony peeps into the room, she looks up, gives him a smile and graciously invites him to come in to listen. Harold clears his throat, nervously smiles at Antony and announces: ' "The stars are brightly shining" from *Tosca…*' With a little thrill up his spine he suddenly realises *he* is the audience – an audience of one! With a sweeping gesture, Liesel plunges into the keyboard with the opening phrase and Harold bursts into song. It is so loud and overwhelming that he reels back into the armchair, transfixed by Harold and his voice. He is rather plump but neatly dressed in a suit and tie. His face is so black it almost looks dark blue and his hair is black and wavy. But his voice is like nothing he has ever heard before, ringing out like a trumpet with such volume and clarity, totally unlike the silvery sound of Irmgard Seefried singing Schubert.

Later in the afternoon, Ian gives him a task that makes him sigh with relief. 'Seeing you don't seem to be planning to sing tonight my boy, you can help by writing out the programme in your best copperplate. Your mother tells me you win prizes for your hand-writing, so this is your big chance. I want twenty perfect copies by six o'clock.'

'Thanks Uncle Ian, I'll get on to it straight away. Harold Blair is a wonderful singer.'

'Yes he's a real talent. He learnt to sing at the aboriginal mis-sion at Cherbourg in Queensland and Liesel has done a terrific job coaching him. I'm arranging for a concert recital tour for them both next year around Australian country towns, and the ABC will broadcast at least one of the concerts. You should come with us for part of the tour. It will be good for your education; I'll talk to your mother.'

In addition to a bracket of three opera arias from Harold Blair, there is a piano trio from the composer Felix Werder, Liesel is to play the *Moonlight* sonata by Beethoven, and one of Jenny's friends is to play some Spanish guitar pieces. There are several other items too but thankfully no Russian revolutionary songs.

People start arriving with instruments and scores and he can sense an unfamiliar authority from the Lloyds as they greet the guests. Aunt Gwenda is wearing a smart dark blue dress and looks completely different as she chats easily with the people arriving. Jenny is wearing shiny black slacks, a black top and a gash of bright red lipstick. She smiles and whispers to the Spanish guitarist who even Antony can see isn't Spanish but a skinny young man with a pale spotty face, straggly little beard and long lank hair. He speaks in a soft whiney voice and seems to be Jenny's boyfriend. Uncle Ian introduces him with a cursory wave as 'Ronaldo, a budding flamenco guitarist.'

His mother hustles him to help with serving drinks and savouries to guests, telling him to take a leaf out of Philip's book in being helpful to the Lloyds. He can't take his eyes off the guests who look unlike any of the adults he has known in the family or in Brisbane. They seem to be either tall and droopy with wispy hair, or short, bald and plump and they talk to each other like spies, sometimes breaking into sharp giggles. One young woman dressed in what looks like a thin multi-coloured blanket comes up to him holding her flute and accepts his offer of a glass of punch and in a soft breathy voice asks him his name. He tells her and she says she is Brenda and is going to play a new piece by Dorian Le Gallienne, as if he should know exactly who that is. He sees close up she is not so young and the dress smells odd.

'Good evening, ladies and gentlemen.' Uncle Ian is standing before the piano, programme in hand. 'Welcome to our home and to our little concert tonight. As I'm sure you are already aware, we are greatly privileged to have some of our finest artists here tonight, both from Australia and abroad. What we will hear tonight is essentially a private preview of some of the fine performances we may enjoy in our public concert halls before long. Some of the music you will know and love, and some will be new and unfamiliar. This is a rare combination; I hope you will reward our artists with your close attention and afterwards with your appreciation. With no more ado, please welcome our dear friend and magnificent pianist from Vienna, Liesel Jorg who will play Beethoven's much loved *Moonlight* sonata in C sharp minor.'

Antony has heard the *Moonlight* before and loves the arpeggios in the first movement that Liesel plays with her right hand after a tiny pause each time. He is exhilarated by the scampering last movement which Liesel dashes off as he watches the flashing of her fingers. The applause is deafening and Liesel acknowledges it with a grave bow, hand on the piano.

Next is the Trio by Felix Werder, and the mood changes dramatically. Felix is a short fleshy man with dark soulful eyes. One moment he is serious and sad looking, and the next he has a wicked grin on his face and is whispering something out of the side of his mouth to the violinist. From the piano, Felix gives a short introduction in a thick foreign accent about the piece. He makes everyone laugh when he tells them he has stacks of pieces in his desk drawer that nobody wants to hear, and the other day he found this trio in the bottom drawer and thought it might be just the ticket for Ian Lloyd's soirée. The violinist, who is a top professional from the Victorian Symphony Orchestra, gives a knowing smile at this and the cellist, a dark-haired lady in a long green dress just looks nervous. It seems like very grim music. There don't seem to be very many notes and they go from the top to the bottom of the scale and back very suddenly. The players are concentrating very hard and each stroke of the bow seems to require a huge effort of will. Felix plinks away at the piano watching the other two like a hawk and giving little smiles of encouragement. After quite a long time, there is a pause and then a great scramble of loud screeching notes, some giant chords on the piano and it's all over. Uncle Ian comes up beaming, wrings Felix's hand and leads loud applause from the audience. Antony finds this very puzzling as he has never heard music like this. He even thinks he wouldn't call it music.

He is thrilled by Harold's bracket of songs who sings the *Tosca* aria again, this time even more passionately. He decides he should shout *bravo* with everyone else. Harold also sings a lovely aria, more peaceful and melodious, called *Il Mio Tesoro* by Mozart, and then an American Spiritual which he makes sound sorrowful but beautiful too. Brenda plays her flute piece accompanied by Liesel. This makes him feel as if he were sitting beside a creek in the bush with the sound of water over the stones and a bird in the background.

The last bracket of the evening is from Jenny's friend Ronaldo. Uncle Ian tells the audience he will turn the lights down low so that there will be no distraction from the intimate sounds of the great guitar music of Albeniz and Granados. He says Ronaldo is a talented young musician, shortly going to Spain for further study. Antony finds a spot in the crowded room where he can sit on the floor leaning against an armchair and see the player close-up. The variety of sounds he can make on the guitar is fascinating; the speeding up and drawing out of the notes to create longing or excitement, mesmerising.

When it is over, there is a great buzz in the room as the women bring in the hot food and serve glasses of wine. The performers are happy and relaxed and those listening are excitedly crowding around asking questions. Ronaldo and Jenny are sitting on the floor in a corner quietly chatting while he fiddles with his guitar. Antony stares admiringly at them from where he is sitting. Jenny looks up and smiling at him, asks:

'Did you like it?'

He feels rather stupid but replies: 'Oh yes, I think … your playing is fantastic, and the music is too.'

Ronaldo looks up and murmurs in an offhand way, 'Yeah, it's great stuff.'

Harold Blair is talking animatedly to Uncle Ian and Antony goes up to them with the bottle of wine to fill people's glasses.

'Harold, I don't think you have met our young house-guest Antony. He's a music lover. What did you think of Harold's singing my boy – any good?'

Embarrassed by the tease, he manages an enthusiastic nod and Harold tells Ian he sang the *Tosca* aria for him alone during the afternoon.

'You know I'm was so glad you were there this afternoon, because I get absolutely sick in the stomach with nerves before I have to sing in front of an audience. Singing it first for you made all the difference and I really felt good singing it in the concert – no nerves at all for once.'

Just before they were due to return to Brisbane, Betty takes the boys to Luna Park. Aimée wants to have a long chat with Mill before she leaves. She hasn't seen her since they went to stay at the Lloyds and she feels she needs her advice. Deep down she just wants to be with her and wishes she lived nearby. She would have liked to take her to lunch at one of the cafes in South Yarra, but it has become impossible to leave Will in the house alone.

Mill has prepared sandwiches and a salad and they sit under the liquid amber in the backyard. Again she notices how old and frail she looks.

'How has Will settled down – since Christmas? Are you managing?

'Oh yes, it's not really any different. He's pretty good at home, as long as we keep a watch on him. But Betty's not happy about it as you probably know.'

'She will be worried about you after she starts the job at the Nurses Centre. Can you get someone to come in regularly to give you some respite? I could ring one or two of the hospitals; they're sure to know people who do this – retired nurses.'

Mill's face is set and Aimée can see she doesn't want to talk about it. 'Don't worry dear, Betty and I will work it out and Jo is offering to come over when I have to go out somewhere. I want to hear what you've been doing during the holidays and what your plans are.'

She regales her with all her doings and the people she's seen. She's had a wonderful time she tells Mill, and the boys have too, especially Antony. Davy has been out of it a bit as there has been nobody really his age. She tells her about the Lloyds and how she has enjoyed so much staying with them, talking to them, hearing about all the remarkable things they do and the people they help. She says she is so impressed with the way they bring up their children, Jenny and Philip, how they talk to them like adults and leave them to their own devices, and how interesting, self-directed young people they are becoming.

'Are you being tempted to come back and live here?' Mill asks. This is what Aimée really wants to talk about. She's pleased Mill has brought it up because she wasn't sure whether she could or should bring it up.

'I don't know, I feel so confused. Gwenda Lloyd thinks I would be irresponsible not to. She thinks the boys would do so much better here.'

'Why? Surely you are the best judge of that. What do you feel?'

'I can understand that Antony would thrive here, but I'm not sure Davy would. Of course Alan wanted the boys to go to Melbourne Grammar and put them both down for the school when they were born.'

'I don't think you should take too much notice of that, and in any case your boys will do well wherever they go to school.'

'So you don't think we should came back here?'

'I didn't know you were even thinking of doing that – do you want to come back? You yourself?'

'In one way I would love to, but in another I don't see how I could. Except I hardly dare tell you that Janet and Hatty Alexander want us to come and live with them in East Melbourne.'

'Really! Would you like that? Is the house big enough?'

'It probably is though I think eventually the boys would drive them mad. And of course their old mother lives there too. No I don't think it would work. But Janet is terribly keen for it to happen and Hatty is wonderful with the boys.'

'Well my dear you do have some things to think about!'

She smiles briefly and Mill takes her hand across the table.

'Don't worry too much about it Aimée dear. When you get back to Brisbane, it'll become clearer. You'll have time to think about it. You don't have to make a quick decision, in fact you shouldn't. And aren't you starting a new job with a doctor when you get back? That's more important for the time being. If you eventually decide to come back to Melbourne, all the family would love it. We couldn't think of anything nicer. Now it's time for a cup of tea. Would you like to put the kettle on?'

She comes back with the tea things and kisses Mill on the cheek. 'Thank you so much dear Mill, you always calm me down.'

'Have you spoken to Betty or Jo about this?'

'No, I haven't and I don't think I should until I know my own mind better.'

'I think you're quite right.'

The warm summer afternoon drowses on and they chat away about the family, interrupted only when Mill goes in to wake Will up from his afternoon sleep. Mill talks about all her children, including Alan, concern about their future uppermost in her mind.

'You know Will was so proud of Alan. He watched his career closely and felt he had far more talent and personality than he had himself, not that he ever said anything to Alan about it. I used to say why don't you tell him. He'd love to know his father was really proud of him, but he always said, no, a father doesn't need to say that to his son. But I know he regretted it in the end – he couldn't believe it when Alan died and it completely knocked the stuffing out of him – he's never been quite the same since, even before he started to lose his memory.'

'It did to me too,' Aimée says in an undertone. 'I've never got over it.'

Mill purses her lips and nods slowly, patting her hand. Aimée senses her frailty and her consciousness that her time is past, and her sadness that she can no longer influence and support their lives as she always has. With a sudden unbearable cramp in the chest, she realises after this afternoon she may never see her again, her closest link with Alan.

When they finally arrive back in Brisbane after the gruelling return trip, the awful reality of school and boring old Brisbane hits him. He sits on his verandah looking out to the backyard; the smell of rotten persimmons and the mundane sounds of the neighbourhood tell him he's no longer in Melbourne. It's almost dark and the mozzies are buzzing. He smiles to himself that when they got back, there was a letter from Philip waiting for him telling him a car got a puncture from the tacks they put across the road. The tacks remind him of other incredible experiences, such as on the last night when Uncle Ian took them to that great restaurant called the Italian Society, where the waiters wear long white aprons and Uncle Ian tries to talk to them in Italian. The only bad thing was eating those horrible oysters Uncle Ian insisted he eat.

He sighs and allows his mind to wander over all the things they did, all the people they met. He remembers the plan he made with himself on one of the last mornings he was in the Lloyd's living room, playing records. He is going to compose his own symphony in his mind. It is now dark and it is almost silent in the garden. Nicky is happily stretched out on the floor beside him. He thinks he will start with a slow introduction. A sad, mournful melody with a falling cadence at the end of the phrase. Not quite right he thinks, a bit too much like the slow movement of Beethoven's 5th that's been in his mind lately. He sort of whistles softly through his teeth to get the sound of the violins, but it's hard to hard to get the oboe sound he wants. The slow introduction ends with some big portentous chords, and the noise he makes for the chords makes Nicky lift his head enquiringly.

By the time his mother calls him for dinner, he has been lost in this process for at least half an hour, and his mood has entirely changed. As he walks into the kitchen, he feels quite jaunty.

Part Two

The Poinciana Tree

Wings Unfold

In the months after they returned from the Melbourne holiday, she began to feel her burdens lifting. It wasn't that circumstances had changed much or her money worries had stopped – they hadn't. But she knew now she would manage and the boys were becoming less dependent. She had made several important decisions: she had changed her job; she had made a firm decision not to go back to Melbourne; she had put *Breffney* up for sale.

The single thing that made the most difference was working in Dan Hart's rooms. It was like spending days in a normal, real world. She drove to his rooms on Wickham Terrace high up over the city, parked in the yard, sat down at the desk behind the counter, and believe it or not usually spent twenty minutes chatting to Dan about his young family or perhaps about some of the challenging consultations the previous day. It made her feel like a real person, and best of all was driving home knowing that the boys would be home waiting for her and eager to chat, and after dinner was over, she could relax, listen to the wireless, even read a book!

Dan was friendly, enthusiastic, always asking after the boys, and had wide interests, well beyond his vocation as an eye surgeon. As his practice was quite new, not as busy as his elder brother Jim's, he liked to sit down opposite her and speculate about his ideas. She talked to her friend Pat Fraser about how much she enjoyed working with Dan, who after all was Pat's youngest brother. Pat was pleased but not surprised.

'Oh Danny has always been the cleverest in the whole family, and he has such a sweet nature. We all loved him partly because he was the baby, five years younger than Phil, and we all spoilt him. He has grown up to be the most family conscious of all of us, organises all our get-togethers.'

'Pat, I owe so much to you and your family – it's one of the main reasons I've stayed in Brisbane.'

'You never really told me why you decided to stay here.'

Aimée shook her head, 'It's odd isn't it. I love all those people in Melbourne and I have such happy memories of the place. But I really feel now it's a page I have to turn. Here is where I lived with Alan, where the boys have always lived, where I've made such special new friends. Life's not very easy these days, but I do feel we belong here' – she looked up with a smile, 'and Dan has changed my life.'

It wasn't only Dan who had changed her life. She had started to find a life of her own, linked to but separate from the boys. To start with, she came to realise how many friends she had. Alan was always a gregarious man, and they had made many friends. Now she could go out occasionally and see her friends at weekends. She realised people liked her. She could tell the people she met in suburban Brisbane thought her a little exotic, a rather brave widow hailing from Melbourne. She even spoke in that Melbourne accent, and had just driven her boys all the way to Melbourne for Christmas. Perhaps she came from an old Melbourne family? She knew people her Brisbane friends had never heard of – and was regarded as *artistic*! Better not tell anyone how dull and ordinary I am, she thought.

She was taken up with enthusiasm by Marjorie McPherson, whose son Paul was a friend of Davy's at Mr Gordon's school. Marjorie was from Sydney's North Shore, and her husband Robert had been a pioneering aviator, though he now looked rather decrepit. Marjorie saw her as a kindred spirit from the right side of the tracks. She invited her to play tennis on Sundays and to rather smart tea parties. She spoke in a wonderful low thrilling drawl that soared into an almost endless high-pitched trill when something excited her. Antony was fascinated and would just stand and stare listening to the vocalise. Was she acting he wondered? She seemed a nice person, but that voice – he couldn't believe it.

She knew her women friends were intrigued about her friendship with Toby. It was clear it had become the topic of gossip.

Women she knew only slightly asked leading questions and she felt annoyed and exposed. When at one of her tennis parties, Marjorie asked in front of the other women whether she would like to invite Toby to Robert's 60th birthday party, she felt quietly furious. The trouble was that it was simply a good friendship with Toby. He was kind and generous, but it wasn't going anywhere. He had too long been a bachelor and had become set in his way as a man without a serious female relationship. Sadly, she thought, because his combination of minor physical disabilities had probably caused this pattern of life-long avoidance of emotional commitment.

For her birthday in May, Toby asked her to dinner at Lennons, Brisbane's best hotel. He gave her a staggeringly large bouquet of gladioli, but Lennons! He was a connoisseur of fine wines, and the head waiter, done up to the nines in his white tie and tails, was delighted to find a customer who actually seemed to know about the wines on offer.

'Will you have red wine with the main course Aimée, I can recommend the 1947 Coonawarra Claret, the best in the country?'

'Thank you, that would be lovely.'

Indeed the wine tasted lovely and the whole dinner was superb but the combination of red wine, rich food and Toby's noisy enthusiasm felt too much for her. She dreaded the prospective outcome when they arrived home, so it was almost the truth when she complained of a migraine headache and fled into the house.

It was her sister Edna in Perth who phoned first.

'Father has just died – this morning, of a heart attack.'

She had never heard Edna sounding so completely helpless. Edna who was so easy and capable, who knew what to do, as she always had when they were young, shuttling across the continent to Melbourne and back.

'Anna rang me, completely distraught. He had got up and had a bath but was feeling ill and went back to bed. She found him dead when she went in to give him a cup of tea. I've spent the day with her and she wants me to do everything...'

Olive rang later, quite calm as usual but concerned about Edna. She had already talked to Owen and they'd agreed that Olive should go to Perth in time for the funeral. She told Aimée that Bruce was trying to book a flight to Perth for her as soon as possible so she could be with Edna. As phone calls crossed the country over the next few days between the three sisters as well as with Owen's wife Honor, Aimée came to realise none of them seemed to care much about the loss of their father, though Edna who'd seen him quite regularly, was genuinely upset. It was the full realisation of what they had all lost so many years before as children and as a family that dismayed them. It was as if it needed Arthur's death to bring home to them the sadness of what had happened to them.

Mourning for their lost childhood didn't last long. Edna rang from Perth a few days later to tell her they had been told by the family solicitor their father had left nothing to any of them – his whole estate, very substantial, had been left to their stepmother Anna. Both Edna and Olive were furious, and had decided to challenge the will.

'I've talked to the solicitor and told him it's outrageous. Anna's a wealthy woman and you and Owen have nothing. Olive's going to talk to her solicitor when she gets back and make a challenge on the grounds of yours and Owen's needs.'

'That's terrible for Owen and Honor, but really, I am managing. My new job makes it so much better than before.'

'But you've no capital. What happens if you get ill? It's so unfair. I can't believe Father could be so callous and neglect his own family like this. It's certain to be her doing, complaining all the time about how she's going to cope.'

Over the next few weeks the issue of the will was never out of Aimée's mind. The curious thing was that never since their childhood had the four of them talked so much, though all by telephone. In a way it was wonderful. It took a sad turn of events like this to realise how much they still cared about each other. During these weeks she felt a kind of illicit delight in talking regularly to her brother and sisters. She was rueful that their physical separation for so many years, their different lives, had diminished their relationships and for that she was regretful, even a little guilty as she was as much to blame as they were.

Eventually Olive announced the solicitor had advised they had a very good chance of winning their case, indeed such a good chance that it was unlikely to go to court, but could be mediated between the solicitors with the aim of half the estate, except the house, being shared between Owen and Aimée. Aimée found the whole idea distasteful and told Olive and Edna, that if the challenge went ahead, it all should go to Owen as she at least had the beach house *Breffney.* Owen point blank refused this option, and after a long conversation, they both agreed to withdraw from the whole thing. Aimée took a deep breath, rang Edna and told her that she and Owen had agreed they should drop the case. A burden was lifted and she knew Owen felt the same.

She was standing at the kitchen sink after breakfast one morning looking out the window, noticing how big Alan's poinciana tree had become, though it could only be eight or nine years since he planted it. Somehow it made her realise the relationship with Toby was going nowhere and she must start to work out a longer-term future – for herself as much as for the boys. First of all, she must make her mind up about the house at the beach. The sad and sordid business of challenging her father's will only added to the need to resolve the question of selling *Breffney.* Putting off selling *Breffney,* because it was too unbearable to even think about, was no longer an option: it was just something she had to do.

Oddly enough it was Toby's enthusiasm for the commercial prospects of Surfers Paradise and other villages on the coast that started her facing the facts. She even asked him rather forlornly if he wanted to buy *Breffney.* His hearty laugh and guilty smile

revealed his hollow interest but he covered his tracks by suggesting she contact Bruce Small, a real estate agent at Surfers who had
the idea of turning the nearby Nerang River into a series of canals
where every house had a water frontage.

'I think we're going to have to sell *Breffney*, Winifred,' Aimée
said one morning.

'Oh dear, what a shame.'

'But you can't Mum,' said Davy, 'we need it for Christmas
holidays.'

Antony looked horrified: 'Why do you have to sell it?'

'Well it's very expensive to look after and we don't use it much
now with me working full time.'

Davy, who never complained for long, put his head on his
hands and leaned on the table. 'I'll ask the Harrises if I can have
Christmas with them on their boat.'

'Oh Davy, you couldn't be away for Christmas,' objected
Winifred.

'Anyhow we went to Melbourne last year and we can prob-
ably rent a house next Christmas. And Ant you've stayed with the
Cappers at the beach and I'm sure you could ask them any time.
Mrs Capper told me you're always welcome.'

'I don't want to be always staying with the Cappers!' he said
indignantly.

'Why not?'

'I just don't want to.'

'He spilt the beetroot,' said Davy.

Aimée frowned. 'What do you mean?'

'He spilt the beetroot on the white table cloth – he told me.'

'You didn't? When you were there a few weeks ago? What
happened?'

'You're a cow David. It wasn't really my fault anyhow. Old Mrs
Trude is so stingy.'

'What did you *do*?'

He took a deep breath and glared at David. 'Mrs Trude gave
John and me a mingy little salad for lunch, hardly anything. Mr

and Mrs Capper weren't there.'

'Yes, go on.'

'Well I helped myself to some more beetroot … and it dripped across the white tablecloth.'

He was grinning now at the appalled faces of Winifred and his mother. He didn't tell them, because it was too shameful, that Mrs Trude was in the kitchen when he dripped beetroot juice on the tablecloth, and when she came back and saw what happened, she scolded him, saying that helping himself behind her back was deceitful and greedy and unworthy of his mother.

'I think that's terrible behaviour – I'm really surprised you could do that. Mrs Trude must have been furious.'

'John thought it was funny and he got into trouble for laughing.'

'Poor Mrs Trude. The Cappers must have been cross about it too. I hope you apologised.'

He changed the subject and told them about Mr Capper whom he found very unusual.

'You know he lies on the window seat all afternoon listening to the races, drinking whiskies. He asked me to get him one and I put soda from the syphon in it and he spluttered and told me to throw it out the window and said you don't ruin good whisky with soda in this house. I said do you put ginger ale in it then, and he just stared at me as if I was mad, and just said 'water'.'

She decided she must get the Frys up to Surfers before she finally sold the house at the beach. She had long ago told Olive they must come up and the children should get to know each other better before they grew up. Olive said Bruce wouldn't come; he might drive them up but then he would go back to Iluka where he would fish.

They came during the June holidays, Olive, Michael, Susan and Jane. Bruce allowed them a week. It was one of those holidays where they felt like children released from all responsibility. There was never a cloud in the sky – perfect winter sun shone the whole time. Michael was now sixteen; she saw him as a young man of such grace and ease, always with a smile and so helpful with everything, going shopping, fetching wood for the fire, looking after the younger children, being 'the man of the house'. The four younger children played endless games in the sandhills, though Susan, tall and quiet, enjoyed hanging around Olive and Aimée, half listening to their conversations.

As with their time at Shellharbour two or three years earlier, she shook off all her concerns, marvelling at how Olive, quiet and undemonstrative, somehow managed to set her free. Perhaps it was her lovely children; maybe it was the sheer orderliness of her life, her ability to shrug off any worry with a wry comment. Probably, she thought, it's mostly the sea, the beach and the light. Each afternoon they walked miles up or down the beach, with or without the children, and picnicked in the sandhills in front of the house for tea with a makeshift barbecue set up by Michael.

Jane was almost fourteen and becoming very pretty. Antony, nearly a year older, had lost his shyness with his girl cousins, and found himself discovering a new world of delight in Jane's company. They found one or two places in the endless sandhills along the Esplanade where they could play a more private game. The game they devised was about pretending to be lovers: lovers like the real lovers they had spied entwined with each other with blankets, towels, and drinks. It didn't take much watching to work out what to do and they found that embracing and kissing on the lips was really very pleasant. They became quite good at saying passionate things to each other in voices like the actors and actresses in the films they had seen. Deep and thrilling voices, like William Holden whom he admired. Jane liked Lana Turner but he thought she was quite wrong for Jane who was brunette anyhow.

After a couple of days, his irritating younger brother David discovered what was going on. They hadn't seen him following them around, but during the picnic in the sandhills in front of *Breffney* one night, he started making out to everyone that he knew what Antony and Jane were up to. David's sing-song smirk made it pretty clear. Michael found this amusing and started teasing them both. Antony hissed at David, get lost you smart arse, but was relieved that the mothers didn't seem to be too bothered, apart from exchanging looks.

The next day, Friday, was the last day before the Frys had to return home and it became cloudy and rather cold. After breakfast, he whispered to Jane:

'Let's go to our best spot near Narrow Neck this morning because it might rain later, and anyhow we are all going to the Pier Theatre this afternoon.'

'Is that the place behind the little cliff?'

'Yes David won't find us there.'

'It's the spot where we saw that couple isn't it?'

'Mm.'

He was nervous, and Jane seemed to be too. Yesterday they had seen a couple in a cleft between a little cliff and a close-by sandhill. They almost stumbled on them and they seemed to have taken off their clothes. The girl gasped and sat up suddenly and grabbed for her towel and he saw her breasts quiver. And the man turned around and looked really angry and shouted at them to piss off.

They didn't talk until they reached the little cliff and luckily nobody was there. He looked around to make sure nobody like David had followed them. They sat down and kissed, rather primly.

'Will we take our clothes off?' he asked looking down at the sand.

'No.'

'I don't think we should either.'

The ice was broken and they laughed and lay down beside each other. He turned on his elbow and in his deepest film star voice told her she looked more beautiful than ever. But she had a very soft look in her eyes. It didn't seem a game any more.

Finally *Breffney* got sold. She drove the boys down to Surfers one Saturday a few weeks later, dropped them at the beach, and went to see Bruce Small the estate agent. He was very business-like, and when she told him where it was and how it was built, he said she would get at least £5,000. She left his office feeling whacked in the tummy. He hadn't even bothered to go and look at it. She went back to *Breffney* and spent the afternoon cleaning it, and packing up a few bits of cheap crockery she liked. She never went there again.

Two years later she heard from George Capper that a company from Sydney had bought the house for £25,000 and planned to build a multi-storey block of flats on the site.

Aimée and Winifred liked to work in the back garden of the house in Creswick Street on Saturday mornings. Winifred felt she needed to work up a sweat after her sedentary job at Dr Scholes' rooms. Aimée liked her company but found the work in the hot garden and the effort of rounding up the boys to help, fruitless and dispiriting. The garden was hardly an impressive place; the main item of interest was the vegetable bed at the bottom where she grew tomatoes, lettuces and cauliflower. On the fence at the side, a wild choko vine thrived, though its produce was scorned whatever she did to try to make it palatable. Next to the back verandah, there was a large wild orange tree with sooty fruit but the juice was sour and the boys turned up their noses at it. The worst part was a huge old persimmon tree in the middle of the garden that the neighbourhood boys liked to climb. It was full of sickly sweet fruit that fell underneath, got trampled and traipsed through the house. If the house wasn't rented, she would have cut it down in a flash.

The flower beds were a disaster. The boys and their friends practised broad jumps into a makeshift pit, and high jumps over the lowered clothes line. It meant that the flower beds were wrecked and the clothes line was always lying broken on the grass.

After sharing the mowing, they were both exhausted and sat

down on the concrete slab in the laundry with cups of tea.

Winifred said: 'Did I tell you I ran into an old friend, Claire Connor from Ballarat in the city last week?'

'No I don't think so.'

'She's a wonderful girl, a bit older than me and an excellent musician. I hardly recognised her when I saw her; she has long red finger nails and smokes from a long cigarette holder and was wearing slacks, and she seems to talk in an American accent. She told me she was driving trucks for the Americans during the war.'

'Goodness me! Were you at school with her?'

Winifred paused: 'Oh no, she's a Roman Catholic and used to play the organ for St Patricks Cathedral in Ballarat. We both played the organ and that's how I got to know her. She always wore the latest clothes and was rather a star.'

'She sounds an unusual friend for the Church of England Dean's daughter.'

Winifred said earnestly: 'No it wasn't like that in Ballarat. Most Anglicans mixed happily with the Catholics.'

Winifred gathered up the tea things and took them upstairs to the kitchen to find Antony grazing at the fridge. 'Why don't you come down and help in the garden? You're big and strong now and should be doing the mowing for your mother'

'I'm doing something.'

'What are you doing? Nothing important. Come on.'

Pause and big sigh: 'Oh, alright.'

Over sandwiches at lunch the mood lifted. Aimée was pleased Antony had cut all the edges; he felt virtuous and Davy had happily gone off for the afternoon to the Harrises. Winifred suggested Claire be invited for dinner and they agreed a date.

The round cedar table in the dining room was set for dinner for five. Davy wandered in and frowned at the setting and called out to his mother in the kitchen: 'What's happening in here – is someone coming?'

She was at the kitchen sink washing up. 'Yes a lady called Claire Connor is coming to dinner. She's an old friend of Winifred's.'

'Claire Connor, what a funny name.'

'Well, it's her name and I want you on your best behaviour tonight. Now go and have a bath and put on that nice blue shirt and your new shorts. And your sandals.'

She was still cleaning up in the kitchen when the sound of loud laughter and shoes clumping up the kitchen stairs made her freeze in alarm clutching a tea towel. She looked at the clock over the stove. It wasn't yet five and they weren't supposed to be here till six!

They tumbled into the kitchen, giggling. Winifred was right: the longest red fingernails Aimée had ever seen, a cigarette in a long holder and a profusion of red hair piled up.

'I'm terribly sorry for landing on you like this. I think we're early. We took a taxi to be on the safe side as I didn't want to trust myself on a tram, and he got us here in no time. Anyhow it's all Winifred's fault. She's a really bad influence and such an old soak. I hadn't been to the Cecil before. It's a nice hotel and she kept plying me with drinks!'

Winifred turned scarlet at the absurd allegations. 'Oh Claire, you're outrageous. Aimée I'm so sorry, I'm not used to drinks in the afternoon.' More giggles. 'Anyhow this is Claire!' With this, Claire gave a huge bouquet of yellow roses to Aimée who scooped them up with a big smile and thanks.

The boys sidled into the kitchen at the commotion, Davy wrapped in a towel.

'You must be David', said Claire, 'I've heard a lot about you. I'm glad you're washed and clean – I hate grubby boys.'

Davy offered a sickly smile. Antony smirked at his discomfort. She turned to him: 'So you're Antony, the one that writes essays and goes to concerts with Winifred. Are they terribly boring?'

He realised he was being teased: 'No of course not. We went to the Boston Symphony Orchestra a couple of weeks ago and heard the Eroica symphony.'

'Did you? I was there too. Weren't they marvellous. You know they're the best orchestra in the US now.' He stared at her with renewed interest and was interrupted by his mother telling him to take Claire and Winifred into the sitting room and to get them a drink while she got into a proper dress.

At dinner Davy sat opposite Claire and played a game with her dodging looks around the large vase of yellow roses in the middle of the table. Claire regaled them all with stories of Winifred's and her own youth in Ballarat, alternating with tales of her time as a truck driver with the American forces. Her stories as an American army driver fascinated them all so much that Aimée made a sign to Antony not to leave his mouth open. 'Claire got to know General MacArthur, you know,' said Winifred proudly.

Claire looked past the roses at Davy and asked him, 'Do you know who he is?'

'No.'

'Well, he's a famous American general who was in charge of all the American and Australian forces in the Pacific during the war. For nearly two years he ran all these army forces from the AMP building in Queen Street. I first met him when one of his staff officers rang the garage in Wilston where I was based. I was the only driver in the garage and I was ordered to go to Lennons where he lived and pick up his cigarette holder as he needed it for a reception he was going to.'

'A cigarette holder like yours?' Antony asked.

'No not like mine at all. I had to meet the house-keeper and go to his room, and in his wardrobe in this beautiful leather case, all embossed with Chinese dragons, was this black ivory holder covered in precious stones, that looked mostly like emeralds.'

She looked conspiratorially at the boys. 'What do you think I did?'

'Steal it?' Davy suggested.

'Put a cigarette in it and have a smoke?' Antony was sure.

'Both wrong. I was so amazed staring at it, I dropped it! But the floor was carpeted so I wasn't shot.' She grinned and they all laughed. 'I took it back in the car to the AMP and reported I had the General's cigarette case, so I was ushered straight through to his office and gave it to him. He took a minute to look up from what he was writing, then he leaned back and asked me point blank, what's your name corporal? I told him and he said with a frown, have you looked inside? I was terrified and thought maybe I will be shot so I told the truth and said it was very beautiful and he said it was a gift from the wife of the President of the Philippines for all his services to the nation. Then he took me around his office, opened up a big glass cabinet and showed me all his medals and treasures. After that he often asked for me to drive him and he always called me Corporal Redhead.

'Wow,' said Antony.

The dinner with Claire was a great success and the boys fell quickly under her spell, especially Antony, who thought he'd never met anyone like her in his life. Aimée was delighted with her too, loved the way she simultaneously teased and involved the boys, her affection for Winifred, her colourful stories and despite all the trappings, she was serious about the world and the people she knew. She asked her to come to see them again, and she did, becoming like a favourite aunt in the family.

At Churchie, Antony was known as Tony. His best friends were Ken Wyatt and Garth Welch; the three of them sat in the back row of the class where they could avoid the gaze of the teachers most of the time. Ken was a clever skinny boy whom Tony liked a lot and they became bosom pals. Garth was rather precious and through his mother's insistence, had become a very competent ballet dancer, even at the age of fifteen. Later he went on to become Australia's leading male dancer.

Tony hated Maths, mostly because he couldn't understand it, but strangely enough he was one of the the Maths master's favourites, along with Donald Orr, a tall prissy boy with a cherubic face. The master was called Kajewski, Kaj for short, and was feared for his sarcastic scorn of laggards and his application of his short whippy cane. He was a tall man with a huge paunch and a sweaty unhealthy-looking face, and he wore a constant sinister smile as if he were about to pounce on some poor unsuspecting boy.

He would write a simple equation on the board and come across to Tony, put his hand on his shoulder, and ask sweetly: 'And what's the answer to that Tone?'

Every time Tony would freeze with a mix of horror and incomprehension as he had no idea of the answer.

'Tone, I'm disappointed with you. I'm sure you can answer that simple question Donal'?' And of course Donal' could always answer the question.

Tony felt for Garth because he was always being asked to dance for a school concert or play, and was on the receiving end of mocking remarks about being a dancer. Kaj was worst and used to imitate him by swirling down the aisle in the maths classroom waving his arms, and even suggesting he should wear a cricketer's box to hide the bulge in his tights. Nevertheless Garth didn't seem to mind the mockery, and the two of them enjoyed whispered subversive conversations in the back row of the classroom.

They gossiped incessantly about the eccentricities of the masters, and the way many of the boys went out of their way to irritate, bait or even ignore instructions. The general view was masters were fair game, and any weakness displayed should be ruthlessly exploited. The new Junior English master Mr Bates, a pale young man with a flop of light brown hair falling over his forehead was utterly lost. In his classroom, a group of boys behaved as if it was lunch time in the playground. He was reduced to leaning on his table with his hands gripping the edge, rocking backwards and forwards pleading: 'Gentlemen, please... please...'

By contrast, the boys in the Latin class didn't dare speak a word out of turn to the Latin master, 'Stiffy' Wade, a thin faced man with a Hitler moustache, a soft, clipped, cultured voice and a serious introverted manner. Tony wondered why he had such complete control of his classes; was it because he never smiled? Ken thought that the eccentric, even deranged behaviour of some masters might be a result of their terrible war time experiences.

On the other hand, Bobby Lanskey hadn't been at the war as he was too old. The very idea of Bobby in uniform made you laugh. He was the head Science master, had a knobbly nose, a red face, and like Kajewski, a large paunch. Everyone knew he had spent his whole career at the school, had been passed over as headmaster, and was now an alcoholic whose antics all the boys loved. There was a fund of stories about Bobby – he had become a legend at the school, even beyond the school. He was the compere at the annual GPS Athletics Carnival, where his rich, gravelly voice playfully poked fun at every GPS pretension, eliciting huge waves of cheers from the crowd for any school mocked by Bobby.

He had mixed feelings about Bobby. With another boy, he had chosen to study French instead of Chemistry. This meant twice a week he had to request permission from Bobby to leave his lab after the Physics class to go to French. Every time Bobby found a new way to embarrass the departing pair, ranging from mock-innocent enquiries about 'What is French?' to elaborate bows to the two boys, or threatening waves of his waddy. One day, as the class sat in the lab waiting for Bobby to arrive, the class captain Kerry Larkin passed the message around that Bobby was drunk, and that everyone should sway in unison. Bobby staggered in looking much the worse for wear and muttered something to the class. The rows of boys started to sway at the sign from Kerry. Bobby looked up, eyes bulging: 'Stop swaying… I know you're swaying.'

This charade was repeated several times during the class that afternoon, with Bobby's response becoming more terse.

'If you twerps don't stop swaying, I'll be up there with my waddy for the lot of you!'

Cheers from the class. Then he seemed to lose heart and took up his long boat hook and went around the lab leaning over the science tables closing the high windows with the boat hook, muttering alright then, you horrible creatures can all go home early. It was ten minutes early so the class cheered again. As he leaned upwards to close the last window, his trousers slipped off the edge of his paunch and fell around his ankles, revealing baggy pale green underpants. More delighted shrieks from the class. He shuffled behind one of the science benches, pulled up his trousers, looked up at the rows of laughing boys and growled: 'All is well.'

While he never felt the need to challenge the masters or behave badly, Tony found it hard to take the school seriously. School was a place you went to five days a week and passed your time in class rooms. It didn't occur to him that in a few short years, he would have to spend five days a week doing much the same but have to actually think and work.

Still there were some parts of it that he looked forward to. He liked French as Miss Baker the French teacher was obviously an expert and when he went wrong she told him exactly what the problem was and how to do it properly, including pronouncing the words. But in his opinion, few of the masters had much idea of what they were talking about. He much preferred sitting around with his friends or finding a good book and reading it in the library.

His true best friend disappeared during his Junior year to live in Melbourne with his family. His name was John Edwards, 'Bagga' to his school friends. The origin of Bagga was obscure though some boys said it meant 'bag of bones.' Certainly John was quite short and slightly built, and he did have a rather galumphing walk. Maybe they thought he was dragging a bag of bones?

He was thirteen when he first met John, in his last year of primary school, his first at Churchie. Despite his small stature, John was nearly two years older and somewhat literary and eccentric. He wrote extensively – all sorts of high flown or absurd pieces – left-handed and with the paper turned almost square on, with a flowery script. His talk was similarly elaborate as if he was an extremely youthful academic expert, though the expertise was often deliberately nonsensical. A year or two after he and his family moved to Melbourne, he wrote Tony long and complex letters of his doings in Melbourne and sent photos of the musical ensemble he had established with equally eccentric new friends. They played Percy Grainger pieces with lawnmowers, vacuum cleaners and various blowing implements. Clearly they had been inspired by Gerard Hoffnung, then the rage amongst clever people.

John was resourceful and went to some lengths to achieve what he wanted. One morning at school he spoke about his friend Merv on the Wynnum bus.

'Who's Merv?' Tony asked.

'The Wynnum bus driver.' As if this was a ridiculous question.

'You don't live in Wynnum. What are you catching a Wynnum bus for?'

'To get to school you idiot. Don't you know about the Wynnum buses?'

Tony was stumped by this. So with a sigh, John explained. 'The Wynnum buses are a private bus company and bring people into the Valley and the city in the mornings for their work, but they return to Wynnum empty because no one wants to go to Wynnum at 8 o'clock in the morning.'

'Some people must want to go to Wynnum in the morning.' Tony said logically.

John struck his forehead and shook his head despairingly. 'They are NOT ALLOWED to pick people up on the return journey.'

'Why?'

'I don't know why but the law prevents them,' John said impatiently.

'I still don't know why you need to have anything to do with a Wynnum bus? You live in Sandgate which is almost the other side of Brisbane.'

'Because the Wynnum buses return to Wynnum through the Valley and past East Brisbane where our school just happens to be, you nincompoop.'

'But you're not allowed to get on them.'

He leant forward with a mysterious look: 'Ah! But I can get on them, through my good friend Merv the driver. We roar across the Storey Bridge bouncing away with me the lone passenger nearly hitting my head on the roof. And he lets me on for nothing and I can save the fare. Pretty smart eh?'

'Can I get on too?'

'Maybe. Meet me outside McWhirters at exactly five past eight tomorrow and I'll ask Merv.'

So it happened that he joined John on the Wynnum bus courtesy of Merv and they regularly bounced like footballs in the empty Wynnum bus across the Storey Bridge each morning. But all good things come to an end and this end was not a good one. One wet morning they bounced and slid across the Storey Bridge and as they came to the other side of the bridge, an almighty blast on a passing truck's horn made Merv come to a slithering stop with the truck cutting across the front of the bus and stopping. A big angry looking man got out of the truck, ran up the bus stairs, grabbed Merv by the scruff of his shirt and gave him a huge punch on the jaw. Merv slumped down with a gurgle, and without a word, the man got out of the bus, back into his truck and drove off. The two boys ran down to the driver's seat and found Merv out for the count. Within a minute, cars were stopping and tooting and people rushed on to the bus to abuse the driver only to find him apparently sleeping. The boys breathlessly told what had happened, but when someone asked them why they were on the bus, they looked at each other and decided it was time for a quick exit and to walk the rest of the way to school, thus arriving both sodden and late.

The next morning, they lined up outside McWhirters hesitantly to wait for the returning Wynnum bus. It arrived on the dot but had another driver, a grim looking older man. Worse, the bus didn't stop, but just drove straight past. They had no choice but wait for a Council bus and pay a fare. It would take much longer and they'd probably be late for school. Worst of all there'd be no

Merv skittering furiously over the Storey Bridge.

Aimée was glad Claire had made an appointment to see Dan Hart. When Claire rang her at Dan's rooms, she had explained an old eye problem with the left eye, but she didn't want to go to Dr Scholes, the eye doctor Winifred worked for. 'He's a pompous old fogey and I hate the way he treats Winifred like she's a young girl. So I thought you could have a word for me with Dan Hart and it's an excuse for us to have lunch.'

'Of course I can make an appointment. I'll tell him you knew General MacArthur; he'll love to know all about that!'

She didn't want Claire paying to take her to lunch so on the day of the appointment with Dan, she made a picnic lunch and proposed they eat across the road in Wickham Park under the Moreton Bay figs. Brisbane in November is hot and steamy and the day usually finishes with a storm. Shady Wickham Park looking south east down over the city will get any whisper of a breeze.

'Your man Dan is terrific. We had a great chat; he knows so much about Brisbane's history.'

'Yes he's like an encyclopedia. How is the eye?'

'Oh, you know – not too bad. I'm shortsighted in one eye and always having problems with the other. But he's a relief after Dr Scholes.'

'It's a relief to me too after spending years sewing and smocking like a slave.'

'I loved meeting you and your kids last month. I'm incredibly impressed with how you manage to do everything with a full-time job. If you want me to do anything I'd like to help. I've got a car and can always take you or them places to give you a bit of a break, and I don't have much to do in weekends.'

'What a lovely thought, but you don't need to worry about the boys.'

'The boys will be a hoot for me. I'm having a party next

Saturday so why don't you come and drag Winifred along too. It'll be a change – I'm having Clive and Kath Barron – he's a doctor who lives near the coast at Tweed Heads. Also old friends from army days.'

'I'd love that.' Though she wasn't sure she would.

The picnic table under the figs was disgusting, covered in bits of broken fruit and cigarette butts all around. They wondered why they had even sat down and laughed at the bad choice. She saw there was an easiness about Claire, a practical knowledge about how things work that none of her female friends seemed to have. She was so open and light-hearted, though somehow also serious. She found herself telling her about Toby and even how she met Alan.

Tony and his mates usually ate their lunches on the shady grass under the trees that ran down to the Flat, the playing field nearest to the school classrooms. They were a pretty seedy lot. In fact 'seedy' was an epithet often used by the more sporty masters to describe one or other of this loose little group of boys whose common characteristic was sporting incompetence. One of this group, Hugh Gore, a country boy from Goondiwindi, was probably the worst tennis player at the school along with Tony. The tennis coach Jack Pyle always had them playing each other as they were no competition for anyone else.

'You know the Pocket is on next Tuesday,' announced Ken.

Garth shuddered. 'I did it last year – it was horrible. I couldn't bear to do it again.'

'You have to,' said Hugh, 'it's compulsory.' He added with relish, 'You know the sewers from all the eastern suburbs empty into it.'

'That's bunkum!' Ken said. He was one of the few people in Bobby Lanskey's science classes who was getting ahead.

'No it's true,' insisted Hugh, 'I heard it from the matron in

Goodwin House, and anyhow I've seen the shit floating by when I did the Pocket last year.'

'I'm going to be sick,' said Garth.

One of Churchie's proud traditions to toughen up the boys was the annual Pocket swim where it was compulsory to swim around a mile-long 'pocket' in Norman Creek, a slow-moving piece of aquatic sludge winding itself around the school's grounds.

'What are you going to do this year Tony? What's your story this time?'

He had never swum the Pocket and had sworn to himself he never would. He thought he would drown if he tried to. But he was worried he had no story worked out for next week.

Suddenly John Edwards appeared from nowhere clutching a red cardboard folder and crouched beside him, looked around at them all and announced cryptically: 'I've been in touch with the bus company and told them the real story about Merv.'

Puzzled glances between them all. 'You mean the Wynnum bus driver who was king hit when you and Tony were coming to school?' Ken asked.

'Yes,' said John, 'you can't have bus companies sacking drivers because some mad truck driver knocks him out.'

'But what can you do?'

'I've written the manager a letter telling him what happened and saying Tony and I want a meeting with him. I also said Merv should be reinstated. I've got a copy of the letter – do you want to see it?'

Hugh said sarcastically: 'Bagga, he'll be quavering in his boots at the idea of you and Tony going to meet him.'

'You can laugh, but as a member of the public, you have to stand up for people who have been treated badly, and Merv was treated badly, wasn't he Tony?'

'Yes,' he replied distractedly. He was far more concerned about the Pocket than about going to meetings with a bus company.

Ken always seemed a bit more practical than the others and said: 'Alright Bagga, let us know what happens when you've been to see him, if you get to see him.'

'You know, it might be best to get a petition up for Merv,' said John, scratching his head, 'I'll see you blokes later,'

The Christmas holidays intervened soon after, and Tony heard nothing more from John about meeting with the Wynnum bus company. At the end of the year John Edwards and his family moved to Melbourne, and with his departure, a slice of colour was lost to Tony and his school friends.

Aimée knew how disappointed the boys were with the sale of *Breffney* and felt she had to compensate by arranging a holiday at the beach over the Christmas holidays. She booked three weeks for them at a large old-fashioned guest house called *Chelmsford* on a rise overlooking the Broadwater near Nerang Street, the main street of Southport. Her new friend Claire rolled her eyes at the idea of *Chelmsford*.

'Darl, you'll be bored stiff there. It's full of retired couples and old ladies and they'll feed you nothing but boiled cabbage. You'll have to take the boys out of there every day or they'll pull the old place apart. I'll come down for a while and take you to see some friends.'

Claire was right: it was like a home for old people, and the food was like hospital food. One morning at breakfast, Clemmie, one of the old waitresses, tottered up and said there was a telephone call for her. It was Claire and she was driving down that morning – to rescue them. As usual, she had mixed feelings of alarm and excitement at the thought of Claire's rescue mission.

The party in Brisbane had been quite unlike any party she'd ever been to. Winifred warned her by telling her she wouldn't enjoy it, and finding an excuse for herself. Despite her misgivings, she went to the party. Claire had a flat in an old weatherboard house high up on stumps in Red Hill, overlooking the city. She had hung red Chinese lanterns and swathes of intricately patterned Indian cotton material everywhere. The garish red-pink glow made it look like what she imagined a brothel would look like and the low lighting made it almost impossible to see who anyone was. She was introduced to everyone by Claire as if she was the guest of honour and after a while realised she was certainly unlike anyone else there. She was shocked to see two youngish women sitting on a sofa kissing, though perhaps the one with short hair was a man; she couldn't be sure. She found herself talking to a very entertaining little man called Ron who apparently was Claire's colleague at Penneys. He told her stories mimicking the customers with a high voice, extravagant gestures and peals of laughter. He went on to heap praise on Claire saying she a natural in retail and was being made head of the kitchen and household goods department.

Waiting for Claire in the lounge at *Chelmsford*, she smiled to herself at recollections of the party, and all the odd people she met. It seemed most were old army friends. One or two came with a wife or husband, but most seemed to be single like Claire, and she wondered if there was anyone special in her life, or whether she and her friends were rather lonely, like she often felt.

Her reverie was broken by Davy racing in to say Claire had arrived! 'Arrived' was the word. She stepped out of the bright blue open-topped Plymouth convertible she had parked at the foot of the stairs of the guest house and greeted the boys looking like a film star.

'Hi ya boys.' She was wearing yellow slacks, a geometrically pattered shirt and her hair was tied up in yellow scarf. Even more special was a tall sun-tanned man beside her in a casual white shirt and khaki trousers.

'Bill, these are my good friends Antony and David Jeffrey. Ant and Davy, this is Bill Cleveland.'

The boys shook his extended hand. 'Good morning boys.'

Antony was very interested in the Plymouth and asked Claire if he could sit in it. 'Ask Bill. It's his, I just drive it,' turning to Bill with a laugh.

After introductions in the lounge, Bill offered to take everyone to lunch at the Surfers Paradise Hotel. Aimée demurred but was shouted down by the boys, and Claire clinched the argument, saying after lunch we'll all go to the new wildlife sanctuary at Currumbin.

The hotel dining room was stylish, decorated with lots of chrome in the latest art deco mode. As the Southport hotels were all pre-war and mouldy, Claire said it was the only place to go on the coast. Davy agreed enthusiastically, and reminded them the Surfers Paradise Hotel had its own zoo.

She felt foolish having thought Claire might be lonely. She even felt a touch of envy. She knows what she wants and clearly she gets it. Bill is a very handsome man and talked to the boys at their level. He was charming to Claire but not too familiar, and she thought how lucky she is. That evening the boys were full of the day's experience: the smart hotel, what they chose to eat for lunch, the Plymouth, and especially the new wild life sanctuary called Fleay's Fauna. Bill Cleveland impressed them with his easy manner of knowing what to do and being able to answer their questions. His presence seemed to make Claire even more glamorous.

Having stayed the night in the Surfers Paradise Hotel, Claire and Bill took her and the boys the next day to lunch at the Tweed Heads home of Clive and Kath Barron whom she had met at Claire's party. The Barrons lived in a modern house with windows all around high up over the estuary of the Tweed with wonderful views up and down the coast. Clive, a genial sun-tanned doctor and Kath, in a voluminous floral sari, welcomed them all while Clive mixed cocktails. Claire was clearly a close friend of the Barrons and there was much hilarity over the less visible doings at her party. Aimée felt rather out of her depth amongst these smart people. At the casual lunch Kath served out on the terrace, Clive apologised that he had to do his hospital rounds after lunch and diplomatically suggested Bill take the boys down to Point Danger to see the wreck and have a swim at Fingal beach.

When the men and boys had left, Kath served coffee and went straight to the point:

'So at last we meet the famous Bill!'

'It was such a pity he couldn't get here for the party. You know the whole idea was to introduce him to my friends.' She turned to Aimée and explained he lived in Sydney. 'He's got this great job where he's in charge of Shell's oil operations in the Pacific and needs to spend most of his time in the islands.'

'Doesn't sound that great to me,' said Kath.

Claire sounded a bit defensive, 'He loves it as he gets to move around all the time, and this was his stamping ground during the war. It's how I met him. He was a Major in the Transport Corps during the war and based in Port Moresby most of the time, but he spent half his time in Brisbane liaising with MacArthur's people.'

'Does he get to Brisbane very often?' asked Aimée.

'Now that he's in charge of the whole west Pacific area, it means he'll be here much more of his time.' She stubbed out her cigarette and looked up with a slightly nervous smile. 'He's hoping he can re-locate full time to Brisbane as his headquarters. I've been telling him he has to – Sydney's so far away from his territory.'

'Ah Claire, that's the way, keep the pressure up. Why don't you both stay with us for a couple of days and we'll work on him.'

'I wish we could but he's got to go back to Sydney tomorrow, but thanks!'

'Is he driving back in that flash car?'

'Yes he's leaving at 6 am and reckons he'll be there for dinner!'

Aimée asked about the Barrons' lives in Tweed Heads. They had a daughter boarding at All Hallows school in Brisbane, but their passion was golf. It turned out Kath was the womens' champion at Tweed Heads Golf Club, known to be the best championship course between Brisbane and Sydney.

The two days with Claire and Bill were a terrific tonic for the boys as they found creeping around *Chelmsford* among pale old people on sticks not at all to their liking. If affected Aimée too, though she knew the lifestyle of the Barrons or Bill and Claire was not for her. It made her think she should make more of her life. The boys were now in their teens and in a few years she might be on her own. She decided to make an effort to connect with friends who were holidaying on the coast and the last week at *Chelmsford* was full of diversion. The boys walked or caught the bus most days to see the Capper boys. The Frasers had taken a house at Narrow Neck and she spent several days with Pat, regretting that Antony and David Fraser seemed to have lost their friendship. There was a big New Year's Eve party with fireworks on the beach at the Hogkinsons further down the coast that they all loved.

Back home she told Winifred how much they had all enjoyed the holiday despite the stuffiness of *Chelmsford*. She told her all about their time with Claire, Bill and the Barrons.

'He's such a nice man and was so natural with the boys. It seems he may be transferring to Brisbane soon.'

Winifred looked worried. 'Did she mention to you that he's married?'

'Married? Surely not?'

'Yes he's married with two children. I had hoped it was all over between them as he hasn't been here for some time. Oh dear.'

Aimée was devastated. She hardly knew what to say. 'I can't believe he's married. That's so sad ... surely she will have to give him up ...?'

'She will have to because she's a believing Roman Catholic, so there's no chance of a divorce and marrying him.'

'Does he live with his wife?'

'As far as I know he does, and I don't think she knows about Claire.'

'Oh, that's an impossible situation.'

She was deeply upset with this revelation. In bed she couldn't sleep tossing around in her mind all the ramifications. At one level she felt desperately sorry for Claire, at another, her innate sense of propriety was appalled that Claire could be so foolish. In her bewilderment, it confirmed her lifelong suspicion and dislike for the Catholic church. Why shouldn't she marry if she was in love with him and he with her? But how could he be deceiving his wife having an affair with Claire in a different city? It was cruel and horribly selfish. She found herself wondering about the wife. Did she know and tolerate it for the children's sake? Did she want a divorce? She liked Claire so much: she was a real breath of fresh air in their lives. She didn't know what to think.

He was finding that life was becoming very different in the Sub Senior year, his second last at school. Many kids had left after Junior and the classes were now much smaller. Everything seemed more important. The homework was more demanding; he realised he was expected to *think*, and work out problems. He also became aware that he actually had opinions, and they often differed from his peers, and even sometimes from the masters. One of the set books they had to read and study was *Wuthering Heights*. It was a revelation: the wild setting, Heathcliff's brutality and the passion of the love affair utterly entranced him. For a week or two he walked around in a dream of the Yorkshire moors. In the English class one morning, the master told them not to bother about *Wuthering Heights*, it was a boring book, not suitable for boys of their age. Much better to study *The Citadel*, or the *Story of San Michele*. Tony stared at him in outrage; he was speechless. How could an English teacher not understand the magnificence of *Wuthering Heights*?

A pattern of keeping his passions and dreams to himself was developing. He didn't dare discuss his love of music with any of his friends, feeling he would be derided.

He often rummaged in the bookshelves at home, looking at and sometimes reading the books his parents had bought years before. When he found *The Fountain*, by a writer called Charles Morgan, he found himself caught up in a fascinating but totally foreign world. It was set during World War I about a British officer who had been interned with a family in rural Holland. He had decided to use his enforced idleness to live a virtual monastic or contemplative life for the period of the war but then fell in love with the family's daughter. The conflict of moralities and profound issues of life and love, jolted him out of childish attitudes, This time he felt the story and the issues it raised were more real to the here and now, and had relevance to his own life, wherever that might take him. He sensed for the first time he was becoming an adult, though with no idea of what he might do after leaving school.

In musical terms, he had become absorbed in the music of Brahms – fallen in love with his music would not be an exaggeration. Two years earlier he had been introduced to his Violin Concerto, played by Yehudi Menuhin with the orchestra conducted by the great German conductor Wilhelm Furtwängler. He had saved his pocket money to buy a recording of the 2nd Symphony and was transported by memory of the great soaring melody from the first movement. He had heard all the symphonies by now and felt he was becoming an expert on them. Also he loved the quiet intro-spective intermezzi for piano Brahms wrote at the end of his life. He wondered what it was about these pieces by an old man that spoke so much to him.

When he got home, he was surprised to find Claire there help-ing David with his homework. David used his arrival as an excuse to disappear, leaving his homework on the kitchen table.

'Well how are you Ant? How's school?'

'Oh alright.' He felt distracted. He needed to air his thoughts about Brahms. 'Claire, do you know those intermezzi opus 117 that Brahms wrote?'

'Yes I used to play one of them as a student. Why? Do you know them?'

'The Lloyds had a recording I used to listen to in Melbourne, and I've heard them a couple of times since, on the wireless. I was just thinking about them on the way home and it seems sort of funny why I like them so much. Usually I like orchestral music most. Do you think it's because he was old when he wrote them and he thought he was dying?'

'Maybe. He was a very romantic composer you know despite the fact he never married. When he was old he looked back on his life with sadness and regret. He had admired Robert Schumann and people think he was in love with Schumann's wife Clara. Many of those piano pieces were inspired or written for her. She was a fabulous pianist.'

'Yes I hadn't thought of that. I think Brahms piano music is much deeper than Chopin's. I think Chopin's music sounds as if he's always playing for a room full of fashionable people in frilly clothes.'

'That's rather hard on Chopin. His piano music is wonderful!'

He liked talking about music and concerts with Claire. It wasn't just that she knew so much, but unlike anyone else he felt relaxed talking about it to her. Nobody else seemed to understand what he was on about, even Winifred. Claire thought he should learn the piano and even offered to teach him, though she admitted it would be difficult without a piano at home. He didn't feel an urgent desire to learn the piano. Playing the music himself didn't feel important. What was important was getting to hear more and more, to absorb it into his mind and body: more of what these great composers had to say about their life experiences through their music.

After dinner, Claire, Winifred and Aimée sat out on the verandah to have a cup of tea and smoke a cigarette. Since Winifred had told her about Bill being married, she had never brought the subject up. It even had affected her friendship with Claire. It wasn't now as warm or intimate. She wondered if Claire knew that she knew: she thought she probably did. It was Claire who brought up the subject of eligible men.

'Winifred, have you told Aimée yet about your new friend?'

'Oh Claire, he's not a friend.'

'Well if he's not a friend, what is he?'

'He's, well, he's a very nice man who's taken me to a concert.'

Claire explained: 'He's a *very* nice man and he clearly likes Winifred. I met him last week and he's manager of a big property outside Roma.'

'How exciting! What's his name?'

'Brian Cox.' Winifred looked pleased but embarrassed. 'I didn't feel I should bother you about Brian just yet.' Winifred was now in her late thirties and not experienced with men.

'That's wonderful Winifred, where did you meet him?'

'He's a friend of Scotty Walker's who introduced us when I ran into them at Rowe's cafe. Then he rang me up a few weeks ago and asked if I'd like to come to a concert at the City Hall.'

'You are a dark horse Winifred! Are you going to bring him here and introduce us?'

Later that same evening, the phone rang and it was Brian Cox asking for Winifred. Aimée and Claire promptly took to the kitchen. She asked Claire what he was like.

'I only met him for a minute. He's not at all smart but you can tell right away he's a strong character, and I think would be good for her. I think she's smitten, even hinted he'd spoken of marriage. She would love to be married and have a baby.'

'I do hope he's suitable for her. In some ways she's quite innocent about men.'

'You don't think Bill Cleveland is suitable for me do you?'

'Oh Claire. What can I say? He seems such a lovely man, but…'

'I know it's a rotten situation, but his marriage is over for all intents and purposes. He only stays for the sake of the children.'

'How old are the children?'

'Early teens.'

She looked out the window at the poinciana tree and shook her head. She looked back at Claire and saw her mouth set and tears in her eyes. She walked across and embraced her.

'If he does separate, I would go and live with him. Whether Sydney or Brisbane.'

Aimée had tears in her eyes now and said gently, 'It wouldn't be much of a life.'

Claire responded bitterly: 'Thanks very much. That's pretty obvious.'

A few days later, Winifred brought Brian to meet Aimée. She immediately liked him. He was a typical 'bushie', ruddy-faced, sandy-haired and with a hesitant slightly awkward manner she put down to shyness. He looked perfect for Winifred and they were obviously delighted with each other. She was surprised at Winifred's determination. At her age, she said there was no need for an engagement, and she wanted to set the wedding date right away and be married by September. It was all so uncomplicated; such a contrast with Claire's awful situation.

How could she help Claire? Since the fraught conversation in the kitchen, she felt more confused than ever. Claire was obviously hurt at her unsympathetic attitude, but she wasn't unsympathetic – quite the reverse. But she couldn't see how the dilemma could be happily resolved and she didn't think for a moment Bill would leave his family. Even if he did, Claire would have a terrible time sharing the children. She resolved to support Claire through this whole thing, however it turned out. At least she had to make that clear to her.

On the bus that took many of the boys to the city from school, he began to notice a small group of younger boys who always sat in the same place with lots of noisy ribaldry and laughter. The ringleader was a plump boy with a mass of bright red hair everyone called Jeremiah. His best friend was a boy called Ned who had black straight hair and a freckly olive complexion. Ned seemed to drift along in a lazy graceful way but had a beautiful smile that set him apart. During the school term he realised he had a strange fascination for Ned, maybe it could be called an obsession. He thought he was beautiful, but he was puzzled why. He wasn't athletic or strong, in fact he was quite an ordinary kid. As the year came to a close, he wondered if what he felt about Ned was some sort of love. But if it was love, it was strange because he didn't want to kiss him or embrace him like he did with his cousin Jane. When he saw Ned, observed him smile or tease his friends, it made his spine tingle and feel happy and sometimes even exalted.

In the January after Christmas that year, his mother was lent a little beach house near Broadbeach further down the coast from Surfers. The cyclones came early that year and much of the time it was wet and the surf was huge and pounded the beach. Even the sandhills were being washed away. After all the fun they'd had during the Chelmsford holiday the previous year, and in Melbourne the year before that, this holiday was miserable. None of his friends was around, it was always wet and there was nothing much to do. On the last day before they had to return to Brisbane for his final school year, he and David caught the bus to the Pier Theatre to see an Abbott and Costello film. At the Pier, he suddenly saw Ned in shorts and tee shirt stroll past in his usual languid way. His heart leapt and he turned and stared as he disappeared along the street.

'Who was that?' asked David.

'Oh nobody – just a kid from school.'

When he and his brother got home from the Pier, and despite a constant rainy drizzle, he set out on a long walk five miles up the beach to the end of the Spit, dragging behind him a huge piece of beach vine as long as a cricket pitch. The channel at the end of the Spit separating it from Stradbroke Island was wild and grim. He stood and watched for a while, revelling in the whirl of the wind. It was dark when he got home and his mother was worried and asked where he had been. The Spit he said and grinned. After dinner, looking through the radio program, he saw there was a performance of Beethoven's 9th symphony conducted by Toscanini to be broadcast at 10 pm. His mother would be in bed so there was nothing for it but put his ear up against the wireless and play it as softly as he could. Because the weather was so stormy, the reception was full of static, he could hardly hear anything. But he pressed up hard against the little radio and the music was thrilling, unforgettable. He went to bed elated. What a day to end the holidays!

Back to school after the Christmas holidays, he was upset to find that Ned had left the school. Deep down he knew it was probably a good thing. He had to be more practical about things and even think about what he was going to do after he left school. Dreaming about kids at school had to stop – it was even embarrassing thinking about it now.

A couple of years later when he was working as a junior assistant at Flack and Flack in Townsville, he read a book by the great German author Thomas Mann called *Death in Venice*. He was astonished to find it was the same story as his experience with Ned. He was barely aware of the complex motivations for the book's protagonist the famous writer Gustav von Aschenbach, but was amazed at Aschenbach's parallel obsession with watching the young boy Tadzio on the Lido beach in Venice. Somehow it seemed to validate the memory of his own experience.

In May 1953, Aimée turned forty-five, an event that made her feel both depressed and worried. If turning forty was a shock, she was now unequivocally middle aged and a frump. Femininity had passed her by. Winifred was now happily married to Brian and living in the bush. Her other women friends were all well set up with husbands and families. There was no man in her life and not likely to be. Worst of all, Davy had started secondary school at Churchie, was in the bottom class and hated it. Antony was in his last year of school, but had no idea of what he wanted to do as a career. He was such a dreamer, she felt sure he wasn't really concentrating on his work despite his protestations. His habit was to lie on his bed with his head propped on his elbow, reading his study books with Nicky folded up in the crook of his legs at the end of the bed.

Pat Fraser told her David was studying hard and determined to study medicine at Queensland University and become a paediatric surgeon like his father. Thomas Brown was already in his first year studying Engineering. Her friend Betty Brown was typically disarming about Thomas.

'Thomas has survived Geelong Grammar in one piece, and believe it or not, he has plumped for mining engineering. Can you really see Thomas out there in the wilds digging holes in the ground? My children continue to amaze me. And of course Erica loves everything at NEGS and is unbelievably grown-up and sensible – where on earth did she get those qualities? Not from me.'

Betty always made her laugh and feel better. But Antony seemed to be hopeless at Maths and was unlikely to matriculate for professional courses such as these. She had been to see Jim Irwin at Flack and Flack, Alan's young colleague who had been such a help sorting her affairs after Alan had died, now shortly to be appointed a partner. Jim told her Antony could start as an audit clerk in the firm and study Chartered Accountancy. He should also go to University and do Commerce. She had been relieved to hear this but couldn't see Antony becoming an accountant.

Her biggest worry was Davy. He hated going to school every day and she knew she had to do something about it. The master in charge of his class at Churchie wasn't really helpful. All he could say was that he's a quiet boy, is a terrific runner and is shaping up well at football on the wing. He admitted most of the boys in his class weren't academic, but loved their sport.

She hadn't seen much of Claire Connor that year, but with pressure from both boys who were so fond of her, she invited her for dinner. As usual she arrived looking a million dollars in a red silk blouse and black pants. She was instantly enveloped by the boys, teasing and joking with them; for a moment Aimée felt a twinge of jealousy. The role of a mother is sometimes – a lot of the time – like a servant. You are there to be exploited, do all the dull things so they can have fun with others.

Claire brought with her a bottle of red wine and after dinner the two of them sat at the kitchen table with the wine and some cheese. The intimacy she used to enjoy with her flooded back, starting with Claire's admission she'd broken it off with Bill Cleveland.

'It was hard to do, really hard, and I felt very resentful about you, even though I knew you were right. In the end I got to realise he was never going to leave her.'

'But you didn't need me to tell you that.'

'Maybe, but you're one powerful lady. When you say something, people take notice.'

'Claire, what nonsense. My boys never take notice of me, though I sometimes wonder if that's their problem or mine.'

'Your boys are terrific and they both adore you. They might not seem to take much notice, but they absorb every word and store up the wisdom. Your problem is yourself. It's time you started looking out for your own life.'

'It's too late for me and anyhow at present I can't think of anything else except the boys. It's a crucial time for them both and I have to work out what I do with Davy. He can't stay at Churchie.'

'Is the problem a comprehension matter? He has problems with reading doesn't he?'

'Yes he doesn't read well, but it's more than that; he doesn't manage any school work properly.'

'But if he isn't understanding the words, he will have trouble with everything. Maybe he should leave school after Junior and start an outdoor type of job? He's becoming tall and strong.'

'I've been thinking of that. He seemed very interested listening to Brian and Winifred talking about life in the bush. He loves animals and Winifred has asked him to come out to Roma for school holidays.'

'If he enjoys that maybe Brian could offer him a job as a jackaroo when he leaves school?'

'Yes perhaps, but he's very shy and lacking in confidence. I don't think he's ready for that.'

Claire scoffed at that: 'Going on the land with someone like Brian in charge would be perfect to bring out the confidence in a boy like Davy!'

Life hadn't been much fun in Tony's last year. His friends

seemed to have become serious about their studies and future careers. His mother was always at him to apply himself, not only at his school work but around the house and garden too. In his last few months at school, he finally got the message and started working hard, though even he realised it was too late to have much effect on his final exam results. He consented to have special coaching for the dreaded maths, and a glimmer of comprehension started seeping into his brain. If only he had started earlier …

After their last paper for the Senior Examination, he and his friend Ken decided to go on a camping holiday to unwind after all the swotting for exams. It was hardly a big adventure as they only got as far as a camping ground beside the Nerang river at the back of Surfers Paradise. At least it was a change from endless exam study, and they enjoyed lying back on their camp beds watching the river roll by. He plied Ken with all sorts of questions about what books and films he liked and what he planned to do in the coming months. Ken was a year older and of a more practical cast of mind. Tony tended to look up to him as if he were an elder brother.

'What did you think of *Roman Holiday?*' he asked. After their last day of exams, they had gone to see the hit new film at the Winter Garden cinema.

'It was quite funny but it's completely unlikely that a princess would ever manage to get around Rome on the back of a motor bike.'

'I thought Audrey Hepburn was gorgeous.' Actually he had thought she was so gorgeous that he was overwhelmed by her and had found tears prickling his eyes in the cinema. He had even gone on his own to *Roman Holiday* four more times in the following week.

'I thought she was too skinny,' said Ken flatly.

As it grew dark, they grilled sausages on the barbecue and potatoes in the cinders, and they talked on, feeling very satisfied with their changing status.

The idyll didn't last long. About midnight after they had gone to sleep, a storm blew up and ripped out the flimsy pegs of their tent. Tony sat on the edges of the flaps in the pouring rain while Ken hammered in the pegs more deeply. It was in vain as the rain and wind increased and half an hour later the tent blew completely away and they were lucky enough to rescue it in the river just before it floated away in the dark.

When he first started work at the end of his Senior Year, barely seventeen years old, his life at Flack and Flack seemed a mixed blessing. Soon enough he became the junior auditor at a quasi-military organisation called Army Canteens located in a large pre-fabricated army hut. Here he was expected to spend most of his day adding up and cross-adding all the columns in the Cash Book, a task he hated at first, but to his surprise he gradually became quite good at it. He proudly admitted to Len, his immediate boss, that simultaneously he could add up, plan his weekend and be quite conscious of both streams of brain action which meant that he could think of three things at once. Len shook his head at him, not sure whether he was a loony or a possible genius.

Later he had a miniscule promotion and became the regular junior auditor at a more prestigious client, the Orient Line, a shipping office. Its office was on Eagle Street, full of mahogany furniture and smart young men in suits attending to customers wishing to book sea voyages overseas. There was a tradition that the best Orient Line men were party goers, and the best preparation for the nightly celebrations was a visit to the pub at lunch time and a more dedicated visit after work for the six o'clock swill. Work finished at five and the pubs closed at six.

The Orient Line men gave him his first hard lessons in pub culture. Afterwards he was never sure whether this was a great life lesson he learnt, or the beginning of a slow descent into a flawed lifestyle. His chief tutor at the Orient Line was the sub-accountant, a lantern-jawed young man a few years older called Allan Drewe.

Allan told him the story of his interview for the job two or three years earlier. The interview was conducted by the Accountant, Mr Montgomery, a middle-aged man prone to walking briskly around the office with a frown, *simulating* (according to Allan) a busy office manager. Allan, who at the time of his interview was as innocent as Tony, was ushered into the general manager's empty but palatial office for the interview by Montgomery. A chair was impatiently indicated, and Montgomery went behind the huge desk and threw himself casually into the general manager's executive chair. Apparently the chair had a mind if its own, tipped up and deposited Montgomery ignominiously in a heap on the floor behind the desk. Allan was so shocked that he stood up and peered over the desk to see what had happened. It was only later that he saw the absurdity of the event and wondered how he ever got the job.

When Tony arrived early one morning at the Orient Line office to continue the audit, Allan whispered to him to come out to the edge of the main office and watch. Curious, he did so and it wasn't long before Keith Cashman, one of the main men in the front office who attended customers, arrived at work looking rather worse for wear. As usual, he stood behind his large desk, and for a minute gazed vaguely at the scene around him as if trying to figure out why he needed to be there. But this morning was different. Allan had tied two pieces of string to the back of both Keith's triple level wooden in-trays and looped them out of sight over the back and under the desk and tied them to the castors on the legs of his chair tucked under the desk. When Keith pulled out his chair on arrival, the subsequent fracas was long remembered in the annals of the Orient Line. It was a reverberant office with a hard floor and the noise was like an explosion; splintered wood and sheaves of paper and invoices, pens and pencils reached almost every corner of the office. Alarmed customers ducked for cover. Tony was particularly delighted by the bemused expression on Keith's face as if someone needed to tell him why his world had come to an end. When a shocked silence descended on the great space, he turned to Allan only to find he had disappeared.

In his second year after school he turned eighteen and was called up for National Service at Amberley Airbase, hardly an hour's drive from Brisbane. On their first day the Squadron Leader met them on the tarmac and told them:

'Well chaps, next week jet flying will start for you all!'

It never did start, and over the two periods of three months, the training regime was laughable. He always felt his greatest achievement at Nasho was to learn to fall asleep standing up holding his rifle safely. It ranked with his ability to think about three things at the same time.

The life lessons were not wasted. Having never boarded at school and not being the tough sporty type, living in a military camp with hundreds of young men of his own age was quite a challenge. He made friends with people from all sorts of walks of life he would otherwise never have come across. Though useful military training was negligible, the tidiness and discipline of military life bred more orderly habits and some vestigial sense of responsibility. His friend Hugh Gore from school was in the same intake and the same hut and they colluded in devising ever more pointless processes to avoid doing the deadly boring work required of them. Hugh believed (he had proof) that you could hold a spade in a certain way and walk around with it all day without ever having to turn a sod.

In the room where he spent his two bouts of three months, in best military precision his room-mates were Jackson, James and Johnson. Brian Jackson was a tough lad from Parramatta, built like a bear and with an insouciant smile that went a long way with the ladies. His descriptions of his exploits while on weekend leave in Brisbane or Ipswich were fascinating. Jacko might have been twenty years older, lived in a world where the day to day transactions of life were immensely more adult, more real and completely scary. Tony felt a great sense of privilege when talking to him. Gordon Johnson was a large benevolent private school boy from Sydney; the fourth denizen was Cedric James.

Cedric, Ced to his friends, was a slight young man, 'weedy' according to the sergeant major. He walked with small steps, held his incessant cigarette in a limp hand and giggled rather than laughed. It was quickly discovered in the camp that Ced was an excellent jazz pianist, and a raconteur of extraordinary stories of newspaper and night club life in Sydney where he was already a senior journalist at age nineteen on the *Financial Review*. He became a popular personality in the camp not only for his prowess as a jazz pianist but for his light-hearted and raffish take on life. He made it clear to the others that he wasn't cut out for the military life, and people would have to bear with him if sometimes he didn't measure up.

The intake at Amberley was told from the beginning that their major task was 'aerodrome defence'. This allowed the authorities at the camp to teach the men nothing but basic drills like marching, handling ancient rifles, foraging in the bush, and keeping the airbase neat and tidy. One day Sergeant McKinnon announced the platoon would be taught how to handle hand grenades. About thirty of the intake gathered under a shady tree in the bush just outside the base, while the sergeant demonstrated the techniques of arming and disarming hand grenades and the all-important technique of throwing them, something like a cricket slow bowler bowling a lob with a straight arm. Not too difficult and much fun was had as everyone lined up again and again to have their go. Soon enough some of the men became bored – boredom threshold was always low – and spread out under the trees having much needed naps.

Sergeant McKinnon looked around and his eye landed on Cedric. 'James, I haven't seen you practise a throw yet.'

'It's very hot Sergeant, and I don't feel very well, so I think I'll give it a miss,' Cedric had an anxious look.

'Rubbish! Come on lad, be a man. Here's the hand grenade. Do what you've been taught to do.'

'I'm not sure exactly what you do have to do.'

'For God's sake, pull the pin, extend your arm straight behind you and bowl it, like this!'

He demonstrated with great precision. Cedric, by now looking red with anxiety, took the hand grenade, pulled the pin, and threw. It wasn't really a throw, it was a kind of push with a bent arm action, requiring so much effort he almost fell over. The grenade went about ten metres to his hard left and fell into the lap of one of his colleagues, Rob Hobbs, sound asleep with his hat shading his face, spreadeagled under a tree. There was a tremendous shout of alarm. Though they were not armed grenades, Rob leapt up in horror with a deathly scream, and Cedric rushed over to apologise, purple with embarrassment. Sergeant McKinnon took Cedric aside and manfully coached him for the rest of the morning, but before long recognised it was a fruitless task.

Two or three times Tony invited Cedric and Hugh to spend weekend leaves at home at Creswick Street in Brisbane. Aimée already knew and liked Hugh from school days, but Cedric's eccentric charm delighted her. Cedric knew exactly how to make her laugh, even to the extent of some 'come-hitherish' insinuation in his manner. Tony invited the prettiest girls he knew, including his special friends Erica Brown and Gail Hickey, to join him with Cedric and Hugh on Saturday night outings. Their favourite place was the illegal night club, the *Gypsy Baron,* entered through a makeshift corrugated iron flap in the wall of a semi-derelict building in a lane off Ann Street. No liquor was allowed on premises after six pm except for a few smart restaurants, but it flowed freely (though at extortionate cost) at the *Gypsy Baron* to the accompaniment of a very ordinary little band. The excitement there was two-fold: you might be raided at any moment, and the dance floor was so small you were compelled to dance extremely close to your partner.

Cedric's advent in his life almost persuaded him he was becoming a man about town, despite being only eighteen, almost nineteen. Yet he knew this new-found image of himself was a sham. He couldn't drive and his mother refused to teach him. While it was easy enough to arrange a night-club outing with girls and his

Nasho friends, when on his own with a girl, he could manage nothing more than a few chaste kisses. After leaving school, his boon companion was another old school friend, Simon Moxon. There was a sort of synchronicity in their lives: they had both become junior audit clerks in accounting firms; they both joined the golf club where they played pathetically bad golf together each weekend, and they both craved more successful female relationships. Simon was extremely tall and lanky; he was a dab hand at imitating the accents and reciting large chunks of dialogue from hugely popular radio comedy shows *Much Binding in the Marsh* and *The Goon Show*. His conversation was a sort of incomprehensible gibberish of assorted radio show dialogue mixed with some ordinary English.

Simon's proudest possession was the family's new Holden. It was not his own but neither his father or mother liked to drive so he became the family chauffeur. Antony would often spend late evenings with Simon in the Holden parked on Bartley's Hill gazing down at the city's lights spread before them, wondering when their fortunes would turn for the better. He admired Simon's ability to drive, so he asked if he would teach him, on his mother's old upright Ford Prefect that went to Melbourne and back five years earlier. The trouble was second gear fell out unless you held it in with your left hand. The clutch was so primitive, that as soon as it was let out, even half an inch, it kangaroo hopped then stalled. Simon was endlessly patient; in the end Antony got his licence and dreamed that one day he would have his own car.

He was determined to spend his first holiday from Flack and Flack in Sydney and Melbourne. Returning to Melbourne was a must: to resume his friendships with his cousins and friends from the memorable time he had over Christmas holidays while at school. Even more important, Hugh now was studying Architecture at Sydney University living at the prestigious St Pauls College, and Cedric had invited him to stay with him in his family's Tara Private Hotel at Coogee in Sydney.

His annual holiday from work being due, he decided he needed an adventure. The answer was to hitch-hike to Sydney and

Melbourne and back. One sunny May morning, he caught the train to the start of the New England highway. The first lift was in a small truck to Warwick on the Darling Downs, about eighty miles. Lifts were interspersed with long walks to find accommodation, usually in the cheapest pubs on the outskirts of towns. The journey was exhilarating: he had enthusiastic conversations with the drivers, mostly long distance truck drivers or travelling salesmen, keen to relieve their boredom by swapping tales of the road with a transient passenger. Sometimes he had brilliant rides, like the drive from Albury on the Victorian border all the way to Sydney in a brand new Mercedes, owned and driven to his amazement by a logger called Karl working in forests in Victoria. But often it was the reverse: being stranded for hours on a dirt track on the almost non-existent Princes Highway in the remote bush of north-eastern Victoria.

Returning to Melbourne was a real thrill. He felt he knew the city, giving him a sense of proprietorship, revelled in its autumn colours and chilly weather, so unlike Brisbane. He loved resuming his friendship with his cousin Anthony and especially his girl cousins Sara and Joanna, both now attractive and lively teenagers. The girls took him to his first VFL match at the Melbourne Cricket Ground. He was astonished at the incredible noise and enthusiasm from the huge crowd, and even more amazed at the screaming and furious antics of his sweet cousins as they expressed their support for the family's beloved team Melbourne playing against their hated rival Collingwood. It sparked his life-long fascination with Australian football, though he disappointed the girls by deciding to follow Footscray, a hopelessly unfashionable team.

He stayed with his old grandmother and his aunt Betty; his grandfather had died since his earlier visit. He soaked up the memories of his earlier stay, even the smells of the soap in the bathroom and the preserves hanging in the laundry. He loved his grandmother and the way she greeted him with such warmth, cooked her wonderful roast dinners for him, asked him so many questions about what he was doing, and seemed really interested in what he told her. His favourite aunt Betty took him to her golf club and they played a game together – he was surprised how much better she played than he could. She took him to a concert at the Town Hall conducted by Sir Bernard Heinze, his first concert outside Brisbane and instantly he knew it was better than the concerts in Brisbane, almost as good as recordings he had heard.

When he arrived in Sydney in Karl the logger's new Mercedes, it was a whole day sooner than he had told Cedric he would arrive. He was apprehensive when he made his way on the tram to Coogee and walked up Beach Street to the front door of the Tara Private Hotel, high up overlooking Coogee Bay. It was already eight o'clock, probably too late for something to eat. Cedric's mother answered the door. She was well dressed and had curly red hair; maybe you could call it frizzy. Clearly she was used to late guests. Cedric was at work with the paper, she told him, but come into the kitchen and we'll rustle you up something. What was rustled up was more like a feast, in quantity at least.

Unpacking his bag after midnight in his room on the top floor looking out at the blackness of the ocean, he was both exhilarated and exhausted. After the feast in the kitchen, he had been taken to the office to meet Percy James, Cedric's father. The office was a small windowless room on the ground floor, packed with surplus hotel detritus, files, cabinets and a couch for guests to sit. In the corner covered in papers and a large typewriter, was a desk where Perce worked. Perce was a constant dynamo, seemingly working round the clock keeping his empire going. He was a corpulent man with a Roman nose, balding hair, heavy horn-rimmed glasses, carpet slippers and bulky trousers hitched very high with braces. Tony was welcomed with an expansive handshake from his shabby swivel chair and gestured to sit alongside two other people who seemed to be residents whiling away their evening keeping Perce company. He was ordered to give full details of all his hitchhiking travels and quizzed about his exploits with Cedric at Nasho. He found himself in the unusual role of entertainer with many oohs and ahs from his decrepit little audience and noisy laughter from Perce.

When Cedric arrived home an hour or so later, the tempo was nearly doubled. His father was scolded for not offering drinks; his mother came in bearing a tray of cakes and other goodies and suddenly there was a party. Glasses were clinked, cigarettes lit, and Cedric regaled the room with his take on the news of the day, scandal, politics and finances. When he finally got into bed in his little room, he realised dimly his life had taken another new turn with his induction into the eccentricities of the James family.

Her job with Dan Hart, an intermittent social life with her friends and occasional outings with Toby had at least banished her dreadful money worries. The undefined black mist future seemed safely in the past. While Antony's life seemed aimless to her, she realised his National Service experience had found him new friends and made him more confident. Getting David out of school and on to the land had been much more challenging but he seemed content being a jackaroo with little indication of homesickness.

Reluctantly she turned her mind to the idea of buying a house. She knew the longer she put it off the less likely she would find something suitable. There was no logic for her delay. She had sold *Breffney* three years ago; there was still a shortage of housing and house prices were rising. It was just that there had been so many changes in her life: her job with Dan, selling *Breffney*, David leaving home, Antony in and out of National Service and leaving her home alone for long periods. She dreaded another upheaval, and where on earth would she look for a house? She couldn't afford Clayfield or Ascot where she'd lived all her time in Brisbane since she had married Alan, and where most of her friends lived.

She was surprised when Antony pushed her into action:

'Mum, when are we going to buy a house? You said we'd buy a house when you sold the beach house. That was ages ago now and now there's just you and me in this dump.'

'*We*' he says, '*we* are going to buy a house.' He'll be off to

Melbourne or overseas any time, she thought. It's *me* buying a house. For my lonely dotage. I hate the idea.

'Do you really want to move somewhere else? We can't afford to buy around here – I know we should buy a house, but where?'

'Yes let's look for a new place, it doesn't have to be here in Clayfield. We can check the ads in the paper on Saturday and start looking.'

For the next few weeks he looked up the ads and went off looking at houses, saying he knew the sort of house to look for. One of his hobbies was to sketch plans of modern houses he saw, telling himself he should be studying architecture. What a strange impulsive boy he is, she thought. Here he is just back from what he says is the best adventure and holiday he's ever had and is always talking about wanting to go overseas. And now he can only talk of us buying a house.

She had to admit in the end his new-found zeal had results. He came back from a Saturday afternoon with Simon Moxon spent driving around in his car looking for houses. They had visited Simon's uncle, who lived in Northgate, a newish suburb a few miles to the north of Clayfield. Simon's uncle told them a builder he knew was building three houses in the next street.

'They're great houses Mum. Simon and I went to see them and walked around the site. They all have three bedrooms and front verandas looking out over the view to the bay. I can take you to see them tomorrow.'

They went to see them together and her heart fell. They were quite pretty weatherboard cottages, painted different colours on concrete stumps, but the long wide street was full of dreary little houses, not a tree in sight. The thought of living her life alone in featureless suburbia was depressing.

Typically Aimée pushed down her misgivings, gritted her teeth and smiled at his enthusiasm. Visits were made over the next weeks as the cottages neared completion. She found that she could afford to buy one without taking a loan, and agreed with him to buy the pale blue one. He seemed delighted, and became absorbed in working out colour schemes.

'I think we need to have a brightly coloured feature wall in every room.'

'Do we? Why?'

'Well this is happening in all the new houses being built. Everybody wants to get away from the boring old cream and green.'

'*Breffney* was cream and green; I thought it looked lovely.'

'Yes, but that was a long time ago.'

Yes indeed it was – how life changes, and not always for the better. On her last morning at Creswick Street, standing at the sink looking out at the garden and the street, as she had done for fifteen years, she gazed at the poinciana tree Alan had planted when they first moved in. It was now fully grown, spreading its shallow red and green fronds across the garden. Every morning she had looked at it with a pulse of pleasure, willing it to grow a little more. It was a sad moment and its significance made her bite her lip.

As they threw themselves into the interior painting, bought some new furniture, and then moved into the new home in Northgate, she joined in his pleasure of living in a brand new house. It smelt new, of paint, sawdust, and oddly, hope. The first day they moved in it was November and hot. She threw open the floor length windows in the front living room and the strong fresh north easterly breeze from the bay blew in like a little gale, giving her a sense of exhilaration. Maybe, she thought, I can make this my own private place and be happy.

Having lunch with Claire one day near Dan's rooms on Wickham Terrace, she told her they both had settled into a companionable routine in the new house at Northgate.

'You must come and see it and have dinner with us. We've become like Darby and Joan.'

'I can't believe that with him being at Nasho and gadding around the country. But you're getting to like it after all?'

'I am. It's very comfortable and fresh and everything works and the neighbours are nice. Actually, I've never felt so companionable with Ant. I suppose it's really that he's growing up and has started to realise that someone else exists in the house beside himself.'

'I think you're a bit hard on him. He probably thinks he has you on your own for the first time without a pesky younger brother. Are you teaching him to cook?'

'Not really, but he does help around the house and believe it or not, he's doing the heavy work in the new garden. The main thing is that we talk a lot more about what we both are thinking. Funnily enough, I am always pushing him to go out more and see his friends and take a girl out. He knows some lovely girls and when I've seen him around them he's so chatty and charming, but I think deep down he lacks confidence.'

'Don't worry, he'll work it out soon enough. They all do. I haven't seen him for ages, is he still passionate about his music?'

'Oh yes, I'm afraid so. Sibelius is his latest obsession. He plays these gloomy symphonies day and night on the huge speaker he has in his room. He says he's writing a book on them.'

'Writing a book! Wow!'

He liked living in the new house, especially the look of his bedroom. It was at the back of the house and he had painted the rear wall charcoal grey contrasting with the pale peachy yellow he remembered with affection from the Lloyd's house in Melbourne. He had a spacious shelf for his growing collection of LP records and had bought a large speaker and relished its big boomy sound. His latest treasure was the complete recording of all thirty-two Beethoven piano sonatas in a huge box set of twenty LPs. Wilhelm Kempff was a serious looking German with a high forehead who played the sonatas with a simple clarity, shying away from exaggerated contrasts in tempo or dynamics. At least that was his own opinion, though he sometimes felt Kempff should give rather more passion to the great late sonatas. He had found a book called Beethoven: His Spiritual Development by an Irish writer called JWN Sullivan which was a complete revelation to him. As Beethoven grew older and more isolated through his deafness, Sullivan described how he entered a sublime world of the imagination where he created some of the most profound music ever composed.

His big project at the time was his passion for the symphonies of the Finnish composer Sibelius who had just died at a very old age. In fact it was Sullivan's great book that had inspired him to write a critique of the Sibelius symphonies. Night after night he listened to the recordings of the symphonies. He wrote down his thoughts about the music, the images they gave him of the bleak nordic landscape, the ideas that must have been in Sibelius' mind. He read everything he could find on the composer and the symphonies but found the excessively technical analysis not much help. He felt most of it completely missed the essence of the music. The Fourth symphony, the most remote and obscure of them all which the critic Neville Cardus had described as like drinking a glass of very cold water, fascinated him the most. Eventually he decided the tragic ending most critics described was not tragic at all but a sliding off into a mysterious contemplative place of peace and joy. At last the symphony made sense to him.

A New Life

The phone rang. 'Is that you Aimée? It's Stephen King here. How are you, I haven't seen you for such a long time. Where are you living now?'

Stephen King! Whatever happened to him after his wife died?

'Hullo Steve, how nice to speak to you. I bought a house at Northgate a year or two ago. Antony and I live here.'

'And young David?'

'He has gone off to the bush as a jackaroo – near Longreach.'

'Really, how time flies. I remember he seemed a little boy when I last saw him.'

'And the same I suppose with Robin and Carolyn, though of course Robin's married now isn't she?'

'Yes that's right and she has two little children, but I really rang to say I have tickets for the Ballet next week and I wondered if you would like to accompany me?'

My goodness, the Ballet! I would never have thought Stephen King would go the Ballet. She didn't know him well but he knew several of their friends, that is the friends she and Alan had made who were still her friends though most had disappeared from her day-to-day life. She really knew him from the little house he and his wife Adele had on the Esplanade at Surfers half a block down from *Breffney*. She recalled he loved fishing in the surf, was down at the water's edge most mornings in the Christmas holidays, dressed like a short bulky tramp in old khaki shorts and shirt, with a rod stuck in the sand and another in his hand, or digging with his feet for bait in the wet sand. It had been very sad about Adele who had leukemia and slowly wasted away over several years.

They went to the Ballet – it was *Giselle* but it was clear Steve had never been before. It had been a ploy! In the ensuing weeks they went out together several times, usually to a restaurant. She could tell he had an agenda from quite early. It was so different from Toby who told stories and jokes and you knew it was never going anywhere. Steve was keen to ask her all the questions about her life, very tactfully, but she knew exactly where it was leading. It gave her time to ponder. Her first impression was how well-mannered he was. It wasn't just superficial charm but a genuine sense of *politesse*, perhaps coming from his long career running the law firm inherited from his father, and listening and being sympathetic to so many clients. She could also sense he was a man of purpose; he had distinct views on many aspects of life. He was probably a person whose views were unlikely to change or would require a well-argued case to shift his position.

She was shocked to discover on their second rendezvous that he had recently had a heart attack, not long after Adele had died. He brushed it off saying he had recovered well. He had changed his diet and lost weight but her questioning revealed how debilitated he had become during the years of Adele's illness. Now he was determined to re-order his life.

'Aimée, the experience of the last few years has taught me I must concentrate on the important things in my life and reduce distractions. Jonathan is now eight and his life has been completely disordered. I now have two younger partners in the firm who are very capable though Connor Gill, my most senior colleague, is not far from retirement. So I must now step back from constant ten hour days. I'm fifty-two and aim to retire as soon as Jonathan leaves school in ten years time.'

'Where does he go to school?'

'He boards at the Southport School. He seems to be happy enough there, but I've booked him to go to Geelong Grammar when he's finished primary school.'

His clarity of purpose was admirable she thought, but oh dear, it wouldn't be easy to share his life. That poor little boy of his. She ran into Betty Brown at the Clayfield shops soon after. She told Betty as casually as she could that she'd gone to the Ballet with Steve. Betty of course clung to every word and was on to the situation in a minute:

'You know he's had a coronary; don't touch him with a barge pole.'

'Oh Betty, don't be silly. I've been out with him once or twice. He's just a bit lonely.'

'I'm joking of course, but Tom tells me he's had a terrible time. You should really be careful – you don't want to go through all that again.'

Betty was right and the responsibility of little Jonathan would inevitably fall to her, whatever Steve intended. Anyhow it was all absurd; Steve had not said anything and even if he did she couldn't seriously think about becoming embroiled in a complex family like the Kings. In addition to Jonathan, she knew his elder daughter Robin was married to a member of the Murdoch newspaper family. The younger daughter Carolyn mixed in the same group of young people as Antony.

Nevertheless her hands-off approach was quickly compromised. Steve was a keen card player and asked her to partner him at social card evenings with Pat and Ken Fraser and Jock and Bertie Robertson, or sometimes Jo and Norman Pixley. The game was usually poker, not for high stakes, but the others were experienced players, and she felt a fish out of water. She had no idea how to assess the strength of her hand of cards, let alone decide what to bet. She just wished it would be over soon.

In a way it was all these confusing experiences, none of which she really wanted, that added up to her gradual realisation that Steve was becoming part of her life in a way that never happened with the gentle and considerate Toby. Antony, with his job, his social life and his obsession with his music, seemed oblivious to what was going on for her. He seemed to behave as if he and his mother were a contented *de facto* couple busily going about their separate lives. So when Steve parked outside the Northgate house after a card evening, then casually asked her to marry him, she felt it was a bit like making an arrangement for their next outing.

She didn't accept on the spot. She talked separately to Pat

Fraser and Betty Brown, her best friends. Pat, so sensible and sympathetic, couldn't conceal her delight at the idea. Betty was wise and supportive despite being aware of Steve's shortcomings, insisting her decision must come from her heart. Rather reluctantly she decided to confide in Claire, whom she knew would be sceptical, partly because she moved in different circles, and partly because she had a more cynical view of men. She invited her to dinner at Northgate with the idea they would talk after dinner when Antony inevitably retreated to his room to play music.

'Hullo Ant, where have you been hiding? You never come to see little old me these days.'

As always she looked spectacular with the long red fingernails and the amazing glasses. He beamed and hugged her, staring at the bright blue floral dress that swirled around her. 'Oh, I've been pretty busy at work and things.'

'Hullo Claire,' Aimée said, smiling with pleasure, 'yes we've been remiss – it seems ages since we've seen you.'

'So why am I here? I got all dressed up for some special occasion. What's going on?' He looked bemused at his mother, who looked embarrassed.

'I don't know,' he said, 'but it *is* my 21st birthday later this month. Want to come? We're going to have a dinner dance at Baxters.'

'Hardly darl, I don't think I'm the kind of gal to wow your friends. At Baxters? That's a bit low class for a smart kid like you.'

'Oh no, Baxters is fabulous. The oysters are brilliant, and I've booked four alcoves seating six people each. It's great! It's where all the bookies take their molls after the races.'

'I know. Well, horses for courses, in racing lingo.'

After dinner they sat at the table chatting, mostly Antony regaling them with his exploits and telling Claire about Sibelius. After a while Claire told him to disappear because she wanted to talk to his mother. When his door shut, she turned to Aimée.

'Alright, what is going on? You're not getting married are you?'

'What on earth made you think that?'

Claire rolled her eyes: 'Who is it?'

'Steve King, I don't think you would know him.'

'You really are?' Her eyes were like saucers.

'Not exactly. I've been going out with him for a couple of months, but he has proposed and I'm ... confused.'

She was whispering so Claire pulled her chair close and leaned in to hear the story. Something about Claire's total reading of her mind allowed her to tell her everything including all the misgivings she was determined not to tell. After more than an hour of confession, Antony emerged from his room and they stopped talking. They went down to her car, Claire got in, took a deep breath and looked up at her:

'Well all I can say is he's a lucky guy, and he's probably a nice guy. But at this time of your life do you really want to bring up an eight-year-old boy? I don't think you do, but it won't stop you being a wonderful mother all over again. You know of course that's what he needs most, a wonderful mother for his boy, and you've passed with flying colours.'

She knew Claire wouldn't approve, just like she hadn't approved of Claire's affair with Bill Cleveland. But Claire understood her better than anyone else she knew in Brisbane so she tried, unsuccessfully, to stop thinking about it at all ... until Steve brought it up again, driving home from a dinner with friends of his at his club.

'Did you think about my ... proposal, Aimée?'

As if I haven't been thinking of anything else.

'Of course Steve, it's such a wonderful suggestion, but there's so many things I have to think about that I wonder whether it's the right thing to do.'

'Do you mean Jonty?'

'Yes Jonty especially but, other things too ...'

'Have you mentioned it to Antony and David?'

Without thinking she said: 'I don't want to talk about it to Antony until after his 21st next week.' Then realising how absurd she was becoming, she blurted: 'Oh Steve I'm sorry for being ridiculous, it would be wonderful to marry you.'

She didn't tell Antony until after his party as it wasn't fair to distract him from his big moment. All his friends gathered at the house for drinks before they took off in several cars to Baxters. Her decision behind her, Aimée loved to see all his friends gather in the house. Some like Erica Brown, Simon, Ken, John Capper and Leith Fraser she knew well, but most were new to her, though she had met his new girlfriend Gail several times and thought her a sweet young girl, so pretty and gently spoken. They are such nice-looking young people she thought. It made her feel she need no longer worry about him.

He loved being surrounded by his friends, and being able to claim Gail as his girlfriend. He felt a little pang of guilty pleasure at the way some of his male friends looked at her. Beside a pretty heart-shaped face and dark *gamin*-style hair reminding him of Audrey Hepburn, she had a resplendent figure. At Baxters, they all gorged on oysters and prawns and a dozen bottles of Wynn's Coonawarra Claret he had brought. They danced the night away to the distinctly unromantic tones of a fat lady pianist in a shiny green dress quaffing gins from the piano lid. None of this bothered him, holding Gail ever closer during dance after dance. Eventually the party broke up and he drove her to watch the moon over the cliffs overlooking the bay at Shorncliffe. It was a balmy night and they talked, kissed and embraced enthusiastically into the small hours, until he gradually realised the feeling in his groin was becoming painful, very painful, and he must take her home and the night come to an end, though not quite as he had envisaged it.

On a quiet late summer afternoon, Antony took his mother's arm and escorted her up the aisle in St John's Anglican Cathedral in Brisbane to be married to Steve King. All morning, indeed for over a month, her mind was a complete jumble of thoughts, worries mostly, but also happiness, horror, disbelief, desire to disappear, relief – everything. Now she just felt wilted like an autumn tree, a dried-out leaf ready to be blown away. Until her son, now so tall and *she* thought … handsome… came up beside her and smiled, a little nervously, but confidently, and led her towards the altar and Steve.

Bill Baddeley, the new Dean of the Cathedral, stood at the head of the aisle, tall, majestic and unbelievably grand as he smiled serenely down towards her. Steve, more than a head shorter than the Dean, his smile even broader, turned towards her and took her hand. The Dean, recently arrived from England trailing impeccable theatrical and aristocratic lineage, was the toast of Brisbane. Now his smile expanded to envelop the couple as he whispered in a rich baritone: 'Welcome Aimée and Stephen.'

Antony loved the whole thing. Being asked to give away his mother; seeing her look so happy even if rather dazed and confused; the elegance of this ceremony in the vast space aided by the patrician style and splendour of the Dean. His step-sister-to-be Robin and her husband Keith Murdoch had befriended the Baddeleys through mutual connections in England. Robin, making the most of the new friendship, had told her father they must be married in the Cathedral by Bill. Antony thought his mother looked very smart, in fact he couldn't remember when she had looked so well-dressed. She always looked neat but she rarely wore what he thought could be called 'good' clothes. She was wearing a dusty pink silk dress with a fine floral pattern and a hat made of fine white straw with a wide brim and a darker pink band. He thought she looked really pretty and elegant, and for a moment he felt he had misjudged her, at least he had misjudged her appearance. He had to admit to himself he had never thought of her as especially pretty or feminine. But now he realised with a tinge of guilt that she was both, even though she was nearly fifty!

The reception was held at Steve's club, the Queensland Club, a huge old grey stone and weatherboard pile opposite the Botanical Gardens, overhung by giant Moreton Bay fig trees, a true relic of colonial times. Though several of her friends' husbands were members, and Alan had once been a member, it seemed to her to be a bastion of male rituals, even pomposity. Her feeling of dazed other-worldliness followed her into the club. She gazed on the smiling faces of their friends as if in a dream. The surge of guests gathered in the big drawing room; waiters in white tuxedos deftly passed around canapés. Silver salvers of scotch and gin with little bottles of soda and tonic were offered everywhere. Part of her felt thrilled by the genuine warmth from the press of people and from Steve's care and attention. Another part wondered what on earth was she doing here. She didn't dare dwell on the contrast with the simple family affair in Melbourne when she was first married over twenty years earlier.

Mercifully after the toasts of champagne and speeches, Steve extricated them both from a party that seemed destined to go on all night, and took her to the Bellevue Hotel on the opposite corner, where a table was booked for them in the dining room.

'I thought you might be a bit exhausted by it all my dear, so the Bellevue seemed the answer,' he said as he handed her the menu.

'Steve, you are so thoughtful, but I don't think I could eat a thing.'

'There's whiting on the menu and the dining room has a good reputation. Why don't you try it grilled?'

'Just one fillet then with some salad would be nice.'

'Will you have some wine?'

'Goodness no, not after the champagne, I'd fall over!'

'But you're up for the plane to Melbourne tomorrow?'

'Of course, I can't wait.'

He had suggested they honeymoon on a cruise from Melbourne to New Zealand, and beforehand spend a couple of days in Melbourne where she could introduce him to her friends and to her beloved old mother-in-law and her daughters. When he had asked what she thought of this idea, she was almost speechless with gratitude. For the first time, she felt sure she had made the right decision.

She looked at him now across the table at the Bellevue with its rich blue carpet and little pink table lamps. Despite his short stature and barrel chest, he was a handsome man with a deep and cultured voice to match his old-fashioned charm. His thoughtfulness was a boon to her and for the first time in many, many years, she felt enclosed and protected.

Not long before Aimée and Steve were married, he had built a house on a steep sloping block overlooking the Brisbane river at Indooroopilly. In fact it was situated immediately below the large colonial Queenslander set in expansive grounds owned by the Pixleys. The Pixleys were great friends of Steve and told him of the vacant lot below their home, so he had bought it and built a compact modern house. It was this house Aimee now moved into, together with Antony.

After the wedding, the *ménage-a-quatre* living in Inga Avenue on the hill slope under the Pixley's house all found the experience strange, even unsettling. She thought the house hot and stuffy facing into the western sun and Steve seemed surprised his new step-son was happily settling in with no apparent desire to move out on his own. His younger daughter Carolyn had itchy feet and couldn't wait to get away. Though pleased her father had married Aimée, Carolyn wasn't as close to him as her elder sister Robin, and their relationship wasn't easy. She and Antony had known each other since they were children and both now took a childish pleasure in being irritating to their parents.

Carolyn had already been to England with a girlfriend for a year and was looking to go somewhere more unconventional. On a whim she applied for a job in Darwin, was accepted without an interview and announced she was off to Darwin. Her father was appalled, and so was Aimée. Nobody from a respectable family, especially a young woman, went to Darwin. Carolyn was secretly pleased with the parental response, and Antony was impressed with her risk-taking. Off she went, and sent back occasional letters telling of her exploits that horrified Steve. She met a man in

Darwin called Les Smith, not an auspicious name for the daughter of Stephen King. In a later letter she admitted Les was twenty years older and had four children. The atmosphere in Inga Avenue became very steamy. Then one day, the letter arrived announcing she was getting married to Les the next week. This was calamity. Robin and her husband Keith were summoned and a family conference was held. Steve thought he should fly to Darwin immediately but Aimée and Robin agreed that was not a good idea. So Steve took a deep breath and picked up the phone.

'Hullo Carolyn.' In a deep sepulchral voice.

'Hello Dad, how nice to hear your voice.'

'I want to say how happy I am for you and offer my congratulations to you and … Les.' Steve's voice had grown even lower.

'Oh dad, I'm just joking.'

'I hope you'll be very happy but I don't think we'll be able to get up to the wedding if it's this coming week.'

'Dad, it's a joke. I like Les very much but we're not getting married. He would have to get divorced.'

'Carolyn, are you telling me you've decided not to get married next week?'

'Dad, I'm telling you it's a joke. You haven't written to me or rung me for ages and I thought this would be a way to make you get in touch. You see it's sometimes lonely up here and I miss you all.'

Now that she was again a married woman living in her husband's new house, she felt almost superfluous, though she thought maybe it was like the eerie calm before the storm. Steve had insisted she resign from her work at Dan Hart's eye surgery, which she reluctantly did. It was good for Steve having the Pixleys close by. She had known them for years: they had been friends of Alan's, but Jo was often critical of people around her, even her friends, and Aimée felt vulnerable around her.

Here she was, she thought, almost hiding in her new house,

sewing a dress for Robin's little daughter Anna, Steve's grand-daughter. Sewing again! After all that terrible sewing for years just to survive, it was almost therapeutic now! How topsy-turvy these last few years have been. It was only three years ago that she went through all that agony with David. She had never stopped wondering whether she had been right in sending him off to the bush. It had been the stay with Brian and Winifred at their place near Roma that really sparked his interest. When he had come home, he hated school even more, not that he really complained. He just looked so burdened when he came home each day, and the awful look of gloom as he huddled frozen over his homework. She used to feel quite sick for him and felt at her wit's end. In hindsight it was a good thing she had run into Jim Irwin of Flack and Flack who offered to arrange for her to see the man he knew at the pastoral company Australian Estates. How ghastly the man had been, so superior and disdainful about David, even before interviewing him. Poor Davy, how he had been slaughtered; he was crushed when he got home. But at least it started the process and maybe she wouldn't have rung Brian Cox if she hadn't felt so desperate.

Toby had been so helpful too. Dear Toby, he had written her such a nice letter when Steve and she announced they were getting married. She had felt sorry about Toby – he had been sweet and attentive to her for so many years. But she mustn't dwell on that. He had really been a saviour for Davy. When Brian had offered to approach Clark and Tait, the pastoral company he dealt with, how relieved she had been when Toby offered to make the appointment for David and had coached him for the interview.

She could never forget the day he left for Longreach to take up the jackaroo's position. The panic on Central Station when they lost of one his suitcases! She was the one who was almost paralysed with worry; he seemed unconcerned and she had to admit that as soon as he heard he had got the job and it meant leaving school, his gloom and depression had lifted like a cloud dispersing. Now he's been there for two years, and how he has changed. Almost unrecognisable! When he came back for the holidays last summer, she could hardly remember the boy who had left for the bush when he was sixteen. Tall and gangly in that bushy's hat, and so tanned. The sun had been good for his acne – almost disappeared. He looked healthy and well, she thought, but still very quiet and saying almost nothing, even less than before. He didn't say if he was lonely, but he probably was, though he seemed to have made a couple of friends.

I must watch the time she thought: I'm due for lunch at Jo's at half past twelve. She wondered how many would be there – lots probably.

It was much easier for Antony when he went off to Flack and Flack without a murmur, though oddly enough she suspected he took longer to get adjusted to it and even now she feels it's just a job for him and his real life is somewhere else, mostly in his music. At least he seems to have made lots of friends and is having quite a busy social life. National Service was good for him. Six months of having to live with other young men with all the discipline of the armed service, though thankfully with no action. And the friends he made were different, very different from the people he met at school. She thought with affection of Cedric James with his jazz piano playing, chain smoking and his charming night-club manner, even to her.

Jo Pixley set up her lunch on the shady corner of the vast veranda surrounding their house, seated around a big table on comfortable bamboo chairs. Aimée was pleased there were only five of them and delighted Jo's daughter Jane was there, up from Melbourne for a brief holiday. Jane was a spirited girl, a champion golfer but found living in Melbourne away from her mother's caustic wit improved their relationship. Also there were Aimée's new step-daughter, Robin Murdoch and Robin's aunt, Bertie Robertson. Jo was in an expansive mood, clearly feeling she had staged a minor coup to have two generations of women friends to lunch linked by Aimée's advent as a neighbour and Jane's visit. Everyone knew each other but rarely saw each other, so it was a perfect chance for Jo to find out the interesting news.

Aimée was fond of Bertie and saw her as a real friend and ally in her new life. Bertie's sister Adele, Steve's late wife, had been a semi-invalid for years, and Bertie had become close to Steve through her tireless support for Adele. Bertie spoke in a gravelly voice and had a wry take on everything going on.

'How's it going down there, dear?' she said out of the side of her mouth nodding at the new house.

'It's awfully hot in this weather. Being under the hill facing the west, it doesn't get the nor-easters. I think Steve thinks he made a mistake.'

'I told him that but of course he wouldn't listen – I'm only a woman. But I wasn't meaning that. I was meaning being so close to you know who.'

Aimée gave her a fleeting smile.

Jo looked across imperiously: 'Aimée dear, will you have whisky or a gin with lunch?' She had a beaky chin and a slightly hooked nose making her look rather like a bird of prey, not inappropriate for her personality.

'Now Robin,' she added, 'I want to hear all about the Baddeleys. He's the new Dean of the Cathedral Jane darling, he's a big man, so elegant and grand, and you should hear his voice. Robin knows them well and organised him to marry Aimée and Steve.'

'Oh Jo, it wasn't like that!' Robin laughed loudly in embarrassment, remembering the resistance she had met with all her suggestions for the wedding.

'Well what was it then? You know them don't you and weren't you the first to meet them? And isn't he prominent in the theatrical world?'

Aimée saw Jo was having a go at Robin – maybe she was piqued at Robin's rising social status around Brisbane. Robin looked uncomfortable.

'We met them through mutual friends in England who asked us to look out for them. They knew nobody when they arrived and are very nice, not at all smart or pompous. His sister is Angela Baddeley, the actress who plays blowsy cockney types in British films.'

Jo changed the subject: 'Aimée I hope you don't mind Antony having drinks with us after work here.' Turning to the others she went on: 'Tony drives Norman home every day and most days they pick up Antony in the city too and we all sit out here and have a lovely time.'

'No of course I don't mind, but do you? Tell him to go home if he stays too long.'

'No we love him coming in any time – he tells us all sorts of things!'

He had taken to going to work with the Pixleys in their car each morning and often coming home with them in the afternoon. She thought if he was telling the Pixleys about Steve and me, he was also telling us about what was happening in their greater world.

Jo's next question was about Jonathan, Aimee's new stepson, aged nine. She knew it was coming and dreaded it, mainly because Robin would be all ears and had all sorts of opinions about how he should be raised.

'I haven't seen Jonty at all since you both moved in – is he now boarding at the Southport School?' She looked at Aimée and then to Robin and back.

Oh Jo, what a loaded question, she thought. 'Yes he's boarding there and seems very happy there, don't you think Robin?'

'Yes it's the best place for him. There's no way Aimée and Dad can be expected to look after him on a day-to-day basis.'

'But he'll come home for holidays?'

'Yes of course and he can spend plenty of time with Keith and me too.'

'But what about your new kitchen shop? You must be so busy – they tell me everyone is buying all their French Provincial ingredients and equipment from you.'

Robin brushed this diversion away. 'There's always plenty of time for Jonty and it's one of the best things about you and Dad living close to us.' Mercifully, Robin didn't bring up the big issue which was to send Jonty to Geelong Grammar when he finished primary school. Aimée knew Jonty should live at home and go to school in Brisbane, but nobody else seemed to agree.

One sunny morning as she sat at the kitchen bench musing about her complicated new life, she jumped when the phone rang beside her. It was Betty Jeffrey.

'I'm sorry to give you bad news but Mum has just died.'

'Oh Betty.' This wrenched her back to another world. 'You must be heartbroken. How did it happen?'

'She died peacefully in her sleep in the early hours this morning. None of us was there.'

She knew they would all feel terrible about that: the woman they had all loved and depended upon, who had always known what to do. Betty sounded flat and exhausted. She had never heard the irrepressible Betty like that before, except of course when Alan had died.

'I'm getting all the family together here tonight to work out the arrangements. At least we know we've got the plot next to Dad. Will you come down?' This was not so much a suggestion as a demand.

'Of course I will.'

She had last seen old Mill and the family when she and Steve had visited Melbourne on their honeymoon nearly a year earlier. In her mid-eighties, she had seemed so frail then, but she knew how hard it would be for her girls, Betty, Jo and Mary who all worshipped her. She did too and there was no question that she would have to be with them for the funeral. She also knew in her heart-of-hearts that if she didn't go right away, there would be arguments amongst the sisters. She had seen it before – in serious family matters, they all behaved much better when she was there. These wry feelings of unbroken family connections were a real jolt for her in her new circumstances with her new husband and new family. In recent months she had barely thought about the Jeffreys. Maybe, she thought, this is one of the reasons why I feel at odds with myself here in Steve's house.

Steve agreed she should fly down the next day and offered to come with her but she said it would be better for her to go alone as she could be close to the girls. She sat down and wrote a letter to David telling him the news and that he should write to Betty. When he got home that night she told Antony of his grandmother's death. She could see he was genuinely upset.

'I loved staying with her when I was a kid and a couple of times when I drove or hitchhiked down later. She just knew what a boy liked and she always wanted to know about everything, not only what I was doing but what I thought.'

'For me she was the real link with your father's family. I often felt she was my mother too.'

To her surprise, the funeral and the whole visit was such a happy time. She was thrilled to see the young ones, six of her boys' cousins, all looking so bright-eyed and grown up, and immediately regretted not insisting Antony fly down too. Betty was back to her best and in complete charge and she had long tearful hugs with Jo and Mary. Flying back to Brisbane, she felt so much better and energised from the reconnection with the family. It was what had been needed for her new life with Steve.

With Carolyn apparently gone for good, and Jonty soon to finish his primary school at the Southport School, Aimée and Steve decided it was time to move from the Inga Avenue house they both disliked. They bought a big Queenslander in Ascot, nearer to most of their friends, and where Steve could set up a workshop under the house for his wood-working. She thought it was far too big but she told herself it was the nicest house she'd ever lived in, and it was a much more suitable place to bring up Jonty.

Jonty was the issue. Despite her new-found happiness and financial security, she worried about Jonty and sometimes felt the hints of that old depressive helplessness, so familiar from the past. Steve was so set on him being sent to board at Geelong Grammar, but in her heart she knew this was wrong. Here he was, now nearly twelve, having boarded several years at Southport soon after losing his mother at six, and being sent off a thousand miles away to board again through his secondary school years. Steve wouldn't hear of her concerns with the misguided belief that it was not fair for her to be saddled with the day to day care of a step-child.

She was sitting alone in the house late one evening – Steve and Antony were both out – thinking aimlessly about Davy, worrying if he was lonely and surely in need of the love and care of the family. It was the same as with Jonty. He was so much younger, but even more he needed the care of his mother. She wasn't his mother, but she could do so much more for him if he were here. When the phone rang she nearly jumped out of her skin, and immediately knew it was Davy. It wasn't Davy; it was the doctor at the hospital in Longreach. Your son is in hospital here, he told her; he has been shot in the thigh and has lost a lot of blood. He has just come out of surgery, but he'll be alright.

I can't believe it, she thought; I must be dreaming. This can't be true.

'Are you there Mrs Jeffrey?'

'Yes I'm here … is he … what happened?'

'I don't know exactly, but it seems he was out in a truck with his friends kangaroo shooting, and a bullet ricocheted off the side of the truck into his leg.'

She could barely manage to form words. 'How could he … is it serious?'

'It's quite a nasty wound as we had to remove the bullet from quite deep in his thigh. But he will be OK. We've got him on quite strong antibiotics and we'll keep him here for the next few days to make sure it doesn't get infected.'

My God, I can't believe it, she thought.

When she told Ken Fraser the next day, he immediately rang the doctor in Longreach, and after consulting him about David's condition, rang her back and told her that if necessary, he would arrange for David to be brought back to Brisbane when he was fit to travel so he could convalesce under his supervision.

'Aimée, he's fine for the present, but the wound is in a vulnerable place and it will need careful treatment for some time.'

Hopefully, she asked: 'Do you think he should be brought back to Brisbane now?'

'Not at this stage, but if there are any problems, we'll bring him back right away.'

'Oh Ken, I'm so relieved you've become involved. Thank you. I can't tell you how grateful I am.'

But she wasn't relieved. There wasn't much Ken could do. She was on the phone to David regularly, at least just enough to check on his progress without seeming to pester him, first while he was in Longreach at the hospital and then back on the property to recuperate. Soon he was walking around but he couldn't do much and certainly couldn't ride. On the phone he was typically vague:

'How's your leg coming on darling?'

'OK.'

'Is it healing well?'

'Sort of.'

'Is it painful?'

'Sometimes.'

'It's not infected is it?'

'I can't really tell.'

'Are you going into Longreach to have it checked?'

'I'm seeing the doctor at the hospital next week.'

She found this sort of exchange deeply frustrating. Steve was reassuring but she didn't feel she should bother Ken. She badly wanted to get on a plane and fly to Longreach, but everyone would think that so alarmist …

He had bought a new car, a brand new Austin Lancer, white on top and bright green below. In reality it was bought half and half with his mother, but he chose it and did most of the driving, even slightly resenting it when his mother drove off to see friends or do some shopping without even telling him.

He felt very satisfied with it, a sign, however tenuous, of his new-found independence. He couldn't wait to drive it to Sydney for his annual holidays from Flack and Flack. His love of Melbourne had diminished as the bright lights of Sydney took an alluring hold in his mind. He would stay with Hugh in the Cross and for a while at the Tara Private Hotel in Coogee with the James household. And Cedric had become engaged! This was big news – his first good friend to be getting married.

Cedric, always the party-goer, had arranged for the three friends, Hugh, Tony and himself, to have an evening at the famous Chequers night club with his fiancée Val, Val's sister and Hugh and a girlfriend. Tony was dazzled with Chequers. It seemed like a Hollywood night club you only saw in films, a huge room with banks of round tables rising around a crowded circular dance floor and a small dance band to the side. Cedric ordered champagne and the silver bucket at the side of the table was kept replenished throughout the evening. Tony thought this is the life; in Brisbane you enter a night club through a hole in the wall and keep the liquor under the table in case of a raid!

Val was bright and friendly and Cedric in his element, leaning back, summoning and chatting to the maitre'd, ordering the food and drinks, cigarette in hand.

'Come on, everyone, let's have a dance. Come on Tone, you take Glen. She's never been to a night club before.'

'Don't worry Glen,' said Hugh, 'Tony usually behaves quite well, but I have to warn you, he's a terrible dancer.'

Glen smiled weakly. Tall, blonde and willowy, she was barely eighteen and in first year at university. On the packed dance floor, he found himself jostled against her and his face exactly on a level with hers, her huge blue eyes two inches away from his. Suddenly, they both staggered, for a second falling into each other. Cedric looked over Val's shoulder with a sly smile: 'I forgot to tell you, the dance floor moves, this way or that – depending where the crowd takes it.' The evening wore on. He was entranced, by Chequers, the champagne but mostly by Glen.

The next few days passed in a daze of wondering how he could see Glen again. As before, the James household was full of colour and events, usually involving Perce's dealings with his permanent guests at the hotel. Cedric solved his problem by announcing they were both invited to dinner on Saturday night at Val and Glen's parents' home. On their way there, he explained the girls' father was a very big wheel: head of the Sydney Water Board. They lived in an unpretentious house far away from smart Sydney. The two girls, their parents and the young men sat around a plain table, a simple roast meal was served and no liquor was offered. He quickly realised they were a strong Christian family surrounded by few luxuries. He wondered how on earth the worldly and sophisticated Cedric found them. Of course it was Val he had found, not her family. But even more to the point, did they approve of him? Cedric's disarming charm and teasing with Val's family must be the key. He made them all laugh, even their stern and powerful father.

Now staying in Hugh's little flat in the heart of King's Cross, and egged on by Hugh, he rang Glen and invited her to come to a concert of the Sydney Symphony Orchestra at the Town Hall. He was delighted when she seemed thrilled to accept. Wearing a new tie bought for the occasion, he drove to her house and was greeted at the door by a vision in a pale yellow jacket and matching skirt, blonde hair curling around her shoulders, and her mother hovering in the background, looking dubiously at him. In the brilliantly lit foyer of the Town Hall, he bought her a soft drink and a programme and explained that the orchestra under their director Eugene Goossens was said to be the fifth best orchestra in the world. He had no idea where he'd heard this arcane statistic, but they both nodded seriously to each other, and it was another chance to gaze directly into her heavenly blue eyes. The Town Hall was packed for an all-Beethoven concert; he was enraptured by the whole thing.

Sitting beside her, conscious of her long legs demurely protruding from her skirt, he was able to seem quite expert in his explanations of the music. When he drove her home, he leaned across the seat and kissed her; in a moment their arms found each other, and again at the front door, a full embrace…

'Are you alright Tony? All those sighs – was it that bad?' Hugh's voice suddenly in the middle of the night.

'Sorry, no I'm fine … just can't seem to get to sleep.'

The next few days seemed to whirl past in five minutes and it was suddenly Sunday evening. He had planned to drive back on Sunday morning as he had to start work on Monday but he couldn't bear to cut short a minute with Glen. She invited him to Sunday tea with her family and he nervously turned up, clearly under the spotlight from her parents, especially her mother. He sensed her disapproval despite polite questions about his family, his work and his interests. She didn't say it, but he was acutely aware of her thoughts: Glen is only eighteen and has led a sheltered life while you are four or five years older and come from a different city and social setting and we know nothing about you.

By 7 pm, he realised he had to go; it was getting ridiculously late. Glen went with him to the car.

'You're not going to drive back now are you?'

'I have to.'

'You mustn't – you'll fall asleep and have an accident.'

'I'll try to sleep for a while in the car.'

'Promise me you will.'

He hugged her as tight as he could, and then looked hard into her eyes. 'It's been wonderful meeting you and getting to know you. I hate going.'

'I hate you going too, especially tonight. You will write to me and tell me you're safe as soon as you get back, won't you?'

'Yes of course I'll write and you'll write back won't you? And I'll come back to Sydney just as soon as I can.'

They kissed again and as they separated she blew him a final kiss and mouthed something. He wondered if it was, 'I lo… …'

Yes he was sure it was!

He set off in a high state of exhilaration, remembering the times they had together, repeating the delicious moments that had flown past in a flash. The day they had driven up to Mona Vale and Avalon beaches. It was too chilly to swim but she was wearing a white cotton dress with pink flowers that seemed to give a rosy look to her face, and as they walked along the beach hand in hand, the wind would blow up her frock showing her lovely long legs. Later he parked the car in a glade overlooking Pittwater, and he asked her had she read Dylan Thomas for her English classes? She said she would be next year. He adored the Richard Burton recording of *Under Milk Wood* and had committed it to memory. Feeling self-conscious, he stood under a tree framing the view of Pittwater and faced her, reciting Dylan Thomas' wonderfully musical narrative, even attempting to emulate Burton's Welsh vowels. She smiled then laughed as she listened. After a while he stopped, grinned and putting his arm around her waist, they walked on. What a moment that was!

Sleepiness eventually intervened and he was reduced to singing the themes from the Beethoven symphonies, then the Sibelius symphonies to keep himself awake as the hours wore on. Past Maitland, he saw a shadowy figure on the side of the road carrying a sack over his shoulder. With a shudder he recalled the news the previous day of a headless body found in Maitland. That man is probably the murderer and has the head in the sack over his shoulder. He sped on – he couldn't stop here for a sleep.

David's leg wasn't healing so Ken Fraser intervened and ordered him back to Brisbane. In a way, she was relieved but as soon as she saw David in hospital, her anxiety grew worse. He looked dreadfully thin and the infection in his leg, to her nurse's trained eye, was terrible. It seemed to have dug a cavern in his thigh like a large insect feeding on him. She went in every day to see him but it seemed ages before the antibiotics started to do any good. The one thing that gave her some comfort was David's good humour and fortitude. He kept on telling her not to worry, that he would be alright, that he had himself seen much worse injuries up in the bush. She could see he was no longer the shy silent boy she had sent off to be a jackaroo; he was actually a man. Despite his pallor and emaciated frame, she could see he was strong, or would be once the infection was beaten. Ken looked in at the hospital most days and joked with David. One day when Steve was with her, the two of them ribbed David, told jokes about hilarious fishing accidents, making her feel completely superfluous.

More seriously, Ken told them that after he left hospital he would have to recuperate for a couple of months in Brisbane before he could think of going back to the bush. She thought it should be six months and even dared to think he should never go back. But she could tell Steve was in agreement with Ken and the medical people: he must get back to his work as soon as he was fully healed, so she said nothing about leaving the bush, even to David.

She noticed she had become curiously calm as David slowly recovered. It took a while before she realised it was because Steve was there, reassuring her, interrogating Ken about his treatment, about his recovery and any future problems he might have. It was different now after all the years of being on her own worrying about the boys' welfare, when she knew nothing about likely outcomes. Steve was beside her now and her decisions needn't be hers alone.

Back in Lancaster Road recovering his strength, David was slow to get involved in Brisbane life. He went to see a couple of his old friends like Jim Harris, now a lively young man around town, but found himself ill at ease. Thin and gangling, with his wide brimmed hat hiding his face, he looked the very image of the bushie. As he became stronger, Antony took him to a couple of his parties but David hated them and had nothing to say except to answer the same question time and again about the gunshot accident.

How totally different her boys had become. There was no hostility between them. In fact all the childish resentment had disappeared, but their lives and interests were diametrically opposed. When it was agreed with his doctor that he was sufficiently recovered and could return to Longreach, he immediately cheered up and she felt proud to see the young man emerge and plan his return with confidence.

The effects of David's accident and the disruption to Steve and Aimée's placid lives masked her other main concern: Steve's decision to send Jonty to Geelong Grammar. It had become a *fait accompli* and now she felt badly that she had stayed on the sidelines and not argued strongly against it. Admittedly both Robin and Steve seemed perfectly happy for Jonty to go, and Steve was quite insistent. Having David at home recovering didn't help but she now told herself she'd been too timid tackling Robin. She liked and admired Robin but from the time she and Steve started seeing each other, she felt uncomfortable about her. Robin was so clever, confident and articulate and somehow she felt dowdy and even stupid in her presence. Of her friends only Jo Pixley and Bertie Robertson knew Robin well. Bertie was her aunt, knew her foibles and her need for success. Bertie agreed it was not a good idea to send Jonty away and said so.

'Are you perfectly happy for Jonty to go to Geelong?'

What was she to say to this?

'Not really but it had to be Steve's decision. He's his only son and he's so proud of him. He seemed to cope pretty well with boarding at Southport.'

'My dear, none of that's a good reason. Did Robin agree with Steve?'

'Yes of course. All along Steve has said it's not fair to me to have to bring up a teenager full-time and Robin tells anyone who asks the same thing.'

'Well yes he's right about that.'

'No he's not,' Aimée was quite cross. 'I worry a lot about Jonty.

He lost his mother as a young child. He's been at boarding school most of his primary schooling, and now he's being sent a thousand miles away. He's had almost no family life. He's a lovely boy and I would love to have him here all the time and go to a school like Churchie.'

'Of course you're absolutely right, but up against Steve and Robin, there's no way you can win that one. Steve has always had his heart set on Geelong. You know, nothing but the best for his boy.'

'Bertie, I feel really bad about Jonty because I never took a stand about it.'

'Look dear, don't beat yourself up about it. It's not your fault and after all, it's a great school. You'll have more than enough time to be a mother to him during the holidays.'

But she continued to worry, not just for the moment but through the whole year. She remembered Betty Brown's feelings about Thomas going to Geelong, though Jonty wasn't introverted like Thomas. The Capper boys had both been to Geelong and both seem to have liked it. She thought perhaps the problem was that as a mother she felt responsible for him. In the end of term holidays, Jonty loved to be home but didn't seem troubled by school. He spent every minute he could with Steve in his wood workshop and followed him round like a puppy. Isn't it strange how different people are, she thought; my boys would have hated boarding school, but Jonty is so far away and yet seems completely untroubled.

Slowly he was given more responsibility at the accounting firm Flack and Flack. He had already qualified as a chartered accountant two years earlier, but he knew he wasn't cut out to be an accountant. Still he had to make a living and he quite enjoyed going out of the office and doing most of his work auditing the books and records of the firm's clients, mostly branch offices of the big companies based in Sydney or Melbourne. What he liked most was observing and chatting to the staff at the client offices, some of the younger females were quite attractive, and some of the older ones rather odd, eccentric or in some cases, even mad. Mr Lipinski, chief accountant at one of the biggest clients, was Polish and reputed to spend all his salary on Golden Casket tickets, frequently winning large cash prizes frequently though his decrepit clothes seemed to belie the fact. Another curious individual, the accountant at the murky office of a spices company had a disgusting habit of spitting the butts of his cigars, still alight, on the filthy spongy floor of the office, grinding them under his shoe when he next bothered to get up from his chair. Walter the portly head ledger-keeper at yet another office, loved talking about his favourite films. Tony found the best way to wind him up was to talk adoringly about Elizabeth Taylor's latest blockbuster as it drove Walter into a tizz of horrified disapproval: 'that *evil* woman!'

He had to admit to himself he had no ambition, though if it were possible, his friend Rollo Davis had even less. Two or three years younger, Rollo had recently joined Flack and Flack because he had nothing better to do. He was something of a celebrity amongst their friends. Tony was secretly delighted, taking it as a mark of his personal prestige when Rollo appeared amongst the Flack and Flack audit staff. He took to saying to friends: '*Rollo* now works for us!' Well he really didn't – do much work.

Rollo was one of those gilded young men who everyone found fascinating. A champion gymnast at school, he was short but strongly built. Not only was he handsome like a film star whose name you can't quite remember, but he had a soft voice and a beautiful smile that made girls feel weak at the knees. His exploits gave him almost cult status amongst his peers, and despair for his parents. Tony was there when towards the end of a heavy drinking session at the National Hotel, Rollo won a bet with his mate Don Rylance to do handstands on the narrow parapet of the hotel five stories up from the trams trundling along Queen Street below. After many dings and worse in his own car before writing it off, he decided it was best to drive his parents' car, chalking up by his own tally forty-three dings before he decided it would be better to go overseas. Rollo was not a drunk; he was a daredevil, testing his prowess with little care for the outcome. Still, Don Rylance maintained he was never the same after he fell from the rings during the GPS Gymnastics.

Tony was the senior audit clerk at one of the clients, a drapery business called D & W Murray. The job was boring and the office hot, airless and sleep-inducing. Rollo was his assistant and dawdled around the office at a snail's pace, looking as if he was falling asleep on his feet. He asked Tony:

'Are you going to be down the coast over New Year?'

'I'm thinking of going down to Sydney.' He was dying to go to Sydney to see Glen. 'Do you want to come?'

'I might. A few of us were going to stay in Rylance's house at the coast but I'm not sure it's a good idea.'

Tony had heard about Rollo's problem. The story was that three girls had been chatting down at Surfers Paradise under an umbrella one recent Sunday and discovered to their mortification and fury that each of them had had an assignation with Rollo the previous night on the beach. On the same night! It was said they were out for revenge.

In the end he went to Sydney, without Rollo. To his delight and surprise, he was invited by Glen's parents to spend a few days with the family at one of the Water Board's guest residences on the dams around Sydney. He was relieved when Rollo decided after all he would brave the scene at Surfers.

The days on Woronora dam with Glen's family were very chaste. Apart from participation in decorous family relaxation, the best he could manage was a stroll around the lake and some nervous kisses when trees hid them from view. He felt a stern and disapproving reaction from her parents was quivering just below the surface. It was only when he got back to Brisbane that he understood the extent of his disappointment and frustration.

For Rollo too, a week at the beach dodging girlfriends, getting boozed with Don Rylance and his friends and playing rounds of very bad golf made him bored and angry. Work at Flack and Flack was always extremely busy in January and both felt exploited by being expected to work late into the evening to meet client deadlines. At the pub where they ate sausages and chips over a beer before returning to the fray for the evening slog, they opened up to each other.

'You didn't seem a happy traveller when you got back from Sydney. What was the problem – women trouble?'

'Well yes, actually it was.' He showed a rueful grin.

'Now he tells me. Come on, out with it. Who is she?' This with a broad smile of encouragement.

'She's the sister-in-law of an old mate of mine from Nasho who's an editor on the *Financial Review*. I met her in Sydney a couple of years ago but she's a uni student in Sydney so I never get to see her.'

'Can't she come up here for holidays and hang out with some of the females we know?'

'That's out of the question. She lives with her parents and they're wowser types who think I'm the big bad wolf. To make it worse, her father's a bigwig in the Public Service.'

'This doesn't sound like your scene at all Tony. What happened when you were down there? Did he catch you playing up with his precious daughter?'

He had already said far more than he wanted to Rollo. He didn't dare mention the whole visit was chaperoned. Nor did he dream of admitting that for months he had been carrying on an exchange of moony love letters with Glen where he fantasized about their walking the endless beach at Surfers Paradise on stormy nights talking about passion and poetry, looking into each other's eyes, before getting down to more serious love-making. All he had to feed his romancing, apart from his overheated imagination, was a couple of photos, one a grainy snap of the two of them in a Kings Cross restaurant with Hugh and a girlfriend of his. The other was a posed photo of Glen in a floral dress and large floppy hat as if she were at a garden party. She looked tall, slender and gorgeous and he hid it safely in his desk drawer at home. For Glen's part, her letters to him were chatty and full of news of her daily doings at home and University. Apart from a few mild expressions of her wish to see him soon and some kiss-laden sign offs, she avoided responding to his purple prose.

Rollo and Tony were united in sensing their lives were aimless and their need for new horizons. Rollo admitted he was wasting his life and he had to leave Brisbane. He was gathering plans to spend a few months travelling overland to Europe and the UK. This echoed Tony's sole unwavering ambition: to travel to London, base himself there and immerse himself in the music, theatre and opera of London and the great European music festivals.

When the two of them started sharing their overseas plans, he was amazed to discover Rollo had a fascination for history. He had recently read Ensor's Oxford British History of the 19th century up to the First World War and was now reading AJP Taylor's British History volume up to 1945 as well as many books of European history.

'I need to find the right books on India and the Middle East so I can bone up on those places before I get going overseas. If you're going overseas soon, we should go together.'

He was instinctively dubious about travelling anywhere with Rollo. He lacked Rollo's daredevil spirit of adventure. 'If you're going overland, how long do you think it will take?'

'No idea, maybe six months, a year. Maybe India will be so good, I'll never return.' He smiled mysteriously. 'Anyhow,' he went on, 'I wouldn't mind trying some of your opera.'

Tony found the Australian Opera Company was coming to Brisbane soon and booked two seats for them to see *Don Giovanni*. They decided it was to be a learning experience for Rollo and they would not invite girls as this would change the whole thing. It suited Tony too as he had first seen *Don Giovanni* in his mid-teens when the theatre was called ***His*** Majesty's, and he could pretend to be an expert. As an operatic experience it was not a great success. In his opinion, the Don was no good and not a patch on Geoffrey Chard who sang the first time he had seen the opera. Also the seats were in the back row of the stalls, and the couple in front of them were canoodling all through the first act, moving their heads all over the place. Eventually Rollo leaned forward and said something in a hissing voice in the ear of the young man. The man cringed and became completely still. At the interval, he and his girlfriend quickly left the theatre, glancing in alarm towards Rollo as they exited.

'What did you say to him?'

'I just threatened him a bit – he got the message.'

It was Robin who first told Aimée that Erica Brown was engaged, even before Betty Brown herself gave her the news. She felt mildly miffed that she heard it first from Robin, not because Betty hadn't told her but because Robin always seemed to know about everything before anyone else. Aimée thought Erica the nicest girl she knew. Everyone did. She had a personality that included everyone and was never known to speak a cross word to anyone. She was also beautiful with honey blonde hair, flawless complexion and a devastating smile. All the girls who knew her considered her their best friend. She was always first to help an old lady across the street. Her only problem was that the young men in Brisbane thought she was a bit like Little Red Ridinghood with her basket of goodies dispensing benevolence to all around her. The reality was that in the eyes of these callow youths, she was so perfect they didn't know what to say to her, let alone touch her.

Antony had known Erica his whole life. She was the only girl he could say just about anything to, and did, but even he knew instinctively that she dwelt on a higher plane than he could aspire to. Holding her close on a dance floor was always the greatest of pleasures, but he felt it had to stop there. While overseas in London, Erica had met a very talented Rhodesian who was doing an advanced medical degree at Oxford. They had fallen in love and become engaged. The news was they were returning to Brisbane to get married and would go back to Oxford to finish his degree before returning to Rhodesia to live. This astonished both Aimée and Antony who shared the common knowledge that Erica planned to get married, have four children and live across the road from her parents, a mantra she had repeated since adolescence.

The view around Brisbane at this time was that Erica's wedding to Mike Denborough was going to be the most important event for years in their social circles. He, as well as Steve and his mother, had received invitations (as had most of his friends.) The wedding was to be at St Augustine's, the local church the Browns had always attended, with a reception afterwards at their home.

He had very mixed (up) feelings about the wedding, but like everyone else couldn't wait to see it all take place. He felt a touch of envy that Erica had found someone so apparently superior to anyone he knew, but in another sense finding a foreigner to marry as far away as Oxford told him nobody in Brisbane was good enough. More directly, he couldn't help comparing Erica's marriage to his own situation with Glen who had none of Erica's poise and maturity. Erica was the toast of a wide circle of friends; Glen was a student in a small close-knit family and no one he knew in Brisbane had any inkling of her existence. The comparison made him feel depressed and inadequate.

The marriage service in St Augustine's was a revelation to him. Watching his childhood friend give her vows with such solemnity as she looked up into her husband-to-be's face affected him so deeply that tears welled in his eyes and he felt dizzy. When the large congregation gathered outside the church after the service and photos were taken, it was a different emotion: delight at their obvious happiness and from being among the throng of well-wishing friends. Walking in the crowd of guests up Windermere Road to the Brown's home was another extraordinary experience. He ran across the road and gazed at them, wishing he had a camera. The setting sun slanted into the eyes of the mass of people strolling up the hill chattering and laughing in their wedding finery, past the ordinary suburban houses. It looked absurd, surreal, like a fairy tale version of the Wizard of Oz disappearing into the sunset.

A marquee had been erected on the big lawn in front of the house with food and drinks, but on this balmy summer evening, guests wandered with their drinks in the garden or on to the large verandas around the house. All his friends were there, weaving in and out of the light while the champagne flowed, creating a miasma of strange sensations like he was walking on wheels. He spotted his former girlfriend Gail – they had drifted apart, though remained friends. Together they sat on a bench under a camellia tree.

'Doesn't she look wonderful,' Gail said dreamily watching Erica float up the stairs into the house on Mike's arm.

'Are you planning to get married too?'

'Certainly not!' He was teasing and knew she was about to go overseas.

'Do you think all this is Erica's dreams come true?'

'I suppose so,' then she sighed, 'Erica's dreams aren't really dreams, she makes them happen. Let's go and sticky beak at the wedding presents.'

The big dining room table in the front room opening on to the veranda was laden with loot like a shiny gift shop: silver cups, jugs, plates, china tea sets, coffee sets, glassware of every description. Gail whispered to him wasn't it all ghastly, she'll never use any of it. Their friend Penny picked up a glass ballet dancer complete with tutu, nudged Gail and hooted with laughter, only to receive a furious response from a large lady in pink insisting Penny put it down as it was *extremely* valuable. Erica appeared from behind them thanking the lady in pink effusively for the ballet dancer. They quietly retreated from the room but Erica pursued them on to the veranda.

'Don't run away you two. Talk to me – I need to be with real people. I feel like a model on a showroom floor.'

They sat on some cane chairs in a corner of the veranda. He could see Erica's face was pink and there were drops of sweat on her forehead.

'Are you alright – would you like a drink?'

'Thanks Antony, anything but no more champagne. Just cold water.'

Off he went. Even getting a glass of water for her was a sort of privilege. He jostled with a dozen red-faced men at the bar competing for their next drinks and bore the precious glass of water back to the veranda. Already she was surrounded by a bevy of guests but gave him one of her delicious smiles when he handed her the glass.

The night went on, the speeches given, and the chairs and tables cleared to one end of the veranda for the dancing. The bridal couple took to the floor and he thought he heard the phrase 'like royalty' spoken aloud. Later in the evening he danced with Erica. He told her in a voice that suddenly quavered that her father had given the most beautiful speech he had ever heard. Tom Brown was a man liked by everyone but a shy and intensely private person who reputedly 'never spoke more than one sentence and none if possible.'

'He seemed to speak about your whole life and said things I didn't know about you and probably nobody does. It was so inspiring and heartfelt. Everyone was amazed, especially the oldies who'd never heard your father like that before.'

'Oh Antony, I don't know how I'm going to bear leaving my family. I love them so very much, all of them – mum and dad, Thomas, Sam and Deb. You know after Mike proposed, I spent days agonising about this. I loved him and I had to marry him, but I couldn't think of moving to another country, leaving the family behind. I just couldn't.'

'But I thought you were going to Rhodesia?'

'No we're not now. We're going to Melbourne – Mike's got a fantastic research job at the University there.'

He felt really happy for her, even happy about her dilemma. She loved Mike and she loved her family – how lucky she was. And they all loved her back. In his own way he loved her and the Browns too. They were like cousins; they had always been there, including himself, his mother and brother in their lives; no fuss, no expectations, just there, welcoming them.

The Poinciana Tree

Setting the Seal

As he stood at the rail on the deck of the *Flavia* with the crowds of people below, streamers everywhere, he looked up for a moment past the Pyrmont wharf sheds and east beyond the Bridge to the main harbour. Smiling to himself, he whispered inwardly: This is it ... at last! We'll be sailing east out of the harbour towards Europe. It seemed now he had been waiting all his life for this moment. The last moment before everything changed. He'd always liked the east; it always seemed more positive than the west. Looking east from the beach at Surfers at sunset had given him the same feeling.

He shook himself from his reverie and shouted farewells to his friends on the wharf below. Pieter, David Eastman, Hannan, Frank Elgar, his new girlfriend Heather, Brian O'Gorman, Caroline ... Ten minutes earlier they were all gathered on the deck with champagne and paper cups. A quick look at his tiny four-berth inside cabin with an ancient mariner type sitting on his berth told him there was no point in a party in the cabin. Champagne in paper cups on a chilly August afternoon was not quite the way to start his new life. Hugs and farewells seemed rather perfunctory. Except for Heather no one seemed to understand how momentous it was for him.

The ship moved steadily out from the wharf with three blasts from the horn. It seemed only moments before they passed under the Bridge and it had become almost dark. He stayed on the deck, relishing the cold and wind. It was odd, but he couldn't put his mind to the long-awaited future. His head was full of the friends he had just left. Most of them he'd only known in recent months since he'd arrived in Sydney. The real fact was his life had changed when he left Brisbane a year earlier. Maybe that was the change he had been waiting for, when he had finally left home for good.

Looking back now in the dark as they sailed through the heads to the sea, he could just make out the lights of the bridge, then turning ahead again, nothing but darkness and the swish of the sea. He realised he knew absolutely nothing about what was waiting for him in London.

Change in his life began nearly two years earlier when he got the letter from Glen. His nervousness as he opened it was quickly borne out: she was ending their relationship. He hadn't dared anticipate it, but actually he wasn't surprised, despite feeling devastated and empty. Almost shamefully he saw how mature and sensible it was, even considerate and regretful. Third year was so much harder – she had to become less distracted. Their lives were so separate; at different stages, different cities. She understood his need to go overseas. She hoped they could stay friends.

He moped around for weeks, telling no one, but Aimée guessed the cause of his gloom. Months before, he had confided to her his strong feelings for Glen and she had made the mistake of questioning the good sense of such a distant relationship. His angry reaction made it clear this was forbidden territory. If Glen was off the agenda she was quietly relieved. Perhaps it was time for him to seriously plan to work overseas. She chose her time carefully one morning over breakfast when Steve had left early for work.

'Ant, have you thought of talking to Mr Irwin about working at Flack and Flack in London for a year or two?'

'It's Price Waterhouse in London, Mum, and here too now actually. But I don't think they'd want me there.'

'Why not?'

This was a good question and he had no answer for it. Maybe he didn't want to be hemmed in by Price Waterhouse in London. Maybe they would tumble to the fact he was a hopeless accountant.

He mulled over this conversation for a few days before deciding she was right. He steeled himself and next morning when he got to work, asked Jim Irwin's secretary for an appointment, but was dismayed when the man himself loomed out of his office with a beaming smile on his face:

'Don't worry about an appointment Tony. Come in now. I've been wanting to talk to you.'

He went in and sat down nervously.

'So what can I do for you?'

'Oh, er, I thought you wanted to see me?'

'You go first.'

He felt a complete fool and didn't know what to say.

'Mr Irwin, I was thinking I should get some more experience and wondered if the firm maybe would be prepared to look at a transfer to London office for a while, sometime ...?'

'Tony do you like working for the firm? Do you see yourself having a career here?'

Oh hell, they've worked me out. His stomach felt it had fallen on the floor.

He replied with fake enthusiasm: 'Oh yes I do – really. It's just that I thought it would be a good idea to get some experience overseas.'

'I'm sure it would be a good idea, but I recall when we had a conversation like this a couple of years ago, you said you'd like to be an architect. Do you remember?'

'Oh. Yes, I think I do remember. But then I decided it wasn't right for me.'

'Why was that?'

This is agony. I've got to get out of here.

'I suppose it was a pipe dream and anyhow I didn't have the maths and science to get into an architecture course at the university.'

'If you'd really wanted to, you could have studied those subjects at night to get into the Architecture degree course.'

He was flummoxed. He didn't know what to say.

Mr Irwin pushed his ruddy face across the desk and bored into his eyes from a few inches away, still wearing the beaming smile.

'Look Mr Jeffrey, I agree a year in London office would be excellent, but there are two 'ifs' before you could even think about it. First we have to be sure you really want a career as a chartered accountant. And second we have to be sure you have the determination to succeed as an accountant in the firm. Therefore I have a suggestion for you. Let's see if we can get the right answers for the two 'ifs'. I want you to go to our Sydney office in July for at least a year. It's a much larger office than this one. It has much bigger clients and most importantly, it has excellent people in the firm there you can learn from. What about it?'

He walked out of Jim Irwin's office stunned. Sydney! This wasn't what he'd gone to see him for. But he understood clearly this was both a threat and an opportunity. What bad luck this hadn't happened a bit earlier – it could have saved his relationship with Glen. Maybe it still could?

In the ensuing weeks, he felt himself becoming a changed man – in reality, becoming a man, not an oversized boy. First, resumption of the Glen relationship was out of the question; it was part of his former life. Going to Sydney to live was exciting and he enjoyed telling his friends he was being 'transferred to the head office in Sydney'! For the first time he thought he could do quite well in the firm; maybe they even expected him to do quite well. Even Rollo seemed impressed:

'Going to Sydney eh? You won't know yourself, and the opera will be better there too. You'll probably never come back Tony. Anyhow I'll be off soon.'

'You mean to London?'

'India first. I'm going to head for Kashmir and maybe Nepal and do a bit of mountain climbing.'

In the last Friday in June, with a freezing westerly blowing, he sorted his stuff and packed the car. The clothes were easy enough but the books and records were something else altogether. He painstakingly packed six large boxes, three for the books and three for the LPs. Four went in the back of the car, one in the front and the last in the boot with his clothes. Early on the Saturday morning he sat across from Steve and his mother for his last breakfast at home, announcing he was all packed and ready.

'You won't know yourselves when I'm gone, rattling around this big house.'

'No, it will be easier for us,' Steve smiled, 'at least I won't have to be waking you up in the middle of the night telling you to put the lavatory lid down.'

'You'll stay tonight in Armidale or somewhere, won't you?' Aimée said, 'Don't drive right through to Sydney.'

'I'll be fine Mum, don't worry. Thanks for everything. See you both soon.'

The disappearance of Antony to Sydney was like the aftermath of a cyclone. To some extent the resulting quiet life was a relief, certainly to Steve. For a long time now she had wondered when Steve's patient tolerance of his stepson's presence was going to wear thin. She felt his absence keenly, not because she felt responsible for him any longer, but she enjoyed his fleeting company and the window into his entertaining world. His departure signified the reality of her changed life; not only had both her sons permanently left home, but they had gone to distant places and were unlikely to live near her again. Her motherhood role to Jonty would be a vital though intermittent responsibility now that he was boarding at Geelong.

She was content in her relationship with Steve. In fact never had her life been so peaceful. He was a true gentleman, treating her with kindness and consideration, despite his gentle insistence on both leading the life he wanted. She saw her friends regularly, she had joined the Moreton Club, and she had learnt to accept the weekly games of poker with grace. However she was also aware of the losses, beside her sons. She never seemed to see her more raffish friends, like Claire; the Jeffrey family had faded from her life. Even contact with her own sisters had become occasional. For some time she had been conscious of a growing need to recharge her life. Soon enough Steve would retire and a move to the Gold Coast was certain. Not that she minded: the idea of living near the beach was wonderful, but she must make more of her life before then.

There was one thing in her life besides her relationships with family and friends that had always been a constant: her art. Most of her life she had been secretive about it, almost repressing it like she had repressed memories of her marriage to Alan. It was not lack of love and commitment to either but a semi-unconscious perception that these feelings about her art were too precious to share with others.

Since she had married Steve and had more time to herself, she had made a habit of visiting the Queensland Art Gallery and the occasional exhibition at a commercial gallery. Usually she went on her own as none of her friends was much interested in art. She had even met and talked to the quiet but urbane Director, Robert Haines. Tall, elegant and with a stutter in his speech, he was an icon in the small Brisbane art world. She had been fascinated with the long running controversy of Picasso's *La belle Hollandaise* which Haines had sensationally managed to buy for the Gallery through generous funding from a reclusive private patron, Major Harold Rubin. Some years later Haines resigned in outrage after a public campaign by his Chairman egged on by politician Joh Bjelke-Petersen to relocate the Gallery and remake it into a commercial operation. Selling *La belle Hollandaise* was proposed as a way to fund the new development.

She was bitterly disappointed at the disappearance of Haines to Sydney, but it galvanised her to overcome her personal reluctance and start painting again. The fact that Haines had promoted artists she loved like Arthur Boyd, Sidney Nolan and Jon Molvig gave her confidence. Finally, it was a retrospective exhibition of flower paintings by Margaret Preston at the Gallery that inspired her into action. She asked Steve whether it was possible to convert a junk room under their house into a makeshift studio. Typically

Steve swung into action and had his regular handy-man/ carpenter help him build a proper room with benches and a large window looking out to the garden. It was next to his own well-equipped carpentry workshop and made for companionable weekend activity for them both.

When it was almost finished and she had completed a few flower paintings of her own, she invited Claire to come and see it one morning. She hadn't seen her for ages and she knew Claire would prefer to see her on her own. She was suitably impressed:

'Darl, this is perfect. This is just what you need to get you going again.' She looked around the room. 'It's pretty bare. You'll need to tart it up with your personal touches. This little one on the easel is yours I suppose – it's very nice.'

Aimée detected faint praise. 'I've only just started and I haven't done anything in oils since I was a student a hundred years ago. I feel a complete amateur so I'm joining a class at the Art Gallery.'

'Have you been thinking about what sort of stuff you want to do?'

'I want to start with still life painting, both in oils and watercolours. I used to be pretty good at that, but it's going to take some concentration and I'm finding it quite hard.'

'You know you've never suited yourself since I've known you. This is the opportunity to give it a real go, but you mustn't get distracted by everyone around you wanting a bit of your action.'

'It shouldn't be a problem. I'm away from everything down here. If I shut the door, I can't even hear the phone.'

'You've got to try some selfishness. Actually refuse invitations.' She gave a cynical toss of her head.

Having Claire over and giving her some lunch was a breath of fresh air. Her laconic suggestions were what she needed, she thought. It made her determined to be serious about deficiencies in her technique and not sink into amateur prettiness. The strength and power in Margaret Preston's work had really impressed her, despite its 'pretty' subject matter.

A few days after arriving in Sydney, he found a bed-sitter in Kings Cross, only a block away from Hugh Gore's flat, feeling sure this was the start of the Bohemian life he had long craved. He was wrong; Hugh now spent all his time with his fiancée Jenny and her family in Rose Bay, planning a suburban life on the upper North Shore. He had already been best man for his other old school friend Ken Wyatt, also living far up the North Shore. His cousin Michael, now a tax expert in the Price Waterhouse Sydney office, was not only married but had become a father. The Kings Cross flat was cold and bare and made him feel lonely.

Price Waterhouse was full of busy young men with brief cases, rushing in and out of the office, all dressed in suits – no sports coats here. He felt insignificant, out of his depth, the only consolation being his new boss, a ponderous middle-aged Scot called Jock Rennie. Jock spoke very slowly in a thick Edinburgh accent, every word well chosen, but the words of wisdom were leavened by his sly wit. In two or three sentences Jock could tell him all he needed to know about the client company he was being sent out to audit. He could also tell Jock was sympathetic; maybe he too felt an outsider amongst these smart young people. The client offices were usually on the outskirts of Sydney requiring long drives to and from work each day, but it suited him as he found the client staff more relaxed and friendly.

One morning in the office, a call was put through to him from a man with a very posh English accent:

'My name's Eastman, David Eastman. I believe you know Vernon Hill.'

'Yes I do. I know him quite well. Is he a friend of yours?' Vernon was an old Etonian who had turned up in Brisbane a year or two earlier, a charming but raggedy young man looking like a sunburnt mountaineer.

'Yes we were at school together.'

'Were you the one who drove out to Australia with him?'

'Yes that's right. Vernon suggested I look you up.'

They agreed to meet after work at the Coogee Bay Hotel.

David was tanned and wiry with penetrating blue eyes and messy blond hair as if he had just got out of bed. He walked with long awkward steps and head thrust forward like an emu looking for its next feed. Some time later Tony discovered this was referred to as the 'Eton slouch', a silent calling card for all old Etonians, where they walk with their hands in the trouser pockets with their jackets pushed back behind their arms. They settled in the beer garden and immediately got on well. David had recently arrived in Sydney after months of itinerant wandering around Australia, picking fruit, serving in bars and had just scored his first proper job as a ground traffic assistant at Sydney airport. He admitted to extreme left wing political views, and for the time being at least, had rejected his aristocratic background.

Tony asked him about the famous journey to Australia through the Middle East and Asia he had made with Vernon in an antique pre-war Volkswagen beetle.

'Oh God, don't remind me of it,' he said with a short loud laugh, 'it was utterly chaotic. I was literally frightened for our lives a few times. You should have seen some of the places we holed up in. I used to sleep with a knife under my pillow.'

'But Vernon told me you had a great time?'

'Vernon is just crazy. He'll go anywhere and happily chat up thieves and murderers. But it wasn't just the people and places. Just driving on what are called roads is a lethal process. One day in Iran we were driving along a narrow road next to a stream, and we could see this large camel-drawn cart with huge old wooden wheels coming straight towards us. We tooted frantically but then saw the driver was sound asleep. We stopped the car but the cart wheel just went straight up over our car! The track over the bonnet and hood is still there.'

He remembered the car well. He had been a passenger in it when Vernon had driven from Sydney to Brisbane the year before. It was the most ramshackle car he had ever seen and it had impressed him that Vernon had driven all day in this broken-down piece of tin regaling his three passengers with stories of the epic journey across Asia. Vernon had bought the VW for almost nothing when serving in the British army in occupied Germany, and had personally converted it from left to right hand drive for the trip to Australia. The trouble was he had never bothered to cover up the holes in the floor, or change over the starter button from the far left of the dash. On the long drive from Sydney, the girl in the front seat several times tried to open the glove box by pressing the starter button, much to Vernon's subsequent fury.

The upshot of the meeting with David at the Coogee Bay was a decision to find a house to live. Also through Vernon, David had met another expatriate Brisbaner, Pieter Wessels, who worked at the ABC. They were a distinctly odd trio, Pieter adding a world-weary professorial manner to David's wild-eyed revolutionary look. As a simple accountant, Tony realised he had to be the practical one and set out to find a place for them to rent. 12 Hopewell Street in a scruffy corner of Paddington had the dominant virtue of being cheap. It had the unmistakeable smell of cat added to damp. The floors were covered in ancient feltex carpet of a mottled mid-brown colour, maybe pink a generation earlier, so that when added to the subterranean damp, it seemed like you were walking on a large sponge.

Seeing he had gone to the trouble of finding the house, he commandeered the front bedroom opening on to a narrow wrought iron balcony. Here the feltex had a pinkish aspect, but it might have been because the light was better. They set about establishing a routine that quickly revealed their personal eccentricities. Pieter took over the kitchen table where he spent most waking hours reading intellectual magazines, frequently sighing despairingly about the world's foolishness. Tony found this irritating as the kitchen table was needed to prepare meals. If you responded to Pieter's pronouncements with an insightful comment of your own, he always squelched it with: 'Yes I know…'

However Pieter and Tony were as one in their alarm at David's very British version of personal hygiene. On Saturday mornings he ceremoniously ran his weekly bath in the mouldy old claw-footed bath. Of even more concern was his habit of airing his clothes. He believed regular washing of clothes was bad for them, degraded the fibres and wasted water. It was better to throw the week's clothes into a corner of the bedroom and let them breathe for a few weeks before picking them up again and wearing them for another week. In David's view this procedure could be followed for a couple of months before all the clothes, now benefiting from several months of alternate wear and airing, could be part of a grand wash in the bath with half a carton of washing powder.

David's colourful eccentricities went far beyond his washing preferences. Perhaps based on his memory of the pre-war VW, he had acquired a bright yellow Holden van of indeterminate age. His departure in it each morning to his job at the airport was the end point in a lightning fast process Tony often observed with fascination from his balcony overlooking the street. David invariably went to bed long after midnight and it was his view that no time should be wasted between enjoying the sleep he needed and the necessity of getting to work. He gave himself two minutes from the moment his cacophonous alarm clock woke him to being in the car and off. In that time he grabbed his crumpled white shirt and navy trousers from the floor, threw them on, put on his black shoes (tying laces had to wait till later), took an apple from the kitchen, raced down the hallway dumping his peaked cap on his head to disguise his unbrushed hair and flew out to the car. Somewhere during its life the yellow van had lost its muffler, so the banging of the door and the terrifying noise as it roared off woke the whole of Hopewell street each morning.

Despite the plethora of odours and the complete absence of cleanliness, 12 Hopewell Street always seemed to have people coming and going. On the whole the neighbours were friendly and had few pretensions. Smart renovation had so far avoided this part of Paddington and the comradely cat smell pervaded most of the houses. There was also a steady trickle of female visitors who could loosely be described as girlfriends, though none would want to claim any special relationship with any of the Hopewell Street men.

Tony had met two nicely brought up women from Queensland who lived a few streets away and were friends of girls he knew in Brisbane. Caroline and Margaret (Loll) were clearly a cut above anyone else who frequented Hopewell Street, a fact not lost on either Pieter or David. On the other hand most of the male visitors were of more dubious origin, mostly expatriates from other parts of the world enjoying the sun and sleazy side of life offered in the stretch from Darlinghurst to Bondi. Typical were Brian O'Gorman, an Irish physiotherapist, both older and wiser than the three residents, and his sidekick Brian Harrison, a person with an uncanny knowledge of every dive in Sydney. These two and other irregular hangers-on seemed to have nothing better to do than spend most evenings at Hopewell St speculating about the world and its women and waiting for something more interesting to happen.

Through one or other of these casual connections, Tony and O'Gorman rolled up at a party one warm December night in a back yard in Willoughby owned by a retired sea captain from the British merchant navy, Captain Elgar. The party was an unusual combination of suburban middle-aged couples, pretty young women, and curiously elegant young men. The Captain was the titular host and sat in a deck chair in the middle of the yard regaling anyone who would listen with stories of the sea. The real hosts were his daughter Margaret, a nurse, and his interior decorator son Frank, handsome, witty and debonair, who darted around introducing everyone. Frank gave Tony an appraising look as if he were merchandise of doubtful provenance, then took him by the hand to the laundry where several young people were gathered getting drinks.

'Margaret, I want to introduce you to Tony Jeffrey who I'm told works for Price Waterhouse – can you believe it! Oh there's Heather! Heather come and meet this gorgeous man. Brian tells me he's very musical so he's just right for you. Heather, meet Tony: it's good of you to come and add a bit of class to all these boring people our dear father gathers around him. Don't you just love Mozart?'

Margaret gave Frank a friendly shove and he dashed off giving Heather a kiss on the way. He discovered Heather was a close friend of both Margaret and Frank and indeed her parents were at the party too. She had deep-set brown eyes and an intense sultry look that he guessed masked shyness. He gave her a glass of wine and they went out into the garden.

'Do you know all these people here?'

'Most are really friends of Frank and Captain Elgar, but yes I know most of them.'

'Frank's rather different isn't he?'

'Oh Frank's sweet, he's the friendliest and most amusing person I know. And in a different way, so is Captain Elgar.'

'So who are your parents?'

Heather pointed to a very glamorous woman laughing and dancing with one of Frank's friends on the back verandah.

'She looks so young, how can she be your mother?'

'She's forty-one and she loves nothing better than partying with my friends. She pretends to be our age.'

'Where's your father?'

'He'll be waiting in the car for all this to end.'

Brian O'Gorman came over with another young man, both laughing.

'Tony, have you met John? He's knows more about the peccadillos of the Catholic Church than anyone I know. My God, I think you must be a priest yourself, John?'

'I've often been tempted, but so far I've resisted their blandishments. Nice to meet you Tony and I see you've already latched on to the lovely Heather.'

John Hannan was an old friend of Frank Elgar's and came from a wealthy family who seemed to be big in the hotel business. He liked to present himself as a cynic who did nothing for a living but sponge on his family. Brian said: 'They must be a generous lot to supply you with ongoing quantities of the folding stuff, John.'

'No they're stingy and bitter and hate parting with any of it. I just love the look on my father's face when I tell him I've run out. Even better when I tell him I've got all these gambling debts. Isn't it right Heather, aren't they just a lot of rich wicked sinners?'

Heather laughed: 'How can you talk like that John. I think your parents are lovely.'

Tony thought John was intriguing, another one to add to his growing collection of oddballs. John prowled around the garden telling outrageous stories of his own bad behaviour, mixed with slanderous gossip about priests and politicians. Yet he seemed proud of his own family's Irish antecedents, telling improbable stories of his ancestry that made Brian roar with laughter.

'It's all true, the Hannans have always believed that you must honour all branches of the family. It's the only safe way to keep your reputation intact. They always have something on you, and they can do you out of your inheritance in a flash. So that's why I have eight Christian names. You don't think my mum and dad just thought they were just nice manly names?'

'Eight names?'

'Actually there were nine but one of them was unacceptable, so I dropped it.'

'What are the eight names?'

John half turned away, in the gloom seeming to strike a theatrical attitude.

'John Daniel Patrick Michael Timothy Cornelius, (pause) O'Neill Fitzhubert – Hannan.'

'Wow?'

Before he had left to come to Sydney, Aimée had told him he must visit his uncle and aunt, Owen and Honor at their little fruit farm at Blaxland's Ridge in the hills west of Sydney. He had fond memories of this reclusive couple from childhood visits. Quickly he fell into the routine of driving up every second Saturday. He decided their shabby but pretty little house – more of a shack than a house – needed painting so he committed to painting it on the Saturdays he visited.

After a month or two of regular visits, he decided they were probably the most interesting and admirable couple he had ever met. Owen was very like his mother with his quiet and dignified manner and even looked and spoke like her. For him the hard and lonely life propagating and picking passionfruit was ideal both for his spirit and his questionable health. Honor worked at the local Holden dealer's office and cooked nutritious food for their dinner. She had a soft voice, a sweet smile and was not averse to poking gentle fun at Owen for his serious approach to life. His great passion was reading. After dinner each night, he read the Sydney Morning Herald, on weekends the Bulletin, all the while with the ABC's music program playing quietly in the background. Later in bed, he read Patrick White's novels and his favourite of all, Proust's *A la Recherche du Temps Perdus*. Proust was Owen's avatar, to be read and re-read with no limit. For him Proust was saturated in wisdom and understanding of the human condition.

After a day's painting, Antony loved nothing better than sitting down with them to eat Honor's delicious food, and to quiz Owen about his world views. It always amazed him that this reclusive man, who saw almost no one, knew more about literature, music, and world affairs than anyone else he knew. Even so, Owen's modesty was such that he seemed to hang on his nephew's opinions about concerts or recordings he heard and his views about life in Sydney. He thought it must be because there was no one else for Owen to talk to about the things he loved.

Honor was the opposite. She wanted to know about what he was doing, who he was meeting, and did he have a girlfriend? She wanted to know everything about his mother and his brother David. She hardly ever saw his cousins Susan, Michael or Jane, and the last two were now married, she said, but of course they have their own lives to live. When he mentioned he had recently met a girl called Heather and she loved music like he did, she insisted he bring her with him one of these weekends.

Driving back to Sydney late on Saturday nights, he was always stimulated and got to thinking about his own future. There was no doubt his life in Sydney was completely different from Brisbane and far more interesting. He had already decided he could never return to live in Brisbane and came to the conclusion he must really make a go of his work at Price Waterhouse. He had heard his cousin Michael was regarded as one of the most talented of the younger people in the firm and would become a partner before long. I suppose I should be ambitious too he thought, but found it hard to imagine. Going to London was still at the front of his mind, and until this particular destiny was fulfilled it was impossible to think of anything else too seriously.

But he was pleased Honor wanted to meet his new girlfriend, if he could call her that. He had seen her a few times now and they had been to a concert together. She was unlike his past girlfriends; she was a committed Catholic and seemed to have a serious attitude about her life. She had recently graduated as a school teacher and loved her new job. The thing that disturbed him about her was her family as he could tell she wasn't happy at home. From several brief visits to her home to collect her for outings, he found her father stern and forbidding, not so much towards him but to Heather his daughter. He had been a major in the army and now ran a big men's club in the city, and exuded a military aspect. Her mother was attractive and youthful looking but she was always giggling and simpering like a young girl. She seemed to like best being a companion to Heather's very pretty younger sister whom she obviously adored almost to the exclusion of Heather.

Heather rang him up and said she was going to a series of lectures at Sydney University on Mahler's symphonies. Would he like to join her? It became a weekly event they both looked forward to. It made it easier for them to get to know each other. He loved Mahler's music, having discovered it as a teenager at a time when his massive symphonies were virtually unknown and hardly ever played. The Professor of Music, Donald Peart gave the lectures, one in respect of each of the nine completed symphonies. The result of these weekly assignations was that Heather became one of the regulars at Hopewell Street, much welcomed by the men like Pieter, David and Brian, and greatly improving the down-at-heel male atmosphere. None of them appeared to challenge the primacy of her relationship with him but they all treated her as a special friend.

One steamy evening early in January, as they all lounged around at Hopewell Street, David said it was time for a party at the house. When Tony mentioned it was Heather's birthday later in the month, everyone agreed they would throw her a birthday party. All the men invited their friends, a motley lot, and Heather was encouraged to invite anyone she wanted. This was when the trouble started. First, she realised that apart from people like John Hannan and Frank and Margaret Elgar, not many of her former well-brought-up school friends would be comfortable at Hopewell St in the company of its much older and lecherous denizens. Worse, Frank had told Heather's mother Patricia about the party who had announced she was coming.

'No she's not,' said Brian, 'she hasn't been and won't be invited.'

Heather was really agitated: 'But you don't know her, she'll still come whether she's invited or not.'

They all looked at each other rather mystified and it was agreed that if she insisted on coming, it wasn't the end of the world. Pieter added: 'I rather like the idea of meeting your mother, especially if she's as awful as you seem to make out. I like awful people.'

Preparations proceeded for the party the following Saturday night. A full scale clean-up ensued. Floors were scrubbed, a powerful vacuum cleaner was hired for the feltex; David brought forward the periodic washing of his clothes and Pieter bought an array of air fresheners to try to counteract the pervasive cat and damp smell.

On the Friday before the event, Heather rang and said she had given her mother an ultimatum: if her mother came to the party, she would not. Tony tried to cajole her into coming whether her mother came or not, but Heather was adamant. By 7 pm on Saturday night, the house was transformed. Fresh flowers were set on the tables, streamers hung from the ceiling, trays of glasses put out, a large tub was filled with ice, wine and beer and the fridge loaded with goodies to eat. Guests arrived, drinks were served, savouries handed around, and the noise level quickly rose. Soon enough, Heather's mother Patricia arrived with a brilliant smile looking around admiringly, followed by a sheepish looking Frank Elgar.

'Where's Heather?' Tony asked Frank.

'I think she's coming with John.' Frank replied vaguely, but John soon arrived with no Heather.

Patricia now sat in the middle of the sitting room with a glass of wine holding court with Frank or anyone else prepared to come and speak to her. Her presence without a thought for her daughter, his girlfriend, outraged him. Several of the women came up to him asking who this strange woman was. He rang Heather's home, but no one answered. He asked Patricia why Heather wasn't here but she only shrugged and said she had no idea. Soon it became clear to everyone the guest of honour wasn't coming and the party atmosphere quickly deflated. He could hardly believe Patricia could be so self-centred. He took Frank aside and told him to take her home right away: she was not welcome. Frank huffed and puffed but before long, led her away. Everyone tried to defuse the situation with jokes, but the party was ruined and guests drifted off.

'Y'know Tony, isn't it time you made a break for it?' Big laugh. This was the way Brian introduced a topic that included an element of seriousness. The Hopewell street men were having a drink at the Coogee Bay after a Rugby match at Cumberland Oval.

'What do you mean?'

Despite his shabby, couldn't care less manner and appearance, Brian was at heart a philosopher. A few years older than the others, he liked to cultivate an aura of wisdom and esoteric knowledge.

'Oh, I don't know, but you seem a bit frustrated around here.

When are you going to throw in the towel with that accounting firm, Price too high or something? Now David here, he's got a real job out at the airport.'

This time they all laughed.

'Oh yes I've got the best job in the world,' intoned David bitterly, 'makes me a fortune and such fantastic people to work with.'

'OK maybe the airport isn't where we all want to finish up in our old age, but at least you've come across the world and seen and done amazing things while poor old Tony is pushing a pen barely a mile or two from where he was born.'

He felt unjustly put upon: 'Sydney's not bad and I've been here less than a year. You two seem to be happy enough with the flesh pots of Sydney.'

'Look Tony, you're not an accountant. You look at me and tell me you're an accountant and all I can do is go into helpless laughter!'

'Well, what do you think I should be?'

'I don't know, but I reckon you're ready to try something else, or some place else.'

Though Brian had a broad grin on his face, this line of talk was quite unsettling. David was also smirking and nodding his head.

'I think this is all ridiculous. Here you both are bumming around the world having a good time with no thought for proper working careers, and all you can say is that I shouldn't be an accountant. I think you're both jealous of my success!'

More laughter.

This conversation bothered him in several ways and made him realise he must be more decisive in thinking about his future. He enjoyed working for Price Waterhouse in Sydney and was dismissive of Brian's teasing, but in a corner of his mind, he did want something better, but what could that be? Soon he would have been in Sydney a year, perhaps it was time to raise the question of London again with his boss? What if they wouldn't hear of it? Should he leave and take pot luck in London? He'd never worked anywhere but Price Waterhouse. Then there was the question of his girlfriend Heather. He could tell she was starting to see him as a lifeline to separate from her family. The fiasco of her party had brought them closer, but he shirked at feeling responsible for her relationship with her family. He mulled obsessively over these thoughts for days, a week, before making a time to see Jock Rennie in the office.

'Good morning Tony. What can I do for you, lad?'

'Well I wanted to talk a bit about my future.'

'Right.'

'You know I planned to go overseas before I came to Sydney?'

'No.'

'Uh, well, Jim Irwin in Brisbane thought I should come for a year here before going to London, and a year will be up in June.'

'Right.'

Pause. 'Do you think I could get a transfer to the London office soon?'

'No idea.'

He knew this was going to be awkward and wished he hadn't bothered.

'Well is there anyone who might be able to advise me about this?'

'You might ask the Staff Partner Mr Burgess.'

Jock said he would have a word with Mr Burgess and let him know.

For weeks he had been really excited about this concert. Lisa Della Casa had been his favourite singer for years. In fact he had to admit to himself he was in love with her voice. Her recording of the Strauss opera *Arabella* with the great baritone Dietrich Fischer-Dieskau was the most beautiful singing he had ever heard. Her Mozart recordings from *Marriage of Figaro* and *Don Giovanni* were hardly less wonderful. Now she was visiting Australia for the first time and he had booked seats in the sixth row of the Town Hall for her concert with the Sydney Symphony Orchestra. Heather looked lovely in a teal blue dress with a high collar and a pretty black wrap as they strolled around the brilliantly lit Town Hall foyer. She listened intently while he explained the background to the Strauss *Four Last Songs* Della Casa was to sing at the concert.

The performance was everything he could have expected. Hearing her voice in the flesh in these glorious songs was even more rapturous than in the recordings. She was beautiful too. Eyes fixed on her face, he leant back in the seat mouthing invisibly the German words of the songs he so loved. Tears came to his eyes – he felt it was almost too beautiful to bear. Heather glanced sideways at him from time to time, aware and slightly bewildered by his evident rapture.

After the concert while he drove her home, she could see he was distracted and after saying how thrilling the concert was, she said little. They kissed quietly in the car for a while outside her parents' house, but soon they said their goodnights and she went inside.

On the drive back, he tried to convince himself it was not the night to tell her of his fantastic news he had just got from Jock that he was to start work in the London office of Price Waterhouse in October.

Aimée was thrilled when Antony rang to say he was flying up to Brisbane for Rollo's farewell party. When he had written a few weeks earlier to tell her he was moving to London, her first thought was dismay that she might not see him for years. Now at least he would stay with them for the weekend of the party and she could find out what he was planning. On Friday Steve had tactfully retreated to the Club for an evening of poker and she cooked Antony his favourite roast. When he arrived, he looked around the house for a minute, shook his head and remarked:

'I'll tell you what Mum, it's nice to be at home again. You

wouldn't want to visit us at Paddington, it's so grotty after this.'

'Yes I heard that from Hilary Bligh.'

'Hilary Bligh? You mean Caroline's mother? She hasn't been to Hopewell Street, at least not when I've been there.'

'I expect she heard it from Caroline. She tells me you and Caroline are good friends.'

'Well, yes, we saw her quite a lot at Hopewell Street and at her flat in Woollahra, but you know she's gone to England with her mother now.'

'So you can see her when you get there?'

'Yes I suppose so.' He seemed to think about this and continued, 'Caroline's great, we get on really well and talk a lot about books and the theatre. Yes it will be good in London and we can go to the theatre together. You know they've just established the National Theatre at the Old Vic and Laurence Olivier is in charge.'

She had never met Caroline, but she knew and liked her elder sister Christine who was a close friend of Erica Brown. The Blighs were a country family and Hilary an elegant woman and amateur actress despite the rigours of bringing up five children in the bush. Aimée thought Antony was in some ways naive and liable to fall in with unsuitable company. Instinctively, she felt Caroline would be the right sort of girl for him. His passion to go to London worried her and she hoped working at Price Waterhouse would give him the right sort of stability. Having a girl like Caroline around could only be a good thing.

Over dinner he talked freely about life in Sydney and he seemed delighted with the oddities of the people who shared his house and their friends. As often with him she found it hard to understand what it was that attracted him to such eccentric people and the bohemian lifestyle.

'I can't wait for Rollo's farewell party tomorrow night. It'll be wild. You know he's going overland via India and it may be months before he gets to England.' She got up to rinse the dishes and he knew she didn't want to talk about Rollo's party.

'How's David going?'

'As far as I know, he's doing very well. He's back to full scale work and he's talking about a better job at another property. But it was a terrible injury and it may be years before he has full strength in his leg.'

'But he loves being on the land doesn't he? And if he's getting a better job, it must be that he has good prospects?'

'I hope so, but what about you Ant? How long will you be in London?'

'At least two years I think. They seem to think that's about the right amount of time. But, Mum, I want to talk about you.'

'Me?'

He was leaning against the kitchen counter smiling at her, sipping his beer.

'It must be about five years now since you married Steve, is that right?'

'Yes I think so.'

'It occurred to me in the plane today that we haven't had a proper talk for years like we used to.'

'Well you're an independent person now and you've been living in Sydney for a year.'

'I suppose so, but it's nice to have a good talk after such a long time.' He walked down the hall and looked into his old room. It looked the same but empty.

'It all looks a bit sad and lonely in this house now. Are you happy here and doing what you like doing?'

She thought about this and put a bowl of ice cream and stewed fruit on the table in front of him.

'No I'm not lonely. Steve and I get on very well and we have lots of friends. It would be lovely if you and David were close by, though I doubt that will ever happen.'

'Will you stay on here indefinitely?'

'No I don't think so. You know Steve has this dream of retiring to Surfers soon after Jonty leaves school and is settled at University. There's a huge residential development scheme happening on the Nerang river behind Surfers, and Steve has his heart set on buying some land there.'

'Would you like that?'

She looked past him. 'I'm not sure. We'll have to see.' After a pause, she said, 'I'd miss my friends.'

Then out of the blue, he asked: 'You know after my father died, you never talked about him.'

How could she answer that.

'Was it too hard to talk about it?'

She looked down at the table, started to say something and stopped. Then she said: 'Yes I suppose it was. I never intended to be like that. I suppose I felt I just had to get on with it – life I mean, looking after you and Davy. It seemed that you were all that was left and there was no choice.'

'Were you able to talk about it to your friends? When I was a kid I always liked seeing you with your friends, sitting in that chair in Creswick Street under the lamplight sewing and talking to your friends like Pat Fraser. Or with Claire or Winifred. You all looked so companionable and absorbed in what you were all saying.'

She looked troubled and for a while said nothing. Her thoughts were spinning. Why was he bringing all this up now? She felt chilly and pulled her cardigan around her, then got up from the table and turned on the heater.

'Yes you're right, they were wonderful for me. In a way they saved my life. But I don't think we talked about your father much. It was more about what they were doing or I was doing and about our children. They were probably thinking how they could make everything seem normal for me. I'm very sorry I didn't talk about your father but I remember so well I just couldn't. It was too pain-ful. Did it affect you very badly?'

'No not really. I just got on with my own life I think. Like any little boy I was completely self-centred.' She could tell he was trying to lighten the mood.

'I know I tried very hard to make everything seem as normal as possible. So did Winifred when she came to live with us.'

'You must have been terribly lonely.'

'No I didn't have time to be lonely. The worst thing was making all these decisions on my own about you boys, or about money when I had no experience of any of it. I never got used to it and I would lie awake all night worrying. This is one of the best things about marrying Steve – I have someone beside me helping me decide on anything that is a problem. But Ant I don't want to talk about those sad times. I want to talk about you and what you're going to do. It's going to be so exciting for you.'

He looked into space with a smile. 'Yes it will be.' He looked up at her and added casually, 'What are you going to do now that you've got so much time?'

She hesitated, then decided he should know.

'I've taken up painting again. Steve's built me a studio. Would you like to see it?'

'How fantastic – where? I'd love to see it.'

She took him downstairs and into the studio. On three of the walls she had hung about twenty of her still lifes, mostly flower or native bush paintings. In the centre was a portrait in oils of Steve, in three quarter profile, looking as if he'd just heard a good joke. He was speechless, until eventually managing: 'My God, have you done all this? When? I didn't know you could paint like ... this is amazing.'

'You like it – I've been working quite hard.'

'Mum I had no idea. This is like a .... an Aladdins's cave.' He wandered around the studio, asking questions about each painting. After a while, he turned and looked at her with a bemused smile, and gave her a long hug.

Eventually they went upstairs and he found a bottle of red wine in the sideboard. He poured them both a glass and toasted her. He had always loved her, even depended on her, but now he felt almost guilty he had under-estimated her. It was a revelation. How remarkable she was.

Soon the slightly solemn atmosphere dissipated. He made her laugh with some of his stories about Sydney. It was obvious to her that going to Sydney had been really good for him and given him far more confidence and maturity. London would surely do even more for him.

She was glad she'd shown him her studio and her paintings. His response really warmed her heart.

Afterwards

After I left for London in 1963, my mother lived for another forty years in a contented relationship with Steve King. His loving consideration for her through their long marriage was unstinted. Even her inclination to let him set the agenda of their lives was true to her instinct and the style of the times.

In 1970 Steve retired from the legal firm his father had founded, then built his dream home on the banks of the Nerang river near Southport. The two of them were the very image of the gracefully ageing couple living in idyllic retirement. Breakfast on the terrace overlooking the river, boat and crab pot tied to the little jetty, fishing on the river, golf for him, for her the joyful continuation of her painting given up thirty years earlier. His son Jonathan (Jonty) had left to study theatre at RADA in England. A growing stream of grandchildren and old friends gave them a busy social life. Several of her friends' daughters adored her and sought her out for advice and friendship.

But her personal circumstances ironically offered and then fate withdrew the happiness and security she so badly wanted and deserved. A few years after their retirement, she developed an extremely painful condition known as 'tic douloureux' manifested as a sharp shooting pain across one side of the face. In her case it was diagnosed from her life-long habit of unconsciously grinding her teeth which probably caused degeneration of the facial trigeminal nerve. No medication seemed able to deal effectively with the condition or the pain. After several years, major brain surgery was attempted to deal with the offending nerves but never conclusively solved the problem. She did not allow the condition to affect the way they lived but it did lead to her becoming more reclusive.

I recall on a later visit with my family asking if she would paint a portrait of one of my children and my surprise when she said she did not paint any more. In hindsight this was an indication of the beginning of dementia, which I suspect she tried hard to conceal from Steve. Not that she would have self-diagnosed, but she hated to confess to any illness or weakness that might affect those she loved. As she moved into her seventies, she succumbed slowly to Alzheimer's disease, almost imperceptible at first, but gradually taking over her life.

In their later years, Steve became very incapacitated with arthritis and could not manage their riverside home. They sold up and moved to an apartment in a retirement village on the Gold Coast. Despite his incapacity and her dementia, they loved having visitors, of whom there were many. To the uninitiated, they were charming hosts with Steve making friendly conversation from his chair while gently instructing Aimée to take the cups from the shelf, fill the kettle from the tap, take the milk from the fridge, pour the tea etc.

My stepsister Robin Murdoch had always been a caring presence and became a tower of strength for them both in these later years. Before Steve died in 1997, he moved them both to a nursing home where she lingered until 2003. She died at the age of ninety five, leaving ten grandchildren and eight great grandchildren at the time of her death.

Acknowledgements

A few years ago I decided to write the story of my mother. I felt her kindness and resilience in the face of so many vicissitudes had never been recognised beyond her immediate loved ones. I thought her story was a shining example of the thousands of ordinary people who faced the Depression and those hard wartime years and their aftermath with stoic fortitude, never asking for help but never losing their love and commitment for those around them.

The task was dependent on memory, mostly that of my brother and myself as the only people still alive who had known her all our lives. Memory is a remarkable facility, especially if we work it hard. I knew the facts of Aimée's life and was clear in my memory of her personality. But opening up her personality meant a leap of faith that I could imagine her thoughts and feelings and add them to the known circumstances to find the real person, or at least an authentic version of the real person.

The really exciting aspect of writing through memory has been the far deeper knowledge and understanding I gained of my mother than when she was alive. It also has given me a new element of understanding of my own early life.

I am deeply indebted to my brother David for letters and photos in his possession and for many of his different interpretations of events in our family's lives. Inevitably as the writer and secondary protagonist, I feature far more than he does. I feel sure he will forgive me as in no way does this reflect the circumstances of our lives with our mother.

Another vital source was a three-hour interview I recorded in Melbourne with my father's three surviving sisters Jo, Betty and Mary some thirty years ago. Aimée was like another beloved sister to these wonderful women. Their remembrances of their early lives, the meeting and marriage between Aimée and their adored brother Alan and their reflections on the subsequent sorrowful events are essential elements of the book. I especially cherish the memory of my aunts and my mother's friends, all of whom seemed to me then and now as the salt of the earth.

It has been a tremendous pleasure to recall the other people who appear in these pages. In some cases, I have changed names to avoid possible embarrassment to surviving family, but in no case is disrespect intended. A few people have been invented to provide necessary connections in the narrative.

Finally my thanks to family and friends who have helped and encouraged me in this self-inflicted task. In particular, I want to thank my son Guy for his beautiful design of the book and my daughter Ann for her idea of the eponymous poinciana tree in her watercolour. I am very grateful for Belinda Grieve's encouragement and editor's eye, Margaret Barbelet's criticism of the book's structure that led to a substantial rewrite, and above all for my wife Sally's scepticism of my wordiness that kept me on my toes throughout.

Antony Jeffrey

*A*ntony Jeffrey has followed a career in arts management for many years. He was the first Director of the Australia Council's Music Board and first CEO of the Australian Chamber Orchestra. He has worked as manager or consultant to a great many arts organisations including five years as Commercial Manager of The Australian Opera. He has recorded more than a hundred interviews with artists and other creative people many of which resulted in his book *Many Faces of Inspiration* (2011). In 2008, he was awarded an AM for his services to the arts.

In recent years he has shared his time between creative writing together with arranging and leading music tours overseas. His book on leading pianist and conductor Roland Peelman (in association with photographer Anthony Browell) was published in 2021, by Connor Court. The *Poinciana Tree* is his first novel.